Praise for
the novels of the Nine Kingdoms

River of Dreams

"Elegant writing . . . An enchanting, vibrant story that captures romance, fantasy, and adventure with intriguing detail and an epic, fairy-tale sensibility."
Reviews

"Aisling and Rùnach's tender r take turns saving each other from p   l be left eager to read about their fut   *kly*

"Fantastic . . . As always, the wor   and vivid and the characters fascinating and well   ueu, which is why Kurland's books are truly awesome reads!"   —*RT Book Reviews* (Top Pick)

"Time after time, book after book, Lynn Kurland crafts a tale vividly alive with imagination . . . She weaves stories with a magic that could only be conjured from dreams."   —*The Reading Cafe*

Dreamspinner

"Fascinating, well-drawn characters and vibrant descriptions of magical situations and locations reinforce a vivid, enchanting narrative."
—*Kirkus Reviews*

"The writing is classic Lynn Kurland—fluid and graceful."
—*The Romance Reader*

"Awe-inspiring . . . The beginnings of a new quest that will be filled with ample quantities of adventure, magic and peril!"   —*RT Book Reviews*

"Lyrical writing, brilliant mental imagery, richly descriptive magic, and larger than life characterization."   —*The Reading Cafe*

Gift of Magic

"The exciting story line is fast-paced from the onset . . . Lynn Kurland spins another fabulous fantasy."
—Genre Go Round Reviews

"A magical combination of action, fantasy, and character exploration that is truly wonderful! A journey well worth taking!"
—RT Book Reviews

Spellweaver

"One of the strongest fantasy novels welcoming in the new year."
—Fresh Fiction

"Kurland weaves together intricate layers of plot threads, giving this novel a rich and lyrical style."
—RT Book Reviews

A Tapestry of Spells

"Kurland deftly mixes innocent romance with adventure in a tale that will leave readers eager for the next installment."
—Publishers Weekly

"Captured my interest from the very first page."
—Night Owl Reviews

Princess of the Sword

"Beautifully written, with an intricately detailed society born of Ms. Kurland's remarkable imagination."
—Romance Reviews Today

"An intelligent, involving tale full of love and adventure."
—All About Romance

The Mage's Daughter

"Lynn Kurland has become one of my favorite fantasy authors; I can hardly wait to see what happens next."
—Huntress Reviews

"*The Mage's Daughter*, like its predecessor, *Star of the Morning*, is the best work Lynn Kurland has ever done. I can't recommend this book highly enough."
—Fresh Fiction

Star of the Morning

"Kurland launches a stunning, rich, and poetic new trilogy. The quest is on!"
—*RT Book Reviews*

"A superbly crafted, sweetly romantic tale of adventure and magic."
—*Booklist*

More praise for *New York Times* bestselling author Lynn Kurland

"Both powerful and sensitive . . . A wonderfully rich and rewarding book."
—Susan Wiggs, #1 *New York Times* bestselling author

"Kurland weaves another fabulous read with just the right amounts of laughter, romance, and fantasy."
—*Affaire de Coeur*

"Kurland . . . consistently delivers the kind of stories readers dream about. Don't miss this one."
—*The Oakland (MI) Press*

"[A] triumphant romance."
—*Fresh Fiction*

"Woven with magic, handsome heroes, lovely heroines, oodles of fun, and plenty of romance . . . Just plain wonderful."
—*Romance Reviews Today*

"Spellbinding and lovely, this is one story readers won't want to miss."
—*Romance Reader at Heart*

"Breathtaking in its magnificent scope."
—*Night Owl Reviews*

"Kurland infuses her polished writing with a deliciously dry wit . . . Sweetly romantic and thoroughly satisfying."
—*Booklist*

"A pure delight."
—*Huntress Book Reviews*

"A consummate storyteller."
—*ParaNormal Romance Reviews*

"A disarming blend of romance, suspense, and heartwarming humor, this book is romantic comedy at its best."
—*Publishers Weekly*

"A totally enchanting tale, sensual and breathtaking."
—*Rendezvous*

Titles by Lynn Kurland

STARDUST OF YESTERDAY
A DANCE THROUGH TIME
THIS IS ALL I ASK
THE VERY THOUGHT OF YOU
ANOTHER CHANCE TO DREAM
THE MORE I SEE YOU
IF I HAD YOU
MY HEART STOOD STILL
FROM THIS MOMENT ON
A GARDEN IN THE RAIN

DREAMS OF STARDUST
MUCH ADO IN THE MOONLIGHT
WHEN I FALL IN LOVE
WITH EVERY BREATH
TILL THERE WAS YOU
ONE ENCHANTED EVENING
ONE MAGIC MOMENT
ALL FOR YOU
ROSES IN MOONLIGHT
DREAMS OF LILACS

The Novels of the Nine Kingdoms

STAR OF THE MORNING
THE MAGE'S DAUGHTER
PRINCESS OF THE SWORD
A TAPESTRY OF SPELLS
SPELLWEAVER

GIFT OF MAGIC
DREAMSPINNER
RIVER OF DREAMS
DREAMER'S DAUGHTER

Anthologies

THE CHRISTMAS CAT
(with Julie Beard, Barbara Bretton, and Jo Beverley)
CHRISTMAS SPIRITS
(with Casey Claybourne, Elizabeth Bevarly, and Jenny Lykins)
VEILS OF TIME
(with Maggie Shayne, Angie Ray, and Ingrid Weaver)
OPPOSITES ATTRACT
(with Elizabeth Bevarly, Emily Carmichael, and Elda Minger)
LOVE CAME JUST IN TIME
A KNIGHT'S VOW
(with Patricia Potter, Deborah Simmons, and Glynnis Campbell)
TAPESTRY
(with Madeline Hunter, Sherrilyn Kenyon, and Karen Marie Moning)
TO WEAVE A WEB OF MAGIC
(with Patricia A. McKillip, Sharon Shinn, and Claire Delacroix)
THE QUEEN IN WINTER
(with Sharon Shinn, Claire Delacroix, and Sarah Monette)
A TIME FOR LOVE

eSpecials

"TO KISS IN THE SHADOWS" FROM TAPESTRY

Lynn Kurland

DREAMER'S DAUGHTER

BERKLEY SENSATION, NEW YORK

THE BERKLEY PUBLISHING GROUP
Published by the Penguin Group
Penguin Group (USA) LLC
375 Hudson Street, New York, New York 10014

USA • Canada • UK • Ireland • Australia • New Zealand • India • South Africa • China

penguin.com

A Penguin Random House Company

This book is an original publication of The Berkley Publishing Group.

DREAMER'S DAUGHTER

Berkley Sensation Books are published by The Berkley Publishing Group.
BERKLEY SENSATION® is a registered trademark of Penguin Group (USA) LLC.
The "B" design is a trademark of Penguin Group (USA) LLC.

ISBN: 978-0-425-26284-9

An application to register this book for cataloging has been submitted to the Library of Congress.

PUBLISHING HISTORY
Berkley Sensation trade paperback edition / January 2015

PRINTED IN THE UNITED STATES OF AMERICA

10 9 8 7 6 5 4 3 2 1

Cover design by George Long.
Cover art by Dan Craig.

One

The palace of Inntrig, seat of power in the country of Cothromaiche, was a very quiet place.

It was difficult, perhaps, to be home to the sort of magic that
flowed through the hills and dales of such a country, an unsettling
magic that was rarely talked about and guarded jealously. More
difficult still was providing shelter for the souls that inhabited
that country, souls who understood that magic and possessed the
means to use it. In the end, it was no doubt best, if you were any
sort of sentient thing, to just keep your opinions to yourself and let
those with the ability to split the world in half with their spells
continue on their way unconversed with.

It didn't help matters any that Cothromaiche found itself so
close to that most secretive of countries, Bruadair. As the residents

of Cothromaiche had discovered, things tended to seep across the border, things that were perhaps not capable of being regulated by sharp-eyed customs agents and burly border guards. Dreams. Strange magic. Tales that stretched back into the mists of time so far that their authors could no longer be named. Those were the sorts of things that respectable library doors simply couldn't bring themselves to discuss in polite company.

Aisling of Bruadair stood in front of a pair of those mute doors and wished that the fixtures in the palace had been perhaps a bit less restrained. Though she wasn't sure anything at that point would have put her at ease, she might have at least had someone to converse with about her troubles. Or some*thing*. In Cothromaiche, she supposed the distinction didn't matter.

Of course, there were two souls on the other side of those doors who would have been more than happy to discuss all manner of things pertaining to her present business, but considering who those two lads were, she didn't think she wanted to hear what they might have to say.

She closed her eyes and wondered how it was that a simple weaver from an obscure village in a country shrouded in secrecy and menace could possibly find herself garnering the notice of any but a well-dressed gentleman who might want cloth woven especially for him. Yet there she was, standing in a Cothromiachian king's palace, terrified to face her future and wondering if it might be possible to run away before anyone noticed. She wasn't quite sure how she'd gotten from where she'd been to where she was at present, but she couldn't deny that a book had been the start of all her troubles.

She shivered. She'd owned but one book, and somehow purchasing it had led to being befriended by the peddler who had sold it to her, then subsequently being sent on a quest by that same peddler to look for a mercenary to save her country. What had happened to her along that journey was unbelievable enough that it likely should have found itself only between the covers of that book. Then again, her lone book had been a faithful listing of the military strictures of Scrymgeour Weger. Where her tale belonged was between the covers of a book on fables and myths.

She looked at the massive doors in front of her. She would have put her hand on the wood to see what it might be willing to reveal about what sorts of books on fables and myths the library contained, but she knew there was no point. The finely carved doors were resolutely silent. If there happened to be a hint of a *sshh* offered as a suggestion, she could understand. She also supposed she could have been imagining that.

That was a thought she found herself clinging to more often than not of late.

She shifted a bit and decided that perhaps the wall near those doors wouldn't mind if she leaned a shoulder against its sturdy self and caught her breath. She'd been struggling with that sort of thing for the past three days, since she had been rescued from an underground river that wended its way under Inntrig and no doubt served the palace gardener very well in his hothouse labors. The rescue had been timely given that she'd been on the verge of drowning.

A day or two of simply eating and sleeping had done wonders for her body, but not as much for her mind. If she'd thought she would find peace and respite from the unrelenting realities of her life in Inntrig's rather silent halls, she'd been thoroughly mistaken. Having the time to think had left her with more questions than answers, and the few answers she'd gotten were ones she hadn't wanted. She didn't want the rest of those necessary answers, but she supposed she would have to have them just the same. No sense in putting off the inevitable any longer.

She reached out and reluctantly put her hand on the wood. It didn't even shush her. It simply stood there, apparently too polite to mention that on its other side lay hundreds of books with potentially alarming contents. Unfortunately, books weren't the only unsettling things inside that library. It also contained a gracious host with details about countries she didn't particularly want to visit and the grandson of an elven king with plots and schemes on his mind.

The door shifted under her hand as only a solid wooden door could, startling her out of her unproductive thoughts. She moved away, expecting to find someone coming out of the library, but realized it had just been the door acting on its own. Perhaps it knew something she didn't. She frowned at it, but its only response was to open soundlessly. Caught, and so easily too.

She sighed, then walked forward only to pause in spite of herself. She had seen her share of libraries over the past several fortnights which she supposed made her a decent judge of their quality. She'd seen collections of books gathered in a university, in a trio of palaces, and in a building so large she'd been almost frightened by its height. But in none of those places had she had the overwhelming urge to pull a random book off the shelf and curl up in a chair to simply spend the afternoon reading for pleasure.

The walls in front of her were covered with shelves that stretched from floor to ceiling; the floors were covered with lovely and obviously expensive carpets. The furniture was heavy and dark, upholstered with leather for the most part. There were either long tables ready to accept large numbers of books or smaller tables set next to chairs, obviously set there to support goblets of wine and plates of strengthening edibles.

The surprising part of the room was the light. There were windows along one wall, true, but they couldn't possibly bring relief to all the nooks and crannies she could see. She supposed the lamps were lit by otherworldly means, though she could see no spells there. Obviously there was magic in Cothromaiche that she simply couldn't recognize.

She did recognize the two men sitting at a table near the windows, though, poring over books. Or, rather, arguing companionably about what they were reading. She leaned against a doorframe that didn't immediately tell her to shove off and supposed the time for avoiding the two of them had come to an end. She had managed it fairly well over the past couple of days, abandoning them in the library while she spent her time spinning, walking in the garden, or simply pacing through the passageways and attempting to convince herself not to up and bolt for points unknown.

Not that she ever would have managed the last, she supposed. Too much had happened to her for her to simply vanish into some obscure village and allow the world to continue on its course unchallenged, though perhaps it had been a single realization that had changed everything for her.

She had magic.

Worse still, those two men sitting there knew it.

One of the men who sat there with a tranquil expression on his face and the sun glinting off his pale blond hair would have only listened to her make excuses as to why she needed to flee and said nothing in response. Then again, that was apparently what Soilléir of Cothromaiche did, that keeping of his own counsel. For all she knew, he'd learned it from the bloody library doors.

She looked at the other man sitting there, dark-haired and rather less disinterested in what she was doing than he perhaps would have admitted. That was Rùnach of Ceangail, son of a black mage and elven princess. If she had told him she was about to run, he would have reminded her that she had agreed not only to allow him to save her country for her but wed him as well and that both would have been rather difficult if she disappeared into the night. He wasn't at all happy with the thought of her coming along on what was in truth her own quest, but he had given up arguing with her. There was no question of his going into Bruadair without her. She knew the country; he did not.

It would have been cowardly to say how desperately she wished she knew nothing at all.

Looking for details about her country was what Rùnach and Soilléir had ostensibly been doing, though she knew they hadn't limited themselves to that. On those fairly rare occasions when she had succumbed to the lure of library chairs, she had listened to them discuss politics, the shifting of country borders, and the antics of the members of the Council of Kings.

Well, those things and magic.

Not only had they discussed magic and all the incarnations of it that interested them, they had occasionally trotted out their formidable skills and indulged in the practice of it. Rùnach, who had been without his magic for a score of years, had smiled a little with each spell tossed out into the midst of the chamber for examination.

She had avoided thinking on how he'd had his magic restored to him. Of course, that had been made substantially more difficult by his affectionate gratitude plied on her whenever possible and the ensuing discussions between Rùnach and Soilléir about her part in the affair.

That discomfort had been added to quite substantially by the distress she'd felt over discussions of things pertaining to Bruadair. It wasn't simply that her country had been taken over by a usurper who strutted about the city as if he were sure no one could oust him from his stolen palace. It wasn't that she had seen for herself paintings of her country when it had been drenched in magic and beautiful because of it. It wasn't even that Bruadair's magic had been drained almost completely from the land, as if it had been a very fine wine siphoned out of the bottom of a cask.

It was that she knew she and Rùnach would have to not only rid Bruadair of its unwanted ruler, but uncover the mystery of where the country's magic had gone.

She couldn't bring herself to think about attempting to get it back.

She had never once considered, all those se'nnights ago when she'd been tasked with finding someone to remove Sglaimir of places unknown from the throne and restore the exiled king and queen to their rightful places, that such might be her true quest. She had thought only to travel to Gobhann and seek out Scrymgeour Weger's aid in selecting a mercenary to see to the business of overthrowing a government. It had never occurred to her that she would fail in that only to find herself taking on the role of savior for a country she had thought she didn't love.

It was odd how one's life could change so suddenly and in ways that were so unexpected.

She had never imagined she would encounter someone like Rùnach of Ceangail or that he would offer to take her quest on himself. As tempting as that had been, she'd known that her soul wouldn't have survived such a display of cowardice. She had agreed to his coming with her in part because he had his own quest that seemed to lie conveniently alongside hers, but mostly because she couldn't imagine her life without him.

She jumped a little when she realized Rùnach was watching her from his spot at the table. It was no doubt foolish to be so overcome by the sight of a handsome man, but perhaps she could be forgiven. The first time she'd seen Rùnach, she'd been rendered speechless by the sheer beauty of his face. Well, half his face, rather. The other half had been covered by scars he'd earned from an encounter with a well of evil, though those scars had done little to temper his elven beauty. Unfortunately for her ability to do anything useful when he was around, those scars had been taken almost completely away when she'd spun his power out of him, woven it into a shawl that she had laid over his shoulders, then watched as the king of Durial had spelled it into him.

Rùnach rose with a welcoming smile. She pushed away from the doorframe and started across the library to meet him—

Only to find herself sprawled on the floor. She caught her breath and lifted her head in time to be whipped in the face by a flurry of what she had to admit on closer inspection proved to be the skirts of an extremely lovely silk gown.

She watched in surprise as that excessive amount of red silk and the woman it encased continued their rush across the floor only to throw themselves collectively at Rùnach with a cry of gladness that soon turned into very expressive weeping.

Aisling sat back and considered this new turn of events. She commiserated with the carpet's disapproval of the newcomer's very sharp heels and considered adding her own opinion about too much silk in the face, but she was distracted from that by the conversation going on in front of her, if conversation it could be called.

"I thought you were dead!" the woman wailed.

Rùnach's mouth worked, but no sound came out. He looked around him for aid, but Aisling didn't suppose she dared offer any. Soilléir had risen from the table as well and was sauntering around the end of it as if he hadn't a care in the world. He didn't seem inclined to offer anything past an amused smile.

"Um," Rùnach managed.

The woman wailed a bit more in a terribly artistic way, then sank back down onto her very dangerous heels.

"You're not covering my face with kisses," she said in surprise, obviously quite unhappy about that realization.

Aisling wasn't altogether thrilled with the idea herself. She looked at Rùnach, but he was still wearing the sort of look a body wears when it's just been walloped across the face with a cricket bat. She knew exactly how that expression looked because she'd occasionally taken the time on her day of liberty to watch lads play that pleasing-looking sport in an open field near the Guild. She'd had little to do with lads and nothing to do with bats and balls, but watching something besides her shuttle endlessly going from side to side on her loom had been at least marginally entertaining.

"Ah," Rùnach offered.

The woman pulled away and put her hands on her silk-covered hips. "Have you lost your tongue or your wits? Or both?"

"I'm surprised—"

"To see me here?" the woman demanded. "I should think you would be overjoyed. Obviously you've lost your wits."

She seemed to realize quite suddenly that she was not alone with her rediscovered . . . well, whatever Rùnach was to her. She pulled away from him, then glared at Soilléir.

"I see you're in the thick of things, Léir," she said, sounding greatly displeased. "As usual."

Soilléir inclined his head. "To my continued surprise, cousin," he said, "I find that I am."

The woman shot him an unfriendly look, then continued her inspection of the chamber. Aisling knew she shouldn't have been surprised to be singled out next given that she was the only other soul in the library, but she was. In her defense, it had been that sort of year so far.

She scrambled to her feet and suppressed the urge to curtsey. Perhaps she should have because it was obvious she was looking at royalty. The gown she had already encountered and been intimidated by. There were endless yards of fabric expertly sewn to give the impression of a terribly tiny waist, a perfect bosom, and an inexhaustible amount of riches. The tiara sitting atop the woman's black hair didn't detract at all from her face, which Aisling had to admit was so beautiful it was almost difficult to look at.

She rethought her decision not to curtsey.

"And who," the woman said, her voice dripping shards of ice, "is *that*?"

Rùnach took a deep breath. "My betrothed."

Aisling felt her own skirts flutter. That was likely because the woman's intake of breath had almost sucked them right off her.

"*That*?" she asked contemptuously, then she turned just slightly and favored Rùnach with a look that would have perhaps brought a lesser man to his knees. "Perhaps you have forgotten in all the excitement of your obvious escape from death at your father's hands, Your Highness, that you are betrothed to *me*."

Aisling felt something sweep through her and it was no longer a desire to curtsey to the woman in front of her. She suspected it was an intense desire to kill the man standing behind that woman.

Rùnach looked profoundly uncomfortable. "That's where things become a little complicated."

"Which is reason enough to take a bit of air," Soilléir said cheerfully, "elsewhere. Aisling, perhaps you would care to join me?"

"Aye," the woman said shortly, "take that creature there with you. I've a desire for private speech with the apparently still-breathing prince of Tòrr Dòrainn."

"Annastashia," Rùnach said with a sigh.

Princess Annastashia whirled on Rùnach. "All I want from

you is the answer to where the *hell* you've been for the past twenty years!" she shouted. "And don't pretend you've been off on some bloody noble quest!"

Aisling was torn between wanting to see how Rùnach would extricate himself from his current straits and wanting to escape having to listen to what she was certain would be a very unpleasant conversation. The one thing she knew with certainty was that she had no desire to be anywhere near that woman while she had her claws out. Soilléir's cousin looked as if she were fully capable of doing damage to anyone who got in her way.

Soilléir paused next to her. "We can back out the doors, if you like," he murmured. "Keep her in our sights, as it were."

"I don't think she can hear you," Aisling said, "if that worries you."

"I think I should be more worried about what will be left of Rùnach's hearing after she's finished with him," Soilléir said with a faint smile.

"Will she stab him, do you think?"

"I don't think she has any weapons. Well, none save her sharp tongue. If Rùnach cannot defend himself against that, there's nothing I can do for him."

Aisling nodded and walked with him to the doorway, wishing she could appreciate his attempt at levity. She paused, then looked over her shoulder. Rùnach was leaning back against the library table with his arms folded over his chest, wearing an expression that very eloquently said he was steeling himself for a conversation he didn't particularly want to have. Aisling found herself the recipient of a look that she thought might have been a request not to rush off and do anything rash, but it had been a very brief look indeed.

Aisling decided there was no point in not taking the opportunity to look at what might be the means of finally sending Rùnach to his grave. Annastashia looked less elegant than perilous, and not because she was currently shouting dangerous things at Rùnach. There was something about her that left Aisling with the intense desire not to be in her sights. She considered the woman for another moment or two, then looked at Soilléir.

"Are you elves?" she asked.

"Why do you ask?"

"Because your cousin is very beautiful, but she doesn't look like what I thought elves should look like." She paused. "When I thought they were nothing but mythical characters, that is."

"Is that what you thought?" he asked with a smile.

"It is," she agreed, "and you're answering me with questions."

"Am I?"

"Rùnach does that. It's very annoying."

Soilléir laughed softly and offered her his arm. "I've tried to stop, but the habit is too ingrained in me by now. Blame Rùnach's mother. I learned it from her."

Aisling didn't wonder, then, that Rùnach had taken the practice for his own, given how much she knew he had loved his mother. She suppressed the urge to look at him one final time and instead walked with Soilléir out of the library. She waited until they had left the shouting far behind before she looked at him seriously.

"Well?"

"My bloodlines are complicated," he conceded. "I'm not even sure my grandfather's bard could identify exactly where we come from. We're a mongrel bunch, honestly."

"Yet possessing magic capable of undoing the world, or so Rùnach says."

"I would say that you, my dear Aisling, are one to talk."

She would have laughed, but she realized he was serious. She shivered. "I can't talk about magic now." Never mind that the reason she couldn't talk about it was because she couldn't bring herself to face the fact that she might have it. Magic, that was. Not in truth. Not when it meant that she might have to become familiar enough with it to use it—

"Let's make for the garden then," Soilléir suggested. "'Tis a truly lovely place to spend the morning, as long as you aren't wearing delicate court shoes."

"How fortunate, then, that I'm wearing boots."

Soilléir smiled and the sting of the previous handful of moments disappeared. "Exactly so. You and the garden will get on famously."

Aisling considered a bit more as they walked without haste through passageways that were simply corridors instead of being hallways determined to deafen her with tales of glory and former traversers. She'd had enough of that in elvish palaces and dwarvish fortresses. The silence was, she had to admit, something of a relief.

"That was my cousin, Annastashia," Soilléir said at one point. "In case you were curious."

Aisling would have preferred to ignore the whole subject, but she supposed it was better to know everything sooner rather than later. "So I gathered. Is she betrothed to Rùnach in truth?"

"I think it may have been discussed," he conceded, "but to my knowledge there was nothing formal between them."

Which could mean several things she wasn't comfortable thinking about. "She has magic, doesn't she?"

"She does," he agreed.

"Is she going to turn me into a garden gnome while I'm not paying attention?"

Soilléir smiled. "She doesn't have those spells, thankfully."

"You sound relieved about that."

"I am, actually, and I imagine Rùnach is as well. Those of us who hold the spells of essence changing are very choosey about the souls to whom we give them. Anna doesn't have the temperament to manage them very well, so she knows none of them. Rùnach, how-ever, is the soul of discretion, which is why he has them all."

"Did you know he had his power hidden behind his scars when you gave him those spells?"

"Which spells?"

"The spells of essence changing."

He frowned. "Those spells?"

"You're doing it again," she warned.

He smiled a little. "I'm trying to avoid answering that."

She looked at him blankly. "Answering what?"

"Whether or not I knew Rùnach's power—" He stopped short and laughed a little. "You almost had me there." He considered, then shrugged. "Perhaps it's best to leave that question unanswered lest I put myself in a position of having to say more than I'm comfortable with at another time to someone else. I can tell you, though, that even if I *had* known what I won't admit to knowing or not knowing, I didn't have the power to draw his magic from him."

She stopped at that. "In truth?"

"In truth."

"But you are so powerful," she said faintly.

"It makes you wonder about the woman who managed the feat, doesn't it?"

Aisling didn't want to wonder about that at all. She also didn't want to think about the fact that Rùnach had spent a score of years thinking that magic was lost to him forever when in reality it had been with him all along, buried by his mother under the scars on his hands and face. Perhaps Soilléir had done him a mercy by never mentioning it to him. She sighed.

"And yet you gave him your spells, thinking he would never use them?"

"I never said that."

She shivered. "You must trust him."

"With my life," Soilléir said frankly. "And believe me when I say there are few whom I could say that about."

She nodded and continued on with him out to the edge of the garden. She paused, then looked at him.

"They aren't engaged?" she asked, because she couldn't not ask it.

"It was discussed," Soilléir conceded, "but nothing more that I'm aware of."

Aisling wondered absently if all women who loved a particular man felt the same sort of queasiness she did upon learning that that man had come very close to wedding another.

"Well, I guess he could help me, then come back for her," she said slowly. "If he decided to formalize what had been discussed."

"He could," Soilléir agreed. "Though that would make it a little difficult to continue a betrothal with you, wouldn't it?"

"But he's a prince. He would likely be most comfortable in a palace." She glanced at him. "Don't you think?"

"He might," Soilléir said with a nod, "occasionally. But not for the rest of his life. That would be a terrible thing for him, I think."

"Do you?" she asked searchingly. "Why?"

"Because he spent twenty years haunting my solar," Soilléir said, "when he could have been having cushions plumped for his royal backside in Seanagarra."

"Perhaps he wanted a look in the library there."

"He could have had that without masquerading as my servant." He shook his head. "He is a man of taste, true, but a life of luxury and ease is not for him." He paused, then looked at her. "It is difficult to step back and watch terrible things happen to other people, isn't it?"

"Is she a terrible thing?"

"I'm not sure I would want to cross her."

She couldn't believe that was true, but she also knew what she'd seen. "Rùnach looked uncomfortable."

"Rùnach looked terrified."

Aisling realized he was teasing her. She smiled at him. "Should I leave him to terrible happenings, do you think?"

"I think you should. We'll see if he manages to emerge unscathed in time for supper. If not, we'll decide whether or not we dare attempt a rescue."

She supposed there was little else to do. She walked with Soilléir along paths that were just paths and under trees that seemed content to silently stretch their branches toward the heavens. Not even the fountain they walked past seemed inclined to do anything but sing softly to itself. She passed by it, then paused and turned back.

There was something caught there on the lowest basin. Aisling plucked it off the stone, then held it up to the sparkling morning sunlight. It looked like a thread from Annastashia's gown, though it seemed a little less like proper thread and a bit more like a strand of magic.

Or a strand of dream.

Whatever it was, it definitely belonged to Soilléir's cousin. Aisling put it in a pocket, then caught up to Soilléir who was simply watching her with a faint smile. Perhaps if she asked him enough uncomfortable questions, he would spend the morning avoiding answering her and she wouldn't have to discuss what Rùnach was doing at the moment behind silent wooden doors.

Libraries.

She'd known there was a reason she'd wanted to avoid them.

Two

Rùnach of Ceangail was swimming in deep waters.

That seemed to be his lot of late, though not a lot he would have chosen. He had almost drowned in the underground river that had brought him along with Aisling to Cothromaiche several days earlier. He'd felt as if he'd been drowning in all the details he'd been attempting to glean from the king's library for the past pair of days, details that he was fairly sure would be critical to any future success. But at the moment, what was about to suffocate him was the torrent of words he was being subjected to from the woman in front of him, a woman he hadn't seen in a score of years.

"You are betrothed to me!"

He hesitated. Perhaps the present moment was not the one to point out that she was mistaken. He had considered it, that was true.

Her father, the second son of the current king of Cothromaiche, hadn't been opposed to the possibility of a match, that was also true. But Rùnach certainly hadn't felt at liberty to do anything until his father had been seen to. He'd only been a score and eight at the time. Man enough, perhaps, but still very young to be choosing a bride.

He was willing to admit that Annastashia had seemed like the perfect choice for him at the time: royal enough to suit his family but far enough away from her own grandfather's crown to satisfy a lad with no aspirations to any throne. Whether or not he had been a good choice for her was still up for debate.

He fought the almost overwhelming urge to bid Anna a pleasant morning and be on his way to find that intriguing Bruadairian lass who had abandoned him without any show of remorse, but supposed he wouldn't make it past the woman in front of him unscathed. She might have looked too elegant to do aught besides direct servants with a languid hand, but he suspected that in a good brawl, she would leave him a bloody mess.

Perhaps he had grown timid during his time in Buidseachd or perhaps he had simply matured enough to understand the true nature of his peril, because he could say without equivocation that she scared the hell out of him.

"It has been a few years," he said carefully, when she paused for breath.

"A few years?" she bellowed. "It's been a *score* of years, you imbecile! Where in the bloody hell have you been?"

He started to speak, then shut his mouth. There was little use in telling her the details of his adventures. She had found the fact of his parentage distasteful enough a score of years earlier. Telling her exactly what had transpired with his father at the well was pointless. Admitting that he'd been lodging at Buidseachd courtesy of her cousin could be, in a word, fatal.

"Father said you had gone to ridiculous lengths to slay your sire," she said coldly, "and that you had failed."

Rùnach nodded. "So we did."

"He also said you'd died in the attempt."

"Obviously not, though it was a very near thing." Again, no sense in cluttering things up with particulars she didn't need to know. She wouldn't care at all for the things he'd had to do to survive as he had crawled away from the well, unable to bury his mother, unable to find his siblings, unable to feed himself save with what he'd been able to catch and kill with his teeth—

"Yet here you are," Anna continued briskly. "Accompanied by some waif of a girl who looks as if she's never in her life had a moment of instruction in deportment."

"She's been sheltered," he conceded. "But what of you? Surely you haven't been swathed in mourning garb for the past twenty years."

She drew herself up. "The shock was not insignificant, of course. In spite of that, I did press on."

He imagined she had. He thought it might not be inappropriate to suppress a shudder at the thought of a life with the woman in front of him. She was lovely and titled and all the things he'd once thought he needed to be happy. Now, he suspected his life would have been an endless procession of evenings spent socializing in clothes that itched and shoes that were too tight.

"I'm surprised you haven't pressed on to the altar," he said before he thought better of it.

"I'm still sorting through all the offers," she said shortly. "And there are at least a dozen."

And that, Rùnach supposed, was the absolute truth.

"Your face is scarred," she said, scrutinizing him with a frown.

"It was much worse, believe me."

"You also seem to have become a bit rough around the edges."

"Blame your cousin," Rùnach said, deciding abruptly to throw Soilléir to the wolves in order to spare himself. "I've been his guest."

Her eyes narrowed. "So I heard earlier this morning. I wonder why he couldn't bring himself to inform me of that fact?"

"Perhaps he thought that telling anyone I was alive would put my life in jeopardy."

"How utterly ridiculous," she said with a snort. "Who would want you dead? Well, save me, of course, when I found out you'd been in hiding all these years. Who else would possibly care?"

He smiled. "No one, of course. But you know your cousin. He tends to be overly cautious from time to time—"

"He's a fool," she interrupted, "with an overinflated sense of his own importance in the world. Now, get rid of that mousey wench and we'll proceed with our original plans."

"Anna—"

"Rùnach," she said, steely-eyed, "don't be difficult."

"I'm not being difficult," he said. "I'm on a quest."

She blinked, then laughed, a tinkling thing that he might have found attractive a score of years earlier. He didn't find it attractive at present.

"You are a silly boy," she said, reaching out to pat his cheek indulgently.

Well, he was certainly no longer a boy and he was sure he'd never been silly. He sat back against the table and held on to its edge, tapping his fingers against the underside of it, beginning with his pointer finger and working outward and back inward. It occurred to him, as he used it as a way to control his temper, that he hadn't had to resort to that in twenty years—or been able to use his hands to do so, as it happened.

His life had changed, indeed.

"I'll arrange for supper," she continued. "Grandfather is still out hunting grouse, or so I understand, not that he would make an effort merely for you anyway. I'll see to it all, as usual. We'll have dancing."

"I think—"

"Yes, you have managed the like in the past and I imagine you'll do so again occasionally in the future, but your input is not required now. Be prompt. That is the limit of your responsibilities tonight."

He continued to drum his fingers silently against the underside of the table because it was somehow soothing. It helped him stay where he was and listen to Anna's plans that seemed to include more than just supper. He bit his tongue as she began to pace in front of him, discussing the arc of his life now that he was back in proper society instead of lounging uselessly about the schools of wizardry.

He shook his head at the realization that at one point, he might have thought that her plans for him sounded reasonable. Residence at either his grandfather's palace in Tòrr Dòrainn or muscling his way into a suite of rooms in Ainneamh. Glorious parties, endless suppers, countless sets of dance, all accomplished whilst using all his charms to propel Annastashia—and himself, it had to be admitted—to ever more astonishing heights of exclusivity.

Perhaps he'd misjudged Annastashia. He wasn't looking at a woman who wanted to simply better herself; he was looking at a woman who wanted to rule a country.

She would have been terribly disappointed if she'd had any inkling what his plans had been less than a handful of months before. Perhaps she would have approved of his having liberated himself from the schools of wizardry in order to attend the nuptials of his younger siblings, and she might have agreed that it was foolish to think he could go back to hiding again in the shadows, but she never would have agreed to the plan to turn his back on his elven heritage and aspire to a life as an ordinary swordsman in an obscure garrison.

He'd had skill enough with a sword in his youth and he'd long since given up the idea of ever using a spell again during the course of what he'd known would be an enormously long life. She would have argued with him when he'd left his paternal grand-parents' house at Lake Cladach and set out to hone his warriorly skills. She definitely would have balked at watching him go inside Gobhann.

Which was, he supposed, just as well. Getting his sorry self inside Gobhann hadn't resulted in acquiring enviable skill, it had resulted in the acquisition of a woman whose eyes continued to haunt him and whose quest for a mercenary had compelled him to offer himself in service to her.

Though perhaps that was simplifying things where he shouldn't have. Aisling had been sent to find a mercenary, but had discov-ered recently that perhaps her role in Bruadair's salvation might be quite a bit more substantial, she who had grown to woman-hood in a country where crossing the border meant instant death, spinning meant more death, and saying the name of her country aloud was a capital offense. She had done all three without harm. Either Bruadairians lied about those sorts of things or Aisling was much more than a simple weaver.

He suspected the latter.

For himself, he'd found himself first drawn to her quest, then to the woman herself, though that wasn't as true as he might have wished. He'd gotten a good look at her, then ruthlessly decided he wanted nothing further to do with her. Falling helplessly into eyes whose color he had yet to determine even after all the time he'd known her had made a mockery of that initial determination. She was artless and honest and courageous.

That and she had thought elves nothing more than pointy-eared myths for at least the first pair of fortnight he'd known her. How could he not have loved her for that alone?

"Are you listening to me?" Annastashia demanded.

Rùnach focused on her, then nodded. Listening to her, perhaps, but being damned grateful that his future wasn't going to include her. He wasn't entirely sure how he was going to make that plain to her without facing her over blades, either magical or steel, but perhaps he could put off worrying about that for another few hours.

"You know, there's still something about you I don't care for." She looked down her aristocratic nose at him. "Something that wasn't there before."

Good sense was on the tip of his tongue, but he was nothing if not politic, so he simply smiled and attempted to look pleasant.

"Something dark and unwholesome," she announced. "Find it and rid yourself of it before we wed." She looked at his sword propped up against a chair. "Perhaps it is that thing there. I can only assume you're still engaged in that foolishness."

"Amazingly enough, yes," Rùnach said. "A useful skill, that."

She snorted delicately. "I daresay." She paused and looked him over. "Bathe before supper."

"When have I ever not?"

"Well, I will allow that your grooming has left nothing to be desired in the past, but I fear that after where you've been loitering recently, you might have forgotten how civilized people live. I shudder to think of the habits you've learned from Léir in that cave he continues to dwell in." She wrinkled her nose. "Who knows what horrible habits you've learned from the company you're currently keeping."

"Please don't disparage her," Rùnach said evenly. "She is on a very difficult quest. If you knew what it was, you might appreciate her efforts a bit more."

"I doubt that. Don't be late for supper."

And with that, she turned and marched out of the library.

Silence descended. Rùnach was terribly tempted to simply stretch out on the sofa near the hearth and have a nap, but that seemed a poor use of his time when he had a betrothed to find.

He counted to an appropriately substantial number to give Anna time to storm off to the kitchens, then retrieved his sword and made his way to the door. He hadn't but left the library behind before he almost ran bodily into someone who looked rather more guilty than perhaps he should have.

"Did you tell her I was here?" Rùnach asked pointedly.

"Who, me?" Astar of Cothromaiche, yet another of the king's grandsons and brother to the elegant if not irritated Annastashia, blinked innocently. "Why would I do that?"

"Because you're a first-rate bastard, that's why."

Astar grinned. "I've missed having you to torment. Why Soilléir didn't see fit to tell me you were still alive, I can't imagine."

"I can," Rùnach said. "You have a loose tongue and no tact. And if you think I'll be sending you an invitation to my nuptials, think again."

"I make a brilliant houseguest. Ask anyone who's housed me."

"Sìle won't let you past the border any longer and Eulasaid is too polite to say what an absolute pain in the arse you are," Rùnach said, then he paused. "Oh, was that too blunt?"

Astar only laughed. "Much, which leaves me no choice but to demand satisfaction from you. Let's go outside and wreak havoc."

Rùnach was tempted to pause and try to count from memory how many times Astar had said that very thing to him, mostly whilst leaning negligently against some wall or other in the posh-est of salons overseen by the most exclusive of matriarchs. How the man had managed so many invitations from such notoriously discriminating hostesses was a mystery, but there was no doubt he was charming. Rùnach suspected he was also his grandfather's best spy, but discretion suggested he keep that to himself.

"Unless you're afraid I'll humiliate you in front of the delight-ful Aisling, of course."

"You know," Rùnach said, "I might like to maintain a bit of anonymity for reasons you don't need to know."

"I can only imagine," Astar said pleasantly. "But you know there are spells brooding over the lists. I'll add to them, if your fastidiousness demands it. Trust me, no one will know we've been there."

Rùnach considered. "I wouldn't mind an hour or two in the lists, true."

"We'll bring our lovely Aisling along with us and allow her to be impressed by me. You, perhaps not so much."

"She is *my* Aisling, not yours, and she's seen enough unsettling things. She doesn't need to watch you attempt to hoist a sword."

Astar laughed as he slung his arm around Rùnach's shoulders and pulled him down the passageway. "You know, Rùnach, if it were me, I would keep a close eye on her. Especially given the fact that my sister is roaming the halls." He lifted an eyebrow. "Then again, perhaps you're the one who needs protecting."

Rùnach rolled his eyes and shook off the other man's arm. "And you're the one to do that? I somehow suspect—still—that you told your sister where to find me this morning."

"She would have tortured me if I'd left that little bit of truth untold," Astar said without hesitation. "She's actually rather adept with a dagger. I believe she keeps them enspelled with unpleasant things and tucked in her reticule just for me. Trust me, you wouldn't have wanted an encounter with the same."

Rùnach had to admit facing her over words had been perilous enough; daggers might have been more than he could have managed.

He walked with Astar through passageways that were comfortingly free of would-be fiancées and was grateful for the peace. If nothing else, he needed another day or two to catch his breath and determine exactly how it was he was going to go off and rescue a bloody country.

"At least your Aisling has had a pleasant morning."

Rùnach glanced at him. "And you would know?"

"I would," Astar agreed. "She and Léir were walking in the garden when last I saw them. She was planning to spend the rest of the day spinning."

"Wool, I hope," Rùnach said, before he thought better of it.

Astar blinked, then looked at him. "I'm not sure I want to know what you're talking about."

"Nay, I don't think you do."

"Who is she?"

Where to start? Rùnach considered all the things he could say about her, then eliminated them rapidly as things he *shouldn't* say about her. After all, it wasn't his place to reveal that he was positive that she was not just a simple weaver who had run away from the most oppressive Guild in all of Bruadair, but instead the missing dreamspinner that no one had the thought to look for save those who had to have known where she was.

The final dreamspinner.

The most powerful dreamspinner.

He looked at Astar. "She is someone who needs to be protected."

"And you're the lad to do it."

It hadn't been a question. Rùnach nodded slowly. "I daresay I am."

"All the more reason to dredge up a few spells and see if you can use them, eh? Though I worry that you'll manage it, honestly. You look distracted."

"It has been a very long year so far."

Astar smiled. "Rùnach, my friend, I think it's been a very long twenty years. What were you thinking to hole up with Léir in Buidseachd? Surely there were only so many pranks you could pull on Droch with your mighty spells poached from your sire's book before you tired of the sport."

Rùnach walked through the gate out into the lists that were obviously well-loved by King Seannair's guardsmen, then waited until Astar had joined him. He could safely say that over the course of his lifetime, he had been very choosey about his confidants. His brothers, of course, and more particularly Keir had always had his complete trust. A handful of his cousins at Tòrr Dòrainn, of course, and even one or two princes of Neroche. But outside that rather small circle, the men he had trusted had been few and far between. Soilléir, without question. And though he wasn't about to burst into tears over the thought, he could safely say that he trusted Astar well enough.

He folded his arms over his chest and looked at Annastashia's brother.

"I take it Léir didn't tell you what happened to me?"

"You know he says nothing," Astar said, frowning slightly. "And tell me bloody what?"

"My father took my magic at Ruamharaiache's well."

Astar's mouth fell open. "*What?* That's impossible."

"'Tis quite possible, as I'm sure you know. He took my brothers' as well." He sighed. "I don't think he took my mother's but I fear by the time he might have tried, she was past—"

"I understand," Astar interrupted quietly. "Còir told me what his father had found there. I honestly thought you'd all perished along with her."

Rùnach supposed he shouldn't have felt such profound gratitude to Soilléir for having kept his mouth shut, but he couldn't help a brief moment of it. He looked at Astar and shook his head slightly. "My mother perished, as did my younger brothers. Well, save Ruith. He was living peaceably in Shettlestoune until events forced his hand, though he did a goodly work with my father—"

"Your *father* is alive still?"

"If you can believe it," Rùnach said grimly. "He's now quite contained, thankfully, behind spells that I would imagine Ruith managed to pry from your cousin. Mhorghain is alive and wed to Miach of Neroche, which I suppose you know."

"I had heard that much at least," Astar said with a faint smile. "A good match for them both, I daresay."

Rùnach nodded. "Our mothers would be pleased. As for Keir, he perished shutting the well and I've been loitering in the shadows of Léir's solar for the past few years, mourning the loss of my magic and looking for replacements for my father's spells."

Astar went very still. "Why would you want them, Rùnach?"

"So I knew how to counter them should they find themselves out in the world," Rùnach said. "And trust me when I say it was a very academic exercise. Or it was until a fortnight ago when I discovered that perhaps my magic wasn't as plundered as I'd feared."

"Should I be sitting down for the rest?"

Rùnach smiled. "I'll tell you if you can best me with the sword."

Astar snorted. "And here I feared you would require something difficult of me. Let's go, then, lad, and I'll try to leave something of you so you might spew out the rest of your sorry tale over a bit of restorative beer. My grandfather's alemaster has had a particularly good year, you know." He paused. "You're sure you wouldn't rather use spells than steel?"

That was tempting, Rùnach had to admit. Astar for all his ridiculous preenings was a very dangerous mage and he had a reputation for having no mercy on the field.

"You hesitate," Astar noted, rubbing his hands together purposefully. "Come now, Rùnach. You weren't such a coward in your youth. Perhaps you've forgotten that you were forever begging me to trot out to the field beyond my granddaddy's glamour and beat on you."

Rùnach laughed a little uneasily, because it was entirely true. He'd been to Cothromaiche at least a score of times he could remember, all whilst on his search for the impossible and powerful, and he'd never passed up a chance to hone his magic against the man facing him. He didn't want to speculate on which of the spells of essence changing Soilléir's younger cousin knew, and he'd never dared ask lest the knowledge not allow him to sleep easily at night. What he did know was that Astar had a penchant for the odd and the elusive, and Rùnach had queried him about both more than once.

"Spells, then," Astar said brightly. "I can tell you're too polite to ask me to leave you on your knees, weeping, so I'll grant your unasked request. Leave your very fine Durialian steel on that bench there and let's see what sort of job was done by whoever took pity on you and restored your magic to you. I can't imagine it was my cousin."

Rùnach had the feeling he might regret agreeing, but supposed he had reason enough to take any opportunity to hone his rather unwieldy magic.

It turned into a very long morning.

Astar proved to be every bit as unpredictable and offensive on the field as he had ever been. His spells weren't so much terrifying as they were full of twists and turns Rùnach very quickly found he couldn't counter easily or even begin to anticipate. It was thoroughly irritating, which he could tell Astar knew very well. And still Astar wove things around him, things that vexed him, poked at him unexpectedly, continually pulled at the ground under his feet as if he'd been standing on the edge of the sea as the tide was going out.

He dragged his sleeve across his face. When had the sun become so bloody hot?

Astar only smiled in a way that tempted Rùnach almost beyond reason to go wipe that smirk off with his fists.

There came a point where he'd had enough, yet holding up his hand to cry peace went unheeded. He opened his mouth to point out to Astar the concession he'd missed only to have a spell he hadn't seen slam into him and wind him. Damned Cothromaichian magic that made no sense. Who had invented such ridiculous spells?

He reached for something to match his irritation that had somewhere during the past half hour become something far stronger. He wasn't so much surprised as rather satisfied to find there were spells there at his fingertips, spells that came readily to his hands, complicated pieces of magic that were worthy of the power he could feel rushing through his veins—

He realized abruptly that he was standing in the midst of terrible spells that were robbing him not only of what breath Astar's spells had left, but almost all movement as well. It took him only a bit longer to realize those weren't Astar's spells, they were his own.

Or his father's, rather.

The tangle that had sprung up around him and was dense and full of thorns. He couldn't move without something impaling him and causing him intense pain. It was, he could admit freely, agony of his own making. A dark, unrelenting, breath-stealing agony that left him feeling as if he were falling into a blackness that had no end—

And then, suddenly it was all gone.

He leaned over and gasped for breath. He saw Astar's boots before he managed to straighten, and felt his sparring partner's hand on his shoulder.

"I'm sorry," Astar said, sounding very sorry indeed. "I pushed you too hard."

Rùnach attempted to shake his head, but he couldn't. He stood there for another few moments, waiting for the stars to clear and the ability to breathe to return. He finally heaved himself upright.

"My fault," Rùnach managed. "My apologies."

"Nasty spells, those," Astar said faintly. "They were . . . dark. And I couldn't stop them, if you want the truth."

"Neither could I," Rùnach said, then he realized they weren't as alone as he might have suspected.

Soilléir was standing twenty paces away, watching him thoughtfully.

"What?" Rùnach said defensively, though he knew the answer himself. He had reached for things he shouldn't have, things that had come too easily to hand. His brother Ruith had warned him he wouldn't want their father's spells, but he hadn't heeded that warning. He supposed he should have.

Yet still Soilléir said nothing.

Rùnach rolled his eyes, trying to save his pride. "An aberration or two. I've been without magic for half my life now. One makes the odd mistake now and again when pressed." That Soilléir had been forced to stop whatever he'd been doing and come to rescue not only him but Astar as well . . . well, he supposed that was something he could avoid thinking about, surely.

"There is that," Soilléir said mildly.

Rùnach shot him a look. "Regretting giving me your spells?"

Soilléir blinked, as if the question not only surprised him, but also wounded him slightly. "Nay, my friend. I know what lies at the bottom of your soul."

Rùnach dragged his hand through his hair. "Forgive me. I'm weary."

"You've had a busy day that looks to be not ending anytime soon." Soilléir smiled. "But perhaps after supper we can escape the madness in the hall and retreat to the library for a bit of peace. I'll go see if I can make that happen."

Rùnach didn't dare hope for it, but perhaps Soilléir had means at his disposal beyond the norm. His spells certainly qualified.

He waited until Soilléir had left the field before he looked at Astar. "I apologize."

Astar clapped him on the shoulder. "Not to worry, Rùnach."

"I'm not sure how things got so out of hand there."

"And I have no idea what in the hell you were spewing at me, but I suppose we could save that for some light after-supper conversation. Let me nap this afternoon and we'll talk tonight when I've recovered. Though if you want to hasten my recovery, you might tell me how it was you regained your power. I'm a little surprised at that, Rùnach, I don't mind saying so. Gair was notorious for not leaving any spoils behind, as it were."

Rùnach retrieved his sword and walked with Astar back to the palace. He paused at the doors leading inside and looked at Soilléir's cousin.

"It was actually never lost," he said carefully. "Apparently, my mother hid it beneath scars on my hands and face."

"Your mother was exceptionally beautiful," Astar said, "and obviously exceptionally clever. I'm assuming you knew what she'd done."

"Hadn't a clue," Rùnach said. "I thought magic was lost to me forever."

Astar blinked in surprise. "How dreadful."

"That's one way to put it."

"So how was it recovered?"

Rùnach looked at him seriously. "It was spun out of me, strung on a loom of fire, and dropped back into my barely breathing form by Uachdaran of Léige."

"Uachdaran of Léige spun your magic out of you?" Astar asked, clearly stunned. "As if such a thing is possible to begin with—"

"Nay, he's the one who enspelled it back into me."

"Who spun it, then?"

Rùnach looked at Astar steadily.

Astar blinked several times, then his mouth fell open. "You jest. *Aisling?*"

Rùnach nodded.

Astar gestured inelegantly toward the field. "And what of that ugly display? This ethereal woman certainly didn't gift you with any of that."

"Nay, nor did the king of Durial, I daresay," Rùnach said. He shrugged helplessly. "Too many of my father's spells rattling around in my head, I suppose."

Though he supposed that wasn't at all what was going on. His father's spells he knew, aye, but those he could control. His magic he could sense sparkling in his veins and there was no evil there. It wasn't anything Aisling had done, nor King Uachdaran. He couldn't believe that his mother would have created such a thing in him either.

But there was something there.

He looked at Astar and forced himself to smile. "I should bathe, I suppose, and dress for supper. Better that than more time on the field."

Astar shot him a look. "Lesser of two evils, Rùnach?"

"Something like that."

"If you're choosing my sister over more time with me, you're choosing the wrong thing."

Rùnach laughed in spite of himself. "That's your sister you're disparaging."

"I know of what I speak. But not to worry. I'll keep watch over our Aisling tonight whilst you're about the heavy labor of negotiating your escape from Anna's clutches."

"She's not your Aisling," Rùnach said, opening the doors and walking inside. "How many times must I say it?"

"A few more at least. The day is young."

Rùnach had to agree that it was, though he supposed he wished it had been otherwise. He wanted to find Aisling, see how she fared, survive supper, then send Annastashia of Cothromaiche off to contemplate her numerous offers of marriage, all of which hadn't come from him.

And then perhaps he would have the courage to face what he knew he wasn't going to want to.

That darkness on the field hadn't come from his father's spells. It had come from his own.

Three

Aisling wandered about the chamber that reputedly belonged to Cothromaiche's chief spinner and found herself too restless to sit but utterly unsure about what to do next. She walked over to the window and looked out. That window overlooked the garden, which she appreciated. Spring was obviously hard upon them even so far north and early flowers had awakened to welcome it.

Cothromaiche was an odd place, she had to admit. She had seen other gardens in other places that had seemed unusual, but in a fairly predictable way. The gardens in Tòrr Dòrainn boasted flowers that were full of pleasure at being of use to the king and queen of the elves. She'd listened to trees in the dwarf king's garden sing half-sleepy dirges with strains of sparkling harmonies running through them, a perfect reflection of the souls who looked inside the earth for their treasures.

King Seannair's gardens were much different. She'd walked in them an hour ago but the stone pathway beneath her feet had been simply stone, the trees and flowers welcoming but not volunteering any conversation past a soft good morning and an invitation to sit amongst them and be at peace. Then again, after watching Rùnach be enveloped in a passionate embrace by a woman who frightened the hell out of her, Aisling supposed peace had been the best the garden could offer.

Soilléir had shown her back to the chamber where she was currently standing, repeating the offer of free rein over its contents that he'd made a pair of days earlier. She found waiting for her on her stool an empty little purse made of marvelous fabric, silent yet somehow quite sentient. She had fished about in her pocket for the thread she'd picked up previously, then put it in that bag. That thread joined something she found earlier, dangling from the flywheel of the spinning wheel set there near the window.

Those tasks seen to, she now had nothing to do but either think too much or make yarn. She looked at the baskets at her feet, baskets full of deliciously soft roving that was nothing more than wool, and decided she would make yarn. It was less complicated that way.

She sat down at her wheel and began to spin a soft cream-colored wool shot through with almost imperceptible strands of gold. It was terribly regal, that bit of business, though she had to wonder what anyone would make with what she was able to spin. But it was lovely under her hands so she kept on with it. Perhaps she would spin gossamer threads and make a shawl for the queen of Tòrr Dòrainn should she ever see her again.

The door to her left opened softly and a throat cleared itself. She looked over, half expecting to see a guard there come to tell her she was lingering where she shouldn't, but it was only Rùnach.

Only Rùnach.

She started to rise but the look of disbelief he gave her had her sitting back down again. He made her a small bow.

"May I?"

"If you like."

"I like," he said, coming in and shutting the door behind him. He found a chair, then set it a discreet distance away from her and sat down.

She had no idea what she was to say to him, so she said nothing. When last she'd seen him, he'd been in the library being inundated with complaints by that woman in the hideously expensive gown. Perhaps he only wanted a bit of peace and quiet for himself.

That, she had in abundance. The only sounds at the moment were the whir of her wheel and the faint squeak of the treadle, but those were soothing sounds, so she didn't complain. She also didn't dare look at Rùnach.

He had stretched his legs out and crossed his booted feet at the ankles as if he had nothing better to do with his time than simply sit there. She waited him out until she thought she would go mad from spinning under his scrutiny.

"So," she said finally, because she couldn't bear it any longer, "I suppose congratulations are in order."

"For what?"

She looked at him then. "Your marriage to Princess Annastashia, of course."

He blinked, then his mouth fell open. "Are you daft?"

"I'm trying to be *polite*." There was no point in saying that she would have preferred to be impolite and heave something heavy in his direction. Perhaps he would sense that without her having to say anything. "What else am I supposed to be?"

He shifted, looking as uncomfortable as she felt. "I'm sorry she knocked you over. I should have rescued you immediately."

"Don't think anything of it," she said. "The carpet and I commiserated about her choice of footwear, then Prince Soilléir took me to the gardens for a bit of bracing fresh air."

He smiled faintly, but said nothing. If only he hadn't been so . . . she sighed. So himself. Familiar and safe and far too beautiful for her peace of mind.

She started up her flywheel and spun for a bit longer until she had to stop again. She looked at him frankly.

"I won't blame you if you want to remain here."

"Why would I want to do that?"

"So you could wed her," she said, gesturing vaguely behind her. "The princess, that is. And nay, I'm not daft."

He straightened, then leaned forward with his elbows on his knees. "Aisling, I have no desire to wed Annastashia of Cothromaiche."

"She seems to disagree," she said slowly.

He rubbed his hands over his face and looked at her. "Will you have the entire tale?"

"I'm not sure," she said. "Do I want it?"

"It paints me in a very unflattering light. Does that help?"

She smiled reluctantly. "I can't believe that's possible, but feel free to try to convince me otherwise."

"I don't think it will take much effort," he said dryly. He rubbed his hands, gingerly, as if he'd done too much with them recently and they pained him. "In my youth, I was a bit of a prat from time to time."

"Surely not."

"Unfortunately, 'tis all too true. Along with my colossal ego, I must admit that I was not, shall we say, unaware of my effect on those of the gentler sex. How I found time for it all, I don't know, but even during my search for terrible spells to use on my father, I managed to attend my share of balls and parties in various locales."

"Here?" she asked carefully.

He nodded. "My mother and Soilléir were very close, which granted us an access we might not have otherwise had. Uachdaran of Léige is fairly choosey about his guests, but he will at least allow the rabble into his great hall. King Seannair is substantially less hospitable. I'm not sure if he fears a guest might elbow him aside at the supper table or nick one of his spells."

"The spells of essence changing?"

"Aye, though why he worries, I don't know." He shrugged. "It isn't as if an enemy could possibly pin any of his progeny down and wrest the spells from them before being turned into something unpleasant."

She didn't like to think about those spells. "Do they all know them, do you suppose?"

"Not to my knowledge. And thankfully so," he added, "else I would have likely found myself turned into a toad this morning by Annastashia. Seannair knows them all, I would guess, as does his son, and Soilléir. What any of the others know, I wouldn't presume to guess. They have magic of their own, to be sure, but its nature is capricious. I'm not even sure how to describe it." He looked at her suddenly. "How does Cothromaiche strike you?"

"Ordinary," she said without hesitation, "though I don't mean any disrespect by that." She paused, then shrugged. "It's just a very quiet place."

"No being kept awake at night by dwarvish stone telling you a millennia's worth of tales?" he asked with a smile.

She shook her head. "Thankfully, nay. Things seem to be polite, but not effusive."

"Soilléir would be impressed with the description, I'm sure."

She waited, but he seemed content to simply sit there and look at the floor below his hands. Perhaps he was contemplating dwarvish tales. Or perhaps he was still looking for a good way to tell her he wasn't going to continue with her on her quest.

She supposed the kindest thing she could do was put him out of his misery. She pushed her stool away from her wheel and rose.

"Well, that's that," she said with a cheerfulness she most certainly didn't feel. "I think I'll beg another meal or two from Prince Soilléir, then be on my way in the morning. Best wishes, of course, for your nuptials."

He looked up at her, seemed to consider for a moment or two, then rose. He clasped his hands behind his back.

"Aisling," he said seriously, "I have no intention of wedding Annastashia of Cothromaiche. I suppose it should have occurred to me that she would be here and our paths would cross, but I hadn't intended that that path run right over you."

"You couldn't have known."

"I could have used my wits and considered the possibility," he said, "something for which I apologize. But now that we have that settled properly, let's turn to other things such as discussing what my heart truly desires."

"Supper?" she asked.

He smiled, then held out his hand toward her. "You know that isn't what I'm talking about. Unless Astar has caught your eye and you're hesitant to break my heart over the fact."

"Break your heart?" she said quietly.

"Shatter it," he said. "Please don't."

She took a deep breath, then sighed. Because in spite of the events of the morning, she knew the man standing in front of her loved her and she felt the same way about him. But there was no point in giving in too quickly. "Prince Astar is handsome," she said thoughtfully. "If one is looking for that sort of thing in a man."

"But like Mansourah of Neroche, sadly lacking in familiarity with soap and brush. I'd steer clear of him were I you."

She put her hand in his. "As usual, you aren't serious."

"Oh, I am," he said. He drew her over to a bench set fully under the window and pulled her down to sit with him. "Let's revisit that moment in that bloody stream full of icy water and Bruadairian magic when you agreed to wed me." He tilted his head and studied her. "Does an aye from you given whilst you were under duress count?"

She considered. "I would say that death looming does tend to leave one perhaps a bit friendlier with honesty than not."

He smiled. "Which is why I'm so damned grateful I wrung an aye out of you whilst you were otherwise distracted. The thought of potentially having to put your father to the sword in order to have the same from him gives me pause, but I'm working up to that."

"I don't think he'll have a say in anything," she said firmly.

"Bruadair, then." He smiled. "Your country may have an opinion. Or at least the magic might. It seems to already have an opinion about several things."

She suppressed a shiver at the memory of being in that underground river with Rùnach, knowing she was about to drown, and finding that Bruadairian magic not only knew her but seemed to . . . well, care for her. She had taken the spell it had given her, used it, and found it responsive to her pleas.

She wasn't sure she would ever forget that moment.

"I suppose we must discuss our plans," Rùnach said quietly. "And come to terms with our magic."

She heard something in his voice she hadn't before. It wasn't so much doubt as it was perhaps unease. She shifted to look at him. "Did something happen to you this morning? Well, besides being deafened in the library."

"Nothing terribly important. I took the opportunity to try out a few spells with Astar in Seannair's lists." He took a deep breath, then let it out slowly. "Let's just say that it didn't go particularly well."

"Are you going to give me details?"

"When I'm sure they won't turn your stomach." He smiled wearily. "It was either too many of my father's spells lurking in darkened corners of my soul or perhaps just being here. For all the peace and quiet, there is something about this country that is . . ."

"Unusual?"

He nodded. "Don't you think? In spite of its façade of ordinariness."

"Absolutely."

"I'm not sure what that means for the remainder of our journey."

She knew exactly what he was talking about. If his magic didn't work as it should have in Cothromaiche, what would happen inside Bruadair's borders? Rùnach's grandfather had, when pressed, admitted that even his magic hadn't worked as it should have within Bruadair's borders. That Rùnach's would likely suffer the same difficulty wasn't something she wanted to think about.

She met his very lovely green eyes. "But we should solve that before too much longer, is that what you're saying?"

"I don't think we have a choice," he agreed. "Perhaps we would do well to make ourselves a bit of a test here. I'm sure no one will notice us at it."

"If Her Highness catches us together, you know she'll turn me into a toad."

He leaned over and kissed her. "I know more spells than she does, I guarantee it."

"I'm not sure why that leaves me feeling so relieved."

"Because I could turn *her* into a toad if necessary." He looked at her. "In honor of that, why don't you try something now?"

"Rùnach," she said with a sigh, "you know I have no magic."

"That stream of something extremely beautiful we encountered in that terribly cold river recently seemed to think so. I wonder what Cothromaiche thinks of what you can do?"

"Are you purposely trying to make me uncomfortable?"

He leaned back against the window and smiled. "Of course not. I'm just curious."

"And we all know where that leads," she said grimly. "Very well. What shall I try?"

"What is your magic called?"

"How would I know?"

"I thought you might have asked it at some point."

She attempted a glare but she feared it had only come out as a weak sort of whimpering thing. "We didn't have time to find ourselves on a first-name basis while you and I were coming very close to dying."

He smiled. "Fair enough. Try Croxteth. It's a very sturdy, sensible magic that Cothromaiche likely won't find objectionable."

"I forgot the spell."

"And I imagine you haven't forgotten anything, but I'll let that pass and give it to you again."

She suppressed a shiver when he taught her the spell, then forced herself to repeat the words. It wasn't terror that gripped her, it was the feeling that she was a child in a roomful of things belonging to her elders and she was contemplating touching something she'd been specifically instructed not to play with.

A ball of werelight appeared in front of them, spluttered, then disappeared.

She looked at Rùnach. "See?"

He frowned thoughtfully. "I don't think that was any lack on your part."

"You try something so we'll know for sure."

He considered, then tried his own spell in Fadaire. The light that appeared there was beautiful, true, but there was something about it that seemed . . . strange. As if she were seeing the light through a window made of glass that was slightly flawed.

The light disappeared abruptly, leaving behind a shadow of something that faded so quickly, Aisling was certain she'd imagined it. She looked at Rùnach, but he was only continuing to look without expression at the place where his ball of werelight had lingered.

"Perhaps 'tis something I did," she offered.

"When you spun my magic out of me, then did me the very great favor of helping to put it back in my veins?" he finished. He shook his head. "Aisling, this isn't anything to do with you. There is no darkness in you. For all we know, Uachdaran decided to drop a shard of obsidian in my veins as punishment for all the spells I poached from him in my youth."

"Perhaps 'tis just a shadow," she said. "From the light coming in the window, of course."

"Of course."

Though she had the feeling it might not be. The look he gave her said he was thinking the same thing.

"I think it might be wise to discuss this with Soilléir before we go any further," he said reluctantly. "I'm not sure he'll offer an opinion, but we can try. I'm sure he's loitering uselessly about somewhere in the palace."

He rose, but she shook her head. "I think I'd like to stay here and spin a bit longer, if you don't mind."

He shot her a look. "Stalling?"

"Absolutely."

He laughed a little, then leaned over and kissed her cheek. "I'll come fetch you for supper, shall I?"

"No need," she said, looking up at him. "I'll find my way there."

"What you mean is that you'll find a way to remain in the kitchens," he said dryly, "which whilst I agree with thoroughly, I can't condone. Come to table or I'll come find you."

"You, Your Highness, are a bully."

"I was hoping to hide behind your skirts, which makes me less a bully than a coward." He walked toward the door. "Pleasant dreams, Aisling."

She looked at his back in surprise. "I wasn't planning on napping."

He turned around slowly and looked at her. "What did I say?"

"You said, *Pleasant dreams.*"

He drew his hand over his eyes, then smiled weakly. "We need to get out from under Seannair's roof," he said. "I can see why Soilléir boards in Beinn òrain. Pleasant *spinning*, Aisling."

She nodded, then rose and wrapped her arms around herself once he'd closed the door behind him. She didn't want to think about her future or her past or what she'd seen just then lingering after Rùnach's spell, something very dark—

She took a deep breath and walked over to her wheel. She sat, but found herself back on her feet almost immediately. She was accustomed to very long hours at her loom, but she wasn't sure she could have managed the same at present with a score of Guild guards standing behind her, their hands on their swords. She had to have a distraction far past what spinning could provide.

She paced around the chamber, bending to touch wool occasionally, more often than not reaching out to touch the strands of sunlight that came through the windows. If she was careful, she found she could wrap those strands about her fingers.

There came a point where she realized she was no longer standing where she had been, taking threads of sunlight and separating them into colors. She was somehow wandering inside

Inntrig, but she felt as if she were wandering in a dream. She saw that while she had imagined that all the non-human things within the palace were silent and only mildly interested in the doings of the inhabitants, that wasn't exactly true. They were silent, sentient guardsmen, unmarked until they were needed. The doors to the library, which she could see as clearly as if she stood in front of them, were wood, but only as long as the inhabitants of that library didn't require their services. She saw with startling clarity how they had on several occasions become an impenetrable barricade to keep safe those inside.

She wandered in the garden, knowing she wasn't really there but feeling as if she couldn't have been more present. The flowers, trees, stones of the path, benches of wood and granite, were in their own way just as vocal as what she'd found in other places. They were simply discreet and watchful, as if they grew and flourished in their own good time, taking pleasure in watching over those who strolled through their midst, unaware and at peace.

The whole country was alive with a magic she had never expected and hadn't seen. It was as if she walked in someone else's dream and saw Cothromaiche through their eyes.

She could no longer tell the difference between dreaming and waking, but saw no way out of where she was. She was half tempted to see if she could spin herself back out of wherever she was, but—

She almost tripped over the spell before she realized it was right there in the air in front of her.

She took it in her hands and examined the whole of it. It wasn't like a book, but rather a rose with petals that seemed to represent steps that had to be followed in a certain way. She peeled the petals back one by one, memorizing their structure as she did so, until she reached the center and saw how the spell could be used. She paused, for the magic was unusual. Then again, she was in Cothromaiche, where it turned out that nothing was as it had seemed at first.

She took a deep breath, then began the spell. She took strands of sunlight and bent them into a flywheel, using the spell to help her. It seemed to be perfectly happy to do her bidding and the sunlight didn't protest being turned into something else. She sculpted a bobbin from the breath of the flowers that bloomed just outside the spinner's chamber, marveling as it took shape beneath her hands and became something other than what it had been while yet retaining what had made it alluring before.

She realized with a start that she was standing quite suddenly back in the chamber where she'd begun her adventure. In front of her was a spinning wheel. Well, it was the flywheel at least, and a bobbin, and a strand of something binding the two together, a band of gold or silver or dream . . .

A commotion behind her had her whirling around with a squeak.

Soilléir and Rùnach were falling over each other to get inside the room. She watched them pick themselves up off the floor, then simply stand there and gape at her. She frowned.

"What?" she asked.

Soilléir looked as if he'd just been in a windstorm. Rùnach looked equally as disheveled. That obviously wasn't because of any piece of weather outside else she wouldn't have had sunlight to create with.

"What did you change?" Soilléir wheezed.

She suppressed the urge to scratch her head. "Change?"

Soilléir and Rùnach both looked as if they needed to find somewhere to sit very soon. Rùnach wound up being a shoulder for Soilléir to lean on. Soilléir struggled for breath for a moment or two, then looked at his support.

"I didn't teach her that."

"Well, don't bloody look at me," Rùnach said. "*I* didn't give her any of your spells."

Soilléir bent his head and laughed. Aisling thought that perhaps what they needed wasn't a chair but a brisk slap or two to bring them back to their senses.

"What are you talking about?" she demanded.

Soilléir pointed to a place behind her. She looked over her shoulder at the wheel that was shimmering there in the air. It was, she had to admit, a spectacular piece of work. It needed a base, but she supposed that could be made. The fact that it was simply hanging there in mid-air was a bit disconcerting, but she thought she might do best to simply add it to the list of other things that had unsettled her. She looked back at Soilléir.

"What?"

"Where did that come from?" he asked.

"I found a spell in a dream," she said. "And I made that out of sunlight."

Soilléir leaned over with his hands on his thighs, apparently trying to decide if he should laugh or continue to try to breathe. Aisling looked at Rùnach.

"What's amiss with him?"

Rùnach patted Soilléir rather too firmly on the back, almost sending him toppling over, then walked over to her. He reached out and touched the flywheel, giving it a gentle spin. He watched it for a moment or two, then looked at her.

"He's coming to grips with what it's like to have a dreamspinner in his grandfather's hall."

Aisling suppressed the urge to go find her own chair. "Why?"

Rùnach was smiling, looking equal parts amused and slightly

unnerved. "Because that, my love, was a spell of essence changing you just used."

"It was just a spell," she protested. "I found it in a dream. As I said."

"Aye, in *my* dream," Soilléir said, apparently deciding on a laugh. "Good heavens, woman, you poached one of my spells out of my *dreams*."

"Just recompense for your being so old that you need a nap in the afternoon," Rùnach said with a snort.

"I have the feeling I'm going to soon need another one to make up for the first."

Aisling would have wrapped her arms around herself but she found she didn't need to. Rùnach had done the honors, pulling her close and giving her shelter she couldn't deny she desperately needed.

But she didn't miss the look he and Soilléir had exchanged.

"What?" she said, finding she was trembling.

"She's going to need a rest, Rùnach," Soilléir said quietly.

"Am I?" Aisling asked, finding that her teeth were chattering.

"Aisling, my dear girl, not only did you just use an immensely powerful spell, you filched it out of my damned head. You ought to go sit in the corner just for that alone."

She winced. "I didn't mean to."

Soilléir shook his head, smiling. "I'm vexing you about it unnecessarily. I am happy to give you spells as you require them, but I have the feeling you'll find them lying along your path at just the right moment without any aid from me." He shot Rùnach a look. "You'd best keep any eye on this one."

"I intend to."

Aisling gestured toward her wheel. "And what am I to do with that?"

"I'll have to give that some thought," Soilléir said with a shiver. "Perhaps after supper."

"Where I'll likely be the main course," Rùnach said grimly.

Soilléir only laughed. "I wish I could disagree, but I'm afraid that may be the case. Take care of that girl there, Rùnach. We'll see to the rest during supper, where hopefully you won't be on the menu."

Aisling watched him go, then sighed and leaned her head against Rùnach's shoulder.

"I'm tired."

"I would imagine you are," he agreed. "Those spells are powerful."

"I didn't know what I was doing."

"The spell seemed to disagree." He hugged her briefly, then kept his arm around her shoulders and led her toward the door. "A nap, love, then we'll see what's left of the world. I'm not sure after that beautiful piece of work that you'll be able to remain anonymous much longer."

Aisling decided she wouldn't think about that until she absolutely had to. She looked over her shoulder once before they left the chamber. The spinning wheel was still hanging there where it would have been resting if it had had a base. It was painfully beautiful and definitely otherworldly.

Something she had fashioned out of Soilléir's dreams.

She had the feeling her life had just been irrevocably changed.

Four

Rùnach's head was spinning.

He supposed that might have been because he'd just been given a bracing slap by a woman he'd once fancied himself in love with. He rubbed his cheek thoughtfully as he watched Annastashia of Cothromaiche stalk out of the great hall, leaving him standing there in front of the hearth. Perhaps telling her that he was honestly, truly not interested in wedding her might have been better saved for another locale, but he had apparently lost many of his social skills over the past twenty years spent in the company of the king's grandson.

It was also quite possible that informing Annastashia in no uncertain terms that he was no longer interested in her whilst in the middle of a dance set had been ill-advised. It had seemed like a reasonable idea at the time given that he was fairly certain if he'd done the same in private, she would have killed him.

He rubbed his cheek thoughtfully and walked across the great hall to the high table where a rather edible supper had once resided. He found an empty chair, collapsed onto it, then looked about himself to see the lay of the land. Astar was monopolizing Aisling, which didn't surprise him. She was very lovely, as usual, if not a little pale. Then again, she had lifted a spell of essence changing from Soilléir's dreams earlier that afternoon and changed sunlight into a spinning wheel, so perhaps she had cause. He sent Astar a warning look, then looked at Soilléir, who was watching him with amusement.

"One task seen to," Soilléir said, his eyes twinkling. "I wonder if you'll fare equally well with the others yet to come?"

Rùnach wiggled his jaw, and wondered if perhaps Annastashia had done damage to one of his teeth. At least it had been a slap and not a close-fisted blow. Or a spell. He found himself rather glad, all things considered, that he'd already eaten supper. He had the feeling he wouldn't be able to eat any breakfast.

"I would have liked to have done that better," he admitted, "though I'm not sure how."

"I don't think you could have," Soilléir said. "I daresay it was a bit of a shock for her to find you alive, then yet another to find you in love with someone else."

"I don't think Annastashia ever loved me," Rùnach said wryly. "The idea of me, perhaps, but no more."

"You give yourself too little credit," Soilléir said, "though perhaps more credit to my cousin than she deserves." He toyed with his wineglass. "She'll move on, I daresay. And it isn't as if you're planning on taking up residence here where you might torment her."

Rùnach sighed deeply. "Nay, I'm not." He looked at Soilléir frankly. "I think we should leave soon."

"Tomorrow, I imagine. The world sleeps uneasily."

"Nay, Léir, that's *you* sleeping uneasily and that was this afternoon."

Soilléir shifted. "I'm not sure I'm equal to thinking overlong on what happened this afternoon." He shook his head. "What that woman can do . . . well, she surprises even me and I'm very rarely surprised."

"The only thing that surprises me is that I have the arrogance to think I can aid her," Rùnach said. "Me, with magic that's not only unwieldy but not exactly what I would have it be. This task would be better suited to someone with more power."

"Ofttimes, great ones aren't called; simple souls are called to greatness," Soilléir said with a smile. "But I wouldn't say you are a simple soul, my friend."

Rùnach studied the fire burning in one of the hearths, then looked at the man who had, he could freely admit, saved his life. "How do I thank you?"

"For what?" Soilléir asked mildly. "My collection of spells that could undo the world and everything in it, or putting you in the path of a woman who could unravel the same?"

Rùnach smiled. "Did you?"

"Might have."

"Why?"

Soilléir shrugged. "Because I know her great-grandmother."

Rùnach realized his mouth had fallen open. "What?"

"What I just said."

"You can't simply drop that tidbit into a conversation without giving me the details of it."

"Can't I?"

Rùnach laughed a little in spite of himself. "Léir, who *don't* you know?"

"A woman daft enough to wed me," Soilléir said solemnly. "And no decent matchmakers either."

"No great loves during the centuries before I was born?"

"I never said that."

Rùnach wasn't sure he even dared speculate, so he settled for holding up his hands in surrender. "Don't look at me for aid, though I appreciate the matchmaking you've apparently done for me." He looked around himself to see who, if anyone, was listening. Astar was still monopolizing Aisling. Anna was definitely not eavesdropping; she was likely in the kitchens looking over a selection of carving knives for purposes he didn't want to think on. He shifted to look at Soilléir. "I can't imagine you don't have thoughts about what lies before us."

"I have thoughts," Soilléir conceded, "but they're not ones I would be comfortable sharing here. Let's collect your lady and repair to the library. I can vouch for the privacy there."

Rùnach nodded, then rose and walked behind the table until he stood behind Aisling's chair. He looked at Annastashia's brother.

"Do you mind if I abscond with my lady?" he asked politely.

Astar smiled faintly. "If you must."

Rùnach pulled Aisling's chair out for her, then took her hand. He nodded to Astar, then led Aisling from the great hall.

"Soilléir is willing to have a conference with us," he said quietly. "I thought we'd best take advantage of it whilst he's so unsettled from this afternoon."

"Him?" she said incredulously. "What of me?"

"I believe you two might be sharing a few of the same feelings." He walked with her for a bit before he dared speak again. "How are you, in truth?"

"I'm not sure how to begin answering that."

He nodded, because he understood that very well. He had never used any of Soilléir's spells, but just having them rattling around in his head was unsettling enough at times. At least he hadn't begun his magical career with a spell that overwhelming.

Then again, he'd had a full morning of magic acting in unexpected ways, so perhaps he had a bit more sympathy for her than he might have otherwise. The thought of that problem being magnified inside Bruadair's unfriendly borders was enough to give him pause.

He walked with Aisling into the library, then shut the door behind them. There were three chairs set there in front of the fire, waiting patiently. Soilléir was there already, standing in front of the hearth. Rùnach waited until Aisling was seated, then sat down himself. He didn't imagine he was going to hear anything he hadn't already discussed with Soilléir, but he supposed he wasn't past being surprised.

"Well?" Rùnach asked. "Or dare I ask?"

Soilléir only smiled at him, then turned to Aisling. "I understand Queen Brèagha gave you copies of her paintings of Bruadair."

Rùnach blinked, then smiled. "Subtle."

Soilléir lifted his eyebrows briefly. "So I am. Aisling, might I look at them?"

She nodded, produced them from the satchel she was never without, then handed over the little folio. Soilléir looked through the paintings slowly and carefully. Rùnach glanced at Aisling to see if he could tell what she was thinking, but she was watching Soilléir peruse the queen's artistic endeavors. He wouldn't have called her expression wistful, though he wasn't sure what else he could have termed it. All he knew was that Bruadair had been one of the most beautiful places he'd ever seen.

Before.

Soilléir finished, then tied the folio shut again. He was silent for quite some time, then he took a careful breath and nodded.

"It looked like that."

"And you would know?" Aisling asked.

"Aye."

Rùnach waited, but Soilléir, damn him, seemed perfectly content to say nothing else. "And?" he prodded.

Soilléir sat back and stretched out his legs, crossing his feet at the ankles. "And I think nothing more than what you and I have already discussed at length, my friend. If it were a lesser country that had been taken over by a man with no right to the throne, we could leave that to the inhabitants to sort in their own good time. But this is Bruadair and it isn't just its inhabitants that are being affected." He hesitated, then shook his head slowly. "I don't like to interfere."

"But you will here?" Aisling asked quietly.

"Will and already have," Soilléir said, "more than I'm comfortable with. But I'm afraid the true work of the day will fall to you and Rùnach. And before you cross the borders, I think you must have a plan in place. I'm mostly here to listen."

Rùnach had no doubt that was exactly what he intended to do unless pushed. He looked at Aisling. "What do you think, love?"

"I would say I was trying not to," she said reluctantly, "but I must admit I've been thinking of little else as I've been spinning. I suppose it might be wise to begin in Beul to see how the fight is progressing." She looked at him. "What do you suggest?"

"I think we need to see if we can't find where Bruadair's magic has gone," he said. He knew he didn't need to add that they would also do well to find out who had taken that magic, though perhaps that would be easier than he feared. All they would need to do was look for any black mages of note lingering in the area.

"And then?"

He looked at her steadily. "I also have the feeling that we might want to find out where that seventh dreamspinner came from."

She looked positively ill. "Perhaps we could put that off for a bit."

"Perhaps we could," he agreed quietly. "Let's first find our way to Beul and see what's to be discovered there. Then we'll plot our course." He looked at Soilléir. "Given all your recent experience with crossing that border, perhaps in this at least you might offer a suggestion or two."

Soilléir smiled briefly. "I suppose I could, for I have rather definite opinions on those borders and the perils associated with them."

"Don't tell me there's a curse attached to Bruadair's," Rùnach said in disbelief. "What absolute rot."

"Let's call them safeguards instead," Soilléir said. "In days past, they were rather benign safeguards, but I can't say the same for what watches the border at present. It isn't pleasant. I would venture to say it's a fairly recent addition, if that eases your mind any. Our good Aisling could walk across the border at any spot and Bruadair would only welcome her, though the land would indeed take notice of her entry."

"And would it tell potential enemies the same?" Rùnach asked.

Soilléir shrugged. "That hasn't been my experience so far, but I'm a very small player in this drama and easily overlooked. I can't guarantee that there might be those watching who would find Aisling reentering the country to be upsetting to their plans, no matter where she did it. I'm not sure Bruadair has the means to prevent that."

Rùnach suppressed the urge to shake his head. He'd been doing too much of that recently. "You speak of the country as if it had a mind of its own."

"It is an unusual place," Soilléir conceded. "The magic is connected to the land in a way that I would say isn't replicated in very many other places." He smiled faintly. "I know far less about it than I would like to claim, but it doesn't lend itself to outside speculation. That so much of the magic has been drained from the country says much about whoever managed the feat."

Rùnach supposed he might not want to think too hard about just who that mage might be. If Acair was behind the theft, then he had grown powerful indeed. Then again, his bastard brother had always been more powerful than Rùnach had ever been comfortable with.

"But if Bruadair knows who crosses the borders and unpleasant mages will possibly know the same, then how will we manage to get back inside?" Aisling asked. "And when you were in Bruadair, how did you manage to move about so freely? Or was I one of the ones still asleep?"

Soilléir smiled. "I can't say that you weren't still blissfully unaware of many things at the time, but even had you not been, you wouldn't have noticed me."

"I noticed your clothes," she said with a shudder. "Blindingly gaudy, those."

Soilléir laughed a little. "One does what one must to accomplish the task at hand."

"But surely clothing wasn't enough," Aisling said. "Was it?"

"Nay, Aisling," Soilléir said seriously, "It wasn't. I took the precaution of hiding my magic."

"Oh," she said, sounding rather relieved. "Then I've nothing to worry about there."

Rùnach couldn't help but look at Soilléir. It was so seldom that he had the opportunity to see the man looking anything but perfectly at ease that he paused to savor the moment. Soilléir scowled, then softened his expression as he turned back to Aisling.

"I'm afraid, Aisling, that that isn't as true as you might wish."

"But I have no magic," she protested. "At least not anything substantial enough to need hiding."

"There's a new spinning wheel fashioned of sunlight in our chief spinner's solar that would disagree."

Aisling rubbed her arms. "I think that was an aberration."

"Some aberration," Rùnach said, half under his breath.

Soilléir opened his mouth, then shut it. "I would have to agree with Rùnach. Aisling, I think as you have been discovering over the past few fortnights, you have more gifts than you suspected. Magic seems to be one of them, whether you care to accept it or not. All I can tell you is that if I am able to see the echo of it in you, unfriendly eyes might see that and more once you're on your home soil. It is best to hide it until the time comes when it can no longer remain hidden. We should choose the proper spell, of course."

Rùnach found two pairs of eyes on him. He held up his hands quickly. "I only have Uachdaran of Léige's spell for the same. I have no idea how it would hold inside Bruadair."

"Did you get that from the shameless king of Neroche?" Soilléir asked with a smile.

"Miach could only dream of having this one," Rùnach said with a snort. "So, nay, this isn't the usual one Uachdaran leaves lying about for those who would like to feel they had plundered his coffers for the exclusive and forbidden. His Majesty gave this to me on my way out his gates a fortnight ago and made sure I knew what I'd been given, though I have the feeling it was for Aisling's benefit, not mine."

Aisling smiled weakly. "He is very kind."

"He would like you stop whatever's running under his floors and through his dreams," Rùnach said seriously, "but, aye, he is very kind. To you." He looked at Soilléir. "Do you care to hear the spell? I'm fairly confident there is nothing attached to it that will destroy me for sharing it."

Soilléir nodded, then listened thoughtfully. "Very powerful, indeed, and something you might want to keep close. I hate to think of what you could send plunging into the depths of the earth with that to hand. But given the rather unusual properties of Bruadair, I would suggest, if I could make a suggestion, that you use something of mine instead."

"A spell of essence changing?" Aisling asked in surprise.

Soilléir rubbed his hands together uncomfortably, as if he had perhaps used one too many of those spells over the years. "Not exactly," he said carefully. "I think you could use Uachdaran's spell of burying if you needed something extra in a moment of desperation, but I'm not sure how dwarvish spells will behave on enspelled Bruadairian soil."

"And you're certain yours will work?" Aisling asked.

"Admitting that will force me to confess how much time I've spent loitering inside your borders, a question that deserves more of an answer than I dare give you right now." He smiled. "The easy answer is, aye, I'm sure mine will work."

Rùnach frowned. "You're hesitating. Why?"

Soilléir looked hesitant. "It is . . . unwieldy."

"Inside your borders," Rùnach asked, "or Bruadair's?"

"Both, which leaves me a bit less comfortable giving it to you than perhaps I might be otherwise." Soilléir said seriously, "But I think we have no choice. Dwarvish magic is, as you well know, straightforward and holds few surprises. Well, save what it might do in Bruadair, which is something I can't account for. The spell I'll give you is not a spell of essence changing so much as it is a spell of essence . . . altering."

"A spell you dug up out of some obscure book you shouldn't have been reading," Rùnach said grimly.

"Just so, which is something you understand all too well, my friend. The spell isn't evil, if that's what troubles you. But it is unusual."

"Oh," Aisling said faintly. "And coming from you, that's no doubt saying something."

Soilléir smiled at her. "Aye, I suppose it is. Nevertheless, I believe both of you have the courage to use it. The courage and the need, if I could be so blunt."

Rùnach sighed. "I've had my sight clarified by my uncle the former wizard king of Diarmailt, my person un-noticed thanks to the ever-helpful king of Neroche, and now I'll be behaving in untoward but courageous ways thanks to you. I can scarce wait to see what happens next."

"The world breathlessly awaits the same, I imagine."

"I imagine so," Rùnach agreed. "Very well, are you going to give us this spell, or simply use it on us and leave us guessing as to how we might undo the same?"

"Oh, I'll give it to you," Soilléir said seriously. "You'll have to use it on yourselves, I'm afraid. Only the one who has fashioned it can undo it. That has its advantages, which I'm sure you'll appreciate once you give it some thought."

Rùnach supposed he wasn't going to have to think too long on that. He leaned forward with his elbows on his knees and listened to Soilléir lay out first the spell in its entirety, then its parts and the sequence in which they were to be used. He was almost sure his ears were failing him.

"And you wouldn't consider that a spell of essence changing?" he asked in astonishment.

Soilléir only smiled. "Are you afraid to try it?"

"I hate to be crass, but after having just had my magic restored to me, I'm not terribly keen to have you take it away from me again. So, aye, I'm damned afraid to try it."

"Let's just say this," Soilléir offered. "It will put a sheen on your magic that—nay, let's put it another way. After several centuries spent in Bruadair, you will both have acquired a certain patina to your magic. I'm simply hastening the process."

"Several centuries," Aisling said with a laugh. "Surely you jest."

Soilléir looked at her gravely. "Elves aren't the only ones who live long lives, Aisling, but perhaps that is something you can think on later, when your immediate task is finished."

Rùnach thought he might like to think on that sooner rather than later, but he kept that to himself. He considered Soilléir's spell, then shook his head. "How can that possibly be construed as hiding our magic?"

"I hadn't gotten to that part yet. We're still working on the patina."

Aisling looked at Soilléir. "Who *are* you?"

"A collector of obscure spells," Soilléir said, "which the connoisseur next to you understands perfectly. I think perhaps we should try now whilst we're here at our leisure." He looked briefly at Rùnach. "This might be uncomfortable."

As usual, Soilléir was the master of understatement, Rùnach decided an hour later. It had been less uncomfortable than it had been profoundly unsettling, which seemed to be the word best used to describe the entire evening. If Aisling had spun his magic out of him and restored it to him in a great, crashing bit of business, Soilléir had him burnishing up his own magic in a way that made him feel as if he'd been stretched on a rack to the point where he could no longer feel anything. Before he could comment on that—or the fact that he'd been willing to do it all to himself—

he'd dutifully repeated Soilléir's spell of concealment that didn't so much bury his magic as to simply set it aside as something not interesting enough to look at.

He promised himself a good faint from exhaustion later because Aisling was still to go and he had the feeling she wasn't going to care for what Soilléir's spells would do to her.

As it happened, it wasn't Aisling who protested the spell, it was her magic. Rùnach would have enjoyed the look of consternation on Soilléir's face, but he was too damned tired to. Aisling's magic was elusive, almost as if it had been something hidden away in a dream. It seemed to look rather narrowly on what Soilléir was asking it to do before it simply shifted out of the way and allowed the spell to toddle on right past it. Aisling finally threw up her hands and indulged in a rather unladylike curse.

"How am I to manage this bloody stuff?"

Soilléir shrugged helplessly. "I would like to say I have all the answers, but in this, I believe you're asking the wrong person."

"You?" she accused. "You're the wrong person?"

"I am not Bruadairian," he said, "my pretensions aside. I'll give you all the spells I know for hiding magic, but you and your magic will apparently need to come to some sort of understanding about them yourselves."

She looked at Rùnach. "I feel like I'm dreaming."

"I think that's only going to get worse," Rùnach said, wishing he didn't believe the same.

"Perhaps one more go," Soilléir suggested. "Put your foot down with the stuff, Aisling, or it will run roughshod over you forever."

She took a deep breath, then tried Soilléir's spell again. Rùnach was a bit surprised by how much he could see, for he did see her magic sigh lightly and step behind her, in a manner of speaking. It pulled itself into itself before it was simply no longer there.

As if it had been a dream that had been vivid enough to touch for a bit, then disappeared as most dreams did. He looked at Aisling quickly but she was neither weeping nor panicked. She looked simply as if she was in terrible need of a good night's sleep.

"Well done," Soilléir said, looking perhaps more relieved than he realized. "Now all that's left is to get yourselves to the border. I believe, if you don't mind, I'll come along at least that far."

Rùnach looked at him in surprise. "Will you?"

Soilléir sighed. "Given how much I've already interfered, I can't imagine one more thing will damage the fabric of the world overmuch. Besides, it's just a ride in a sleigh. How much trouble can that cause?"

"Depends on who's pulling the sleigh, I suppose," Rùnach said with a smile. "I suppose Iteach wouldn't be opposed to it."

"If he is, I imagine I can find a pony or two here who might be up for an adventure." He rose with a groan. "I'll leave you two to your digesting and packing. Sweet dreams, friends."

Rùnach watched him leave the library, then looked at Aisling. "And?"

"I don't feel well."

"I understand, believe me. I think it will pass."

"I wasn't talking about the magic. Or supper. Or anything I can almost bring myself to face." She looked truly quite ill. "I'm not sure what to call it."

He rose, pulled her up and into his arms, then held her close for a moment or two. "I always think the most difficult part of any daunting task is those hours that come immediately before the battle is launched. Once you're in the heat of things, that feeling will pass. A good night's rest will help as well, I imagine."

"Nay, you don't imagine that at all."

He pursed his lips and pulled back. "Very well, I think it will take more than sleep to put either of us at ease, but what else can we do? At least we're embarking on this business together. That's worth something, wouldn't you say?"

She leaned up and kissed him quickly. "Quite a bit. Though I don't think I'll sleep tonight."

He wasn't going to contradict her, but he imagined she would sleep rather well, actually. She had used not one but two extremely powerful spells that day and she would pay the price in exhaustion. As for himself, he could scarce put one foot in front of the other. There was something about Cothromaichian soil that was simply . . . odd.

He wondered just how they would find Bruadair's.

Five

❧

Aisling was grateful for the rain as she had never been grateful for it in the past. It allowed her to keep her hood up over her head as she followed Rùnach along the main street in Beul, the one that led away from the border crossing. For all she knew, her hood also hid the fact that she was finding herself increasingly incapable of drawing a decent breath.

"Breathe," Rùnach murmured.

She would have tried, but she wasn't sure she would manage it. Desperately sucking in breaths would have required more energy and attracted more attention than either of them wanted. Rùnach was already garnering attention enough by having styled himself a successful trader. She, however, was merely his servant so perhaps if worse came to worst, she could simply slink back into the shadows and escape death. Cowardly, true, but she didn't think anyone would blame her.

It was the height of foolishness, of course, to come back to a place she had sworn she would never set foot in again, but she had a quest to fulfill. Rùnach had grave suspicions that his bastard brothers were somehow involved in Sglaimir's affairs, and the two of them were mad enough to think they could accomplish what no one else could. Rùnach's magic was buried. Hers, such as it was, was hidden with as much success as she'd been able to manage. She honestly couldn't say she felt any different. Then again, she was so cold with fear, she supposed she wasn't a good judge of anything. All she knew was that for all intents and purposes, they were walking into the fiercest part of a battle with nothing to defend themselves save harsh words.

Rùnach had discussed the twistings and turnings of Beul's sorry streets with Soilléir after they'd landed, which had left her with nothing to do but wish that instead of riding Iteach to Bruadair, they had been riding Iteach anywhere else. Soilléir had left them a mile from the border, then bid them good fortune. Aisling had succumbed to the temptation to beg him to come along with them, but he'd only smiled and shaken his head. He had casually let it drop that he was off to find Ochadius of Riamh, peddler extraordinaire and instigator of all manner of insurrections, which perhaps said all they needed to know about Soilléir's worries over the outcome of what she and Rùnach intended to do.

Crossing the border had been less terrifying than the last time, but only just. If Rùnach had felt any hesitation, he hadn't shown it. He had simply produced the license Soilléir had given him, tucked a bit of gold discreetly into its fold, then watched blandly as the border guard examined their credentials with a practiced eye. If the gold went first up the man's sleeve, then down into his glove, then into a pocket, who was she to argue? She was relieved when he simply waved them through without comment. It occurred to her as she slid past him that it was the same man who had pocketed her gold the last time. Perhaps he was laying up something against the time he would no longer be able to be so dexterous with his hands.

That had been almost half an hour ago. She had hoped at some point that her nerves would cease screaming that she was walking toward certain death, but that hadn't happened yet.

"Recognize anything?" Rùnach asked.

Aisling pulled herself away from her unproductive thoughts and concentrated on her surroundings. Unfortunately she did indeed recognize where they were. It was the same street she'd walked along for at least a dozen years, perhaps longer, after she'd been granted one day a week of liberty from the Guild. She felt suddenly as if she were floating.

Rùnach's arm was immediately around her shoulders in a comradely fashion. She was, after all, nothing but his servant and it wouldn't do for anyone to think anything else. She forced herself to feel the cobblestone beneath her boots and breathe in air that smelled faintly of peat mixed with something rather more foul. That didn't help much, but it was better than feeling as if she were no longer in her body.

"Better," she managed.

Rùnach patted her reassuringly, then folded his arms over his chest as if he surveyed a battlefield to see where the best spoils might be had.

"Where now?"

She gestured with a shaking hand in the direction of the pub. "There."

"Keep your hood close round your face," he murmured, "and let us see what there is to see."

Aisling felt as if she were walking over her own grave. She followed Rùnach across the street, avoiding puddles and the leavings of horses, then almost ran into Rùnach's back as he stopped at the pub's doorway.

"Out of the way," a voice snarled, then interrupted itself immediately. "Oy, beg pardon, sir."

"No worries, mate," Rùnach said easily. "Doorway's big enough for two, aye?"

Aisling almost tore something in her neck looking up at him. Where he'd acquired that less-than-posh accent, she couldn't have said, but she fully intended to ask the first chance she had.

"Buidseachd," he said over his shoulder, winking at her. "All sorts of rabble there to imitate."

"Did I ask?"

He only smiled, then stepped inside the pub, bidding her follow him. She did, then flattened herself against the wall because it was her habit. It was suddenly as if none of the preceding fortnights where she'd acquired a spine had occurred. With the brush of her foot across the threshold of a place she'd spent every workweek's end for at least a decade, she had once again been thrust back to a place where she was nothing more than a slave—

Rùnach put his arm around her shoulders and pulled her up to stand next to him. If he held her more tightly than was polite, perhaps no one noticed.

"Lovely place."

She would have answered, but her mouth was so dry she wasn't sure she could.

"No worries, mate," he murmured. "This is just a visit, aye? We're not planning on looking for a flat here."

She looked at him briefly and saw in his eyes that he understood exactly what she was thinking. And perhaps he did. He'd spent his own share of time in places he hadn't wanted to be. She nodded, then concentrated on breathing in and out. It also helped to remind herself that once they had found what they needed, she would never need set foot in her current locale again.

She took as deep a breath as she dared, then looked at the gathering room to see who might be there. Surprisingly, none of her usual companions was present. The table where they were accustomed to sitting had been taken over by another group, which for some reason was more distressing than perhaps it should have been. Rùnach nodded toward a table in the shadows. A barmaid met them there, took their order and coins, then departed with all due haste. Aisling sat down uneasily, happy to keep Rùnach between her and everyone else. Rùnach waited until their ale had arrived before he sniffed, then frowned.

"It's terrible," she murmured. "Sorry."

"We'll find luncheon later this afternoon," he said. "See anyone interesting?"

She studied the patrons as unobtrusively as possible. "I see familiar faces, but none of my band." She found that her hand was shaking too badly to hold her cup, so she set it down and held on to it for courage. "You don't think something happened to them because of me, do you?"

"Hopefully not. We'll add it to the list of things to find out. And we won't linger here, I don't think."

She wasn't about to argue with that even though Rùnach was the match of anyone in the common room for size and she had the feeling he wouldn't be matched in swordplay. That and he hadn't been the one to enspell that knife down the side of his boot. Who knew what sorts of things Sìle's spells might find objectionable about the conduct of the other patrons?

She sat with Rùnach for another quarter hour, then followed

him happily from the pub, happier still not to feel a hand grasping the back of her cloak to pull her back into those well-used depths.

That feeling of respite lasted no more than five paces before she had her hand on the back of Rùnach's cloak to stop him.

"That's Quinn ahead of us."

Rùnach turned immediately and pretended great interest in the contents of what turned out to be a shop selling what had to have been the worst meat pies in the entire Nine Kingdoms. Rùnach leaned closer to her and pointed in an exaggerated fashion at what was being displayed in the shop window.

"Who?" he murmured.

"One of my friends," she said, "if that's what he could be called. It was his trader's license I used to cross the border." She had to take a deep breath, which she immediately regretted because it acquainted her nose more fully with the smells emanating from the shop in front of them. "He knew the most about everything that seemed to be happening with the government."

"Well, it would seem there's a reason for that. Aren't those palace guards he's currently hobnobbing with?"

"Aye," she said uneasily. "Unless those are Guild guards sporting uniforms that aren't theirs."

He looked at her sharply. "The Guild has guards?"

"Many."

He closed his eyes briefly, then considered. "I'll give you my thoughts on that later, when no one can hear me shouting. Let's continue on our way past them as if nothing were amiss. Stay on this side of me."

She had no intention of doing anything else. She supposed the smell from the shop that was now clinging to them would keep anyone with sense away from them.

Or so one would have thought. One of the guards looked at
Rùnach as he passed, then stopped him and held out his hand.

"License?"

Rùnach smiled easily, then dug in his purse for his license. He
looked at the guard gravely as he handed it over.

"All in order?" he asked with just the right something in his
tone that suggested that it should be.

The guard frowned, then handed the paper back. "It seems to
be," he said, sounding slightly disappointed. "Never can be too
careful, though. Strange happenings these days. Which is why,"
he said sending Rùnach a dark look, "foreigners aren't welcome
here."

"I'm assuming traders are," Rùnach countered politely, obviously ignoring the warning. "Considering how much time I spend
here, it feels quite a bit like home. Though I will admit I don't
recognize some of the goings on these days."

"Perhaps you would be wise to find somewhere else to call
home," the man said bluntly. "Beul is no longer a pleasant—"

"Shut up, you fool," Quinn said. "You know *he* doesn't like tales
told."

The guard shot Quinn a disgruntled look before he turned
back to Rùnach. "I'd be about my business, friend, and be on your
way before something bad happens to you."

"A very useful piece of advice," Rùnach said. "Allow me to buy
you and your mates lunch in return?"

The others seemed to find that an acceptable display of gratitude. Aisling forced herself to breathe carefully as she stayed next
to Rùnach while he purchased enough food to keep half a garrison busy for quite some time. She kept herself apart as Rùnach
directed a pair of shop hands to give the guards their lunch,
offered a banal comment about the weather, then bid them a good

day. She followed him without hesitation, forcing herself to simply walk instead of bolting as she so desperately wanted to do.

By the time they reached the restaurant where she had almost been seen by her parents before Soilléir had hidden her, she wasn't sure she could go any farther. Rùnach glanced casually at the citizens going about their business on the street, then put his hand under her elbow.

"A rest here," he said quietly. "A brief one, though. I don't think we dare linger."

She nodded, then waited with him inside the restaurant as a table was prepared for them. She had to admit it was something of a novelty to think she would actually eat in a place she never could have afforded while she'd been a slave to the Guild. She looked at Rùnach.

"I will have to make something lovely for you in return for all the gold I've cost you."

"A crown of flowers for my hair on our wedding day," he said with a smile. "Or dreams, or whatever it is you lassies of your particular persuasion create. Color it gold if it suits you."

"You are a very kind man."

"And you are a very brave woman," he said, "for more reasons than just enduring me—oh, here is our server."

She followed him to a table in a private corner, sat, then found that she didn't recognize half of what was on the menu. Rùnach seemed to have no such trouble. He ordered for them, then sat back and simply watched the other diners. She would have thought he had forgotten she was there if it hadn't been for the way he occasionally tapped the side of her boot with his own. For herself, she could do no more than look at the pale amber ale in her cup and hope it wasn't poisoned.

If she ate any of the meal that arrived in short order, she certainly didn't taste it. The only thing that gave her any pleasure at all was wondering if it might have been her parents' last decent meal before they realized she was not where they'd left her.

Rùnach was happy to accept the proprietor's invitation to examine his collection of fine wines and suggested that perhaps a discreet exit out the kitchens might induce him to come back and purchase a bottle or two in the very near future. Aisling knew nothing about wine and couldn't have cared less about rain—or lack thereof—in the area of Shettlestoune that seemed to produce the perfect grape for something renowned for its dryness. That made no sense to her at all, but it was a decent distraction for a moment or two.

She was just as happy to leave it all behind, though, and be free of the man's cellar. Their exit was made, as promised, out the back where there fortunately seemed to be a dearth of guards of any sort.

"So," Rùnach murmured as they made their way down the alley behind the restaurant, "that was interesting company your friend Quinn kept back there."

"I can hardly believe he's one of *them*," she said. She looked up at him. "I was very naive."

"I think you were trusting and innocent. And watched over by very powerful people." He studied the alley for a bit before he looked at her. "I wonder about your other mate. Euan, was it?"

"The last time I saw him, he was being swallowed up in a large group of city guards. He's no doubt either dead or wishing he were dead." She shook her head. "Perhaps he's in league with them as well."

"I hope not," he said, "but I suppose we'll discover that in time. First, let's find some sort of lodging commensurate with the stature of a rich trader and his faithful servant, then we'll see what we can discover about the rooster lounging on a perch that isn't his."

She would have preferred they do anything but either of those two things, but she realized there was nothing else to be done. She pretended not to notice when Rùnach examined the inside of a carriage he hailed, then put her inside first while at the same time keeping hold of her. She supposed if things had gone awry, he would have hauled her out just as readily.

She was enormously grateful not to be in Beul by herself.

A suitable accommodation was eventually found and a very expensive chamber taken in a part of town she had never managed to visit. It was even possible, she supposed, to take a walk in the surrounding environs without fearing for her safety, but she wasn't sure she would have attempted it very often. Beul was, after all, still Beul and full of ruffians and scoundrels of the worst sort.

She had lost most of her gear at some point during the journey through that underground river, though Soilléir's servants had been kind enough to replace most of it. Rùnach had fared better with his own things, but he seemed rather less eager than she would have suspected to leave much of it behind. Then again, he seemed to travel very lightly, which she supposed served him well if he needed to make a hasty getaway.

She kept her pack with her and her satchel pulled across her body, then left the inn and walked with Rùnach along streets as if they had every right to be where they were.

"Where now, do you think?" he asked at one point.

She nodded at the hill plainly visible from most parts of the city. "The castle is there."

"Have you ever gotten close to it?"

She shook her head. "No means and no desire."

"It might be a good place to start."

She couldn't disagree with that, so she walked with him without protest, hoping they would be mistaken for simple travelers out for a look at the city.

The closer they came to the castle set there on the hill, though, the thicker the clusters of guards and the more nervous she became. There came a point where even she could see that they wouldn't get any farther without engaging more guards than they cared to. She stood with Rùnach and simply stared at Sglaimir's lair. She couldn't say she even had any memories of it looking any different from how it appeared at present. She suspected, however, that the grey tone of the entire city was seeping from under those ugly stone walls.

"I think we can go no farther," Rùnach said with a sigh. "Let's find a place to sit and think."

She wandered with him back the way they'd come until they arrived at a public park of sorts. They found the only stone bench that seemed to have escaped decay, and sat before it was appropriated by any of the rather cheeky-looking youth loitering there. Rùnach sent the lads off with a look that even she had to appreciate for its fierceness.

She sighed. It was surprisingly difficult to imagine that the expanse in front of her had ever been anything but an unkempt park full of noxious weeds. Even the trees were silent.

Aisling looked at Rùnach. "It's unpleasant."

"I've seen worse," he said slowly, "but I will concede this holds few charms at present."

There were times she forgot who he was and where he'd come from. "I'm sorry," she said quietly. "I'm sure Ceangail was much worse."

He smiled briefly. "I suppose it depends on how you look at it. Ceangail is evil, whilst Beul is merely grim. Let's just say that neither locale inspires a burning desire to set up house within its confines."

"I wouldn't live here again if the inducement were all the gold in the world."

"What if the inducement were me with a shop on some seedy street where I peddled paltry magical spells?"

She couldn't help a brief smile. "Well, I might reconsider for that."

He took her hand in both his own. "I would never ask. Just testing the waters, as usual." He watched the lads playing ball in front of them for a moment or two in silence, then turned to her. "So, what do you think?"

"I'm not sure why this surprises me, but I think things are worse than when I ran."

"More soldiers than one might reasonably expect, to be sure," he agreed. "'Tis obvious we're not going to be able to simply walk up to the palace and toss Sglaimir off his perch. Not that we ever expected it to be that easy."

"Do you think King Uachdaran was correct about who he is?" she asked. "That he's the grandson of that terrible mage whose name escapes me?"

"I have no reason to disbelieve it," Rùnach said slowly, "but I'm not sure it matters whose grandson he might or might not be. He is the problem we must solve. I asked Soilléir for details about him, but he had none to give. I suppose I should have asked Mother Fàs about him, but I was too busy worrying that we might not escape her back porch alive."

Aisling smiled in spite of herself. "She is very fond of you. And nay, it isn't simply because you built shelves for her greenhouse."

"When her alternative is her beloved youngest son Acair as a houseguest, perhaps she has reason to prefer you and me," he said with a smile. He studied something in the distance for several minutes, then sighed. "I'm not sure it would be wise to ask too many questions here. Sglaimir isn't going to be noising about any of his secrets to his underlings, I don't imagine, but I suspect he's perfectly happy to learn about anyone who asks questions about him." He frowned thoughtfully. "Did you ever hear any gossip about him at the pub?"

"None that I remember," she said, "but I'll confess I wasn't paying all that much heed to what the lads were saying. I was too busy trying to forget the Guild."

"I imagine you weren't the only one," he said, "which is perhaps something Sglaimir counts on. Easier to control the populace when it's distracted with endless amounts of work." He looked off into the distance thoughtfully. "'Tis a pity we don't have Ochadius here with us. Or a way to connect with Freàm's niece in the palace."

"Is it worth trying to find either of them?"

"I don't think so at the moment, not that there would be any guarantee we would manage it even if we tried. I wouldn't recognize the king's niece if she appeared in front of us and introduced herself. And for all we know, Ochadius is dead."

She started to agree that such might be the case, then realized it might not be true. She closed her eyes, stilled her mind, then saw without effort things that didn't belong to her dreams. It took a moment before she thought she could speak.

"He's not," she said hoarsely. "He's dreaming."

His mouth fell open. "How in the *hell* do you know that—nay, never mind."

"I fear they aren't pleasant dreams, if that makes it more palatable."

"Aisling," he began, then he shook his head. "Let's just say that if I didn't know you better, you would terrify me."

"I promise only to use my power for good."

He smiled, as if she had either amused him or pleased him somehow. "Somehow, love, I never doubted it." He leaned back and studied her for a moment or two. "Well, now we've exhausted this idea, why don't we consider others that might be less pleasant?"

"Such as?" she asked reluctantly.

"Finding a certain group of spinners missing one of their number might be useful."

Which was, as it happened, the very last thing she wanted to do. It was difficult enough to deny that she actually had magic, something she had ignored for as long as possible. To be forced to admit that she might have more than just an obscure bit of power running through her veins—

She attempted to swallow, but she failed. "Why would we want to do that?"

"Because they might know what had befallen the seventh of their number," he said quietly. "They might also be able to tell us if she's connected at all to the current political situation. And there are other questions you might be interested in putting to them."

She wanted to say she couldn't think of anything she wanted to ask, but she could think of at least one question she *needed* to ask, namely if she herself might be—

She pushed the thought away. It was such a ridiculous idea, she could hardly entertain it, no matter the conversations she'd had with Rùnach at Inntrig. There were seven dreamspinners, or so 'twas said, and the most powerful of them all had reportedly been slain twenty-seven years earlier. The position held by that seventh dreamspinner had lain empty for—well, she couldn't say for how long. It was a mystery. But presumably there would be another dreamspinner in the world destined to take that place. It also followed that the person destined to be that spinner of dreams would need to have particular skills.

Spinning skills, perhaps.

Those were in short supply in Bruadair, actually. She supposed the thread she had once used to weave endless amounts of cloth had come from somewhere, but she'd never thought to ask where. Someone was spinning thread, but she had only ever known weavers. Spinners were rare. Actually, spinning was considered a capital offense. Those who set hand to wheel were slain immediately by a terrible curse that attached itself to anyone brazen enough to attempt such a thing.

Only she had spun without dying.

Unfortunately, it was also true that in a country of weavers, she could not only spin wool, she could spin all sorts of interesting things using wheels made of yet more interesting and unusual substances. It was also true that she had spent all of her life she could remember in a weaver's guild—nay, not just any weaver's guild, but the most brutal and notorious of them all. Of all the places in Bruadair, it was the last place where anyone would have looked for a spinner.

But none of that meant she was a dreamspinner.

It certainly didn't mean she was that missing seventh dreamspinner.

She looked at Rùnach. "I'm afraid."

"Now that," he said with a faint smile, "is perhaps the most sensible thing either of us has said all day."

She had to simply sit there and breathe until she thought she could speak without shrieking. "What should we do?"

"Find your parents—or the pair masquerading as your parents—and ask them a pointed question or two about the past of a certain girl who can do things others cannot."

"Sensible," she managed. "Useful, even."

"I have the feeling it might be. So, let's discuss our direction. Where is your village?"

"How would I know?" she asked.

He looked at her blankly, then he frowned. "I was going to say because you were raised there, but that isn't true, is it? I'm assuming you know your parents' names."

"Riochdair was his name, Dallag hers. But more than that, I don't know." She looked at him bleakly. "We could perhaps find the nearest library and look through maps until we see something interesting."

He nodded. "We could, but that would take time."

"I'm not even sure they have libraries here in Beul."

"Appalling."

"You would think so."

He smiled. "Aye, I would." His smile faded. "What do you want to do, Aisling?"

She shifted uncomfortably. "I want to go hide back in Durial."

"You'd never get a decent night's sleep for the rocks and veins of ore fighting each other to most loudly declare their magnificence to you. We'll have a holiday each year in Inntrig, if you like. The surroundings there seem to be of a more modest mien. And you're stalling."

What she wanted to do, as she had very honestly said, was run to Durial and hide behind the king's very sturdy door. At the moment, she would have braved Annastashia of Cothromaiche's wrath to seek asylum in Inntrig. But she knew she couldn't. She also knew that the only way to find out anything about dreamspinners was to find out things about herself. And there was only one place to do that. She looked at Rùnach.

"Don't want to lay siege to the castle?"

He shook his head slowly.

She closed her eyes briefly, then looked at him. "The Guildmistress would know from whence my parents hail."

"Could we get inside, do you think?" he asked. "Is there magic there?"

"I have no idea."

"Don't you?"

She thought it was impossible to feel any more terrified than she felt at present, but she realized that wasn't at all true. "Are you asking me to try to determine that?"

"I fear I am."

She closed her eyes and forced herself to relive her memories. She walked through the gates, heard them click shut behind her, heard the heavy metal doors of the building close behind her as well and felt something come down behind her that wasn't visible. She walked to the dormitory where she'd slept for the whole of her life with three score other girls and women. She forced herself to look at the weaving room and the Guildmistress's chambers, then follow along the stark white passageways until she found herself standing at Mistress Muinear's doorway.

She sighed deeply, then opened her eyes and looked at Rùnach.

"There is a spell of watching surrounding the outer walls," she said, trying not to shudder. "I'm not sure what else to call it but that. There is no action to it; it simply watches what comes and goes through the gates. There is another much more powerful spell of containment that closes behind you when you enter the Guild building. Mistress Muinear had, I think, a different sort of spell in her chambers. A more pleasant one, but the magic is unfamiliar to me. Twisted beyond what it was meant to be, perhaps."

"And the Guildmistress herself?"

"Something very unpleasant there. Not Olc, I don't think. I can't name it now, but I think I might be able to if we were closer to her chambers. Not that I'd ever find myself in that place again, of course."

"I wouldn't think to ask you to go," he said quietly. "Leave that to me."

She felt her mouth fall open. "Leave it to you?" she repeated. "What does that mean?"

"What it means is that I'll be the one to go inside and ask the Guildmistress where your parents live."

She turned to face him fully. "You can't be serious."

"Actually, I am," he said carefully. "I won't have you subjected to that place again. I'll find you a safe place to stay whilst I see to what needs to be done today."

She had thought, a fortnight earlier, perhaps a pair of fortnights earlier, that even thinking to take up her quest to find a way to save Bruadair was taxing the limits of her courage. Actually putting her foot to that path had required yet more digging deeply into her heart for the strength to ignore her fear. Coming to Bruadair with Rùnach hadn't been as hard as she'd suspected it would be, mostly because she had assumed they would find what they needed to overthrow Sglaimir, Rùnach would use a few handy spells to put him in his place, then they would hurry off— well, she hadn't considered exactly where they would hurry off to, but she'd been fairly certain it would be a pleasant place.

She had never once considered walking back into the Guild. That was something else entirely.

"Or we could try a library," he said quietly.

She looked at him, grandson of elven royalty and a powerful wizardess, a man who could have easily taken up a place as an equal to any number of lovely if not sharply heeled princesses and lived out his life in splendor and ease. Yet there he sat on a rotting bench, waiting for her to decide what she was willing to do so he knew what unpleasantness was left for him.

She closed her eyes briefly, then looked at him.

"I'll come."

He looked as if he intended to protest, then he sighed. "I'm not sure you would be any safer tucked away in an inn than you would be with me which is the only reason I'll agree to this." He shot her a look. "We might make a bit of a mess getting out if things go south."

"Don't expect me to clean it up."

He smiled faintly. "Nay, I'll see to it."

She chewed on her next words for far longer than perhaps she should have. "I'd like to see the Guildmistress with boils or some other nasty ailment."

"I'm not sure I can manage that and everything else," he said thoughtfully. "You might have to see to the festering sores."

"Have you a spell for that sort of thing?"

"I have spells for all sorts of things, love."

She smiled in spite of herself. "Off we go, then."

Her good humor lasted approximately ten paces, but no more. She knew what lay ahead of her and could scarce bring herself to enter those terrible gates voluntarily.

Then again, Rùnach had done the same thing twenty years earlier when he'd walked into a glade to try to keep his father from unleashing an incalculable amount of evil.

She took a deep breath and kept walking.

Six

Rùnach walked behind a pair of very burly guardsmen and wondered if he'd just walked into hell.

He supposed he could thank his uncle Nicholas for the spell of clarity that had seemingly only been enhanced by the recent return of his magic, though thanks were not precisely what he was interested in offering at present. Being able to see the spells that hung like filthy drapes over the entire Guild was extremely unpleasant. How Aisling had borne it so long was a mystery to him.

Perhaps she was blessed not to have been able to see at the time.

She was half a step behind him, close enough that he could turn and pull her close if something went wrong, but far enough away that it didn't look as if that were his intention. She was, after all, merely his assistant and he a very rich, rather annoyed trader come to find out details about a customer who owed him money.

He walked along floors of dingy grey tile and suppressed the urge to flinch at the relentless whiteness of the walls. At least in Ceangail, there had been blood, a decent layer of fear, and the shrieks of lesser mages coating the castle walls. It had added a bit of interest to the relentless grey of the stone. Here, there wasn't even that. How Aisling had survived so long in such stark surroundings, he didn't know. He fully intended to be in and out of the place in less than half an hour. He didn't think either of them would survive any longer than that.

He was just sure it was his imagination, but he felt as if the passageway were constricting the farther along it they went until there was finally nowhere else to go. The guard stopped in front of an unremarkable steel door, rapped smartly, then stepped aside. Rùnach was very grateful for all the years he'd spent perfecting the ability to remain still and, when warranted, paste a neutral expression on his face.

The door was wrenched open and a tall, austere woman stood there. She was dressed in black, which surprised him slightly. She was wearing an expression of annoyance, which didn't surprise him at all.

He found himself sized up expertly in the space of a pair of heartbeats. The Guildmistress glanced at Aisling, but immediately dismissed her. Rùnach supposed the close-fitting hat, the dirt-smudged cheeks, and the hood pulled close to her face was disguise enough. As he had said, despite it all she was safer right next to him than waiting in some seedy inn. Perhaps he'd spent too much time imagining the horror of returning to their lodgings and finding her gone. Besides, if things truly became dodgy, he could release his magic and save them both.

Assuming his magic worked as it should.

The Guildmistress stepped back and welcomed him into her office with a sweeping motion. "Do come inside, Master Buck."

Rùnach felt a little as if he were going into Droch of Saothair's chambers at Buidseachd, but there was nothing to be done about it now. He found himself regretting sorely having brought Aisling along even though he couldn't have done anything else. He would die before he left her behind to be yet again imprisoned, though he sincerely hoped it wouldn't come to that. His goal was to slip in and out of the Guild whilst garnering as little notice as possible, not raze the place.

The Guildmistress reached out suddenly and took Aisling by the arm. "Do not sit."

"Oh, I wouldn't think to have him dirty one of your chairs," Rùnach drawled in his best imitation of his grandfather, Sìle. "I know I never let him dirty any of mine. He spends more than his fair share of time trotting behind the carriage, as you can see."

The woman pursed her lips. Perhaps she was smiling. Rùnach had no idea. She sat down behind her extremely large and heavy desk, then motioned for him to take a seat on the other side.

"My men said there was a trader here to see me on business that required my immediate attention. I had assumed it would be someone here for large quantities of cloth. Is that your need?"

"Actually, I'm here for an exchange that I hope will prove mutually beneficial," Rùnach said smoothly. "Weighted, of course, more heavily on your side of the scale."

The Guildmistress studied him for several minutes in silence. Rùnach didn't begrudge her that examination. Aisling hadn't told him much at all about her, but he hadn't needed the details. He could immediately see that there was a woman who took pleasure in small things: intimidating those weaker and poorer than she, sending fear rolling through the passageways to bring her workers to heel, no doubt torturing small animals. He'd seen his father do much worse, so he was less intimidated by it than perhaps he should have been.

"So," she said, leaning her elbows on her table and clasping her hands in front of her. "What do you have to offer me?"

Rùnach smiled. "Why don't we discuss what I need first?"

"Because I am not particularly interested in what you need," she said with a very slight lifting of one of her shoulders, "only in what you can provide me. Perhaps you might begin with your trader's license."

Rùnach removed that from the purse at his belt, making sure to brush the coins lingering there in a way that could leave no doubt as to their quantity. He slid the paper across the desk toward her.

"There you are."

"Gold?"

"I have plenty," he assured her.

"Allow me to admire some of it."

He reached in and pulled out several gold sovereigns minted in an equal number of locales. He put them just within her reach and watched as she picked them up one by one, examining where they had been struck. She looked at him calculatingly.

"You have traveled far."

"Exclusive goods are my delight," he said easily. "And one travels where one must to find them."

"Pricey goods, are they?"

"Extremely."

"What did you bring with you today?" she asked, fingering one of his coins.

"A question and ample payment for the answer."

She frowned as if that answer had displeased her somehow, but she examined his license just the same. He only watched with as bored a look as he could muster. Soilléir had obviously gotten himself in and out of Bruadair many times with the same sort of thing. Rùnach had no doubt the current sheaf in question would survive even the Guildmistress's scrutiny.

She didn't shortchange the process, which Rùnach appreciated. She was obviously waiting for him to shift first, if shifting was to be done. He didn't move. He'd learned that much at least from all his years as his father's son.

She finally shot him a glare, then shoved the license back at him. She gathered the coins onto her side of the desk.

"Ask," she said briskly.

Rùnach removed the purse from his belt and put it on the edge of the table nearest his knee, which he'd propped up against the wood. He also took a packet from within his cloak, set it on the table, then opened it partially to reveal the contents. It was nothing more than a silk scarf, but the fabric had come from a Cothromaichian loom, so perhaps the Guildmistress would find that rare enough for her tastes. He set it next to the gold, then looked at Aisling's former jailor.

"As I said," he said, "I deal in only the most exclusive of goods, and my clientele is equally discreet. I was persuaded by a third party to engage in a piece of business with a man I'd never met before and had not interviewed myself."

The Guildmistress snorted. "I can see where this is going already."

"I would imagine you can," he said. "Unfortunately, I was far less perceptive at the time and I found myself swindled over an exceedingly rare and valuable piece of carving. Elvish, of course, and almost impossible to come by. Once I realized my prize was gone but my payment not forthcoming, I set about tracking down this cagey lad and his lady wife."

"Tracking them down where?"

"Here."

She looked momentarily confused, then she frowned. "There are no married couples here at the Guild. Only women."

"I was led to believe they had done business of some kind with you," he said. He reached for his package and his gold. "My mistake, obviously—"

"Don't be so hasty," the Guildmistress said, holding out her hand. "I do business with many."

Rùnach released the prizes and sat back. "Then hope remains."

"How long ago was the crime?"

"Three months."

"Why didn't you come to me three months ago?"

"I only discovered the fraud a pair of fortnights ago, of course," Rùnach said coolly. "Why else would I wait so long? While the theft was an annoyance, I have had other, more profitable transactions requiring my attention. I am just recently arrived in Beul with time to see to the matter. I called at their reputed lodging to find them gone, of course. Unfortunately, no number of threats jogged the innkeeper's memory as to where they might currently find themselves."

"You didn't threaten me."

"I am a gentleman."

"So you appear to be." She looked at him. "Very well, what are the names of this unwholesome pair?"

"The husband's name is Riochdair. The wife had a very unusual name. Dannar, Dagnar, Dannemar." He shrugged. "Something akin to that."

The Guildmistress had gone very still. "And you didn't bother to find out the particulars of this pair?"

Rùnach drew himself up slightly. "Perhaps I wasn't clear before," he said evenly. "I do not screen my clients personally. I have trusted, very ambitious tradesmen chosen especially for that pedestrian labor. It is their business to seek out suitable buyers for me."

"I'd suggest firing the one who set you up with this pair."

"Oh, he's no longer in the business of trade," Rùnach said with a shrug. "I believe his convalescence will be long and unpleasant."

The Guildmistress snorted, then seemed to realize they weren't alone. She looked at Aisling, who was standing by the door, then seemed to consider things she perhaps hadn't before.

"Their daughter was one of my workers," she said thoughtfully.

Rùnach merely looked at her politely. "And?"

"I thought you might find that interesting."

"I don't deal in human prizes," he said, wrinkling his nose in distaste. "They squirm too much."

The Guildmistress pursed her lips, then reached for a piece of paper. She scrawled something on it, then shoved it across the desk. Rùnach looked at it.

Riochdair and Dallag of Malcte. He frowned, then looked at the Guildmistress. "This is the pair?"

"I said it was," the Guildmistress snapped. "And they owe me as well. Their brat is a runaway. If I find her, I'll do worse than simply put her back at her loom."

Rùnach shook his head. "Again, too much work," he said. "Much easier to deal in inanimate objects." He considered the paper again, then pocketed it. He pushed the bag of coins across the table, then placed the wrapped package next to it. "A pleasure."

The Guildmistress spilled the coins out onto the table. Rùnach rose, glancing behind him at the guard standing in front of the door. The man hadn't moved, which wasn't particularly encouraging, but perhaps he was waiting for a signal from his employer. Rùnach turned back in time to see the Guildmistress pull the scarf from the packet. She froze briefly, then looked at him in surprise.

"Cothromaichian silk."

He nodded. "You have a keen eye."

"How on earth did you come by this?"

"Fairly," he said mildly.

"Traders lie."

"Which is why most of them only have substandard goods to

sell," he said, "which I do not. There's a reason for that." He inclined his head. "A pleasure, madame."

He walked over to the door, nodded for the guard to move, then let himself out. He was, he had to admit, vastly relieved that Aisling had exited with him. He put her one step in front of him and loosened both his sword in its sheath and the spell surrounding his magic. First and last resort, respectively, but he could feel the hair on the back of his neck prickling, so they were most certainly not out of the woods yet.

He wasted no time in walking down the hall, though he went out of his way to make it look like a saunter and not a hasty retreat. He heard nothing behind him, though he expected to have someone raise the alarm at any moment.

He nodded to the guards at the front door and was allowed out. Good, but not a complete escape. He didn't relax fully until they were outside the stone wall and the gates had clanged shut behind them. He looked up and down the street, but there wasn't a damned carriage in sight.

"We'll have to walk for a bit, I imagine," he said with a curse.

"I know shortcuts."

He smiled grimly. "I wouldn't expect anything less. Can you get us back to the inn—or, nay, perhaps just to a main street. We'll find a carriage there, I'll warrant."

She nodded. Rùnach followed her, glancing casually over his shoulder now and then whilst doing his damndest not to be obvious about it.

"Are we free?"

The tone of her voice startled him. He slung his arm around her shoulders, pulling her close to his left side. He could fight with either hand because his swordmasters in his youth had been without peer, but he preferred the right, which was handy given that

he wasn't about to put Aisling closest to the street where she could
be snatched away before he could do anything to stop it.

"We're close to free," he lied.

"They're behind us, aren't they?"

He took a deep breath. "I'm afraid so."

She panicked. He'd never heard anyone utterly lose their ability to breathe before and honestly had no idea what to do. He
looked for sanctuary but there was nothing on their side of the
street save abandoned buildings crawling with spells that made
him queasy. He looked across the street, spied an open door, then
hurried with Aisling through mud and horse droppings to present
himself at what looked to be the only inhabited building on the
street.

He realized, once they had stumbled inside, that it was a house
of ill repute. He would have laughed at the ridiculousness of where
he currently found himself, but he was too damned unnerved to.
He brushed aside the feathers he was assaulted by as the proprietress swirled a very fine, feather-encrusted cape around her less-
than-clothed self. Obviously his best company manners were
going to be called for.

"Good afternoon," he said, suppressing the urge to sneeze.

"A visitor," she said, looking terribly pleased. "And his young
companion."

"Who are looking for a back door," Rùnach said. He held up
two gold coins. "And discretion."

"Discretion's me middle name, pet," the woman said, relieving
him of his money without delay. "Unless they're Guild guards
hunting you, then all bets are off."

"Just the back door will do," Rùnach said. "And directions to
somewhere else."

The woman lifted Aisling's hood back from her face, studied

her very briefly, then shook her head. "It'll take more than a request prettily spoken, me lad. We have a runner here."

"How could you possibly assume that?" Rùnach asked in surprise.

She looked at him shrewdly. "I live across from the bloody place, don't I? Don't have many runners these days. Herself rules with an iron fist, don't she?"

"This is merely my servant—"

"Bollocks," the befeathered woman said briskly. "The whole damned town's been looking for this one for weeks now. Guildmistress wants her bad, I'd say—oh, nay, missy, don't you dare faint."

Rùnach continued to hold Aisling up. "What do you want?" he asked the madame grimly. "More gold? My sword? My firstborn?"

She laughed, a robust sound full of good humor. "Wouldn't dare take the last from the likes of you, but your packs seem a bit heavy. Let's start there."

"I don't think I have time to divide the spoils with you."

"Whatever you can pull out in haste, then. 'Tisn't often I have an elven princeling in my front parlor along with a gel the whole of Beul is looking for."

Rùnach made sure Aisling was able to stand unaided before he quickly rummaged through his pack for the most valuable and least enspelled items he owned. He shoved a pair of socks and a fresh tunic back inside, then handed over the rest of his gear. He put his hand out, though, when the proprietress reached for the satchel Aisling wore slung across her chest.

"Not that."

The madame frowned. "What do you have in your pack then, dearie?"

"Just clothes and wool," Aisling whispered.

The woman sighed heavily and looked at Rùnach. "I suppose I'll make do with your things."

Rùnach watched her dump his offerings along with another infusion of his gold into a trunk that was promptly pulled behind a false wall. She nodded toward the back of her house.

"This way, and hurry."

Rùnach put his arm around Aisling and followed the proprietress through the kitchens and into a rather less-than-tidy back garden.

"Through that gate, bolt to your left down the alleyway, then duck through the garden at the end of the street. I'll send a lad to show you. Free of charge, that last bit."

Rùnach had no choice but to trust her. He thanked her for her care, then took Aisling's hand and did as instructed. Unfortunately, it was far too soon that he heard crashing and shouting going on in the house they had just left. He could only hope that that was nothing a woman with the cheek to operate a brothel down the street from the Guild wouldn't be unaccustomed to.

"Through here."

Rùnach looked at a lad standing suddenly before them, panting with a sort of nonchalance that said he'd done this sort of thing before—and more than once. Rùnach tipped the lad a sovereign because his mother had taught him good manners, then followed the directions and hoped he wasn't running them into a clutch of guardsmen.

They emerged onto what had to have been Beul's main street. Rùnach took the first carriage he found and gave the driver the name of their lodging. The carriage had uncommonly large windows, which he didn't particularly care for, but there was nothing to be done about that. He kept his head down, kept his arm around Aisling, and turned over his mind what he'd heard.

They'd searched for Aisling?

Soilléir couldn't have known or he would have said something. Rùnach supposed they were fortunate to have gotten as far as they had. Perhaps the Guildmistress had recognized Aisling from the start but had decided there was no practical purpose in holding her hostage there when there was more gold to be had from him. Either that, or the woman had simply sent guardsmen after them as a matter of course.

The driver suddenly slid open a small window. "Sir," he said politely, "I see a pair of n'ere-do-wells behind us."

"N'ere-do-wells?" Rùnach asked, wincing.

"Thugs," the driver said distinctly. "They roam the streets, to be sure, but these are a bit tougher than the usual breed. Perhaps the fineness of your cloak has attracted their attention."

"No doubt. Still the inn, if you can manage it. A sovereign for your trouble."

"The strike?"

"Name the kingdom," Rùnach said dryly. "I have a selection."

"Neroche."

"Done."

The driver continued on for a bit, then spoke again. "I can drop you outside the city, if you'd prefer. For two pieces of gold I can lose those lads behind us."

"Discreetly?"

"That'll cost you three."

Rùnach supposed he didn't need the clothes he'd left at the inn. He looked at Aisling. "Opinions?"

She took a shaky breath. "I'm too terrified to have any."

"Well, my plan had been to duck out through the inn's kitchens and roll liberally in the compost pile before blending in with the seedier elements, which doesn't sound all that appealing the more I think about it."

"Then three coins sounds like a bargain."

He agreed, then soon found himself rather grateful he hadn't had lunch yet.

An hour and a torturous route through the most impossibly small closes that surely hadn't been meant for anything but foot traffic, he happily jumped from the carriage, following Aisling to solid ground. He looked up at the carriage driver and was faintly relieved to see he didn't recognize him.

"Thank you, friend."

The man inclined his head. "My pleasure, Your Highness."

Rùnach sighed. "You have me at a disadvantage. I apologize, but I don't recognize you."

"I'm Ochadius's son," the young man said with a smile, "Peter."

"Of course you are," Rùnach said, then he looked up at Peter in surprise. "You accepted my gold."

"As I said, I am my father's son," Peter said with a smile, then he sobered. "I wish I could render more aid, but I fear you're on your own from here. I'll return to Beul and see if I can't at least throw them off the scent."

"The Guild guards?" Aisling wheezed.

"Them too."

Rùnach nodded, then moved out of the way with Aisling and watched Peter wheel his carriage around and head back the way they'd come. The noise faded eventually, leaving him standing with a runaway weaver in the middle of a road that seemed to be at least marginally well traveled. He looked up at the darkening sky, then at Aisling.

"Well."

She handed him a map. "We might need this."

"Where did you find this?" he asked in surprise.

"That little boy who gave us directions handed it to me before we started running."

"I didn't notice that."

"You were too busy swearing."

Rùnach smiled, then tucked the map into a pocket of his cloak, then pulled off his pack and took out a finely carved wooden statue of a horse. The statue hopped a reasonable distance away, then suddenly became a full-sized horse. Iteach stretched his neck, then turned around and walked over to look at Aisling. She laughed a little as he snuffled her.

"He's making sure you're well," Rùnach said.

"Nay, he's telling me there's something in my pack he wants," she said. "I think I'm happy I didn't turn this over to that woman."

"I almost hate to ask what he wants," Rùnach said. "Carrots?"

"Astar said he had a gift for me," she said, looking at him and blinking innocently. "Was I wrong not to refuse it?"

Rùnach pursed his lips. "As long as it isn't a betrothal ring, I suppose I don't have anything to say about it, do I?" He helped her out of her pack, then set it on the ground for her. "Rummage, woman, and let's see what he gifted you."

Aisling opened the pack, then froze. She considered for a moment or two before she reached inside and pulled out another statue of a horse. She held it up and studied it.

"Spectacular," she murmured.

Rùnach had to agree. He watched her set the statue on the ground, then moved out of the way with her. The statue, unsurprisingly, became something quite a bit larger. The resulting horse, an absolutely stupendous blond chestnut filly, looked at Aisling and bowed her head all the way to the ground.

"Well," he said, nonplussed.

"She's glorious," Aisling said, reaching out to stroke the filly's neck.

"Fit for a queen," Rùnach agreed.

Aisling looked at him quickly. "Not that."

"Then worthy of a dreamspinner," he said quietly, reaching for her hand. "I believe, my love, that your filly there is a gift from the king of Cothromaiche, though I'm sure Astar will take credit for her every time he can. I'm guessing that's Seannair's way of saying he'd like to be invited to your wedding since he was out hunting during your visit."

"A generous gift," Aisling said weakly.

"Very," Rùnach said. "She looks as if she's made of gold."

"Rùnach, look at Iteach."

Rùnach did and laughed a little. Iteach was, well, the only word for it he could find was *gaping* at the new addition to their company as if he had never seen another horse before. "My horse without a single thing to say. A miracle has occurred."

"I'm sure he'll get over that soon enough." She pulled her cloak more closely around her. "What now? Do we fly or simply ride like demons?"

"How easily you've become accustomed to having magic at your disposal."

"Not easily," she said with a sigh, "but easily enough, I suppose. Terror is a very useful means of persuasion."

"I think we should ride, only because we'll attract less attention that way. The horses will tell us if something untoward comes nearby."

She nodded. Rùnach settled their gear, shook his head over Seannair's generosity facilitated no doubt by Soilléir's suggestion, and steeled himself for a long night in the saddle. He supposed their lingerings in Beul could have been more productive, but perhaps not. They knew where to go, collected a bit of information that would serve them, and had gotten out alive. They were one step closer to what they needed to know.

Perhaps that was all they could hope for at the moment.

Seven

Aisling stood in the stables and shivered. Her hair was wet from her recent bath, true, and there was frost on the ground just outside the doors, also true, but she didn't think that was what was chilling her to the bone. It had everything to do with what had been a profoundly uncomfortable pair of days. Unfortunately, she had no reason to believe things were going to improve anytime soon.

She watched Rùnach ready the horses until there was nothing left to do but ride off into the gloom. Only she didn't feel at all like a Nerochian lad off to do mighty deeds. She felt like a very insignificant weaver off to attempt impossible things that she wouldn't manage.

"Ready?" Rùnach asked.

"Of course," she said, wishing she'd sounded a bit more confident. As it was, she thought she sounded exactly what she was: terrified.

Rùnach put his arm around her shoulders and drew her close. "They can't hurt you, Aisling."

"They can send me back to the Guild."

"Your birthday was two days ago," he said confidently. "In fact, I was so sure of it, I celebrated it by treating you to a hasty exit through enemy-infested streets, then a subsequently quite miserable journey on the back of a very lovely and no doubt very rare horse my horse is gobsmacked by." He pulled back and smiled at her. "Name another lad who could do better."

She couldn't help but smile a little. "It was an interesting escape, true."

He tucked her hair behind her ear. "I'll build you a house this summer and provide you a better day to celebrate next year. The point being, however, that 'tis too late for your—well, I don't think we should call them parents, should we?"

"I don't know who they are."

"Let's go find out. And we'll make it clear it's too late for them to do anything but apologize."

She wanted to do that almost as much as she wanted to return to the weaver's guild in Beul and turn herself over to them for another seven years, but she knew through Malcte was where her path lay.

The journey took only half the day, which was actually not nearly long enough to her mind. The countryside wasn't lovely. In fact, it bore almost no resemblance to what she'd seen depicted in Queen Brèagha's paintings. It was as if a terrible wind had come through and breathed death on everything. The pines still had their needles, barely, but there was no hint of rebirth in anything deciduous. The road was terrible, causing even Iteach to turn his head and give Rùnach a narrow look. She didn't dare ask either horse what form they would prefer to take.

It was actually a little surprising that the horses seemed to have magic that worked perfectly well inside Bruadair when anyone else's seemed less than reliable. She considered that for a bit, then finally put it aside as something to think about later. For all she knew, their horses were not bound by the same rules she and Rùnach were.

She suppressed the urge to snort. Even thinking she might possess something as lofty as magic . . . well, it was ridiculous.

Though she couldn't deny that something had happened to her when she'd used Soilléir's spell of essence hiding on herself, never mind that it hadn't worked as it was supposed to. She wasn't ready to believe she had any magic, truly, but she couldn't deny that there was something that now lingered inside her, just beyond where she could sense it. Something that felt like a beautiful dream that wasn't forgotten upon waking, but as unreachable as if it had been.

Something that felt a good deal like magic, truth be told.

She woke suddenly from her thoughts and realized she was not on a road that wound through rather ugly countryside but on the outskirts of a village that was not pretty in an entirely new and unpleasant way.

Rùnach had reined in Iteach next to her. Her horse, the lovely and indeed quite golden Orail, seemed to agree that the sight before them deserved cessation of motion to truly appreciate. Aisling swallowed with difficulty.

"Well," she said. "Perhaps Beul was a step up."

Rùnach looked at her, then laughed a little. "I'm afraid I would have to agree."

She shifted uncomfortably. "I'm sorry to bring you here."

"Why?" he asked in surprise.

"Because of who you are and where you were raised. Part of the time, at least."

"Aisling, trust me, I have seen things . . ." He shook his head. "I'm only sorry that this is what you were subjected to. Again, I'll build you a house on the edge of the sea. I'll wheedle saplings and seeds out of both sets of grandparents. Perhaps even a gardener, if such an adventurous soul can be found."

She took a deep breath. "Thank you, Rùnach."

"You're welcome, love." He nodded toward what appeared to pass for civilization in the current bit of ugly countryside. "Shall we?"

"I'm terrified."

"I think you should be enjoying this," he said. "Returning triumphant to a former battlefield."

"I would feel better if I had a sword," she said grimly. "Or magic."

"Well, I have the former," he said with a shrug, "and we both have the latter if things go completely awry. But perhaps we should limit ourselves to stern words. I imagine we have enough of those to serve us at present."

"I'm not sure I'll be able to get any out."

"I think you might surprise yourself," he said with a faint smile. "I'll get you started if you hesitate."

She nodded, then realized the implication of what he'd said. She shifted in the saddle to look at him. "And here I thought you were going to fight my battles for me."

"Do you *want* me to fight your battles for you?"

"It would be the chivalrous thing to do, I think."

He swung down from Iteach and looked up at her, putting his hand on her boot. "I would fight all your battles for you, Aisling, if you would allow it, but I'll not rob you of victories that should be yours by right and responsibility."

She pursed her lips at him. "Why must you be so noble?"

"Penance for my youthful prattishness," he said solemnly. "But because I want you to feel properly championed, why don't we solve the tangle this way? I'll clear the field of lesser opponents, leaving you free to come along behind me and see to the captains of the mayhem. And I'll keep my sword loose in its sheath in case they become too feisty for my taste or your patience."

"In truth?"

"Actually," he said, "I would prefer to see to it all for you, but I'll do what pleases you."

"What I want and what should happen appear to be two separate things at the moment."

He smiled and took her reins from her. "Well, when you decide which will have the upper hand, let me know."

She dismounted with far less grace than he had, then held on to the very lovely saddle Orail had provided for her. "I wish I had your courage. You know." She paused. "When you went to the well."

"I was young and arrogant," he said, "and as I've told you before, too stupid to be afraid. I also had a fair idea of what to expect, having seen my father at his craft innumerable times before. And we had a plan in place that we had discussed until we were all heartily sick of it."

"Is that what I need?" she asked. "A plan?"

"It might help," he agreed. "Not knowing what to expect does put us at a disadvantage. I suppose we could have ourselves a drink in the local pub and try to pick up a bit of gossip, but I fear given the size of this village that we would immediately *become* the local gossip and then the element of surprise would be lost to us."

She forced herself to breathe normally. "Is that what we're counting on?"

"Surprise?" he asked, then shrugged. "It seems prudent. Do your parents—or whatever they are—have magic, do you think?"

"I don't think so," she said. She shook her head. "I'm not sure I want to know."

"Then we'll assume they don't or they would be living in a far more exclusive village than this one. If they've no magic, then we have nothing to worry about except that someone might drop a brick on my head from an upstairs window and you'll be forced to use my sword to defend us. I'll keep a weather eye out and you knock on the door. When they're overcome with surprise, we'll have out of them the details we've come for, then be on our way."

She supposed there were worse plans than that one. She also supposed it was possible she would find that the two they were preparing to visit were in truth her parents, she had no magic, and perhaps she and Rùnach would go off and live their lives according to his original plan of disappearing into the employ of an obscure lord. She could weave, he could wield his sword, and they could live unremarkable lives filled with unremarkable things.

She took a deep breath. "Do we hide the horses?"

He put his hand on Iteach's withers and studied his horse. He shrugged. "He claims they'll shapechange if they sense danger. Apparently Orail's progenitors stretch back into the mists of time, a line of rare fillies bred on the steppes of the Blàraidh Mountains where magic covers everything like fine dew and flavors the water in a particularly delightful way." He smiles. "His description, not mine."

Aisling looked at her horse and suddenly saw with perfectly clarity just where she had been foaled and the lush, green pasture where she'd spent her weaning years. There was definitely magic involved, a magic that spoke to her own.

That magic she wasn't quite sure she was ready to accept.

It was almost enough to make her weep. She put her hand on her horse's withers and felt the connection deepen. She blinked a time or two at a gentle look from her mount, then looked at Rùnach. She found that words were beyond her.

Rùnach smiled. "How are you, Aisling?"

"Staggered."

"I can say with absolute honestly that I understand just how you feel."

She jumped a little as their horses slipped into the shapes of two great eagles, then sighed as they swept up into the sky and vanished. She watched the spot where she'd last seem them, then turned to Rùnach.

"I'm assuming they'll return."

"At just the right time, I imagine," he said. "Shall we?"

She hesitated, then stepped forward and put her arms around him. She didn't want to shake, but she supposed she had reason enough. Rùnach's hand on her hair was pleasing, but she wasn't sure anything would have truly soothed her at present. Her stomach was churning as if giant waves of fear were being created and crashing inside her belly just to torment her. She finally pulled away and took hold of herself.

"I'm fine."

"I never thought anything else."

She shot him a quick look because she supposed he had thought all manner of things he hadn't wanted to say about her lack of courage, but he was only watching her steadily, as if he sought to gift her a bit of his own strength. She took a deep breath, then nodded. There was no other choice but to walk on.

The first score of steps wasn't nearly as unpleasant as the second score, simply because she hadn't realized at first where she was. She did soon enough.

The memories were very vague but undeniable. It occurred to her as she walked through that village green, which was anything but lush and inviting, that twenty years of distance hadn't changed things much. The buildings surrounding the square were sadly in need of care that wasn't limited to a fresh coat of paint. There were windows that obviously didn't shut very well, doors that had been poorly repaired, flagstones that were cracked and uneven. The well in the middle of the square was definitely being used, but also in need of extensive masonry work.

She looked up at Rùnach quickly, but he was only watching their surroundings with no expression on his face. He glanced at her, smiled briefly, then went back to his watching. It occurred to her that he was perhaps looking out for things that weren't as they should have been, so she left it to him and continued to put one foot in front of the other.

She paused at the far edge of the square. "I'm not sure where to go now."

"I'll ask someone."

She watched him look around for a likely suspect. He stopped a young lad and held out a coin.

"The goodman Riochdair," he said pleasantly. "His house?"

The lad gulped. "Straight on, my lord, and bear to the right." He pointed with a shaking hand. "There against the forest is his house. Biggest in the area, of course, and the finest."

Aisling didn't doubt it. Rùnach handed the lad the coin and watched him run off before he turned to look at her.

"Ready?"

"I'm not sure I am, but there isn't anything to be done, is there?"

"Paths can be thorny."

She grimaced. "I'm sorry. This seems a trivial thing."

"It isn't," he said simply. He took her hand. "I suspect our little friend will be collecting another coin soon for informing our future hosts of visitors, though, so perhaps we shouldn't dawdle."

Aisling nodded and forced herself to continue on. Rùnach's hand was warm, which was helpful, and she didn't feel even so much as a twitch of unease in his fingers, which was comforting. Or at least it was until she realized she could no longer claim that she didn't recognize her surroundings.

She had to force herself to walk with Rùnach up a path to a house. Biggest in the area, of course, and the finest, though Aisling couldn't see that exactly. To her mind, it was a poorly constructed thing set in the midst of an untended garden through which ran an uninspired path of cracked grey stone.

"Saplings and seeds," Rùnach murmured under his breath. "I promise."

She would have smiled at him, but she was too sick to. She nodded, barely, then spent the rest of the trip to the front door fighting to keep herself from turning and vomiting into the weeds.

Rùnach reached out to knock on the door. Before he could manage it, the door was wrenched open and a woman stood there, wearing the sort of welcoming smile a body puts on when preparing to greet someone very rich indeed. Obviously Rùnach's clothing had done its job.

The woman—Aisling couldn't bring herself to call her *mother*— only glanced at Rùnach before her gaze fixed upon Aisling herself. And then Dallag of Malcte took a step back as if she'd been slapped very hard, her eyes rolled back in her head, and she fainted.

Aisling didn't move to catch her. Surprisingly enough, neither did Rùnach. She looked at him but he only shrugged.

"Happened too quickly," he said, then turned back to his bland contemplation of the woman lying unconscious there in the entryway of a house that was just as shabby as the rest of the town.

A little girl appeared in the vestibule, gaped at her mother, turned that openmouthed look on them before she shrieked for her father. Aisling didn't recognize the child, but that perhaps wasn't surprising given how long she'd been away from the family seat. She could only assume by the way the girl was dressed that she was one of the brood.

A man appeared in short order, glanced at the woman lying there at his feet, then looked out the doorway to investigate the cause of the mishap. Aisling watched him look at them both, freeze, then close his eyes briefly. He opened his eyes and looked at her.

"I wondered when you'd come."

"Did you?" Aisling returned. "I wonder at that, given that you knew where you'd imprisoned me."

She listened to the words come out of her mouth and was slightly surprised at their venom. Perhaps too much time spent in the unrelenting chill of Gobhann's exposed courtyards had sharpened her tongue past where she would have suspected.

Riochdair's mouth had fallen open slightly, but he seemed to regain his composure after a moment or two. He held the door open fully, then welcomed them inside.

"Please," he said quietly. "Come take your ease."

"That'll be the day," Aisling muttered, perhaps not as under her breath as she should have. She looked up quickly at Rùnach but he only lifted his eyebrows briefly, then waited for her to go ahead of him. She was rather glad, all things considered, to know he was standing behind her in all his terrible beauty. Soilléir might have helped him bury his magic, but that had done little to take the edge off what he obviously was. There was a part of her that almost wished he'd still been wearing his scars. Her former parents, who were apparently neither surprised nor pleased to see her depending on which one was being asked, might have been more intimidated by those than his non-pointy ears.

She followed her—well, she certainly couldn't call him her father, because she simply couldn't believe she could be related to that person. She followed their host into what proved to be a salon of some sort. She was invited to sit upon a sofa, which she did. Rùnach joined her there, froze, then shifted a bit.

"I'll see to my wife, then return," Riochdair said.

Aisling waited until he was gone before she leaned closer to Rùnach. "Are you unwell?"

"There is a spring poking me quite vigorously in the arse," he whispered. He shot her a quick smile. "Put bluntly, that is."

She sympathized with him, for she wasn't entirely sure she wasn't enjoying the same sort of treatment from the furniture. She shifted a little, perhaps a little more relieved than she should have been that she was dressed well, albeit in lads' clothing. At least she had washed her face that morning. Best that they see her in something besides rags.

She waited with Rùnach as various souls she could only assume were children belonging to the family came into the salon to gape at them. Or, rather, at Rùnach. She couldn't blame them, for she had a hard time not gaping at him as well. She supposed the only time she would look at him and not wince would be when her eyes were too dim to see anything. He was handsome enough on his own, true, but that coupled with the faint echo of elven glamour that came not only from the magic shimmering in his veins but the runes on his hands and brow made him almost difficult to look at.

Loud voices were suddenly raised in the kitchen, which lent an air of distinction to the place. She was slightly unnerved to find she knew where that kitchen lay, but she supposed that wasn't the first thing she would be surprised by in Bruadair.

She looked at the children, young and not so young, who had gathered to observe them. She studied the oldest first only because she wondered if she might recognize her. She didn't, though she supposed that shouldn't have surprised her. She had been almost eight when she'd been sent to the Guild. If that child had existed at the time, she had been a wee thing.

She tried not to think about how that girl's life had been spent in contrast to hers.

There were five children there, four girls ranging in age from perhaps ten and four to a score and a bit, then a lad of about ten summers who looked thoroughly spoilt.

It occurred to her that perhaps she should be grateful she hadn't grown up with them.

The young lad looked at Rùnach and stuck out his chin. "You have a sword."

Rùnach nodded. "So I do."

"I bet you haven't a clue how to use it."

The eldest girl hissed at him to be silent, but the lad was apparently beyond any mending of his manners. If that little lad only knew whom he was attempting to insult.

"I suppose that's up for debate," Rùnach said. He considered the child standing in front of him. "I would guess by your stance that you have trained."

"Obviously," the lad said scornfully, "but not with a heavy, ugly blade like that. I use a rapier."

"A very elegant weapon," Rùnach conceded. "You're fortunate that your father has seen to your education so thoughtfully."

The boy seemed not to know how to take that. He gestured clumsily at Rùnach's sword. "Where'd you get that?"

"It was a gift."

"From whom?"

"I'll tell you if you can best me in the garden later." He stood up. "Here are your parents."

Aisling would have crawled to her feet, but Rùnach shot her a look that told her two things: she should most definitely keep her seat on her uncomfortable sofa spring, and that he would handle her, ah, *parents* if they got out of hand. She supposed he also wanted to make a point that the people walking into the salon were not worthy of her notice.

She didn't lean back—no sense in ruining her spine as well as her backside—but she did relax just the slightest bit. Dallag swept into the salon as if she were entertaining important guests; Riochdair followed more slowly, looking as if he would rather have been anywhere else.

Dallag sat, then apparently had a proper look at Rùnach. Her mouth fell open and she came close to pitching forward out of her chair again. Riochdair put his hand out but she waved him away impatiently.

"I am well," she snapped at him before she turned a much more polite look on Rùnach. "Welcome to our home, good sir."

Rùnach sat, almost without wincing. "Very kind of you to offer us hospitality."

Dallag looked from him to Aisling and back, obviously confused. "Of course," she said. "I'm curious about who you are and where you met our, ah, beloved Aisling."

Aisling suppressed the urge to snort. Beloved, indeed.

"The tale is long and very interesting," Rùnach said smoothly. "I will naturally be happy to share it with you in detail. And as you might imagine, we have questions for you as well."

Aisling wasn't sure whom she found more fascinating, Dallag

or Riochdair. Dallag looked as if she were torn between a desire
to murder and the need to fawn, while Riochdair simply looked as
if he wanted to disappear. Aisling supposed if she were to be
caught alone with either of them, she would have chosen Riochdair. With Dallag, she had no trouble imagining just how things
would end for her.

She studied the man who was possibly her father. He looked as
if he had been carrying a heavy load for years and it had suddenly
become too much for him. Aisling would have felt some small bit
of sympathy for him, but she'd spent the whole of her life she could
remember feeling impossibly tired. That he should finally have a
taste of that himself was likely nothing more than he deserved.

The children seemed to find him more accessible than their
mother for they gravitated to him. The girls continued to look at
Rùnach as if they'd never seen a man before and the little lad was
still eyeing Rùnach's sword with undisguised envy. That dwarvish
sword had somehow taken on a sheen that she imagined it was
producing itself. Rùnach was, of course, his usual self, mesmeriz-
ing and very hard to look away from. She knew she shouldn't have
cared that he had taken her hand in his, but she couldn't deny that
she did. Her sisters, if that's what they were, were shooting her
looks of furious disbelief.

It was terribly satisfying.

She turned her attention back to the matriarch of the clan,
mostly because it seemed foolhardy not to keep an eye on her. Dallag had recovered well enough and was now watching Rùnach calculatingly. Aisling wished her well in her endeavors, for she knew
that Rùnach wouldn't share more with them than he had to.

But then Dallag looked at her and she had the feeling things
were about to take a turn for the worse.

"I believe perhaps some refreshment is in order," Dallag said

suddenly, rising. "Aisling, darling, surely you wouldn't mind helping me in the kitchen?"

Aisling had the feeling more would be going on than the brewing of tea, but she hadn't spent several days under the tutelage of
Scrymgeour Weger without having learned a thing or two about
defending herself against an enemy. If Dallag proved feisty, she
would have absolutely no trouble at all trotting those skills out for
the benefit of the woman in front of her.

A woman who had obviously never loved her.

She wondered who the hell Dallag of Malcte was.

Rùnach rose immediately and held down his hand to help her
to her feet as if she'd been a grand lady. She smiled politely at him,
then followed Dallag into her kitchen. She had only the most
vague of memories of the place. Actually, the truth was, she had
one less-than-vague memory and it had to do with the last time
she'd seen that chamber on the morning when she'd been handed
her cloak and told she was going on a special journey with her
parents to Beul. Little had she known what lay in store for her.

She stood in the middle of the kitchen and watched her erstwhile guardian boil water and prepare a pitcher and cups. Aisling
found herself easing toward the back door only because she wasn't
entirely sure Dallag wouldn't throw that kettle full of boiling
water at her.

"You do realize," Dallag said, idly stirring tea in a glass pitcher,
"that we can make arrangements for the Guildmistress to come
and fetch you."

Aisling found herself horribly tempted to unravel Dallag's
gown, then wrap her up in it, accompanied by a spell that would
make her itch for the rest of her natural life. The impulse was so
strong, she had to take a physical step backward from the seduc-
tiveness of the thought.

"I suppose you might try," Aisling said, "but I don't think you'll succeed."

"Oh, your elvish lad in there could be overcome easily enough."

Aisling didn't bother with a response, though she had to wonder briefly how Dallag could possibly be that stupid. Perhaps she had no means of sensing any magic at all.

"As you say," Aisling said with a shrug. "As for the other, why would you?"

"Send you back?" Dallag spat, whirling on her. "So you wouldn't be here of course, you stupid girl."

"And you think I have any intention of remaining here?" Aisling asked, finding it not as difficult as she thought to toss off a disbelieving laugh. "Surely not."

"Then why are you here?" Dallag demanded. "To remind me of those first horrible years when I was forced to look at you each and every day and know that you'd been foisted off on me as a babe I was required to care for against my will?"

Aisling leaned back against the door because it seemed a handy way to rest her feet a bit. She'd suspected, of course, that her mother had never loved her. She knew it shouldn't have come as a surprise that her mother had never even *been* her mother. At the very least that made the events of her youth seem much less terrible and quite a bit more logical.

Logical, but brutal nonetheless.

She folded her arms over her chest because it was less tempting that way to use magic she wasn't sure she could either call upon or control. "Was it so terrible then? To care for a helpless babe who wasn't yours?"

"Every moment of every day until I was able to rid myself of you," Dallag said coldly. "You with your spooky eyes and mindless stare."

"Your compassion astounds me," Aisling said flatly.

"Why would I have affection for a child who wasn't mine?"

Aisling said nothing, because there was nothing to say. She simply stood there and watched as Dallag slapped spoons onto the tray, looking as if she'd suddenly been vindicated in an opinion she hadn't been all that sure of to that point. Explaining to the woman that she understood her actions because it was obvious she was a person with no heart would likely be a waste of breath.

She caught sight of a movement near the kitchen entry and realized that Rùnach had come to stand in the doorway. Dallag's back was to him, which Aisling supposed might bode ill for the woman's desire to make a good impression on him. She didn't dare look at him, though, lest she give him away. At least he might keep her from becoming scalded.

"Is he my father?" Aisling asked. "Your husband?"

"Of course not!"

Aisling frowned over that. She supposed that shouldn't have come as a surprise either. Obviously neither of the two masquerading as her parents had ever wanted her, unwitting burden that she'd been. "Then why did you take me in?"

"Because I had no choice. But trust me, I have a choice now. I will have word sent to Beul and then you will indeed find yourself where I need never look at you again."

"I don't think you'll manage it. My birthday was two days ago."

"Of course it wasn't; it was a fortnight ago—" She closed her mouth abruptly. "I mean—"

"Exactly that," Rùnach said coolly. "Thank you."

Dallag whirled around and saw him, then lifted her chin. "It doesn't matter, of course. She has a contract left to fulfill at the Guild. Surely her honor demands she return."

"I would say her contract had already been fulfilled," Rùnach said mildly, "and several years ago, at that. I suggest you rethink your opinion on the matter."

Aisling watched Dallag consider and wondered what she thought she could possibly do to turn the situation to her favor.

"Are you threatening me?" the woman asked in a low, rather dangerous tone of voice.

"I don't think I was the one doing the threatening, do you?" Rùnach asked. "You vowed to sell my lady and I merely expressed doubt that you would manage it."

"And you'll stop me?" she scoffed. "With what magic?"

Rùnach shrugged. "I imagine we don't want to examine the possibilities too closely. Perhaps instead you would be interested in seeing if a better bargain might be in the offing."

Aisling watched Dallag go very still for a moment before an expression of calculation appeared on her face.

"And what sort of bargain might you be speaking of?" she asked softly.

"Dallag," another voice said sharply. "We're finished with bargains."

Aisling realized the lord of the manor had appeared, as it were, perhaps to make certain things didn't get out of hand. Rùnach merely shifted to one side to allow the other man to step inside the kitchen and join the group.

"Be silent, you fool," Dallag said sharply. "Perhaps there is gold to be made here."

Riochdair leaned back against the wall and folded his arms across his chest, but he said nothing. Aisling supposed that told her everything she needed to know about how willing he'd been to fight for her in her youth.

"I'll give you something of value to display," Rùnach said,

"something that will be visible only to those who are willing to pay for the privilege."

"And what sort of thing might this be?" Dallag asked. "It had best be valuable or your *lady* will indeed find herself sitting at a loom come morning."

"An elvish rune," Rùnach said. "Plastered over your front doorway."

Aisling watched Dallag consider.

"And exactly what would you know of elvish runes?"

"More than you, I'll warrant." Rùnach pushed away from the doorway and started across the kitchen. He paused next to Dallag and looked down at her. "Elvish runes are curious things," he said. "Some come accompanied with curses. I could tell you why I have such a thing with me—a rune, not a curse—but then if you spoke of my identity, that rune would do you injuries you would never recover from. Death would be a mercy."

"I'll have word sent to the Guildmistress," Dallag said angrily. "This afternoon."

"And lose the chance for something capable of making you a true fortune? I imagine you'll do no such thing."

"And who are you—"

Riochdair took his wife by the arm and pulled her out of the kitchen. Aisling listened to the curses fade, then looked at Rùnach.

"That was entertaining."

He smiled briefly. "Let's have what we came for, then be on our way. Perhaps a stay at a nice inn would be reward enough for our time here."

"I'm not sure there are any nice inns left in Bruadair," she said with a sigh. She shook her head. "I hope it's worth saving."

"I didn't say you had to save everywhere," Rùnach said, walking over to take her face in his hands and kiss the end of her nose. "We'll leave this bit as a wreck."

"You are a terrible man."

"But you love me."

She put her arms around his neck. "Desperately. Even if you are engaged to Annastashia of—"

He only laughed. "I am not, which you well know. We also won't invite her to the wedding, not that she'll notice. She'll be too busy checking potential husbands off her list to pay the slight any heed."

"Does she have a list?"

"She was holding it in the hand she didn't try to flatten me with at supper the other night."

Aisling nodded, grateful for the distraction. She closed her eyes and allowed herself a moment of peace, enclosed as she was in the embrace of someone who actually did love her. The respite was brief, but perhaps she could hope for nothing more at the moment. The heavy tread of someone coming back down the passageway was enough to send a thrill of fear through her, though she knew it was only her foster father. She pulled away from Rùnach and smiled wearily.

"Thank you."

"A quick question or two, then we'll be on our way," he said quietly. He reached for her hand and held it securely in his own. "We won't linger."

She nodded, grateful for a man who loved her enough to keep her safe, then turned to wait for the man who hadn't possessed the courage to do the same.

Eight

Rùnach sat on a worn stone bench with a bit of late spring sunlight falling weakly down on him and wrestled with the impulse to unhide his magic and use a bit of it on Dallag of Malcte. The woman who had sold Aisling into slavery deserved a brief display of unpleasant spellworking, just enough to make her rethink her greed. He wished her discomfort to be very visible for Aisling's sake, but perhaps that was a little too dark even for his current state of mind.

Aisling seemed slightly less opposed to the man who had masqueraded as her father all those years than she was to the woman who had pretended a similar role. Rùnach rose briefly and put his cloak around Aisling's shoulders as she sat on a different bench, watching the man who had been an accomplice to her incarceration in the Guild pace in front of her. He wished for magic to create a cloak for Aisling so luxurious that the man would have winced, but perhaps there was no point. He didn't dare and he supposed neither Aisling nor Riochdair would have noticed. She did glance at him briefly, smile even more briefly, then turn back to watching her erstwhile foster sire. What she was thinking, Rùnach couldn't have said. He imagined they weren't pleasant thoughts.

He resumed his seat without fanfare and glanced around himself for the dozenth time. He saw nothing, heard no shrieking from inside the house, felt no shiver telling him an enemy was approaching from behind. None of Aisling's supposed siblings were hiding in the bushes behind them that he could tell. He had dispatched the youngest of Riochdair's brood after a lengthy battle, then promised the boy details about the sword later if he would go inside and do all his chores. The lad, apparently David by name, had hurried back into the house without argument. No one else had come to offer a challenge, though Riochdair had glanced his way enough times to leave Rùnach wondering if he were considering the same.

In time, Rùnach decided that he himself was far less interesting than finely folded dwarvish steel. He'd wondered more than once if the sword said clearly to a Bruadairian exactly who had made it, but he wasn't about to ask Riochdair. The man looked as if he might soon have an attack as it was. No sense in pushing him on to a faint prematurely.

Riochdair made a small circle near the bench where Aisling was sitting, then turned to face her. He took a deep breath. "I'm not your father."

Rùnach pursed his lips, finding himself thoroughly unsurprised. A quick glance at Aisling said she was as well.

"So I gathered," she said. "Who are you, then?"

Rùnach supposed he would have to take her aside at some point that day and tell her how damned proud he was of her, if that would even matter. He rested his elbows on his knees and studied her, wondering when it was she had changed from an unsure, innocent miss to what she was at the moment.

Regal.

Even Weger might have cracked a smile at the sight.

She was sitting on a bench that was even more worn if possible than the one that struggled to hold his own weight, but she might as well have been sitting on a throne. Her back was straight, her eyes up, her hands folded demurely in her lap. That same weak sunlight that fell on him fell on her as well, but it seemed to like her better. It gathered itself around her, as if it wrapped her in a warm embrace and was pleased to be able to do so.

Riochdair looked over his shoulder, then took the added step of looking around the garden. Rùnach could have reassured him that they were quite alone—Aisling's sisters who were apparently no longer her sisters were at the window in the upper story of the house with their noses pressed against the glass, and Dallag was standing at a window in the kitchen, glaring, but that was the extent of the eavesdropping.

Riochdair looked at Aisling, then paused. "Would you prefer to sit next to your, ah, next to . . . er . . ."

"I believe I would," she said.

Rùnach was happy to welcome her over to his side of the garden. It was perhaps better because the bench was more fully in the sun. Well, that and the fact that the sun seemed to be willing to include him in its embracing of Aisling. He put his hand on her back and smiled at her. "Thank you."

"For what?" she asked.

"For coming to sit with me."

Aisling nudged him with her shoulder, then looked at Riochdair. "We're ready."

Riochdair glanced about himself one more time, then took a seat on the bench opposite them. He sighed and leaned forward a bit with his elbows on his knees. "As you have surmised, I am not your father. I am, however, your cousin."

Rùnach felt Aisling stiffen next to him. He couldn't blame her for it. He met her gaze and saw a dreadful hope there. If this was her cousin, then perhaps he would know her family.

"Your father brought you to us when you were a babe," Riochdair said. He looked at Aisling, no doubt to judge if she intended to say anything to that.

She simply watched him silently.

"I'm afraid I can't give you the details surrounding that decision on his part," he continued, "though that is simply because I don't know them. In fact, I can't even say that I knew *him* very well; he's a bit of a hermit. All I know is that your mother had died and he was unable to care for you. He begged me to claim you as my own and never tell anyone anything else." He rubbed his hands together as if they bothered him somehow. "I have kept my word, not even telling Dallag my connection to you."

"And yet you broke your word and sent me to the Guild," Aisling said flatly.

"I couldn't keep you here any longer," he said, looking pained. "Not with my wife. She is . . ." He paused, then shook his head. "I couldn't keep you here any longer."

Rùnach watched Aisling out of the corner of his eye. She looked unsurprised, which he understood. He was even less surprised by her next question.

"Who is my father?"

"His name is Bristeadh," Riochdair said slowly. "I can suggest places to search for him, but I honestly have no idea if he's still alive or not."

Rùnach wasn't about to ask Aisling if she could sense the man's dreams. There were some things he supposed she just wouldn't be prepared to do. She looked at her cousin for several moments in silence.

"Nothing else?" she asked.

He looked at her helplessly. "As I said, they keep to themselves, those folk. I am very distantly removed, I will admit, but I believe I was his only choice." He paused, then looked slightly pained again. "Perhaps his last choice."

Rùnach watched Aisling consider the man. She watched him for so long in silence, Rùnach wondered if she would ever speak again. Riochdair, to his credit, only sat there on his bench and waited for her to perhaps come to terms with what he'd told her. Aisling finally took a breath.

"Was there no other place for you to send me, then?"

Riochdair looked for the first time slightly unsettled. "I considered many things once I knew I could not safely keep you here," he said, "but . . . well—" He broke off and shook his head. "You'll think I'm mad if I tell you the truth, I imagine."

"I've become accustomed to all sorts of things over the past few weeks," Aisling said seriously. "If you give me the truth, I'll believe it."

Riochdair took a deep breath. "I was warned not to send you anywhere but the Guild in Beul."

Aisling looked at him in shock. "Warned? How?"

He looked profoundly uncomfortable. He cleared his throat several times before he seemingly mustered up the strength to say what he needed to. "In a dream," he said finally.

Aisling blinked as if she hadn't heard him. She bowed her head for a moment or two, which Rùnach wasn't sure was a good thing or not. He still had his hand on her back and could tell she was still breathing, which he supposed was better than the alternative. He realized after a moment or two that her shoulders were shaking. He leaned over to look at her face only to realize that she wasn't weeping.

She was laughing.

It wasn't laughter tinged with hysteria, so Rùnach thought perhaps that was progress. She shook her head finally and put her hands over her face briefly. Rùnach exchanged a look with Riochdair.

"Dreams can be interesting," he offered.

The man looked as if he found them less interesting than terrifying. He cleared his throat. "I normally would have dismissed such a thing, but the dream was so vivid. It's still in my mind so strongly, it's as if I just awoke from it." He paused. "I couldn't ignore it."

"Of course not," Rùnach agreed quietly. "Of course not."

Riochdair seemed to regain some of his color, perhaps the result of having gotten such a secret off his chest. "I would be happy to lodge you both tonight—"

"No."

Rùnach couldn't blame Aisling for that. He had absolutely no desire to spend more time than absolutely necessary under Riochdair's roof and it had everything to do fearing he might find himself poisoned at luncheon.

Riochdair nodded, as if he also understood. "Very well. How can I aid you, then, beyond simply answering questions you deserved answers for?"

"I need to find my father," she said quietly. "If you can help us with that, that will be enough."

Riochdair nodded. "As I said, he's a bit of a hermit, but I'll make a list of places you might try. I don't know if you have a map—"

"We do," Aisling said.

"Then let me fetch at least something for you to drink while I get you what you need."

Aisling rose. "I'll do it."

Rùnach didn't argue with her. He supposed that she might have a thing or two to say to her erstwhile foster mother—or perhaps not. He wasn't sure which would have troubled the woman more, but he had the feeling Aisling would determine which it was and do exactly that.

He realized Aisling's cousin was simply standing there, not watching Aisling go into the house, but watching him instead.

"You love her."

Rùnach nodded. "Very much."

Riochdair studied him for several moments in silence, then nodded at Rùnach's sword. "Lovely blade."

"It is," Rùnach agreed.

"Care to divulge more pertinent details about its maker?"

Rùnach considered, then supposed there was no reason to not be honest. "Ceardach of Léige."

Riochdair's eyes widened. Perhaps he might have made a noise of surprise at another time, but he looked at present as if even such a simple thing were well beyond his capabilities. He stared at the hilt for several minutes in silence, then turned the same scrutiny on Rùnach.

"Paid a pretty price for it, did you?"

"Actually," Rùnach said easily, "I didn't."

Riochdair studied him for a moment or two. "I don't suppose you'll tell me more than that."

"I think it best not to."

Aisling's cousin nodded absently. "I did the best I could, though perhaps that's not as obvious as I'd like it to be."

Rùnach nodded slowly. "I believe you did."

"The Guild is a hellish place," Riochdair said with a shiver. "I didn't want to leave her there."

"Was there nowhere else to send her?"

Riochdair looked as if he would have preferred to take that dwarvish blade and fall upon it rather than answer. He attempted speech several times before he simply looked at Rùnach, defeated.

"Dallag has very strong opinions."

"I imagine she does."

"And then there was the dream to consider." He looked at Rùnach closely. "Do you dream?"

Rùnach smiled. "Only recently."

Riochdair looked completely unsettled. "Bruadair was once a land of dreams. In my youth, it was a very lovely place. But now . . ." He shook his head. "I'm not sure what happened."

"Aren't you?"

The man looked at him sharply. "What do you mean?"

Rùnach leaned forward with his elbows on his knees. "The king and queen were ousted two decades ago. Why?"

Riochdair pulled back and looked at him in surprise. "How do you know that?"

"I'm a student of history."

More attempts at speech ensued. Aisling's cousin finally settled for a few garbled noises before he managed anything useful. "Who are you?"

"Someone your niece trusts."

"Why are you here?"

"For my own purposes."

"Do you ever answer a question forthrightly?"

Rùnach smiled in spite of himself. "Sorry, bad habit. My errand is private, but not nefarious. I'm interested in what you've seen. And who, if I can be that frank."

Riochdair considered his clasped hands for a moment or two, then looked up. "I had interest in the happenings in Beul, of course, because Aisling was at the Guild."

"Not that you would have gone to rescue her."

The man flushed. "I have children, as you can see—"

Rùnach waved away his words. "I'm interrupting, unpleasantly. Please continue."

"Well, no one wants to see his country overrun," Riochdair said defensively. "But what was I to do? I have no sword, no magic, nothing but the force of my commerce and position here in the village to bring to bear anywhere. I am the mayor, you know."

"I didn't know. Impressive."

Riochdair looked as if he wished it were. "There are rumors that the current, ah, *king* has magic."

"And what do you think?"

"I think he is evil and he wants nothing but the destruction of my country. But what am I to do about it?"

Rùnach smiled gravely. "I believe, Mayor Riochdair, that you've done what you could. The fight now must be taken up by those who have the weapons to fight it." He paused, then looked at Aisling's cousin. "Have you heard any names bandied about? Sglaimir, of course, but any others? Anything unusual?"

"How do you know Sglaimir?"

"I've simply heard his name mentioned." There was no reason to burden the man with anything else he might know.

Riochdair glanced around him, but he'd been doing that for the past hour so perhaps it was nothing new. He rose and nodded for Rùnach to do the same. "Let's walk back to the house," he said loudly.

Rùnach retrieved his sword and did as he was bid.

"Sglaimir is very visible," Riochdair said, almost under his breath. "Loud, brash, and cruel. But I'm not sure he's bright enough to destroy an entire country."

"Have you any ideas who might be helping him?"

Riochdair took a deep breath. "I've heard there is a darkness in . . ." He looked at Rùnach. "You won't believe this and perhaps you've never heard of the place, but I understand there is a darkness in Ceangail that extends into Bruadair."

Rùnach put his hand over his mouth on the pretext of rubbing his lips. "Have you heard the name Acair?"

Riochdair staggered. He looked at Rùnach in horror. "How do you possibly know that name?"

Rùnach put his hand on the other man's shoulder. "Smile and don't be a fool. I assume we're being observed."

"I imagine so. Nothing surprises me anymore."

Rùnach wished he could say the same thing. "I know many things. Where I learned them isn't very interesting. I'm simply curious what you've heard and how recently."

"Why would I tell you?" Riochdair asked through a very tight smile. "I don't even know who you are, unless you feel a sudden inclination to share that information with me."

"I'm not sure the knowledge would serve you," Rùnach said, "and perhaps 'tis a detail you wouldn't want to have to reveal under duress. If I'm not assuming too much."

Riochdair shook his head. "I'm a dead man anyway. Have been for quite some time now. Men from the Guild were crawling through my house for days after Aisling disappeared." He looked at Rùnach bleakly. "I told them nothing."

"Is that why you limp?"

"Noticed that, did you?"

"You hide it well, but aye," Rùnach said mildly, "I noticed. What did they want?"

"What you want," Riochdair said wearily. "Tidings about Aisling's father. I didn't tell them anything, if that atones for anything I did before." He paused. "I'm not sure it will for Aisling."

Rùnach wasn't about to offer any opinion. That was Aisling's forgiveness to tender if she cared to, not his. He belted his sword around his hips, then looked at Aisling's cousin.

"My father is Gair of Ceangail."

Riochdair actually took a step backward. "Why does she keep company with you, then?"

"Because I am not my father."

Riochdair didn't look at all comforted. "Then you know of the evil that comes from that place."

"All too well," Rùnach agreed, "unfortunately. And though my father is contained, I have several bastard brothers who are at liberty to involve themselves in things that interest them. I can think of several who would give much to have their own country to rule." Or more than just Bruadair, admittedly, but he supposed there was no reason to burden Aisling's cousin with that thought.

"And you think that has happened here?"

Rùnach hesitated. "I don't want to believe it, but I have my suspicions."

Riochdair gestured inelegantly toward Rùnach's sword. "Do they know your parentage in Durial?"

"Very well."

The man accepted that with a thoughtful frown. "You have no pretensions to Bruadair's throne, then."

Rùnach smiled in spite of himself. "Assuredly not. Pretensions to making your niece my wife, most definitely, but nothing else."

"You'll have to ask her father."

"I had considered that."

Riochdair blinked suddenly. "Wait. If your father was Gair of

Ceangail, then that makes your mother Sarait of Tòrr Dòrainn . . . your grandfather is King Sìle . . . Sgath . . . Eulasaid—"

Rùnach allowed the man to mentally investigate the branches of his family tree, then smiled faintly. "So it does."

The man looked as if he wanted something very strong to drink. "And you're here for my cousin."

"And to see if a black mage or two can be set outside the borders like the refuse they are."

"I have no sword to offer—"

"I'm not asking for that from you," Rùnach said quickly. "Suggestions on where to find the man we're looking for is enough."

Riochdair didn't move. "I'm not sure, if you'll have the entire truth, that simply telling the truth that I had no idea where Aisling was is enough." He paused, then straightened. "I will offer my sword, if it would be useful."

Rùnach nodded. "I'll remember that."

Aisling's cousin didn't seem in any hurry to go back into the house. "I don't know much about that side of my family. Where Aisling's father comes from. We're related through our grandparents, so perhaps that's only to be expected. But there was always something odd about them." He paused. "Odd in a magical sense, if you want the truth. Hard to believe, isn't it—well, perhaps not for you, of course."

"There are many odd things in the world," Rùnach conceded, "and many normal things that take on characteristics we imbue them with. Perhaps that's all that happened there. You say yourself that you didn't have much to do with your cousins. Perhaps they simply wanted to lord over you an imagined bit of something they made up."

Riochdair nodded hopefully, looking as if he wanted nothing more than to believe just that. "It isn't as if Aisling has any magic, is it?"

"Why would she?" Rùnach asked. "Most people don't." Actually, he was continually surprised by how many people had at least some spell or charm tucked away in their cupboards for an emergency, but he supposed there was no reason to clutter up Riochdair's dreams with that thought.

"She has her father's eyes," Riochdair added. "Very odd, but perhaps that's what leads them to make claims that couldn't possibly be true." He nodded toward the kitchen garden door. "I'll go make that list for you. It might take you a bit if you're walking, though I'm not sure you'd want to buy horses here. They've taken all the good ones for use in the city."

Rùnach assured him they would manage on their own, then walked with him back to the house and into the kitchens.

Dallag was there, hissing at Aisling. To his surprise, Aisling looked rather paler than he would have suspected. The second thing that surprised him was the anger that flooded through him. He realized there was a hand on his arm only when it realized it was Aisling's.

"I am well," she said loudly.

He drew his hand over his eyes, then nodded. He let out his breath slowly, forcing the tension to leave him as well. He took Aisling by the hand and drew her with him after her cousin. He had no idea what Dallag had been saying to her, but he supposed it didn't matter. The sooner they were free of the place, the better.

He kept Aisling nearby as he closeted himself with the master of the house in his library. He forced himself to pay attention to the map laid on the table there and to commit to memory the places indicated. He supposed what he needed was something to eat, but couldn't bring himself to blame his ire on that.

Perhaps he was tired.

He made the polite conversation required as they took their

leave, but couldn't deny he was thrilled at the thought of leaving the house and its occupants behind.

"But my gift," Dallag protested suddenly.

Rùnach paused on the path leading away from the front door. He considered, then pulled the knife from his boot. He then took the echo of the rune his cousin Còir had gifted him and caught it on the tip of the blade. He turned, flung that shadow up over the doorway of Dallag's house, then nodded to Riochdair before he turned to Aisling.

"Finished?"

"I think we'd best be." She glanced at the rune over the door, then looked at him. "A rune of opening?"

"'Tis a pretty thing, isn't it?"

She smiled and it was as if the entire world around her smiled as well. "It was just an echo of one, though, wasn't it?"

"It would appear so."

"Has it any efficacy left, do you suppose?"

"They won't ever manage to shut their damned front door, that's what I suppose."

She reached for his hand. "I love you. And let's go before Dallag realizes what you've given her."

"I think we should pause and discuss your feelings for me," he said. "I'm always more interested in that than endlessly open front doors."

She only smiled and pulled on him. "I need to be away from here before I'm no longer successful in stifling my reaction to your gift. And look, here come our horses."

Rùnach watched Iteach and Orail swoop down, then change themselves into horses with outrageously bejeweled tack right there in the front garden. He was half surprised the ponies weren't staggering under the weight of it all. There were various gasps and a shriek or two from the house. He wasn't entirely certain he hadn't heard the particular thump a body makes when it faints without anyone to catch it, but he didn't care enough to look over his shoulder and make certain.

Iteach lifted his tail over the flowerbed but Rùnach stopped him with a look. Iteach tossed his head in disgust, but figuratively sat back on his heels and waited for them to exit the garden first. Rùnach gave his horse an approving look, then walked with Aisling out the low front gate. He waited until they were out of eavesdropping distance before he looked at her.

"I wonder if we shouldn't head back toward Beul."

She paled. "Why in the world would we want to go back there?"

"Because I have the feeling Dallag wasn't trotting out her front door to see what I gifted her." He took a deep breath. "I think she intends to sell us to Sglaimir. We should give her a reason to think we're headed in a direction we don't value. Back toward Beul seems reasonable."

"And where do you think we should end up?"

"Anywhere else," he said with feeling. "We'll double back under cover of darkness and find a safe place to sleep for a couple of hours. Then we can study Riochdair's map and see where it leads us."

"And if Sglaimir finds us?"

He suppressed the urge to drag his hand through his hair. "We'll have to use magic."

"I don't know how to use mine."

"Neither do I, but I think we'd best unhide ours and figure it out sooner rather than later, wouldn't you agree?"

"Would Soilléir approve of that?"

"He's not here to give us that look he has that says volumes whilst he remains perfectly silent." He found it in him to smile a bit. "I can't imagine he would expect us to do anything but what we must to see our present business accomplished. And I don't know about you, but I feel as if he not only applied a bit of patina to my magic, he applied mold to me. Do I look older?"

She pursed her lips. "You look no more than a score and ten, and I imagine you'll look that way for the rest of your life. How I'll look in fifty years, we can only imagine."

"Ethereal," he said with a smile. "Like something from a dream, as always." He nodded. "Let's go make a spectacle of ourselves in the town square, then ride off in the direction of Beul. When we're a mile or two out, we'll let our ponies do what they do and flap off into the distance. Perhaps we'll even manage supper."

She nodded and walked on with him. He spared a glance over his shoulder, ostensibly to see if the horses were following them, when in reality he simply wanted to see what sort of chaos he'd left behind.

The entire family was standing in the front yard, looking up at the rune that was almost visible, sparkling there in the sunlight. The door was, unsurprisingly enough, open. Còir would have been proud.

He looked at Aisling, winked, and continued on with her. He was tempted to ask her what Dallag had said to her, but he supposed that was something he could safely put off for a bit. There would be time enough later to discuss that as well as runes, anger, and the fact that her cousin had been dreaming as well.

He couldn't begin to imagine how they were all connected.

Nine

Aisling sat in front of the fire on a stool, Rùnach's sword propped up against the chair facing her, and tried to take her mind off her current straits by looking at the runes engraved upon not only the blade itself, but also the hilt and the crossbars.

It was a lovely sword, to be sure. She studied the runes there and wished she had the skill to decipher them all. She supposed most of them were runes of the house of Tòrr Dòrainn, though she only recognized a pair of them because she'd seen the same on the backs of Rùnach's hands. They were beautiful and sharp, as if the magic of Sìle's kingdom had been taken and translated into something fit for battle. Beautiful and deadly, indeed.

She frowned thoughtfully as she leaned forward to study things there that didn't seem as familiar. She reached out to touch the blade and a different set of runes flashed. Not a lovely inter-

twining of gold and silver but rather a more sparkling sort of business, as if they'd been diamonds crushed beyond recognition, then
mixed in a medium that allowed that glittering to be formed into
lines and shapes that spoke of power and majesty. She considered,
then smiled. Runes of the house of Ainneamh, apparently. She
might have suspected that King Uachdaran had ordered those
engraven there to irritate some elven king or other, but perhaps
the truth was no more complicated than the fact that Rùnach had
claim to both thrones in one way or another.

That was something she tended not to think about very often.

She leaned forward to study the hilt and crossbar. There were
other things inscribed there, but she had never seen anything like
them before. She reached out and pulled the sword over into her
hands. It was long, much longer than she supposed she ever would
have been comfortable using, but she managed to get the hilt
propped up against her knees. She leaned over it and traced the
markings there. They glowed briefly as she touched them, then
faded after a moment or two. They weren't like anything she had
seen before, either on Rùnach's hands or in the dwarf king's palace. They were . . . different. Harder, yet somehow not giving the
impression they were carved of stone, while at the same time soft,
as if it had been an echo of a dream. The runes whispered to her,
but she couldn't quite hear what they were saying.

She wondered if they were Bruadairian runes.

A knock at the door startled her so badly that she leaped up
and almost sent Rùnach's sword into the fire. She would have
reached for it, but it was quite suddenly in Rùnach's hands and he
was between her and the door. She put her hand on his back to
steady herself, though he was the one who had not a heartbeat
before been sound asleep.

He glanced over his shoulder, but she shrugged. She hadn't

asked for anyone to come bring them anything and she suspected neither had he. They'd checked in the night before, truly in the middle of the night, but they'd asked for nothing but a room. Rùnach had locked the door, then insisted that she sleep first while he kept watch. She had tried to argue, but she suspected she would never outlast him in a contest of stubbornness. She'd woken at dawn only because her dreams had been troubled, full of things following her that she couldn't see, full of things lying in wait for her that she couldn't find.

She'd woken to find Rùnach simply sitting in front of the fire, staring into the flames. She'd almost sent him tumbling into it by touching his shoulder. He'd risen, embraced her briefly, handed her his sword, then cast himself on the bed. She'd half suspected he'd been asleep before his head had touched the pillow.

He was fully awake at the moment. He reached for her hand, pulled her forward to stand next to him, then pointed to a spot behind the door. She nodded and walked silently across the chamber, pausing only to draw her knife from her boot. It was something Soilléir had given her, no doubt for his own perversely secret reasons. She supposed in the end she would do nothing more with it than cut twine that kept batts of wool together, but what did she know? If she could be of any use to the man standing in front of the door, a man who looked as if he fully intended to do damage to anyone who walked inside their chamber, she would.

Rùnach opened the door and there was a sudden crash.

"Oh," a girl squeaked. "I was just bringin' ye a meal, milord. No need to stab me!"

Rùnach didn't put up his sword, but he did smile. "My apologies, lass, of course. Old habits die hard."

Aisling heard the girl collecting bits of shattered crockery and listened to someone else come with a rag to wipe the floor.

"We didn't order a meal," Rùnach said finally.

"Compliments of the master himself," the girl said. "I'll bring ye another straightway."

"That would be much appreciated," Rùnach said politely. "And many thanks to the master." He shut the door, then put his hand on it and looked at Aisling. "That was interesting."

She slid her knife back into its sheath. "Do you think that was poisoned? Or are they saving that for the next round, do you think?"

He laughed a little. "Aisling, my love, we need to find a place in our lives where when we look at something, we don't suspect it of being something else entirely." He paused. "I'm not sure that makes any sense. Am I awake?"

"I think so, but perhaps you should sit."

"Perhaps I should."

She waited until he'd collapsed into the chair there in front of the fire and propped his sword up against its arm before she sat down on the stool in front of him. She started a little at the look on his face.

"What?"

He shook his head with a faint smile. "Just looking at you."

"You *are* still asleep."

His smile faded. "How are you, Aisling?"

"Fine."

He pursed his lips. "How *are* you, Aisling?"

How to answer that? She had gone back to the Guild, a place she had sworn she would never set foot in again, survived escaping Beul, then faced the people who had sold her into slavery only to discover that one of them was a relative. She had listened to her former foster mother spew horrible threats at her, then had the satisfaction of riding off on a shapechanging horse worth a king's ransom. It had been a very eventful pair of days, to be sure. She looked at Rùnach and managed a smile.

"I'm still thinking about front doors that will never close."

"A stroke of genius," he said modestly, "if I do say so myself."

She rested her elbows on her knees and her chin on her fists. "It was."

"We can still try to find a mine for her to labor in, if you like. Your cousin as well."

"I'm not sure either of them is worth the trouble," she said with a sigh. "And I'm not sure I can hold Riochdair entirely responsible. Her, aye, I think I can, but not him."

"She'll be cleaning her entryway endlessly, if that's a comfort. I hate to think of what will crawl in her front door whilst she's asleep." He frowned thoughtfully. "Perhaps I should have seen to that as well. I did spend quite a bit of my youth in Ceangail, as you know. I have a great store of terrible memories to draw on if necessary."

She attempted a smile. "I'm sorry for it, but you already know that." She sighed. "As for Dallag, I suppose just never being able to shut her front door will be enough to drive her mad. I'm just happy I won't be there to hear about it." She considered her hands, then looked at him. "I'm not sure the visit was worth what we went through to have it."

"Oh, I wouldn't say that," he said. "We now have several ideas about where to go look for your father and, again, thoughts of blisters on her hands from too much sweeping to keep us warm." He paused. "I will admit I am hesitant to set off searching in the dark, as it were, lest we disturb a hornet's nest, but I'm not sure what else we can do."

She frowned. "What do you mean?"

"I'm thinking that if there were those interested enough in

Zayden

your whereabouts to look for you as far as Malcte, perhaps there might be those interested still."

"Leaving the Guild is very serious business," she said, because it was. "Surely it was nothing more than that."

He looked at her steadily. "I suppose that's possible, but your cousin seemed more unsettled than he should have for being someone who had merely been questioned about a simple runaway worker."

"Perhaps they mistook me for someone else."

"Aisling, they almost crippled him when he refused to divulge your whereabouts," Rùnach said seriously. "I didn't question him about the colors the guards were wearing, because I imagine they weren't guards but private soldiers sent out to find information or else."

She looked at her hands that he had leaned forward and taken in his own, then met his eyes. "I didn't know."

"Perhaps there is some comfort in knowing he didn't betray you. Not this last time."

She ignored the shudder that went through her. "Then you think they were looking for me."

"What I think is that we were fortunate to escape the Guild-mistress's office with our lives," he said, rubbing her hands absently, "and aye, I think they were looking for you. For reasons I don't imagine we need to discuss."

She squeezed his hands briefly, then rose. She paced for a bit until even that became almost unbearable. She stopped in front of Rùnach and looked at him.

He was leaning back in his chair, watching her with his clear green eyes. She wrapped her arms around herself.

"So, if you don't want to accidentally stumble into something we won't like, what do you suggest?" she asked.

"I suggest we take our magic out of mothballs and see how it shakes out. At this point, knowing what will likely be following us sooner rather than later, I think we both need our magic readily available."

"Do you—"

The knock startled her so badly that time, she jumped. Rùnach rose with a smile.

"Not to worry," he said easily, then walked toward the door. "I'll see to it."

Aisling didn't share his sense of ease, so she pulled the knife from her boot and walked over to stand behind the door again.

Thankfully it was nothing more nefarious than breakfast. Rùnach thanked the maid, took the tray himself, then shut the door with his foot. Aisling bolted it and went to find a small table to put in front of the fire. Rùnach fetched another chair for her, waited for her to sit, then joined her there. He smiled.

"Very domestic and normal," he noted.

She would have laughed, but she hadn't slept well and she wasn't quite sure she would ever get to the point where there wasn't a great knot in her belly. It was all she could do to grimace.

"Is it poisoned, do you think?" she asked uneasily.

"Can you tell?"

"The question is, do I want to look?" she said. "And the answer is, nay, I do not, but I suppose I would rather look than be dead."

Rùnach leaned over and sniffed a fried egg. "It doesn't smell poisoned."

She looked at the feast spread out before her and wondered if he might be right. It was more than she would have seen in a week's time at the Guild. It was almost more than she could bring herself to believe someone would ruin on purpose. She looked at Rùnach.

"This inn must be very expensive."

"It is," he agreed cheerfully. "Well-heeled clients have certain expectations of security. And food free of suspicious substances." He lifted one eyebrow. "You could have a peek with a magical eye to see what you can see, though, if you like."

She wiped her hands on her leggings. "The thought is appalling."

"I can't imagine," he said, his smile fading. "Frightening?"

"Terrifying."

He reached over and held out his hand, waiting until she put hers into it. "Terrifying, perhaps, but think on what awaits you past the terror."

"Death?"

He laughed a little, leaned over and kissed her hand, then released her and sat back. "I don't think that is your fate, love, but I'm a hopeful sort of lad. You could try a spell of revealing."

"Could I? Why don't you, instead?"

He started to speak—no doubt to protest—then shrugged. "Very well, why not? I suppose I'll have to attempt something eventually, so there's no point in putting it off." He considered the chamber, then shook his head. "We should likely draw some sort of spell over our spot here, though. To keep what we attempt private."

"That would be useful—"

She stopped speaking. Rùnach did as well. She wasn't sure where to look first, but she chose the floor first only because she blamed it for forcing her to pull her feet up so quickly that she almost gave herself a fat lip by knocking her knees against her mouth. Apparently she wasn't as anonymous inside Bruadair as she'd dared hope she might be, but perhaps that wasn't as terrible a thing as they had feared.

Bruadair's magic had spread something beneath them, then over their heads. A thin, shimmering sort of curtain then dropped down around them. It was so faint, she wasn't entirely sure she wasn't dreaming the whole thing. She reached out and touched what she thought she saw.

She almost wept, though she couldn't have said exactly why.

She looked at Rùnach to find him looking at her as if he'd never seen her before. There were tears standing in his eyes.

"I'm not sure I'm at all worthy of any part of you," he managed.

She pulled her hand back and tucked it under her other arm. "Don't be ridiculous."

He smiled, and the look of something—awe, perhaps— disappeared to be replaced by the utter charm of the dimple she had noticed more than once before. "If you insist."

"I didn't do this."

"I know, love," he said gently. "It's just Bruadair, recognizing a treasured daughter." He looked at the magic surrounding them, then back at her. "I suppose we're safe enough now. Shall I go first?"

"Considering you're the one with magic, I daresay you should," she said with a snort.

He looked at her, faintly amused. "You know, Aisling, you're going to have to come to terms with this at some point. Sooner rather than later, I'd say."

"Tomorrow."

He laughed a little. "Very well, if you like. Let's see what happens to me, then you can decide if you want a go."

She wrapped her arms around her knees and listened to him unravel the spell Soilléir had given him to hide his essence. He wasn't undoing the spell Soilléir had used to give his magic a bit of moss around the edges, he was removing the one he'd used on himself to hide his birthright, though perhaps *hide* was the wrong term for it. His magic was still there, she was certain, she simply couldn't see it. It was as if it lingered just out of sight, a bit like she imagined hers did as well. She watched him as he took a careful breath, then said the last word quietly.

And quite suddenly instead of just a man sitting across from her, there was an elven prince with all the glory of century upon century of Fadaire running through his veins. There were other things as well, magic from Ainneamh, the silver-shot power of Camanaë, something from An Cèin she couldn't put a name to. It was all his, yet somehow it was all *him* as well.

She felt a little awestruck, actually.

He looked at her with a faintly puzzled smile. "What is it?"

"You."

"Are all my warts showing?"

She shook her head. "Fadaire, rather. Other things I'm not familiar with as yet."

"Darkness," he asked casually.

She had to take a deep breath. "I don't know, Rùnach. Perhaps a bit."

He drew his hand over his eyes, then smiled. "I am my father's son, after all. I'll work on that part, along with taming my colossal ego as time goes on. You could help that by not looking at me any longer as if I were the most handsome man you had ever laid eyes on."

She realized he was teasing her only after she realized she was staring stupidly at him. Then she laughed, because he *was* the most handsome man she had ever seen.

"I'll try not to overindulge you with the fawning deference you seem to feel is your due," she promised.

He reached over, took her hand, then leaned over and kissed her over rather runny eggs. "I think my mother would thank you for that, were she here to do so." He sat back and considered the table for a moment or two. "I could try to hide those eggs. I think I'd be doing the world a favor."

"Rather," she agreed. "Have at it, lad."

He took a deep breath, then wove Miach's spell of un-noticing over the large plate of fried eggs.

Half the plate disappeared entirely.

The other half shattered.

She gaped at Rùnach. Or, rather, she did after she wiped the egg off her face. She was extremely grateful she wasn't wearing shards of plate as well. Rùnach had egg in his hair. He looked at her and blinked.

"Hell."

"Perhaps your grandmother was right," she ventured. "About your magic being a bit unwieldy here in Bruadair."

"But that was Wexham, not Fadaire," he protested. He frowned thoughtfully. "Let me try something else."

She listened to him use a Fadairian spell of concealment. He spoke the last word with less enthusiasm than she might have expected, but she couldn't blame him. She watched the rest of the eggs—accompanied by what was left of the plate—fling themselves into the fire and disappear with a bang and a spray of sparks. The table vanished only after sending its legs shooting across the chamber as if they'd been bolts from a crossbow. She looked at the four pieces of wood now protruding from the wall, then at Rùnach.

"That's going to be expensive."

He rubbed his hand over his face and sighed. "Damn."

"I'll clean up the mess."

He caught her by the hand before she could rise. "You sit; I'll clean."

"Nay, let me," she said. "I need something to do with my hands."

She cleaned up, then sighed a little as the Bruadarian magic that had hidden them disappeared. She looked at Rùnach standing in the middle of the room watching her, then paused with her hand on the back of her chair.

"What is it?"

He looked at her seriously. "I think we need help."

"And where do you think we'll find it?" she managed.

"Your father might be a good start."

"And what will he have to tell us?" she asked uneasily.

"Perhaps where the local mage's library is, so we might either find a book of spells or something else with suggestions on how to use spells from other magics."

"Would such a thing exist, do you think?" she mused.

"Honestly, I have no idea," Rùnach said. "In any normal situation, a mage would be breathlessly awaiting the time he would have a reason to jot down his contributions to the art of magic. Here in Bruadair, I have no idea what a mage would do—if you even have mages here."

"Has Soilléir written his spells down, do you think?"

Rùnach started to speak, then shut his mouth. "If you would have asked me that a score of years ago, I would have said absolutely not. Now? I'm not so sure. If he has made note of them, I can't imagine that book is easily accessible."

"Are his spells that powerful?" she asked. "Truly?"

"Aye, they are, truly," he said. He rubbed his hands over his face, then sighed. "I'm not sure I want to think about what would happen if they fell into the wrong hands."

"And if someone tried to pry them from you?"

He looked at her steadily. "Death first."

"If I asked nicely?"

He blinked, then he smiled. "Would you?"

"Death first," she said seriously. "I can scarce bear the thought of knowing the one I already know." She paused. "I'm trying to forget it. Unfortunately, it was a very useful spell."

"I daresay it was," he agreed. "I wonder if Bruadair's magic has anything like it."

"Sìorraidh," she said without thinking.

"What?"

"That's what the magic is called."

He smiled. "I wish you'd stop that sort of thing. I'm running out of things to do besides gape at you."

She walked across the chamber and into his embrace. She closed her eyes and was simply happy to have his arms around her.

"It has been a very long spring so far," she said.

"So it has, my love," he said with a sigh, though he didn't sound unhappy about it. "What does that word mean, do you suppose? Sìorraidh?"

"Everlasting," she said, finding the word there on her tongue without having called for it.

"Fitting."

"Am I losing my mind?"

He laughed a little, then hugged her tightly before he pulled away. "I don't think so, but we could find a dreamspinner and ask her opinion. And to do that, we need to find your father. Why don't we have a look at the map Riochdair gave us and you see if anything strikes you in particular. I know what he told me, but I'm interested in what you think."

She waited until he had fetched a map out of his pack and spread it out on the bed. It was a more detailed map than she'd been given by the madame's runner boy, so she supposed it might serve them best at present. She sat down on one side of it and looked at him sitting on the other.

"Do you see anything?" she asked.

"Roads and rivers. You?"

She scowled at him. "Chicken scratches, rather. I have no experience with reading anything save the odd weaving chart. What did my cousin tell you?"

Rùnach pointed to three places, then turned the map so they were facing the right way for her. She trailed her fingers along roads and, aye, rivers as well. And then she blinked.

"Did you see that?"

"See what?" he asked.

"That sparkle there," she said. She pointed to a place on the map where the roads and rivers were not so well demarcated. "That little glade there—" She looked at him. "Why does everything always end in a glade?"

"Because foul deeds are often wrought in forests and apparently sunlight is useful for revealing them," he said dryly. "Hence the need for a spot missing trees." He peered at the map. "So, you see something there?"

"Unless I'm imagining things."

"Do you think you're imagining things?"

She had to take a rather deep breath. "Nay."

"Then let's go investigate."

"I'm not sure I know how to get there. Maps are not my strong suit."

"That's why you have me," he said cheerfully, rolling the map up and reaching for his pack. "I love maps."

She put her hand on his arm. "It isn't just for maps, Rùnach. Loving you, that is."

He paused, then looked at her seriously. "Will you remember that when I'm on my knees in front of your father, begging him to let me wed you?"

"I'm not sure he'll have anything to say in the matter."

"Well, that may be true, but I imagine there will be someone somewhere in the next fortnight or two who *will* have something to say about it. Perhaps even you."

She looked up at him as he rose and started to stuff the map

into his rather empty pack. "You know," she said slowly, "I've
spent so much of my life not having any say over my life." She
paused and met his eyes. "I think I want a say."

He reached over and pulled her to her feet, then into his arms.
He smoothed a stray hair or two back from her cheek. "Of course
you do. And I will, of course, acquiesce to all your demands."

"You will not," she said with a snort.

"Well, probably not," he agreed, "but what would you do with
a man you could walk all over?"

"Wonder where *you'd* gone," she muttered, pulling out of his
arms. She picked up her pack she hadn't even opened, then looked
at him. "Shall we?"

He smiled, kissed her briefly, then reached out and opened the
door for her. "We should. Perhaps the innkeeper will prepare
something for us to eat before I anger him by paying him for the
effects of my magical adventures. Next time, I think I should
attempt the same out in the open."

"In a glade?"

"It worked for my father," he said wryly, "though I'd like to
hope my spells are slightly less objectionable to the surroundings
than his would have been."

She nodded and left the chamber with him, hoping that would
be the case. She wasn't exactly sure what they would do if hers
was the only feeble magic they had to rely on.

Two days later she walked into a clearing with Rùnach. It was
the place she'd seen on the map, of that she was certain. She'd
found that she hadn't needed to consult the map more than a time
or two that first day before she realized she knew where she was

going. She had looked at Rùnach often during their journey, but he'd only been watching her gravely.

She wondered if he could possibly be as unnerved as she was.

The horses currently loped along behind them in the form of enormous, ferocious-looking hounds. She supposed Iteach couldn't be blamed if he spent as much time looking at Orail as he did Rùnach. Her shapechanging horse was glorious as a horse, but her golden hound's coat was truly something to behold. That said, she wouldn't have walked up randomly to those two beasts for any amount of gold.

Rùnach had stopped and was simply standing there in the glade, a little off to one side, watching her. She supposed she wouldn't have walked up to him either, if she hadn't already known him. He looked lethal enough with that terrible sword at his side and an aura about him that warned he wouldn't be trifled with. He also seemed perfectly content to simply stand there and wait for her to do something, damn him anyway.

"Well?" she demanded.

He smiled briefly. "Don't look at me. This is your country."

She wrapped her arms around herself. "I don't like being the one making the decisions."

"I don't think I can make that any different for you," he said seriously. "What do you think we should do now?"

She blew out her breath. "Continue to look for my father, if he's still alive."

He clasped his hands behind his back and simply looked at her.

"Well?" she said crossly. "Just how am I supposed to do that from this point?"

"I don't know," he said slowly "How are you supposed to do that from this point?"

She would have glared at him, but she couldn't bring herself to. "Do you always answer a question with a question?"

He opened his mouth, but she shot him a warning look. He smiled. "Very well, I'll give you an honest answer. I think you should attempt a bit of magic. Perhaps Bruadair will hide us long enough for you to unhide what you need to use at this point."

"I never hid that magic I don't have," she said firmly, "because, as I said, I don't have any."

He looked around himself, then fetched something and put it on a small, flat rock. "A pinecone," he said seriously. "Why don't you see if you can hide it."

She started to deny that she knew how to do anything of the sort, but realized that wasn't precisely true. She surrendered her backpack to the elven madman who put both hers and his in a pile and then looked at her expectantly. She closed her eyes briefly, then laid a spell over the pinecone. She knew what to say because Bruadair's magic told her.

The pinecone faded, then disappeared.

"Hmmm," Rùnach said thoughtfully, stroking his chin. "Can you undo that spell?"

"Undo it?"

"Either reverse it, or perhaps use a spell of revealing?"

Aisling found that the words were there, again, ready for her use. She looked at Rùnach. "I don't like this."

His smile was terribly gentle. "I know, love. But if it eases you any, I think your country's magic seems fairly determined to have you take note of it."

She couldn't even scowl at him, he'd said it so gently and with such a conspiratorial smile. She rolled her eyes on principle, then took the spell the magic had given her and used it on the spot in front of her where she'd hidden—

The pinecone that was again revealed.

And then the world rent in twain.

The pinecone exploded. So did the spell covering a path that led from the glade into the woods. Rùnach shouldered both packs, called for the dogs, then looked at her.

"Well, let's follow that then, shall we?"

"Are you mad?" she gasped. "We're to simply up and walk into that forest there?"

He took her by the hand. "Let's go and see where this leads."

She wanted to balk, truly she did. It would have been much easier, even at that late date, to simply turn around and run the other way. But she knew she couldn't. Rùnach was watching her. She had two shapechanging horses watching her.

Bruadair's magic was watching her.

She took a deep breath, gathered what scant courage she had, and nodded briskly. "Off we go, then."

Rùnach said nothing. He simply waited for her to move. She did, eventually, though it was perhaps one of the more difficult steps she had ever taken. After all, it was just a path . . .

Through an obviously enchanted wood that had revealed the path in question thanks to a spell she hadn't known ten minutes earlier but had used as easily as if she'd known it all her life. She could accept that, with enough time.

She wished she could accept the fact that she had the feeling she wasn't going to like what they found at the end of that path.

Ten

Rùnach followed the faint path with a fair bit of caution, with a ferocious equine-born hound in front of him, Aisling next to him, and his own pony-turned-canine bringing up the rear. He hadn't been surprised that Aisling's spell had turned up more than she'd cared for it to. He also hadn't been surprised that the true extent of her magic had been revealed in her home country. In fact, he was half tempted to say he was no longer surprised by anything.

But that would have been a lie because as he stopped fifty paces away from a house, he found himself too surprised to continue on.

"Well," he said, nonplussed.

"I couldn't agree more."

He glanced at Aisling to find her wearing the same expression he was sure was plastered to his own visage. He turned back to the house in front of him and wondered if they would have walked right into the side of the house without Aisling's spell or simply wandered into the stream running alongside it and drowned.

The house itself looked like the sort of house one might find in the mountains: steep roof, rough timbers, utilitarian with the odd touches of whimsy here and there. It looked as if it belonged to someone who made his living from the land, but not in any magical way. A stream, which on second glance turned out to be fairly large, flowed along one side of the house, turning a large waterwheel. Rùnach had no idea what the owner of the house did to earn his bread, but perhaps he ran a mill or a woodshop or something that required a fairly steady, unmagical source of power.

He watched the wheel for a moment or two, then realized that was where the circles began.

Rùnach found himself walking with Aisling up the path to the gate set in a low rock fence. That was the last thing he saw that didn't have some sort of curve to it. They entered the gate to find circular stones leading up to the house, curves in the edges of the flowerbeds, stones encircling a dozen different varieties of fruit trees. He was half tempted to ask Aisling if those trees had any stories to tell, but he didn't have the chance.

The front door had opened.

That perhaps might have been unremarkable, but Aisling had come to a staggering halt and was gaping at the man standing there.

"Recognize him?" Rùnach murmured.

She wheezed out something that he was fairly sure was a curse. He looked at the tall, unfortunately quite intimidating-looking man standing there, then wondered if it might be wise to release Aisling's hand. The moment the thought crossed his mind, she tightened her fingers with his and glared at him.

"Don't you dare."

He supposed when she put it that way, he shouldn't. He nodded toward their potential host.

"Who's that?"

"One of the Guild guards!" She looked torn between raging and weeping. "He handed me off to the fop—or, rather, to Prince Soilléir, who then dragged me down to the border where Mistress Muinear got me across into the tender care of Ochadius of Riamh. And here, after a very circuitous route, I find myself facing *that* man again!"

Rùnach ventured a look at the man standing in the doorway. He looked . . . haggard.

But he seemingly had no lack of courage, for he stepped out into the sunlight just the same. Rùnach would have winced at the sight of hair the same color as Aisling's, but he supposed he shouldn't. She had to have inherited it from somewhere. It was obvious she had inherited it from that man there.

The man continued down his path, away from his house, until he was standing a handful of paces away.

"Aisling," he said quietly. "Welcome home."

She looked at him, mute. Actually, she looked as if she were wrestling with the intense desire to kill him.

Rùnach couldn't blame her. There was a man who obviously knew her, who had obviously sent her away, and now had the gall to welcome her *home*? And just what did he expect her to do? Fall on his neck and weep with joy?

Rùnach found himself the object of a quick, brutal assessment that began at his boots and ended at his face, with a practiced check conducted along the way for weapons. It was at the end, however, that the man's whole demeanor changed. He glanced at Aisling's hand in Rùnach's, then gave him a look that was tinged with something it took Rùnach a moment or two to identify, and he wasn't unaccustomed to warning looks from fathers. This was something else entirely. He rather strongly suspected that if his hand strayed to his sword or he looked as if he might spew out a spell, he would find himself rather dead.

"Who," the man said very carefully, "are you?"

Aisling offered no opinion. Rùnach supposed he might have to have a chat with her about that later. She did, however, squeeze his hand and shift a bit closer to him. That didn't improve her father's opinion.

"My name is Rùnach," Rùnach said slowly.

"You resemble someone I've recently seen."

Rùnach wished he could have said he was surprised. "And did this person have a name?"

"None that I could discover, but he looks a damned sight like you." The man considered, but his expression didn't soften. "Acair, I think. Something along those lines."

Rùnach sighed. "My half brother—"

He supposed the only reason he continued to breathe was because Bruadair thought his death might grieve Aisling and it had spared him from the spell that slammed into him—and only him—and knocked him flat on his back. Once he could see again through the stars swimming around his bloody stupid head, he found that Aisling was standing in front of him holding off a spell of death with her mere presence alone. He gaped at the shards of spell that were hanging over him like scores of portcullis spikes and supposed he couldn't be blamed for indulging in a shudder.

"He is my betrothed," Aisling said distinctly. "I do not want him harmed."

The spikes hesitated, then tucked themselves rather reluctantly back into what he could see was a canopy of death still hanging over his head. He shot those lethal shards of spell a wary look, then accepted Aisling's hand back up to his feet. He stood there and did his damndest to catch his breath without looking as if he were desperately trying to catch his breath.

Perhaps it was time to revisit the ability to keep his mouth shut he'd learned so well in Buidseachd.

Aisling's father was pointing at him with an unfriendly finger. "Do you have any idea who that is?"

"Do you think you have any right to ask that question?" Aisling countered.

"His father is Gair of Ceangail!"

Rùnach glanced at Aisling to see how she was reacting to that piece of truth. She merely shrugged.

"His mother was Sarait of Tòrr Dòrainn. I know his grandfather and several of his cousins. Very handsome, those lads, but I like this one the most."

And then that blessed girl glanced at him and winked.

Rùnach rubbed his free hand over his mouth because he needed something to do besides laugh. He looked at Aisling's father.

"I am Rùnach of Ceangail," he conceded, "and while I am my father's spawn, I am my mother's son." Or so he hoped. Given how his magic had been behaving since Aisling had restored it to him, he was beginning to wonder if somehow some of his father's madness had found its way into his veins as well.

The other man didn't look terribly pleased, but he wasn't spewing out spells so perhaps they would at least manage conversation before things went south again.

"I don't like this," he said crisply.

"I'm not sure you'll have anything to say about it," Aisling said. "My life is my own to share with whom I choose. And I choose this man here."

The spikes of death rattled once more, sounding like crisp, icy snow falling in the dead of winter, then disappeared.

Aisling's father looked at her. "Very well," he said slowly. "Be it as you will. I suppose I have no right to tell you what to do. I do, however, have answers that you deserve. I have waited many years to give them to you."

"They had best be *damned* good answers," she said curtly.

The man sighed deeply. "I'm not sure you'll find them such, but they will at least be the truth." He looked at her seriously. "If nothing else, perhaps I can assure you that you weren't completely alone all those years."

Aisling looked as if she were on the verge of simply having heard as much as she could bear. Rùnach squeezed her hand and wished he could take the pain he knew she was facing away from her. She looked up at him.

"I suppose I must do this."

"It's why we came," he agreed. "And thank you for my life."

She shivered. "What a nasty spell. And I wish I could take credit for saving your life, but that wasn't entirely me. Well," she amended, "I was alarmed, which I suppose Bruadair knew." She smiled at him. "I think it likes you."

"Thank heavens."

"I like you too."

"I don't think your father does."

"I don't think he's allowed an opinion."

Rùnach thought she might be surprised, but he wasn't going to argue with her. He merely smiled, then walked with her behind a man who looked absolutely shattered. Obviously he'd been expecting Aisling. Whether or not he'd realized how difficult it would be to see her at his home or relished the thought of giving her the answers he surely knew she wanted was perhaps another tale entirely.

The house was as unremarkable on the inside as on the out. There was something about it, though, that seemed strange. Rùnach saw no other spells, but he hadn't seen the first one coming either. He took a deep breath and added that to the list of things he was definitely going to have to come to grips with very soon.

Aisling's father's house looked as if it had been inhabited only recently after a long absence. It wasn't so much that it wasn't clean as it was that it was empty of the sort of usual clutter that accompanied a family living in a home. He walked behind Aisling, forcing himself to leave his hands down by his side instead of putting one on his sword, not that his sword would have served him. He didn't even have his magic as anything to count on at the moment.

That was something he was going to have to address sooner rather than later, truth be told.

He watched their surroundings, perhaps more closely than necessary, simply out of habit and a desire to make certain there wasn't someone hiding in the shadows he might not particularly want to encounter.

Aisling looked over her shoulder periodically, as if she wanted to make certain he was still there. Finally she simply reached behind her and took his hand. He didn't argue. He kept her hand in his as they walked along a short passageway, made a quick turn, then paused as Aisling's father opened the worn wooden doors and walked into the chamber there.

Rùnach paused at the doorway to admire. Admittedly, he had a fondness for libraries, but this one was truly spectacular. The shelves lined the walls from floor to ceiling in proper library fashion, of course, and there were lamps and chairs and all manner of comforts made with the lover of books in mind. Oh, along with one enormous spinning wheel in the corner.

Which wasn't, as it happened, the only wheel there.

He realized with a start that there were wheels everywhere. He could have walked around the room and every two paces reached out to touch something that spun. He hazarded a look at Aisling to find that she had noticed as well. She looked at him, her eyes wide.

"Well," she whispered.

"This is going to be interesting," he murmured. "For more than just the usual reasons, I daresay."

"I can scarce wait to see how," she agreed.

Rùnach supposed he should have at least had the manners to have found a sturdy bookcase to lean against, but all he could do was walk out into the middle of the chamber and continue to turn around—

As if he were the center of a wheel that was continually spinning.

That was a slightly unsettling realization, actually, considering where he was and whom he was with.

He looked around himself, marveling at what the library contained. The whole place was full of wheels, either things that were spinning at various rates or things built in the shape of circles or spokes radiating out from centers into shapes that might be bent into circles with the right amount of force. It made him wonder who in the house was so fixated with things that spun.

Aisling's father excused himself to fetch them something to drink, or so he said. Rùnach looked at Aisling, who was now standing in the middle of that chamber of wheels and books, and winced at the haunted look on her face. He gathered her to him when she walked into his embrace. If she was holding him so tightly he was tempted to flinch, so be it. He kept watch on the door and didn't say anything about how badly she was trembling.

"Don't leave me."

"Never," he said quietly. "Not until you tell me to go."

She pulled back and met his eyes. "Well, that won't happen."

He smiled and bent to kiss her cheek. Her father was standing at the door, after all. He looked at her. "He's returned."

Aisling sighed deeply, then pulled away from him. She turned and looked at the man standing at the door, holding a tray of tea things. His expression was less haunted than it was rather sad.

"You look like your mother."

Aisling didn't move. "Do I?"

The man walked over and set his tray down on a table. Rùnach pretended not to notice that table was in the center of the chamber and that when they sat down, they were merely spokes in its pattern. He poured because neither Aisling nor her father looked equal to the task. He considered what was in his cup and couldn't tell if it were poisoned or not. Aisling traded cups with him, then looked at her father pointedly.

He only shook his head. "Just tea."

Rùnach sipped and was relieved to find it was just that. He sat back and watched Aisling's father begin his tale. It was obviously something he'd considered more than once.

"I am Bristeadh," he said gravely, "and Aisling I am your sire."

Aisling set her cup down and sat back in her chair. She said nothing, but only waited. Rùnach supposed he shouldn't have been impressed with her ability to remain silent. She'd obviously done it for years in the Guild.

He looked at them with a frown. "Do you want something to eat first?"

"I don't think I can," Aisling said quietly. "Rùnach?"

"I'm fine," he said. He thought he might be fine for at least another hour or two until he'd forgotten the sight of scores of spikes hanging over his head whilst he'd been too dumbfounded to do anything to save his own sorry arse. "Please, go on."

Bristeadh sighed again, as if he'd been holding on to his breath for years. "I'll give you answers to all your questions about Bruadair later, if you still want them. For now, I'll tell you about your family. Your mother was Cridhe, who was the daughter of Cuilidh of Cairadh, granddaughter of Muinear of Cairadh—"

"Wait," Aisling said, holding up her hand. "Who? The last one, I mean."

"Muinear of Cairadh," he repeated.

"But," she said slowly, "I know a Muinear."

He looked at her steadily. "Indeed you do."

Aisling stared at him for a handful of moments in silence, then her mouth fell open. "Are you talking about Mistress Muinear? The *weaving* mistress?"

Bristeadh nodded. "The very same."

Aisling pushed herself back against her chair. "I can't believe it."

Bristeadh looked like a man who wanted to divulge all his secrets as quickly as possible before the storm brewing unleashed its fury. Rùnach couldn't say he didn't understand the sentiment.

"Your mother died shortly after your birth," he said quietly. "They refused to leave you here with me, of course—"

"Of course?" Aisling interrupted. "Who are they? And why *of course*?"

"I'll answer the last first," he said. "They refused to leave you with me because I have no magic."

"You appeared to have a damned fine bit of it outside when you almost killed my future husband," Aisling said tartly.

Bristeadh smiled. "I can't take any credit for that. Muinear left that for me years ago. I wasn't precisely sure it would work as it should, but apparently I was wrong. Or, rather, I would have been wrong had it worked." He shrugged helplessly. "So you see why they thought it best not to leave you in my care. The miracle is I was allowed to wed your mother, of course, she being who she was."

"And who was she?" Aisling asked.

"Well, a dreamspinner, of course," Bristeadh said. He looked at her, obviously puzzled. "Didn't you know?"

"Of course I didn't know!" Aisling exclaimed. She took a deep breath. "Rùnach and I have speculated on things, but how was I to know who I was? I thought I was the unwanted daughter of those two miserly fools from Malcte!"

Bristeadh shook his head slowly. "Your grandmother Cuilidh is—or was, rather—the dreamspinner. *The* dreamspinner. The final Dreamspinner who holds all the strands together and blends them as is called for. Muinear was that for centuries before her. Your mother . . . well, your mother—" He sighed and looked briefly at the ceiling. "I'm not sure it was ever meant for her to take that place even if she'd wanted it, which I'm almost afraid to admit she didn't. What she wanted was to have you." He smiled. "You were her dream."

Rùnach closed his eyes briefly. He wasn't sure if he felt sorrier for Aisling that she had never known her mother, or her mother that she hadn't had Aisling for as long as she had no doubt wanted her.

"How did she die?" Aisling asked hollowly.

Bristeadh shifted uncomfortably. "I would like to say that it was from illness or accident, but it wasn't. She wasn't unwell. She simply . . . passed away. Your grandmother died soon after. At that point, we began to suspect that perhaps there were other forces at work than nature."

Rùnach suppressed the urge to rub his hands over his face. If the tidings weren't terrible enough for Aisling, they were for him. He needed the infallible ability to protect her, yet there he sat with magic he wasn't sure would work when necessary in a country

that was likely still home to souls who had apparently slain Aisling's mother and grandmother. He was going to have to come to
an understanding with Bruadair's magic sooner rather than later.

He looked at Aisling to see how she was taking it all. She was
very pale, but he wouldn't have expected anything else.

"Muinear was convinced we had to hide you," Bristeadh continued carefully.

"In the Guild?" Aisling asked.

"Where is the last place anyone would have looked for the seventh, most powerful dreamspinner?"

"But you were there," she said flatly.

"I wouldn't agree to sending you there unless that was part of
the bargain," Bristeadh said grimly. "Not that I was able to do anything useful. I certainly couldn't draw attention to either of us." He
looked at her seriously. "Perhaps this won't ease you any, but there
were more souls watching over you than you might realize."

"If you tell me Quinn and Euan are my brothers, I will scream,"
Aisling warned.

"Quinn is working for Sglaimir," Bristeadh said. "But Euan is
your cousin."

"He knows me?" she asked in astonishment.

Bristeadh nodded. "Indeed he does, though he was sworn to
secrecy. I believe Soilléir threatened to turn him into a pile of
manure did he breathe a word of either your identity or his."

"You know Soilléir as well?" Aisling asked incredulously.

Rùnach couldn't decide if he were surprised or not, though he
supposed he would eventually come down on the side of not. It
said something about the seriousness of the situation, that Soilléir
was willing to be so involved.

"I know many people," Bristeadh conceded. "Soilléir is one
with an interest in the happenings in Bruadair, which I understand

he indulges with great caution. His threats, however, did leave an impression on Euan who definitely kept your secret for as long as he was free. I think he's paid a steep price for that."

"Free?" Rùnach echoed. "What do you mean?"

"Sglaimir's had him at the palace for the past pair of months. Fortunately, he hasn't broken."

"And how do you know that?" Rùnach asked cautiously.

"We have our spies." Bristeadh looked at him. "We know who comes and goes inside the palace, who comes and goes across the border. Your bastard brother Acair has been a regular visitor over the years. A very frequent visitor of late, but perhaps you suspected that already."

Rùnach sighed deeply. There was nothing to add to that.

Bristeadh looked at Aisling. "You can ask Muinear for more details, of course—"

"She's dead!"

Bristeadh blinked. "Well, of course she's not."

"I saw her be slain by the Guildmistress with my own two eyes," Aisling said in disbelief. "I *saw* her fall."

"She's alive, daughter," Bristeadh said gently. "She sat in that very chair not a month ago. Prince Soilléir sat where your friend is sitting and Lord Freasdail made up the fourth place."

Rùnach suppressed the urge to purse his lips. Soilléir yet again in the thick of things. He was going to have a few simple words with that one the next chance he had.

"Lord who?" Aisling asked.

"Freasdail," Bristeadh said. He smiled very faintly. "He has been acting as the First's steward for the past several years."

"The First?"

"The First Dreamspinner. That is what we call the one who holds all the strands. He or she is the final dreamspinner, but the first in power and might." He looked at her with a grave smile. "You."

Aisling shoved herself back from the table without warning. Rùnach caught her chair and pulled it out of her way before it went over backward, taking her with it. She was trembling so badly, he could see her shaking. She looked down at her father with an expression so akin to horror, Rùnach felt his eyes begin to burn. Perhaps she could have denied who she was before . . .

He found his hand taken and he was pulled up out of his chair so quickly, it did tip over.

"I need air."

He wasn't about to argue with her. He shot Bristeadh a questioning look and had a subtle pointing toward the doorway in return. He didn't do anything but hurry along with Aisling as she fled from the library. She didn't seem to have any idea where to go, but that didn't deter her. Before long, he found himself standing in a garden at what was obviously the back of the house. It was, again, full of circles.

Aisling paced—in circles, it had to be said—then suddenly stopped and looked at him as he sat on a bench in what sunlight he could find.

"It's true, then."

"It?" he ventured.

"All of it." She waved her hand about with a jerky motion. "This. Dreamspinners. Bruadairian magic. All of it."

"Aye," he said carefully, "I daresay it is."

Her eyes were as haunted as her father's. "Then what am I to do?"

He sighed deeply. "Keep walking forward, I daresay."

"What if I don't like what's at the end of the path?"

"You don't have to accept your destiny."

She reached out and absently plucked something from the air, looked at it, then put it in the bag Weger had given her all those many se'nnights ago in Gobhann. Then she froze. She looked at him. "I can't help myself."

"So I see," he said faintly. He'd been watching her do that for the past few days, but there was something profoundly unnerving about watching her absently pluck strands of magic out of thin air. He almost didn't want to think about what she was capable of, he who had grown to manhood watching his father trying to undo the world. "It's in your blood, I daresay."

She considered, then seemingly came to a decision. She walked over to him. A collection of pebbles rolled over to congregate at his feet, fashioning themselves into a small stool. Soft moss swept up to cover it. Rùnach wasn't altogether certain that a wee flower hadn't sprung up to wave at Aisling as well.

"I was going to throw myself at your feet and beg you to run with me," she said faintly.

"Bruadair apparently prefers that you be comfortably seated whilst about your begging."

She pursed her lips at him, then reached out to touch the flower. It leapt up into her hand, rested there for a moment, then vanished into a hint of a song that even he heard. The song lingered, then wafted off into the woods, where it was welcomed into a chorus that hummed just out of hearing and memory.

Rùnach bowed his head and laughed. He honestly couldn't think of anything else to do. He lifted his head to find that Aisling had sat and was scowling at him.

He reached out and tucked a lock of hair behind her ear. "You were saying?"

"I was wondering how best to run," she said crossly. "Which you seem to find rather amusing."

"Oh, I think it's anything but that," he said, his smile fading. "'Tis anything but that, my love."

She looked at him bleakly. "What am I to do, then? I was fully prepared to flee, but that was before. I don't see how I can now." She rubbed her arms. "I just don't know how I'll manage any of this."

"One step at a time," Rùnach said. "Bruadair seems to have an interest in your path, if I might offer an opinion."

She took his hand in both her own and looked at him seriously. "And when you knew where your path lay, what did you think?"

"I was arrogant and stupid," he said, "so I'm not sure my thoughts would be worth knowing. And I couldn't let my mother go there alone." He paused, then sighed. "The thought that we were mad crossed my mind more than once, but what else was there to be done? My mother and older brother believed the fate of the world hung in the balance and I shared that belief. We did what we had to."

"I don't have your courage," she said very quietly.

"Aisling, my love, you don't," he agreed. "Yours is far greater."

She shook her head. "All I want to do is run."

"Why don't we shapechange instead?" he asked. "Well, once we come to an understanding with your magic. I don't want to fling myself off the roof of your father's house in dragonshape and become part of his garden path where I land."

Her look of misery hadn't faded. "I thought I was alone. There in the Guild."

"I know," he said softly. "But it sounds as if they did the best they could not to leave you by yourself, doesn't it?"

But what he didn't say was that if they had resorted to hiding her out in the open in a bloody weaver's guild, she must have powerful enemies indeed. If those enemies had been able to slay her mother, that was one thing. That they'd apparently slain her grand-mother the dreamspinner . . . well, that was something else entirely.

If those wishing Aisling's mother and grandmother ill could slay those two women, one of whom was perhaps possessing pow-ers far beyond the norm, how would Aisling fare in their sights? Worse still, if no Bruadairian had been able to save them, who the hell did he think he was to suppose he might manage it?

"Let's walk."

He let her pull him to his feet, then kept her hand in his and started around the garden with her.

Perhaps he had an advantage that the others didn't have. He might not have been Bruadairian. He might not have magic that was completely manageable on Bruadairian soil. He also might have more than a passing familiarity with the lad who was mak-ing the mischief they were facing.

All he knew was that he loved the final dreamspinner who had been so carefully and painfully kept out of sight for almost three decades.

Whatever he had to do, whatever power he had to call on, whatever spells he had to use, he would do it all to keep her safe.

Eleven

❧

Aisling walked through the garden and wondered absently how it was she could have lived her entire life in Bruadair and been so utterly oblivious to her surroundings.

Or, rather, the souls peopling her surroundings. She'd been acutely aware of how miserable the Guild was. She had memorized every ugly crack in every passageway she'd walked down day after miserable day. She had never not been cognizant of her surroundings as she'd wandered within a small part of Beul on her day of liberty each week because she hadn't had time to roam farther afield. But she had never looked at any of the people there, never made note of anyone potentially being someone unexpected, never considered that those around her might be friendly.

Euan was her cousin and Bristeadh was her father. It was almost unbelievable.

Perhaps in time the memories might reveal themselves, but for the moment all she knew was that she'd done her damndest to forget everything she'd ever seen during those hellish years of her youth and young adulthood, and apparently she'd done a very good job of it.

She looked at her father's house and felt absolutely no connection to it. Perhaps that shouldn't have surprised her given how little time she'd obviously spent in it. There was magic surrounding it, that much she could see. It wasn't magic that came from her father. He had again freely conceded his lack of the same without hesitation the night before at the supper he'd cooked for them by very ordinary means. He volunteered that his lack of magic had been something of an impediment to his marriage, but his extremely noble though not royal bloodlines had made up for that.

Not that it matters here in Bruaдair, he'd said with a smile as he'd stirred his soup.

She had no idea what that meant and actually no desire to ask him. Perhaps she had spent too long with Rùnach, who considered first a man's mettle before his station and only trotted out his own royal connections to tease her. Asking her father to explain the possible caste system of Bruadair was more than she'd been willing to do.

She'd been happy enough to simply sit in his parlor next to Rùnach and listen to the father she hadn't known and the man she had grown to love talk politics. It was a little startling to realize she knew several of the players in the grand councils of kings and queens. It was also a little surprising to realize that she looked more like her father than she ever would have suspected. His hair was the same color as hers, a color that she decided wasn't without redemption especially when viewed by lamp and firelight. He fidgeted the same way she did, restlessly looking for things to do with his hands. Once he had decided that Rùnach wasn't worthy of death, he stopped fingering his dagger and started carrying on friendly conversations.

Rùnach, for his part, had been deferential. She supposed he thought permission for marriage might potentially need to be obtained from Bristeadh of Bruadair, a notion she had briskly disabused him of as he'd later left her in front of a guestroom door. She had decided that she liked him very much and even Bruadair didn't seem opposed to him. That was enough for her. Rùnach seemed to think there might be permission to be requested from others further down the road, but she couldn't bring herself to think about that. She was still trying to swallow the tidings of who her father thought she was.

She glanced around the corner of the house, hoping to catch sight of that very handsome elven prince, but he was nowhere to be found so she left off with her pacing and wandered back toward the kitchen. Both her father and her would-be betrothed had stated their intention to simply wait for her to make up her mind about what to do, a remarkable idea all by itself. She wasn't accustomed to making decisions of even minor import. She honestly hadn't a clue what she was supposed to do—

Actually, that was less true than she would have liked. She did know what to do. She simply didn't want to do it.

She entered the back door to find only Bristeadh there, chopping vegetables for lunch. He smiled at her.

"Nice walk?"

She leaned against the doorframe and looked at him seriously. "I know I should remember you."

He shook his head. "Nay, love, you shouldn't."

"Why not?"

"Because I was the Guildmistress's personal guardsman," he

said slowly. "I did my damndest to make sure you were as often out of her sights as possible."

"Thank you."

He smiled grimly. "Cold comfort, I know, but if you knew the identities of the people who were—and still are—searching for you . . ." He paused, then shook his head. "I'll give Rùnach a list at some point. I'm not sure it's anything you need to see. And speaking of seeing, you wouldn't have recognized me anyway at the Guild. Soilléir made sure of that once the plan was decided upon."

She looked at him in shock. "He used a spell on you?"

"Just to change the color of my hair and eyes. Surprisingly painful, actually, though I don't think he took any pleasure in it. He was good enough to restore things to their proper color once we were sure you were safely away."

"Have you told Rùnach any of this?"

"We've chatted about several things this morning," he conceded. "Briefly, though. He's had things to do."

She could only imagine and she imagined those things had to do with digging through books in the library for things he likely shouldn't know. She considered her father. "How well do you know Prince Soilléir?"

Bristeadh smiled faintly. "Our families have known each other for centuries. Personally? For all of my adult life, surely. I think when your grandmother was slain, he was forced to heed Muinear's call for aid. I know he wouldn't have come on his own for anything other than a social call. He doesn't like to interfere."

"Did you know Gair?"

"Sarait, rather. I knew *of* Gair, of course. But I never had the pleasure of an introduction."

"So you didn't know Rùnach was with Soilléir at Buidseachd?"

"Soilléir never even so much as hinted at it and I can't say that

I paid all that much heed to the goings on out in the world. I was busy enough with the task I was allowed, which was to keep you as safe as I could." He paused, then shrugged. "I do remember hearing a rumor that Gair had been about a piece of foolishness at Ruamharaiche's well, but as you might imagine, there were few who felt to mourn just deserts richly dished out. Good riddance to bad rubbish, and all that. It was common knowledge that Sarait and the children had been slain with him, but I had no connection to them. I grieved for their lives lost, but nothing more."

"I thought Gair was a myth."

He smiled. "I don't doubt it. And why is it I suspect Muinear was the one who filled your ears with that sort of thing?"

Aisling smiled in spite of herself. "She did. I'm not sure if I should be grateful for that or not. I looked for pointy ears on Rùnach for at least a fortnight before I came to grips with what he was."

"I'm not surprised." He smiled, then his smile faded. "And to answer your question directly, nay, I had no idea Rùnach had survived the well, though it doesn't surprise me somehow. He's a canny one, that lad."

She had to agree, though her thoughts were perhaps a bit more substantial than that one. She sighed and looked at her father, trying to place him. She supposed she had perhaps learned too well to simply keep her head down and her thoughts to herself at the Guild.

"I don't remember you. I'm sorry about that."

"I'm not sure you would want to," he said quietly. "Let's say that I did several things I wish I could take back and couldn't stop many more I wish I could have."

She felt a little ill. "I'm not sure if I should pity you for that or loathe you."

"You would be justified in the latter," he said seriously, "but I did what I could to mitigate the horrors there." He stopped chopping and looked at her. "It wasn't just the fate of Bruadair, Aisling, that hung in the balance, though that was grave enough. 'Tis the fate of the world is at stake."

"So says Soilléir," she said weakly, "but surely not."

He set his knife down. "Do you know who Sglaimir is?"

"Rùnach says he's the grandson of a very evil mage."

"Carach of Mùig," Bristeadh agreed. "One of the viler of the black mages to slither through the Nine Kingdoms over the centuries. Sglaimir is his grandson."

"What does he want with Bruadair?" she asked. "It isn't as if he's gone out of his way to improve the condition of the palace or surround himself with immense riches. Admittedly I've only seen him from a great distance, but he didn't have dozens of courtiers with him or a grand retinue."

"He wants what every mage wants," Bristeadh said with a shrug. "Power."

She would have disagreed with him, but she couldn't. She'd seen that for herself.

"And you think he's taken Bruadair's for himself?" she asked.

Bristeadh considered his veg for another moment or two, then looked at her. "I don't know. If he has, I agree it certainly doesn't show."

"Do you think he had help with his scheme?"

"Absolutely. From whom is the question. I would say Acair of Ceangail is in the thick of things. He's been closeted with Sglaimir up at the castle far too often for it to count as simple social calls."

"What is to be done about him, then?" she asked uneasily.

"I believe, daughter, that your would-be fiancé will have to give us aid there."

She frowned. "And what if he hadn't come?"

Bristeadh only smiled. "Soilléir's sight extends far."

Aisling would have laughed, but she realized the man was utterly serious. "You mean to tell me Soilléir saw *us*?"

"Ask him next time you see him."

"He won't tell me!"

"Then I suppose you'll be left with speculation. Unless you decide to wring the answer from me, which I beg you not to do." He looked at her with a weak smile. "I have no magic, remember?"

She snorted. "And I do?"

"Aye, Aisling, you do."

She shivered and wished her cloak had been thicker—

Her father laughed at the heavy wool she was suddenly swathed in. "You had best learn to be careful what you wish for, my girl. Bruadair takes a special interest in her dreamspinners. As for anything else, I believe you and Rùnach have a few things to work out before too much more time passes."

"Do you like him?"

"Do you care if I do?"

A question for an answer. She sighed. Perhaps she was doomed to be surrounded by men who weren't capable of simple *ayes* and *nays*. She looked at her father and felt something inside her shift. He looked like her, she had to admit, and he had suffered perhaps even a bit of her own pain in the Guild. He could have just as easily sent her off and not thought of her again.

"I find," she said finally, "that I do."

He smiled. "Then I'll tell you that, my earlier reaction aside, I'm thrilled beyond measure. It is a very lovely family. Well, with the exception of Sìle who is the epitome of an arrogant, blowhardish elf, but perhaps that can't be helped."

"He is fairly magnificent."

"Which is the first thing he tells anyone who'll listen," Bristeadh said promptly. He shook his head gently. "Nay, Aisling, I'm very happy for you both. You deserve someone who will cherish you, which I think Rùnach will. He, I must admit, deserves someone who will value him for who he is apart from his bloodlines, which I daresay you will do. I suppose between the two of you, you'll manage to keep each other safe."

Aisling walked over and put her arms around his waist before the impulse was chased away. He hesitated but a moment before he enveloped her in a return embrace. She thought he might have sobbed, just once. It was enough to bring tears to her eyes, hardhearted wench that she was. She pulled away and cleared her throat.

"I'd best go see that Rùnach hasn't ransacked your library. He's not to be trusted with that sort of thing."

Bristeadh had tears standing in his eyes, but he nodded, smiled, then made a great production of going back to chopping his carrots and potatoes. Aisling left the kitchen before she became more maudlin than spring soup deserved.

She wandered through the passageway, running her fingers along the wall as she did so, touching patterns that were painted there. Not everything was circular, but so much was that she thought she could safely say the house had been built by someone obsessed with spinning wheels. She would have to ask Bristeadh— er, her father, rather—who had built the place and for whom.

The door to the library was open, so she eased inside, then simply stood at the back to see what Rùnach was doing.

He was sitting at the table, poring over a robust selection of things open and spread out in front of him. She wasn't unaccustomed to the sight, so she ignored the books and looked at the man. Well, elf, rather. He was, she was the first to admit, rather handsome, all things considered.

Very well, he looked almost a bit like what she'd always pictured the kings of Neroche to look. Not the current one, whom she knew, of course, but the kings who had lived centuries before. Impossibly noble, terribly majestic. That sort of thing.

Only the truth was, Rùnach would never look like a king of Neroche. No matter how handsome Miach and his brothers might have been, Rùnach surpassed them all. Even if he didn't have pointed ears as she had once believed all elves must have, mythical creatures that they were.

"Are you looking at my ears?"

She realized he was leaning back in his chair, looking at her. She smiled.

"Might be."

"Come closer where you can see them better."

She smiled and met him halfway across the room. She realized that somehow the table had been moved to a different location, which left them standing in the center of a carpet whose pattern radiated out from the center like spokes on a wheel.

"A dreamspinner's house," she said with a sigh.

"Or built by someone who loved one," he agreed. He pulled her into his arms and held her close for several minutes in silence. "Finish your think yet?"

"I think I was finished before I began," she said with a sigh. She pulled back and looked at him. "And you?"

His eyes were bright with excitement. "Want to see?"

She laughed a little. "You look like you're about to open a large collection of presents."

"Just one and it's for you. Come watch."

She followed him over to the table, smiling at his enthusiasm. He pushed the books to one side, fetched a candle, then rubbed his hands together.

"Watch this."

She listened to him weave a spell over the candle, though she supposed it was less an entire spell than just a simple command. She realized immediately he was using not Fadaire, but rather Bruadairian magic. The flame atop the candle came to life and burned with a soft, dreamy sort of beauty that soothed her just to look at it. She looked at Rùnach in surprise.

"Impressive."

"Wait."

He extinguished the flame with his fingers, then took a deep breath. The next flame was of Fadaire, springing to light in all its elven beauty. She watched it for a moment or two before she realized what was unusual about it.

"You didn't burn the house down," she said in wonder.

"I know," he said, sounding thoroughly pleased. "We've come to a bit of an understanding, Sìorraidh and I, about my birthright. Well, about Fadaire, at least. I'm trying not to push my luck about anything else."

"And what was the understanding?" she asked.

"I keep you safe and it doesn't try to kill me anymore."

She smiled. "A lovely truce, that."

He laughed and threw himself into the chair at the end of the table. "You might be surprised how many things I had to promise to get this far."

She sat down around the corner from him, leaned her elbows on the table, and her chin on her fists. "Have you been talking to Bruadair behind my back again?"

He leaned over and kissed her softly, smiled, then kissed her again. "Aye. And I think we should both count ourselves fortunate that I was born in Seanagarra and grew up accustomed to all manner of mythical happenings or at this point, I might be looking for a swooning couch."

"Is that where you were born?"

"Whilst my father was off making mischief of some kind, aye." He shrugged. "He always seemed to have an excuse for never being at our births, but I have the feeling my grandfather's glamour would have ruined his dignity somehow had he attempted to cross the borders after wedding my mother. For the first time in my life, I can say I understand."

"Bruadair let you in."

"Because I love its daughter," he said. He leaned back and tangled his feet with hers. "And how is that daughter today, in truth?"

"Having fewer murderous feelings than usual toward my father in particular and Bruadairians in general."

"That's good of you," he said, his smile fading. "And I mean that, Aisling. You would be justified in being more than angry."

"He did the best he could," she said with a sigh.

"I believe he did."

She considered for a bit, then looked at him. "Do you find it curious that he has no magic or do you think he has magic but is unwilling to admit it?"

"I think, my love, that if he had had magic, he would have used every last drop to keep you with him and safe," he said seriously, "so aye, I think he's telling the truth. Uachdaran told me once that whilst magic might be in the air and water here in this lovely, accommodating country of yours, not everyone possesses the ability to use it. Perhaps they can only appreciate what others can do."

"All the more reason for them to have something to appreciate," she said.

"Besides dingy grey everywhere?" he asked. "Absolutely."

She fingered the cover of one of the books lying there, then looked at him. "So what do you think we should do now? We've found my father, but I'm not sure he has the answers we need." She met his eyes. "I'm still not sure I can believe anyone was looking for me."

He was leaning back in his chair with his knee propped up against the edge of the table. "Your cousin Riochdair certainly believes it. There's a madame in Beul who would say the same." He looked at her seriously. "Someone knows who you are, Aisling."

"I didn't think to ask my father who," she said, finding herself rather grateful all of the sudden for the heavier cloak Bruadair had provided her. "Perhaps he doesn't know."

"I don't think he does," Rùnach said slowly. "I think, Aisling my love, that there are some very curious events surrounding your birth and the deaths of your mother and grandmother. I also think that you are without a doubt the most ethereal creature I have ever clapped eyes on."

She blinked, then smiled. "You're changing the subject."

"I like this one much better."

"You didn't ask my father for my hand."

"I'm working on it. He says he won't give you to me if I can't keep you safe."

She felt her smile fade. "Things are odd here."

"And that, my love, is an understatement that might not even be surpassed by the master of understatement, Soilléir of Cothromaiche who, it seems, is far more familiar with the innards of your country than he let on."

"We should scold him for lying."

"Hedging, he would call it," Rùnach said dryly. "I believe you and I are perhaps a little too familiar with the practice ourselves to reproach him overmuch."

She sighed and looked up at the ceiling. It was circle after circle after intersecting circle, all carved from a glorious dark wood.

"Rùnach?"

"Aye, love."

"Are you frightened?"

"For myself? Nay. That I'll fail you? Terribly."

She looked at him. "You won't."

He lifted his eyebrows briefly. "You have more faith in me than you should, perhaps. But I don't think my faith in you is misplaced. You certainly spared me a skewering yesterday."

She shivered. "That was a rather nasty spell of death, wouldn't you say?"

"I would," he agreed. "Very unpleasant."

"Who do you think put that spell there?"

"I didn't look at it long enough to discover that," he said, "but I suspect we could find out, if you're curious. I would guess it was either your mother or grandmother. Or perhaps your Mistress Muinear."

Aisling looked at him thoughtfully. "I wonder how she managed to be at the Guild for so long without being marked for who she was."

"She must have power we can't begin to imagine," he said, sounding a little uneasy, "which leads me to believe I should perhaps ask your father for your hand before she's there to offer an opinion. I'm not sure how long I would last against her in a duel of spells. As for the other, I imagine pulling the wool over the eyes of the Guildmistress was child's play for her."

"I can't believe she was there," Aisling said quietly.

"She obviously loves you very much."

She shook her head. "It is very strange to think I do have a family of sorts that tried to look after me."

"I hope it will be comforting to you, in time." He glanced out the window, frowned, then looked around the library. "It must be clouding up outside. I'll light the lamps."

She looked at him quickly. He was obviously chewing on his words quite thoroughly. "And?"

"I don't want to burn the house down."

"I thought you and Bruadair had come to an understanding."

He took a deep breath. "So we have." He rubbed his hands together and looked at her with a faint smile. "I'm nervous."

"I could go get a bucket of water."

"Well, between that thought and the one of my sire laughing himself sick over my straits at present, I think I've just found the courage to press on." He considered, then spoke a spell.

Lights sprang to life on candles and in lamps. They burned with exactly the right brightness for her comfort, with a cheery sort of light that felt like sunlight captured inside the library walls. She looked at Rùnach.

"A thumb in your father's eye?"

He smiled affectionately. "I appreciate the thought, but I daresay they're tempering themselves simply to please you. I'm just the happy beneficiary of that."

She enjoyed the light for a moment or two, smiled to herself at the feel of Rùnach's boot pressing against hers, and wished quite heartily that they could spend the next year with nothing more pressing in front of them than soup at her father's table. But she knew that wasn't possible. Never mind what Rùnach was able to do inside her father's library, the rest of the country was being drained of what made it lovely.

She closed her eyes briefly and considered the magic of Bruadair. It seemed intact enough, but she could see where there was a part of it that was becoming . . . well, *threadbare* was the only word she could think of to use to describe what she was seeing. As if it had been a tapestry stretched out to its full length while one corner was becoming slightly less dense than the rest of it. She had no doubt that the whole thing would unravel if the damage wasn't stopped.

She opened her eyes and looked at Rùnach. "We have to stop the unraveling."

He looked at her blankly. "The what?"

"I think Bruadair's tapestry is beginning to unravel in one corner."

"Oh," he said, nodding. "How do you suggest we go about stopping that?"

She had to take several deep breaths, then a pair of less deep breaths, because she felt light-headed, before she thought she could speak with any reasonable confidence. "I think I need to learn to use my magic."

He reached over and took her hand, no trace of anything on his face but compassion. "I think you're right."

"Where do I go to learn, do you think?"

"Where do you suggest?"

She attempted a scowl, but she didn't suppose she'd been all that successful. "You're doing it again."

"Love, this is your country. I'm just the guest."

"You're more than a guest, Rùnach."

He leaned over, kissed her hand, then sat back. "Then as a hopeful inhabitant, I'd suggest we find your great-grandmother and see what she has to say. I would hazard a guess she taught her daughter how to use her magic, perhaps even your mother as well. For all we know, she's waiting for you to make an appearance on her doorstep for just such lessons."

"Well, she *did* loan me that book on myths and fables as often as I wanted it."

"She obviously has a finely honed sense of humor," he said solemnly.

"She may check your ears."

He laughed. "As long as she's not doing it after having slain me with a pointed spell, she can look all she likes." His smile faded. "I think, if I could offer an opinion, that we probably need to go fairly soon. I hate to rush your reunion with your father, but I am a little queasy over the thought of what mischief Acair might be combining as we sit here."

She couldn't argue with that sentiment because she felt the same thing. She glanced toward the window. "Nasty weather for traveling, unfortunately."

"Iteach will complain, I'm sure, but perhaps we'll find him and his lady a dry stable soon enough."

She nodded, then looked at him. "You won't put a rune over Bristeadh's door, will you?"

"Only one of welcome, if it pleases you," he said, then he smiled. "I'm trying not to think about Dallag and how thoroughly she must be cursing the both of us right now."

"As long as she didn't vent her ire by telling the Guildmistress where we were headed, I'll leave her to her cursing," Aisling said, "and happily so."

"She couldn't have known," Rùnach said.

She looked at him in surprise. "You don't sound entirely convinced."

He considered his hands for a moment or two, then looked at her. "I don't believe either Dallag or Riochdair has any idea if your father is alive or not. And we had as much privacy as possible when your cousin was giving us ideas where to go looking for your sire."

"And if someone had been eavesdropping?"

He shrugged helplessly. "I hesitate to think."

"Do you think they know where my father lives?"

"Impossible," Rùnach said confidently.

The word was hardly out of his mouth before the world sounded as if it had rent in twain.

Twelve

✤

Rùnach thought the house might be coming down around their ears. He put out the lights almost without thinking and leapt to his feet.

"Stay here," he said to Aisling.

"Are you mad?" Aisling said with a gasp. "Of course I'm not staying here!"

He supposed she wouldn't be any less safe with him than she would be if he left her behind, so he nodded briskly and reached for his sword. He ran for the door, trying to ignore how the floor seemed suddenly to be spinning beneath his feet. He looked over his shoulder at Aisling, reached for her hand, then continued on, ignoring the sense of vertigo. Perhaps whoever was trying to assault the house was suffering far worse.

He jerked open the door and looked out into the passageway.

There was nothing there, but that was hardly reassuring. Whatever spell was laid over Bristeadh's house was shrieking as if it were being torn at in a way that caused it pain.

"Stay close," he threw over his shoulder at Aisling before he sprinted down the passageway. He almost knocked himself unconscious near the front door by abruptly encountering Aisling's father.

"The parlor," Bristeadh said grimly. "We'll manage to make a stand there."

Rùnach didn't want to know exactly what he meant by that or why he would know what could or could not be done in his parlor, so he followed without comment.

He made certain Aisling was safely out of sight, then joined Bristeadh at the window, taking one side whilst Aisling's father took the other. He let out his breath slowly, then eased forward until he could see out.

The spell of protection had become visible, almost completely obscuring what he could see past the gate. Almost. He could only hope those on the other side of the rock fence were having that same experience, but he didn't dare hope for it.

"Who is it?" Aisling asked from behind them.

"Sglaimir," Bristeadh said. He took a deep breath. "I think the Guildmistress is with him."

"Impossible," Rùnach said in disbelief. He shook his head. "I can't believe it."

"They've had twenty years to hunt me down," Bristeadh said. "I suppose it was a matter of time."

"I can't imagine Sglaimir can use Sìorraidh," Rùnach said. He looked at Aisling standing against the wall to his right. "Do you think?"

"Perhaps he's trying," she said, gesturing toward the window, "and that's why the magic is protesting. I wonder if the Guildmistress has magic?"

Rùnach looked at Aisling's father. "You would know. What say you?"

"I've never seen her use any," he said slowly, "but I'm not sure that's an answer we can be satisfied with. All I know is she's not Bruadairian by birth. What that means for any magical abilities, I can't say."

Rùnach wasn't sure he wanted to know at the moment, truth be told, but he knew better than to go into a fight not knowing the abilities of his opponents.

He found Aisling standing next to him and put his arm in front of her before he realized what he was doing. Aisling put her hand on his arm and pushed it gently down, then moved to stand next to him.

"I'll look."

"Carefully," he stressed.

She smiled at him briefly, then looked out the window. She went very still.

"It is the Guildmistress," she said faintly.

Rùnach put his hand on her back. "And?"

"At least a pair of black-garbed guardsmen." She glanced at Bristeadh. "Not from the Guild."

"Nay, daughter," he said. "From the palace."

"And the man with the finely embroidered tunic and ermine-trimmed cape?"

"That would be our illustrious ruler," Bristeadh said with a snort. "I'm surprised he managed to leave his soft seat at the palace to come this far—" He stopped suddenly and looked at them. "That is unusual, I must say."

"It makes you wonder what he was told, doesn't it?" Rùnach asked, though he didn't want the answer to that.

"How did they find us, do you think?" Aisling asked.

"Someone obviously didn't care for not being able to shut her door, perhaps," Rùnach murmured.

She laughed a little, but it was without humor. "Surely not. I can't imagine anyone would listen to her."

"She could have sent a messenger to Beul," Rùnach said carefully. "It isn't that far away with a fleet horse."

"Or magic."

"Or magic," he agreed. "Though that makes me wonder what sort of magic they're using that Bruadair isn't stopping. I have absolutely no idea how any of this works." He looked at Bristeadh. "What's your opinion?"

Bristeadh pursed his lips. "As I said, I've never seen Iochdmhor use magic—"

"She has a name?" Aisling interrupted in surprise. "I've never heard it used."

"She doesn't like it," Bristeadh said. "Thinks it's too pretty. Sglaimir imported her, though from where is anyone's guess. If you were to press me, I would say that she is a wizardess of some sort, but I've been told I have an overactive imagination. Sglaimir came to Bruadair, I believe, with his own magic and he's certainly had ample time to experiment with using the same inside the borders."

Rùnach suppressed the curses that were on the tip of his tongue. What he needed was the same amount of time to discover what he could do, but obviously he wasn't going to have that luxury. He knew unfortunately very little about Carach of Mùig or from what insignificant hamlet he and his spawn had emerged. There were, as his father likely could have attested to, numerous places in the Nine Kingdoms where dark magic was the norm and black mages the acknowledged masters. Countering their spells was possible, as his father likely also could have confirmed, but the power and skill required was not insignificant.

What he needed was a day with Muinear to see if he could even begin to use his own magic inside Bruadair's borders.

The spell's shrieks suddenly became louder. Aisling clapped her hands over her ears and Bristeadh looked as if he'd been struck by someone who had intended it to be fatal.

"Go," he gasped. "Out the back. I'll distract them for as long as I can."

"But you can't," Aisling protested. "What if the spell fails?"

"Then I will have done what I could for you and will rest in peace."

Rùnach found Aisling looking at him, but he didn't have to ask what she was thinking. They couldn't leave her father, but there was no guarantee they would manage to get themselves all out alive. He dragged his hand through his hair before he looked at her grimly.

"I don't think I should do this," he said, "simply because whilst I might be able to avoid burning the house down, I'm not sure how Bruadair would react to any more aggressive spellweaving."

She nodded, a jerky motion that spoke eloquently of her distress. "What spell do I use then? And please know that I can scarce believe I'm asking that."

"I believe it and what spell you use depends on what you want to do." He looked at Bristeadh. "Who fashioned the first spell? Muinear?"

Aisling's father nodded. "She laid it over the house and grounds before Aisling was born. It has seen its share of abuse, which has led me to wonder over the years if perhaps we weren't as careful about hiding the house as we should have been. There's nothing to be done about it now. What I can tell you for certain is that I haven't a bloody clue what the spell is or how to repair it."

Rùnach resheathed the sword he hadn't realized he was still holding, then looked at Aisling. "Let's go out the back and see if we can identify what was done. You can decide then to either shore up what's still there or create something new."

She nodded, though she looked as if she might rather be puking. He'd seen that look on her face before very early in their acquaintance when she was being poisoned by a cook with a foul sense of jest, so he thought he might be in a position to recognize it.

She looked at her father. "Should we try to save this house?"

"You were born in this house," he said with a smile. "It has good memories, if not brief ones. Your lad there might want to come back at some point and investigate the library. He's scarce scratched the surface of what's there. But in the end, it is just a house. If it comes down to a choice between escaping and saving it, there is no choice."

She took a deep breath. "I've never been able to save anything before."

"Then start with the place of your birth if it's possible," Rùnach suggested. "But whatever we do, I think we should do it quickly."

"You two make your escape," Bristeadh said. "I'll hold them off—"

"Nay, you'll come with us," Aisling said firmly. "But we'll need our horses. Have you seen them?"

Bristeadh looked at her blankly, then he blinked. "Oh, the hounds? I fed them in the stables this morning. I suppose it didn't occur to me to wonder why they preferred to bed down there."

"Shapechanging gifts from my grandfather Sgath and Seannair of Cothromaiche," Rùnach said. "Let's fetch them and go. I think they can ferry us away without any trouble." He glanced out the window. "Aisling, did you see Acair at the gate?"

She shook her head. "He's not there unless he's wearing a spell I can't see through. I can't imagine Bruadair would allow him to hide. Being who he is," she added.

Rùnach listened to the words come out of her mouth and felt himself go very still. "What did you say?"

"I said I don't think Bruadair would allow Acair to hide." She looked at him in surprise. "What are you thinking?"

He chewed on his words. "I'm not sure, but I'll let you know when I decide."

Actually, he thought he might have a fairly good idea of where his thoughts were taking him. Sglaimir seemingly had no appearance of magic, so perhaps he hadn't simply been refusing to use Bruadair's magic out of a sense of decorum, he hadn't been *able* to draw Bruadair's magic to himself. It was obvious he hadn't been using it to hide himself, but perhaps that too wasn't because he didn't want to but rather because he was unable.

Which begged the question, why had Acair visited openly enough that Bristeadh at least had recognized him? Had he been bold enough to do so or simply unable to hide who he was? And if he realized he couldn't harness Bruadair's power inside its borders, then perhaps there was a reason to drain the country of magic instead of trying to use it on the steppes from whence it sprang.

Rùnach had the feeling his bastard brother just might have an opinion on that, something he thought he might need to discover sooner rather than later.

"I think I should save the house," Aisling said firmly. "If for the library, if nothing else."

Rùnach pulled himself away from impossible thoughts and nodded. "Agreed. Any thoughts on how?"

She took a deep breath. "Bruadair is leaving that choice up to me."

He wasn't at all surprised. He pulled away from the window. "I'll go fetch our gear, then—"

"*I'll* go fetch your gear," Bristeadh said, "and my own. You two decide what miracle you're going to indulge in."

Rùnach waited until the man had left the salon before he looked at Aisling. "Well? What do you want to do?"

"A spell of disinterest? Or perhaps un-noticing, like the one Miach gave you. We could hide the house so no one could find it again. Or disguise it, so no one would want to come inside even if they did see it."

"You could," he agreed.

"Or I could change the spell Muinear laid over the house and make it so no one could ever break through it." She paused, then looked at him with haunted eyes. "Change it permanently."

He pulled her into his arms and held her. He wasn't sure which of the two of them was shaking harder, but supposed in the end it didn't matter. He felt her arms come around his waist and supposed neither of them needed to breathe very well anytime soon.

"Do you remember the spell of essence changing you used at Inntrig?" he asked.

She took a deep breath and let it out. She sounded as if that breath was very close to a sob. "I don't need Soilléir's spell."

Rùnach shut his mouth because it had fallen open. He groped for the right thing to say, but found absolutely nothing. He pulled back far enough to gape at her. "Aisling . . ."

Aisling looked at him miserably. "Well, I don't."

"Good heavens," Rùnach said weakly. He fought the urge to simply sit down and rest. "Aisling . . . good heavens."

She pulled away from him and wrapped her arms around herself. "What am I supposed to do? Ignore what I'm being given?"

"Absolutely not. Just don't tell Soilléir. It might lessen his opinion of his own magnificence if he thought someone else might be able to make mighty magic more easily than he can."

"I'm not sure it will be easy."

He reached out and put his hands very lightly on her shoulders. "What can I do?"

"The magic wants you to come with me and drop your spells over Muinear's while I change what's left of hers to something more permanent." She looked at him blankly. "How do I do that?"

He put his arm around her shoulders and led her toward the door. "Do you remember what the front looked like, with the stream and the front garden?"

"Aye."

"And the back, including the stables?"

She nodded.

"Then let's go have a look at the spell outside the back door, round up the ponies, and be ready to fly. I'll tell you how I will weave my spell only to include Muinear's spell and not us, which is what you would normally need to do with yours, but I'm not sure that will work for you here. I suggest you try not to catch us up in your spell, but you'll have to negotiate that with your magic, I suppose."

"I feel faint."

He tightened his arm around her shoulders. "I can't blame you, love. Let me buy you a bit of time, shall I? I'll put something distracting over the top of Muinear's spell first. Elvish glamour, or some such rot."

She smiled briefly. "You're trying to distract *me*."

"Is it working?"

"Not very well."

"I would pour more effort into my efforts, but I want something left of you to do your work."

Her eyes narrowed. "I think you're far too aware of the fairness of your face."

"Nay," he said easily, "far too bemused by the fairness of yours. Let's argue about it later at length."

Later was, as it happened, quite a bit later than he would have wished for. His magic was, his earlier successes in the library aside, thoroughly unwieldy. It was a bit like trying to drag a spoon through solid rock. Frozen honey would have been a simple thing by comparison.

His grandfather would have been appalled by the condition of the glamour Rùnach managed to spread over Bristeadh's property, but Rùnach was just grateful something had worked at all. Muinear's spell at least seemed to find his efforts acceptable. Aisling had woven her spell of essence changing well if not a little untidily. He'd memorized it, of course, because that was just what he did, but he had the feeling he would never dare use it. Bruadair would likely turn him into a toad for his trouble if he did.

He had no idea what would be left of Bristeadh's house when— if—they returned, though Aisling's spell seemed to be, from all appearances, impervious to assault. His own spell of un-noticing that he'd drawn over them—fashioned from Fadaire in deference to Bruadair's delicate sensibilities—had seemed to be working as intended. There had been nothing else to do but be relieved to be away on a horse with magic of his own, accompanied by a very lovely golden filly whose parentage he fully intended to discover sooner rather than later.

Sooner, he supposed, would also be quite a bit later than he would have liked. At the moment, he was simply flying into the sunrise, Aisling sitting behind him so he blocked the wind for her, with her father riding Orail and looking rather green. Flying was obviously not the man's favorite activity. Like father, like daughter, he supposed.

Aisling wasn't entirely sure where they were going and Bristeadh looked so perplexed that Rùnach half suspected that if he left their direction up to the two of them, they would all land in Beul where they would find themselves joining Aisling's cousin Euan in Sglaimir's dungeon. He had posed a silent but very deferential question to Bruadair's sentient self, then decided perhaps he would simply leave it up to Iteach to sniff out a nest of dreamspinners. His pony seemed to know where he was going—either that or he was simply doing his damndest to make certain Rùnach had nothing but sun in his eyes. At the moment, Rùnach wouldn't have been surprised by either.

Aisling's finger was quite suddenly alongside his face.

"There," she said, pointing to the right.

Rùnach couldn't see anything at all for the sun, but Iteach at least seemed to agree with her. His horse began a slow, downward spiral. Rùnach would have accused him of showing off for that lovely filly, but the reality was, he and Orail were no doubt simply sparing Aisling's father any undue distress.

Rùnach looked over his shoulder yet again—he'd lost count of how many times he'd done so during the night—but saw nothing. He was still turning over the possibility that Sglaimir *couldn't* hide himself thanks to Bruadair's magic not being willing to allow it. He didn't want to count on that, but even just the thought of it was almost enough to allow him to take a deep breath instead of endless shallow ones. To have such an advantage might mean the difference between success and failure.

Assuming Bruadair didn't decide that he deserved the same treatment.

He realized Iteach had landed and exactly what that meant only as he found himself dismounting and staring in astonishment at the sight in front of him. He collected himself enough to give Aisling a hand down from their horse, but that was the extent of the courtesy he found himself capable of at the moment. Her father could no doubt see to himself.

"Oh," Aisling said quietly.

He couldn't have agreed more. He supposed he should have taken a bit more time over the past few fortnights to at least come up with expectations about what a dreamspinner's palace might look like, but he doubted that even his wildest imaginings would have prepared him for what he was facing.

Admittedly, he was used to a fairly limited range of buildings. Buidseachd was surely a seat of power and only a fool would have approached it without a great amount of either deference or power. But while it was definitely immense and intimidating, it was not precisely beautiful.

Seanagarra was another vision entirely, immense but giving the impression that it was nothing more than a handful of beautiful gardens surrounding an admittedly fine collection of lovely chambers, halls, and kitchens.

The keep at Ceangail was a wreck, but he seriously doubted anyone expected anything else when they made a visit there. Tor Neroche, Léige, even his favorite place of Chagailt . . . they were each beautiful in their own way, but all were, in the end, simply buildings.

He wasn't quite sure what to call the thing in front of him.

It was enormous. He craned his neck to try to demarcate where the roof ended and the sky began, but that was more difficult than he would have expected. The glade they stood in was less a glade than an enormous expanse surrounded by mountains and forests set at the perfect distance to provide a stunning backdrop yet not interfere with the perfection of the creation in front of him.

A place that looked as if it were made solely of glass that only existed because his poor mind demanded that dreams take some sort of solid form.

He felt Aisling grope for his hand, but since he was groping for hers at the same time, he supposed he couldn't be accused of any unmanly weakness.

He looked at her father, who had come to stand on her other side. "Are we at the right place?" Rùnach managed.

Bristeadh nodded, looking perhaps less overwhelmed than he might have if he'd had a modicum of compassion. He clapped Rùnach on the shoulder briefly, then turned a gentle look on Aisling. "Here we are, daughter. I hope you'll find it to your liking."

Aisling looked as though what she would have found to her liking was to bolt. Rùnach recognized the expression. It wasn't, of course, that he shared the thought fully. He was just having sympathy for her, no more.

She looked at him uneasily. "What do I do now?"

"Well, our horses seem to think you should press on."

"Alone?" she asked in horror.

"I'll come along behind you with the horses," Rùnach said promptly. "At least a dozen paces behind, perhaps a score. Not to worry."

She looked at him in surprise, then her eyes narrowed. "Coward."

"I'll take the horses," Bristeadh said with a smile, removing Iteach's reins from Rùnach's hand. "You two go ahead."

Rùnach looked at Aisling's father seriously. "I wonder when might be the appropriate time to discuss my intentions with you— if Aisling will permit it, of course."

"I would accuse you of stalling, but I imagine you've more courage than that."

So he hoped. He took a deep breath. "I thought I might run the idea by you before I attempted to approach any potentially less corporeal entities with my plan."

Bristeadh smiled. "I'll consent to the match, though I daresay Aisling doesn't need my permission. Bruadair, however, is another story entirely and Sìorraidh will have its own opinions beyond that." He shrugged. "The dreamspinner's magic will slay you if you cross the threshold unworthily. Or it doesn't like you. Or you're catching it on an off day."

Rùnach pursed his lips. "I wish I thought you were having me on."

"Try it and see, I suppose," Bristeadh said.

"How is it you're so comfortable?"

"I'm not the one thinking to marry the First," Bristeadh said with a shrug. "Not this time. I'm just bringing in the horses. You two go ahead. I'll wander off to the stables and leave you to your comfortable breathing. Or not, depending on the hall's preference, I suppose."

"Is *everything* sentient here?" Rùnach asked in surprise.

"Everything," Bristeadh confirmed. "But considering where your mother was from, that shouldn't come as much of a surprise."

Rùnach supposed there was no point in listing all the things he found surprising, mostly because in the end, none of their present business was about him. He watched Aisling's father walk off with the horses, then looked at her.

"How are you?"

She took a deep breath. "I'm not sure." She paused. "I suppose this is it, isn't it? I'll either walk through the doors and continue to breathe or I'll walk through the doors and I'll die on the spot."

"Somehow, my love, I don't think you'll find yourself slain."

She didn't move. She simply held his hand and looked at the palace in front of them. He supposed he could understand that very well. Everything she had learned about herself, everything she might become in the future, indeed the future of her country rested on what happened to her when she walked across that threshold.

She looked up at him. "The moment before battle is the hardest?"

He brought her hand up and kissed the back of it, then continued to hold her very chilly fingers with his. "It is."

"Does it get any better?"

"After a few paces, aye."

"You won't really walk twenty paces behind me, will you?"

"I'll walk wherever you want me to," he said quietly, "but I have the feeling, my love, that you'll eventually need to walk ahead."

"Briefly."

"If that suits you."

She took a deep breath, then nodded. He watched her put her shoulders back and steel herself for the short journey. He would have had more sympathy, but he was worried enough for his own damned self. He could think of many unpleasant ways to meet his end, but he suspected that perishing on the threshold of his betrothed's . . . well, whatever it was—

He took his own deep breath. He didn't want to die. He wanted to wed the woman next to him, have a handful of children who had her eyes, and spend the rest of his extraordinarily long life not walking twenty paces behind her. If that suited her.

Aisling looked at him once more and smiled faintly. She looked more confident than she had before, which was reassuring.

He only wished he could find that same reassurance for himself, because he had no idea whether or not he would manage to cross the threshold of those massive glass doors and continue to breathe.

And he'd thought facing Acair would be the true test of his courage.

Thirteen

❄

Aisling walked up the handful of smooth, wide steps and paused before she put her hand on the enormous doors to what had to have been the largest building she had ever seen. It looked less like a palace than it did a cathedral. She had seen a building very like to what was before her within the walls of the university at Lismòr, though that had been a fraction of the size of the hall she faced at present. Beul had a cathedral, though she'd never been inside it. It had been shuttered for as long as she could remember.

Perhaps there was a good reason why.

The structure before her was so large, she wondered how human hands could possibly have constructed it. She looked up but couldn't see the spot where the roof terminated. She supposed even the doors were three times her height. She considered the heavy golden doorhandles, each perhaps two feet long, attached vertically but somehow looking as if they simply floated in front of the glass that was not cloudy but rather infused with something that was impossible to see through.

Magic, she supposed.

She looked for Rùnach and realized he was standing on the step below her, his hands clasped behind his back, simply watching her. What she wanted to do was turn, fling herself into his arms, and whisper in his ear that *away* would be a good direction to take at present. He lifted his eyebrows briefly as if he understood exactly what she was thinking. Then, damn him, he stepped backward onto a lower step. She shot him a warning look because she didn't dare tell him aloud not to go any farther.

He only inclined his head as elegantly as he would have to his grandmother the queen of the elves. Then he simply looked at her, beautiful elven prince that he was, and waited.

She wondered if he would catch her and hold her once more if she soon found herself breathing her last.

She turned back to the doors because there was no time like the present, she supposed, to find out if your life was going to end or not. She reached out to touch the golden doorhandles, wishing her entire arm wasn't trembling so badly, but before she could touch anything, the great doors swung inward all on their own.

Something rushed through her she couldn't identify: terror, dread, or perhaps even relief. Doors opening was a good thing. Then again, perhaps even wells of evil extended their welcoming embraces to those they wished to smother. She dropped her arm to her side and forced herself not to clench her fists. She knew she should have been looking up, as Weger had shouted at her so often to do, but she thought that might be slightly beyond her courage. It was one thing to step across a threshold; it was another thing entirely to look up as one did so while fearing that death might be lying in wait there.

She kept her eyes on her boots as she stepped forward, then continued to look down as she ventured another pair of paces. Then she stopped, but it wasn't from feeling her life being taken from her.

It was because of where she stood.

She supposed that she might look back on that moment at some point and be able to relive it without having so much invested in not finding herself slain or offending whomever might have been there watching her walk into a hall that wasn't hers. At the moment, though, all she could do was look at the floor.

It wasn't glass, but it was like no polished stone she had ever seen. It was very dark, giving the impression of being solid while at the same time reflecting the depths from whence the stone had been hewn. There was also somehow a faint layer of something that seemed to contain each footprint that had passed over it, particular to the souls making those footprints. She was part of history, yet standing to the side observing it.

Then she blinked, and it was simply a floor. It was, however, a floor she suspected Uachdaran of Léige would have salivated over.

Bruadair was a strange place.

She realized there was a pathway there, a part of the floor that was a less blackish blue than the rest of the floor, as if it knew she had come and wanted her to reach the other end of the grand hall without undue trouble. Or anyone blocking her path, apparently.

She looked up and realized that such might be more of an issue than she would have expected.

The hall was full of people, people who were all looking at her. She who had done her best over the course of her life to simply disappear and escape scrutiny was apparently the focus of their attention.

She flinched a little, then stepped backward, though fortunately not over the threshold. She glanced over her shoulder to find Rùnach standing where she'd left him, outside the hall, his hands still clasped behind his back, an expression of utter seriousness on his face. She was tempted to go hide behind him, which she supposed he knew. He simply watched her, silent and grave, as if he wanted to give her the support of his presence but leave the rest to her.

Which she knew was his intention, damn him anyway.

She took a deep breath, nodded just the slightest bit, then turned back to the path. She put one foot to it and it began to glow above and beyond what it had done before. She was tempted to look around herself and see who else the floor might be welcoming, but she didn't have to. Everyone in the hall was looking only at her.

She took a deep breath, then walked a dozen steps forward. She counted, because that seemed to help. There was a dais at the end of the path, so she supposed that was as good a place to make for as any. There were people standing on that raised bit of the hall as well, but she didn't dare look at them too closely lest they think poorly of her. She would know soon enough who they were.

She looked over her shoulder one more time to find that Rùnach and her father were standing at the doorway, obviously following her. Well, if things totally unraveled, she supposed they might at least offer her sympathy on her way out of the world.

She could bring to mind any number of other ridiculously long passageways she'd traversed over the course of her life, mostly ones finding themselves in the Guild. She had slunk down them, keeping to one side, shrinking as far as possible into herself that she didn't garner the notice of anyone in authority. She had perfected the art.

Only now, that art was useless to her.

She knew, based on too many evidences to deny, that the souls in that glorious hall were looking at *her*. There was nowhere to hide, nowhere to run to, nowhere to go but forward. She also knew, with the same sort of resonance in her soul, that the choice was hers to either accept a birthright she hadn't asked for or to walk away from it. The world would continue to turn, no doubt, and the Nine Kingdoms along with all the other undiscovered places that didn't crave a seat on the Council of Kings would continue to march doggedly along as they had for millennia before she'd been born and would no doubt for millennia after she was dead.

Only they would do it without dreams.

Unbidden, she caught the faintest glimpse of just exactly what she could do if she continued forward.

She looked up at the vault of the ceiling above her and felt herself sway slightly as the realization struck her. She had spent the whole of her life locked in the Guild, trapped in a large chamber with an unwholesome number of looms and weavers, but never in her life had she imagined that the world could be any bigger. Her life had been in that room, her task the very small one of continuing to weave endless reams of ugly cloth, her future nothing but more of the same. It hadn't occurred to her that her life could be made up of something else.

Something like the place she was standing in.

She continued forward, then hazarded a glance at the people flanking the path she was traversing. They all looked different, true, but there was something about them that was hauntingly the same. It took her a moment or two to realize what it was, but when she did, she found herself less surprised than she would have thought.

They all had the same look in their eyes, as if they saw things that perhaps just weren't visible to others.

She continued on her way to the dais, comforted by knowing that the choice to continue on was hers. She could have stopped, turned, and then walked back down that beautiful, faintly sparkling path, out the door, and back to an ordinary life. It would have been safe, perhaps. It also would have even been comfortable, if she looked at it in the right way.

But it would have been small.

Now that she had stepped out beyond the Guild, stepped into the dreamspinner's great hall, she knew that taking a step backward was simply unthinkable, no matter where her steps forward led.

She thought about that until she was a score of paces away from the dais, then she looked to her right at the souls lining that side of the path. She blinked in surprise, for she recognized more of them than she would have thought possible.

Ceana was there, the king of Neroche's spinner. The woman whose chambers she'd used in Cothromaiche, leaving her a spinning wheel made of sunlight in payment, stood there as well though Aisling didn't know her name. She recognized a dwarvish man who had loaned her a wheel in Durial, and she wasn't entirely sure she didn't also see an elven maid she had almost run into bodily in Tòrr Dòrainn.

She looked to her left. She didn't recognize any of the men and women standing there, but she suspected they all had one thing in common.

They spun.

She looked up at the dais. There were several people there, six, seven perhaps. She didn't know any of them, yet they seemed familiar, as if she had seen them lingering at the edge of her dreams for years. They were watching her gravely, then a thin, white-haired woman stepped from behind one of them.

Muinear.

Aisling almost wept.

Muinear walked down the pair of steps and drew Aisling into an embrace. She said nothing, she simply held her so tightly, it was almost painful.

"You came," she said, finally.

Aisling nodded, because speech was simply beyond her. She closed her eyes and tried not to weep. She had loved the weaving mistress first because Muinear had been kind to her when no one else had been and later because she'd taught her everything worth knowing about negotiating not only the Guild, but also life. But now to know she was clinging to her great-grandmother . . .

She found it very hard to let go.

Muinear seemed to have an endless amount of patience. Aisling supposed she might have stood there all day if it hadn't occurred to her at one point that there was a hall full of people watching her and perhaps even something left for her to do. She pulled away from her mother's grandmother and looked into blue eyes that were quite a bit less watery and vague than they had been in times past.

"Thank you," Aisling whispered. "For staying with me at the Guild."

Muinear kissed her on both cheeks. "I'll respond to that properly, my love, when we have privacy. For now, there is choice laid before you. Bruadair has held its breath for this moment for many years, but it won't make any decisions for you. Neither will I. If you choose to step forward, it must be because you've chosen to do so."

Aisling felt a little winded. "I'm not even sure what I'm committing to."

"Aren't you?" Muinear said with a gentle smile. "Still?"

Aisling took a deep breath to answer, then realized there was no need. Perhaps she didn't know what the particulars were of the path that lay before her, but she knew that if she continued forward, she was going to be accepting her birthright.

As a dreamspinner.

Muinear stepped aside and off the path that was still glowing faintly on the floor. Aisling took a deep breath, then looked at the souls standing there on the dais.

There were, she could now say, six people standing there watching her. There was nothing unusual about their clothing; it was nothing she couldn't have found in the shops of Beul. They ran the gamut in looks, some very ordinary, one not particularly handsome at all, and the others almost too difficult to look at. But that wasn't the most remarkable thing about them. The most remarkable thing was they had *her* eyes.

She couldn't say she had spent all that much time looking at herself, but she knew what her eyes looked like.

She continued forward, then paused at the edge of the platform. She looked, one by one, at the six souls standing there. They didn't look displeased to see her; they were simply there waiting. And then they eased apart, three to one side and three to the other.

A spinning wheel sat there behind them.

Aisling put her foot on the dais and stepped up. All the people standing there, the six closest to her and the others who had apparently come to watch the spectacle, made absolutely no sound. She didn't dare look behind her to see if Rùnach was still there in the building, because she knew he was.

She walked forward until she was standing in front of the wheel.

She realized she was surprised by the sight only after she had stared at the thing for what seemed like an eternity. Perhaps she'd allowed herself to speculate too much over the past pair of days about what the wheel of a dreamspinner might look like, but what she was seeing was not at all what she had expected.

It had been fashioned of sunshine and moonlight and deep rivers of cold water that ran beneath the earth, hardened into a substance that couldn't possibly be wood but had the appearance of it. She took a deep breath, then realized that she knew exactly what she would be committing to if she reached out and touched that wheel. She knew what the First Dreamspinner's responsibilities were because Bruadair had been teaching them to her slowly and patiently for weeks, first reaching out after her as she'd been standing in an old granny's house on Melksham Island, daring to risk death by touching a simple wooden wheel.

A throat cleared itself softly from her right.

She looked up in surprise to find a man standing there. He was impossibly thin, rather tall, with a long, beaked nose and hands that fluttered like a pair of restless butterflies.

"My lady," he said, inclining his head, "if I could make a suggestion."

"Who are you?" she asked.

"Freasdail, my lady. Steward to the First."

"Oh," she said, unable to put any sound behind the word. "I see."

"I think that perhaps it might be a handsome gesture to those who've come to watch the ceremony if we were to perhaps move behind the wheel where they can watch the events proceed."

"Is that what we should do?" she asked faintly.

"I think it would be meaningful to them," he said, inclining his head again.

She supposed that if anyone wanted to watch her be struck down for her cheek, they were welcome to it. She looked at Freasdail. "And what do I do once I've stepped behind the wheel?"

"Lady Muinear will instruct you."

Aisling supposed she couldn't go wrong there, so she walked around the wheel and placed herself where Freasdail indicated with a series of lifted eyebrows and slight nods. Muinear smiled at her, then stepped to her side and looked out over the company gathered there.

"You are all come to witness the beginning of a new First," she said in a clear, unwavering voice. "My great-granddaughter, Aisling of Bruadair, whose right this is."

Aisling saw Rùnach standing at the doors of the hall with her father. His hands were still clasped behind his back but tears were rolling down his cheeks. He still breathed, which she supposed was all she could ask for. She looked at her great-grandmother, who was still facing the crowd.

"The history of the wheel is long and illustrious," Muinear said, "but not necessary for understanding the significance of the moment. Suffice it to say, the wheel stopped spinning as my daughter breathed her last and it has not spun since. Bruadair locked its revolutions partly in mourning for Cuilidh, partly as the final test for the lad or lass with magic enough to become the First."

Aisling felt her mouth go dry. She looked at Muinear as she turned and smiled.

"Have others tried?" she whispered.

"Do you really want to know that right now?" Muinear murmured.

Aisling closed her eyes briefly, then looked for Rùnach again. He was only still watching her, steadily. She realized she had nothing to lose at the moment besides her life, so perhaps there was no reason not to plunge ahead and cast her fate to the wind.

She reached out and put her hand on the flywheel. She looked up quickly at the faint sound, then realized it had been Bruadair to sigh lightly. The wood was cold under her hand, but that seemed to be from nothing more than the chill in the hall. She closed her eyes briefly, then gave the flywheel a firm spin.

Bruadair paused.

And then the world burst into song.

She supposed she might not have noticed that if it hadn't been so loud right next to her. The hall had erupted in applause and a few undignified cheers. But the world?

It sang a melody she was certain she'd heard before, but she couldn't for the life of her remember where. She found her hand taken and subsequently shaken heartily by the tall man who had been standing several feet behind her—perhaps to catch her if she fell. Muinear embraced her.

"Ah, my darling," she said, hugging Aisling. "A long road to this place, aye?"

"I thought you were dead!" Aisling said, before she thought better of blurting out the first thing that came to mind.

Muinear laughed. "Not yet, love." She pulled away. "Let me release you to those who have come to greet you. And I think there might be a lad at the back of the hall who has an especial interest in your future."

Aisling wasn't sure where to begin, but fortunately Freasdail seemed to know the most appropriate way to greet the souls who had come to witness what she was very happy to find wasn't her death.

She had the feeling it was going to be a very long morning.

She realized, several hours later, that *long* wasn't exactly the right word for it. *Endless* was likely a better choice, but she had survived it well enough thanks mostly to Freasdail, who always seemed to know exactly when to hand her something to eat or drink, or find her a chair, or clear his throat politely if a well-wisher carried on too long. She wasn't entirely sure that she hadn't received the odd gift or two, but she had lost track of them. She was quite certain that Freasdail hadn't.

A reception was announced outside in the garden and the flock of spinners deserted the hall with alacrity. Aisling found herself standing in the middle of the hall with her great-grandmother. It was then that she realized they weren't exactly alone. Rùnach and her father had apparently been holding up the wall nearest the front doors.

"Ah, a creature from myth," Muinear said, smiling in Rùnach's direction.

"You know that's what I thought elves were for the longest time," Aisling admitted.

Her great-grandmother winked at her. "I'm well aware of that, darling."

"I was surprised to find that his ears were perfectly normal."

"Well, we all make do sometimes with less." She linked arms with Aisling. "We'll wait for them to come to us, I daresay. It's good for them to make the effort."

Aisling thought Rùnach's reputation might benefit from a recounting of all the efforts he had made for her, but perhaps later when she felt a bit more grounded. At present, she felt as if she were not quite where she was.

"Prince Rùnach," Muinear said extending her hand to him. "A pleasure."

Rùnach took her hand and bowed low over it. "Lady Muinear, it is an honor."

"You've taken very good care of my great-granddaughter, I see."

"That, my lady, has been not only an honor, but a pleasure."

Muinear smiled. "Such lovely manners. Your mother would be gratified and no doubt your grandmother Brèagha is unsurprised." She looked at Aisling's father. "Bristeadh, love. I'm not surprised to see you here."

"My lady Muinear, nothing you've ever said has surprised me less."

Muinear laughed merrily. "I've no doubt of that, laddie." She looked at Aisling and her eyes were bright. "Perhaps the moment demands a bit more soberness, but I am so happy to see you that I can hardly muster up an appropriate amount."

"How did you survive?" Aisling asked, because she couldn't sit on the question any longer.

"Iochdmhor is not as clever as she thinks she is," Muinear said conspiratorially, "and I am, if I might say as much, a wonderful actress. I'll give you the particulars when we're at our leisure. For now, you need something to eat, then perhaps a day spent resting in peace and safety. Tomorrow is soon enough to lay our plans and see what's to be done about the mischief Sglaimir has combined. Bristeadh, if you would care to escort me outside? We'll leave these two a bit of privacy before guests start to wander back inside, looking for their First."

Aisling watched her father escort his late wife's grandmother from the hall, then took a deep breath before she turned to look at Rùnach.

He was only watching her with a small smile, the same smile he'd been giving her for weeks. It was a smile that said he loved her, she knew, only this one was slightly bemused, as if he were seeing her for the first time after a long absence.

"What?" she said, wrapping her arms around herself.

He shook his head, unwrapped her arms, then wrapped them

instead around his waist. He drew her close and rested his cheek against her hair. "I love you."

She smiled. "I love you back."

"Thank heavens. Does Bruadair approve of us, do you think?"

"We're both still breathing."

"I suppose that's endorsement enough," he agreed. "How are you?"

"I'm not sure," she admitted. She pulled back and looked up at him. "Staggered, perhaps."

"That, I can understand perfectly," he said. He bent his head, then paused. "Will I be struck down for stealing a kiss, do you think?"

"I'll keep you safe."

He smiled. "I believe, Aisling my love, that you will. I'll return the favor as often as possible."

She was happily distracted for several minutes until he pulled away, shaking his head.

"I don't think the danger is over for me today, so I'd best keep my wits about me."

"Danger?" she asked in surprise.

"Your great-grandmother wants to talk to me later." He paused. "I think I should be afraid."

"I think perhaps you should be."

He laughed a little, then released her and took her hand. "Let's go have something strengthening, then perhaps a nap in a sunny corner. I actually think your great-grandmother has challenged me to a duel, but I'm not exactly sure. And here I thought it would be your father I would need to keep an eye on."

She nodded and walked with him. She glanced at the floor as they walked, seeing how their footprints became part of the history of the palace. Rùnach's were, unsurprisingly, adorned here and there with hints of Fadairian runes. She saw that hers were more than just footprints as well, but wasn't sure how to describe what she saw.

She paused at the door to what was apparently the garden, then looked at the wheel sitting there on the dais, unattended—

Or, perhaps not so unattended. She watched spells shimmering around it and decided that the world was in no danger of having any stray twelve-year-old lads coming along to give an irreplaceable spinning wheel a go.

If only the rest of the world could be so protected from things that might either intentionally or unintentionally do it harm.

"We'll make plans later," Rùnach said quietly. "A pair of hours, Aisling, of peace and quiet. The world won't be destroyed in that time."

She nodded and hoped he was right.

Fourteen

✦

There were several things, Rùnach conceded, that he had never thought to find himself doing over the course of what he knew would be a very long life. Becoming a black mage was one of them. Living out his life in a palace surrounded by servants and having nothing better to do with his time than eat, drink, and dance his endless evenings away had been another.

Facing a diminutive, Bruadairian great-granny who had just told him to stop being such a woman had honestly never entered his mind.

He supposed it had just been that sort of day so far. The journey to the dreamspinners' palace, Ciaradh, had been long and not precisely restful. He'd spent an anxious half hour mentally walking with Aisling up a path the floor seemed to demarcate for her without reservation, only to watch her put her hand on a spinning wheel and hope the bloody thing wouldn't kill her. He'd hob-nobbed with spinners from all over the world, many surprisingly not spinning for those rulers sitting on the Council of Kings, and eaten perhaps more than he should have in preparation for any other activity besides a robust nap.

He'd watched Aisling go off to what he hoped was a very soft bed. The use of a different chamber where he might avail himself of the same was what he'd hoped for. What he'd found was him-self getting the opportunity to face a woman who should have been undertaking nothing more vile than the scolding of a servant.

He paused. Perhaps trying to exercise chivalry by telling her that had not endeared him to her.

He set that aside as something to be examined—and poten-tially apologized for—later, then considered further where he'd gone wrong that morning. After he'd apparently obnoxiously, though inadvertently, patronized Mistress Muinear to his own satisfaction but obviously past hers, he'd been invited to take a stroll with her where she thought he might not need his sword, but he was welcome to bring it if it made him feel more secure.

That should have been a warning.

All of which had left him where he was, facing a woman who had just told him to engage with her in a bit of light exercise before supper. He looked at her, then shook his head.

"Mistress Muinear, I just don't think I can do this."

"What, my boy," she asked with a smile that made him very nervous. "Find the courage to raise a sword against me?"

"It isn't courage that concerns me," he said honestly. "I just have never . . . I don't . . . I can't imagine—" He took a deep breath. "You're a woman."

"No weapon you have, my lad, will harm me. Not Sìle's dag-ger, not Uachdaran's sword, not even your mighty magic."

"But—"

"Not even your spells made to counter less pleasant ones created by your father. Those spells won't hold here, no matter what you might think."

He didn't want to be rude, but he'd seen what his father's magic could do. "I hate to contradict you," he said carefully, "but my father's spells—"

"Brutal," she conceded, "but not insurmountable."

He looked at her in surprise. "But, my lady, how would you know?"

"Lad, I am as old as your father," she said frankly. "If you think I haven't faced him, think again."

Rùnach blinked. "I can't begin to imagine that."

"Neither could he," she said with a merry laugh, "which is why I managed to crawl away from that encounter with my life." She shivered. "A very powerful, clever mage, your father."

"As well as a man who would fight a woman," Rùnach said firmly, "which I am not."

Muinear sighed and looked at Bristeadh. "What am I to do with him?"

"Be grateful he wants to wed Aisling, I suppose," Bristeadh said with a shrug from where he leaned against a low wall with his arms folded over his chest. "You know I can't help you with him."

"I suppose we could bring all the Council together and attack him simultaneously," she said thoughtfully. She eyed Rùnach. "What do you think of that, my boy?"

"If it means I won't have to face you over spells, my lady," Rùnach said, "I think I would prefer it."

It was amazing how quickly a group of spinners could gather, huddle together, and apparently invent a strategy. Rùnach took the opportunity to accept a cup of wine from Aisling's father, who it had to be said looked far too comfortable in his role as sommelier.

"You aren't going to help me?" Rùnach said.

"Didn't I tell you I had no magic?"

Rùnach rolled his eyes. "Use your influence with your granny-in-law and convince her to just watch someone take me to pieces instead of being the instigator of the devastation. She's brought all her helpers and some of them are women as well."

Bristeadh smiled. "You have no idea who any of them are, do you?"

"I see women," Rùnach said grimly, "and I do not fight women."

"Because you fear they'll best you?"

Rùnach shot his future father-in-law a dark look. "Because I am a gentleman."

Bristeadh clapped a hand on Rùnach's shoulder briefly. "Indeed you are, Rùnach, but consider the women in your family. Your paternal grandmother is Eulasaid of Camanaë. She was, and still is I imagine, no wilting wallflower. Her battles fought against Lothar of Wychweald are legendary."

"I'm not Lothar," Rùnach said evenly, "and I can't raise a hand against a woman."

"Consider Muinear a diminutive troll, then. She can be passing unpleasant when she hasn't had her four o'clock libations."

Rùnach eyed him narrowly. "I can see why they hesitated in giving Aisling's mother to you."

Bristeadh only laughed. "Son, you are only scratching the surface of my unsuitability. Someday I will tell you all, but until then, I suggest you gather up your best spells and bring them to the battlefield. Nothing else will do, I fear."

Rùnach drained his cup, thanked Aisling's father for the drink and the utterly useless advice, then supposed there was no point in bringing his sword. He had the feeling he wasn't going to have the chance to use it anyway. He left it propped up against a bench and considered the very short walk back onto the battlefield.

That Ciaradh even had lists of any sort was a bit surprising. Then again, he'd seen guards roaming through the forests surrounding the palace, so they would obviously need somewhere to train. He wondered if those lads might be prevailed upon to rescue him if things went awry.

He watched Muinear invite the rest of the mob to make themselves comfortable on quite lovely benches set against that low wall that was holding up Aisling's father, then walk out into the midst of the field with a spring to her step that made him rather uneasy. He made himself a mental note never, ever to take her invitations at face value again.

That was the last useful thought he had for some time.

He hardly had time to gather his wits about him before he was being assaulted by spells. Perhaps there was no reason not to note that initially they weren't terribly complicated or intimidating spells. He countered them easily enough with whatever magic seemed to come to hand. Perhaps there was also no reason not to reassure himself that his store of spells was rather extensive, so digging up the odd thing to use for something he hadn't expected caused him no great amount of exertion.

Or at least it didn't until the sun began to turn for home, as it were, at which time things took a decided turn for the worse.

He suspected, as a volley of unpleasant things came at him from not only Muinear but a few of the dreamspinners who had apparently decided to stretch their legs a bit, that he might have been wise to have a wee chat with *all* the players on the field before he agreed to engage in anything with them besides a late lunch. It was too late at the moment, though, and he was left with increasingly complicated magic fashioned into increasingly complex spells, which required ever more difficult countermeasures.

He spent a good deal of his time fighting the urge to reach for something of his father's. He revisited the necessity of sending a thank-you to whoever had gifted him with his father's book of spells and insisted that he rememorize them. He wasn't altogether certain that hadn't been the witchwoman of Fàs, which he supposed didn't reflect particularly well on her character.

And then Muinear stepped out again in front of her companions.

Rùnach wondered how long he would last against her before she slew him, and he realized almost immediately that that span of time was too small to be measured. He found himself flat on his back, thoroughly winded, staring up at the sky above him before he could open his mouth to blurt out a protest. His love's great-grandmother was soon peering down at him.

"That didn't go so well for you, my boy, did it?"

"I cannot lift a hand . . . against . . . a woman," he wheezed.

"Pray that little wretch Acair doesn't shapechange into one, then."

He started to argue with her, but two things stopped him. One, he had no breath for arguing, and two, she was right. He studied the late-afternoon sky as his wind returned, then finally heaved himself back up to his feet. He looked at Muinear, who was standing in front of him, watching him with a smile.

"You are asking almost more of me than I can stand," he said frankly.

"And if your father's youngest bastard—and I'm only saying he's the youngest from Fionne of Fàs, mind you, not anyone else— were a girl, what would you do?"

He dragged his hand through his hair. "Weep, I suppose."

Muinear smiled again. "Your chivalry does you credit, Rùnach, and yet more credit to your lovely mother who raised you so well. But you cannot hurt me."

"I don't want to try."

"Then pretend I am your schoolmistress and you may only have your supper if you can show me all the proper and correct answers to the puzzles I put to you."

He studied her. "You're painting a very lovely picture of it now, but I have the feeling you may suddenly discover you've changed your mind once I'm so deep in the mire of my father's spells that I can't escape."

"Or your own, I daresay," she said mildly.

He wasn't quite sure how to answer that, but he supposed if there were anyone to ask about the state of his own magic, it would be the woman in front of him. The rest of the rabble had resumed their comfortable seats by the wall so perhaps he would have privacy for questions he didn't particularly want to ask.

"Do you see the darkness?" he asked very quietly. "In me?"

She looked at him gravely. "Rùnach, there is darkness in each of us."

"Not in my magic," he said. "Not before."

"Are you sure of that?"

He opened his mouth to tell her he was most assuredly convinced of that but something stopped him. Good sense, perhaps. An uncomfortable encounter with self-reflection, definitely.

"I'm not entirely certain," he admitted. "The last time I had magic to hand, I was young and arrogant." He shrugged helplessly. "I don't know."

"Then consider that your father is a prince of Ainneamh," she said mildly, "and he was not always as he is now."

Rùnach felt a little winded. "I'm not sure I wanted to hear that."

"Perhaps not, but we don't always want to hear about the less appealing parts of ourselves. Your father comes from a long line of noble souls. You have aunts and an uncle, I believe, who didn't choose darkness, and their heritage is the same as his. The choice is always yours, Rùnach. As for anything else, I think you had best be prepared for whatever comes your way, hadn't you?"

He considered, then sighed. "Very well, then. Another spell or two."

It turned out to be far more than a spell or two and at one point he realized that he was using far more serious spells than he likely should have been using. Muinear didn't seem to be at all surprised by anything he countered with. She also didn't seem to be working very hard to counter anything he was using.

Yet another thing to set aside for examination later.

He couldn't say Bruadair was particularly happy with him and what he was spewing out—at one point he wasn't entirely sure a cloud hadn't sprung up just over him and drenched him out of spite—but it seemed resigned to allowing him time to learn what he perhaps needed to.

It took time, but he realized as he continued to spar with Muinear that he was actually learning to manage what he was doing. Not fully, not even partly, but marginally. Not enough for it to perhaps make a difference, but perhaps enough to keep him from killing himself.

It was so completely foreign to anything he'd ever done that he felt as though he was standing outside his body, watching someone who looked like him doing things he certainly wouldn't have thought up on his own. The spells he was using required a lightness of touch that reminded him so damned much of Soilléir of Cothromaiche with his single words and happy thoughts that it was no wonder Sìle hadn't been able to do anything inside Brua-

dair's borders. His grandfather would have been left cursing furiously hours earlier.

By the time Muinear announced that it was enough, he was
absolutely drained of energy and magic. He could do nothing but
stand there and shake.

Muinear was suddenly standing in front of him. "Not bad,"
she said thoughtfully. "For an amateur."

Rùnach would have laughed, but he didn't have the strength
for it. He could only lean over and wheeze.

"You know, I tried to lure your grandsire Sìle out here and
teach him what I knew," Muinear said. "Several hundred years
ago, if memory serves."

Rùnach looked up at her from where he was standing hunched
over. "And?"

"You're a better student."

"He's stubborn," Rùnach said, not sure the word had the
strength to apply itself to his grandfather but very sure he wouldn't
dare use the word that would in polite company.

"That's one way to put it," she agreed, "and very politic indeed.
I would call him a pompous ass, but I'm old and have no need to
watch my tongue any longer."

He heaved himself upright. "What were you trying to teach him?"

"How not to stomp through Bruadair as if he'd been tromping
through his stables at Seanagarra. Magic here, as you've seen,
requires a lighter touch."

Rùnach looked at the rest of Muinear's henchspinners. They
had been brutally efficient at pushing him in ways he hadn't particularly cared to be pushed, but they hadn't left him with a desire
to wipe them out of existence permanently. He considered, then
looked at Aisling's great-grandmother.

"And if one needed to attack another mage inside Bruadair's borders," he asked slowly. "What then?"

"That is another lesson entirely."

"I think I'd best learn it sooner rather than later, don't you agree?"

"Unfortunately, I daresay you should." She studied him in silence for a moment or two. "You realize that if this muddle was created by someone of Gair's blood, it will need to be solved by the same."

Rùnach sighed deeply. "That seems to be how things work, doesn't it?"

"I thought you might have your own thoughts on that."

"I daresay."

"I'd be interested in hearing them, but perhaps not tonight. Let's go fetch your sword, Rùnach my lad, and you go find your lady. Perhaps a walk along the shore would soothe her. She's had a longer day than even yours, I suspect."

He didn't doubt it in the slightest. He nodded, then paused and looked at Aisling's great-grandmother. "Shore?"

"What do you think that roaring is just through those trees there?"

"I thought that was simply the echo of my muscles screaming from the exertion."

Muinear laughed. "I'm afraid only you can hear that shrieking. We're right on the coast, though a bit inland. Makes for lovely sea breezes but perhaps less violent storms than in other locales." She smiled and took his arm. "Aisling's mother loved the sea. I think her Bristeadh intended to build her house on the edge of it, but never had the chance. Perhaps you'll manage it, aye?"

He nodded, but found he couldn't speak. He remembered something Aisling had muttered in a fevered dream at Gobhann all those se'nnights ago, something about a house with no doors on the edge of the sea. He had promised her something like it more than once. That he should be almost close enough to even consider such a thing was sobering indeed.

He looked at Muinear. "Would you be willing to work again tomorrow?"

"Lad, I'd light torches and come back out this evening if I thought you could stand the work."

He took a deep breath. "I think I must, but I will tell you that my mother would be appalled at my asking you if you wouldn't mind indulging me."

"What are grannies for," she asked with a smile, "if not to indulge their children? Go have a walk with your lady, find something to eat, then we'll return and see what's left of you by the time the moon's overhead."

Rùnach would have offered to walk her back to the hall but she seemed perfectly happy to skip over to her compatriots in torture with the energy of a ten-year-old lass and no doubt delight them with the details of his humiliation at her hands. He shuffled over to retrieve his sword only to have Aisling's father hand it to him. He took it, then looked at Bristeadh.

"Have you any advice for me?"

Bristeadh smiled. "I don't have magic, remember?"

"You continue to say that," Rùnach said crossly, "and I begin to wonder if you aren't trying to distract me with a falsehood."

"Now, Rùnach, why would I do that?"

Rùnach suppressed the urge to snort, settling for a stern pursing of his lips. "To finish off what your granny-in-law there left of me, no doubt. Why else?"

"Oh, for my own perverse reasons, I imagine," Bristeadh said cheerfully. "Let's see you back to the house—do you need a shoulder to lean on?"

"Decorum suggests I refrain from telling you what I think of your offer."

Bristeadh laughed and put his hand on Rùnach's shoulder. "Such a polite lad. I'll consider the possibilities while you find my daughter and see how she fares."

Rùnach nodded and walked with him back to the hall. He paused at the doors and looked at Aisling's father. "I'm not sure I want her to see anything tonight."

Bristeadh looked at him out of eyes that were a perfect copy of Aisling's. "I don't think she would love you any less."

Rùnach shook his head. "I don't think so either, but still I would prefer that she not see what I need to do."

"Why do I have the feeling you had this same conversation with your mother *about* your mother?"

"My mother, if you can believe it, had this conversation with me. About *me*."

Bristeadh sighed deeply. "I didn't know Sarait, of course, but based on her reputation, I would say you were fortunate to have her as your dam. A remarkable woman of terrible courage."

"She was," Rùnach agreed, "and still, nay. If possible."

"You don't want me out here to keep Muinear from killing you?"

"You don't have any magic, remember?"

"I was thinking my way with words might accomplish the same thing," Bristeadh said with a smile. "But let it be as you wish. I'll keep Aisling distracted tonight while you're about your dastardly business. For now, I think I'll go see if your ponies are still in the stables. That Iteach was already trying to corrupt the lovely Orail with thoughts of dragonshape and sea breezes."

Rùnach didn't doubt that for a minute. He nodded to Aisling's father and watched him absently as he walked away. He put his hand on one of the golden doorhandles and studied the forest beyond the gardens that surrounded the palace and the lists beyond those. He could hear the sea, but it was definitely hidden.

A bit like the running of something he could now hear himself.

He thought of all the people he had talked to over the past several se'nnights who had mentioned the same thing. Captain Burke, whose ship had carried Aisling and him to Melksham Island, who had complained about things running through his belowdecks that weren't mice but dreams. Scrymgeour Weger, who had complained of his dreams being troubled by things running he couldn't identify. Even the king of the dwarves, who had asked Aisling to discover what was running beneath his kingdom that stretched down into the earth, far below where dwarf or man could dig.

He and Aisling had been cast into an underground river that had carried within its bounds a stream of magic. Bruadairian magic. Magic that should have been safely residing inside Bruadair's borders, not finding itself running off in directions it had never been meant to go.

He wondered if Bruadair would tell Aisling where the leak was, if leak it could be called, or what it would say to him if he asked it the same question.

Perhaps it *couldn't* say.

He turned that over in his mind for a bit, then shook his head. He would consider it later, when he'd taken an hour to feed himself, make sure Aisling had eaten something, then enjoy her company before her great-grandmother tried to kill him. Again.

Fifteen

❋

A isling stood in the dreamspinners' hall, feeling absolutely torn in two. It was the oddest sensation, that of feeling as if she were still herself with her past hanging about her like a shroud, yet not at all herself with her future hanging in the distance in front of her like mist draped on a lovely forest she wasn't allow to enter.

And still there on the dais sat a spinning wheel.

She turned away from the sight and continued to wander about the hall itself. Supper had been announced and the guests seemed to have decamped for a dining hall she hadn't yet seen. She'd been invited as well, but she'd demurred, hoping she wasn't giving offense. She wasn't sure she was hungry. In truth, she wasn't sure of anything except she felt as though she were dreaming. Appropriate, perhaps, but unsettling nonetheless. What she wanted was to escape for a bit and look at something else, but she wasn't sure how she would manage it. Freasdail was solicitous, but seemingly very anxious that nothing happen to her. She was perfectly confident that he was hovering somewhere just out of sight where he could rush to the rescue if she stubbed her toe.

No wonder Rùnach shunned the life of a pampered prince.

Well, they would come to an understanding at some point, hopefully. Perhaps when she stopped shaking from the events of the morning she wasn't quite ready to think about. She looked at the hall instead, because it was the best distraction she could invent at the moment.

It was an enormous place, full of light, built to perhaps even intimidate. She stood in the middle of it and turned around slowly, trying to number it among the places she'd seen before, but no amount of turning seemed to make that possible. It wasn't like anything she'd seen to that point.

Tor Neroche had been not so much rustic as it had been solid and immense, as if it had been fashioned from the elements of the land: trees, stone, water running endlessly. The dwarf king's palace looked as if it had simply been carved of the mountain itself. Rùnach's grandfather's palace of Seanagarra was more like something out of a book of fables, impossibly beautiful, full of trees that murmured and flowers that sang and all of it wrapped up in an elven glamour that lingered on in memory long after it was left behind. She thought she might have once likened it to having walked in a dream.

Now, she knew better.

The chamber where she currently stood was enormous, but also almost not quite there, as if it had been so slathered in the echoes of dreams that it no longer found itself in reality. It wasn't where the spinning happened, or so she understood. She had been given a tour by Freasdail, who apparently took his duties very seriously. She'd seen the whole of the great hall, then been shown where the chambers for spinning lay and who inhabited them. She immediately forgot their names and what they did, but she supposed she would have ample time to become acquainted with them in the future.

Her future, as the First Dreamspinner.

She sat down finally on the top step of the dais and looked back down the path that had faded into something far less grand than it had been before. It was barely demarcated, as if it weren't quite sure if she intended to use it or not but feared not to be ready at a moment's notice should she decide to jump up and run out the front doors.

She considered it briefly, then let the thought continue on just as quickly. She wasn't going to leave, no matter how terrified she was. Her future, such as it was, lay where she was. She could only hope that future might continue to include a certain elf . . .

Who had apparently come into the hall while she had been otherwise occupied.

He was leaning against one of the pillars that held the roof up scores of feet over her head. He was doing nothing more interesting than watching her, which she supposed wasn't very interesting at all, but he seemed to be committed to the exercise so she wasn't going to argue with him.

She forgot, from time to time, who he was. She had known him such a short time in the grander scheme of things, but she felt as if she'd known him for the better part of her life. Perhaps she had become too comfortable with him, she a simple weaver and he the grandson of an elven king.

Only she wasn't a weaver any longer and perhaps the spinning she would eventually do was less than simple, but she was still who she was and he was who he was and how was it possible she could ever look at him and not see him for what he was?

She supposed he would stand there all day, smiling faintly,

waiting for her to decide what she wanted to do. She took a deep breath and held out her hand toward him.

He pushed away from his pillar and walked over to her, sat down next to her, and took her hand.

"Comfortable perch," he noted.

"More comfortable than a stool at the wheel behind us, I daresay."

He smiled. "I imagine that will become familiar in time."

She wasn't sure how that would ever happen, but she appreciated his confidence. She looked at his hand wrapped around hers, then at him. "It isn't my spinning wheel. That one behind us, I mean."

"Isn't it?" he asked, looking faintly surprised. "What do you mean?"

"Freasdail told me there's another wheel in a different chamber where the true work is accomplished. That one there is just the one they set out for spinners aspiring to the position of First."

"Are there spinners who aspire to that?"

"Apparently so."

"I never would have guessed."

"Me, neither."

"What's the purpose of that wheel, then? It's a pretty thing, if I could offer an opinion." He smiled. "Though I never thought to have an opinion about a spinning wheel."

"Its purpose is to kill you if you aren't the right lad for the job," she said solemnly, then she did him the favor of patting him firmly on the back until he stopped choking. She looked up to find Freasdail standing there with a cup of something.

Rùnach took it, drank, then set the cup on the floor. "Thank you, ah . . ."

"Freasdail, Your Highness. The First's steward."

Rùnach smiled. "You must be pleased to have someone to look after."

Freasdail made Rùnach a bow. "Very, Your Highness."

"You know," Rùnach said, "if you need to go find something to eat, I think I can take care of her for a bit."

"Oh," Freasdail said, looking as if the thought hadn't occurred to him. "Oh, I couldn't. You see, we've been without a First for so long and we don't want anything to happen to the lady Aisling, seeing as how she's not only the First, but Lady Muinear's great-granddaughter, and perhaps you don't know that her mother and grandmother—"

"We know," Rùnach said gravely. "But perhaps you would be amenable to discussing the details with me, perhaps after our lady has sought her rest?"

"Of course, Your Highness."

Rùnach smiled. "Sustenance, my good Freasdail. You'll be of no use to her if you faint."

The man looked horribly torn, but he seemed somewhat reassured by the sight of Rùnach's sword lying next to him on the pair of steps. He looked at her.

"Five minutes, my lady. I'll return posthaste."

She waved him on to his meal, supposing there was no point in trying to talk him into a longer respite. She watched him go, then looked at Rùnach.

"He'll send someone else to watch over me, won't he?"

"Absolutely."

She considered. "Is this why you wanted to go hide in a garrison?"

He smiled. "Partly. I'd had a happy amount of anonymity with Soilléir, so I wasn't perhaps as desperate for it as I might have been otherwise, but I will admit the thought of living the life of a pampered elven prince did give me pause. I'll see if I can't put myself in the rotation of those guardsmen charged with looking after you. That will no doubt satisfy my desire for the lack of servants hovering at my elbow."

"Guardsmen?"

"Haven't you noticed them?"

She shook her head. "Are you sure?"

He smiled. "Two at the front door, another pair at the garden door, another very intimidating-looking lad by the passageway leading elsewhere."

"How did you notice?"

"I checked the hall after I entered—after I almost ran into the scowling fiends by the doorway—because I thought you might prefer it if I kissed you without an audience. And after, perhaps, I washed up."

She leaned closer to him, kissed him herself, then smiled. "There. I've now shocked lads I didn't know were there. And where have you been to look so wrung out?"

"Wrung out?" he echoed, tugging at the neck of his tunic. "I can only hope I don't look as wrung out as I feel, but to answer your question, I've been entertaining your great-grandmother in the lists."

"Do we have lists?"

"Apparently so." He lifted an eyebrow briefly. "She knows where they are. And so, it would seem, do the rest of your thoroughly merciless dreamspinners. Muinear gave me a minute to catch my breath, magically speaking, then they all came at me like a damned pack of vultures."

"Was it terrible?"

He sighed, then shook his head slowly. "I won't say it was pleasant, but I learned many things I didn't know and was shown things I hadn't considered. So, I would say it was a success." He shook his head again. "I'm still trying to get over the fact that I was facing a tiny woman in the lists and she left me almost in tears."

"I like her."

"So do I," Rùnach said.

She looked around the hall for the alleged guardsmen but saw nothing. Perhaps that was just as well. If she'd known they were there, perhaps she would have been less willing to roam freely. She supposed she would accustom herself to it in time.

Accustom herself to her life, in time.

She was, she realized, enormously grateful for the man sitting next to her. She looked at their hands together, for the sight comforted her in ways she hadn't expected, then looked at him to find he was watching her gravely.

"Still want to, ah, well . . . you know?" she asked.

"I think I need to put a *you know* on your finger so you don't ever have to ask that question again."

She smiled because she loved him, she was sitting in a place that was safe, and for the moment, she could put off thinking about more of her future than what the next quarter hour contained. She shifted a little, then smiled into his very green eyes.

"You're wearing a crown, you know."

He reached up, looking very surprised, and patted the top of his head. Then he looked at her with a wry smile. "The visible world doesn't think so."

"Bruadair has an interesting perspective."

He didn't move. "And how am I supposed to learn to tell the difference between dreams and reality?"

"You're asking me?" she said uncomfortably. "I haven't a clue."

"Is it a very large, impressive crown?"

She blinked, then realized he was teasing her. "Less gigantic than magnificent. Your grandfather would approve, I imagine." She reached up and pulled off his head what she could plainly see. It became solid in her hands. She almost dropped it, truth be told.

Rùnach's sharp intake of breath was followed by a bit of a laugh. "Aisling, I think you're terrifying me again."

"How do you think I feel?" She handed the crown back to him. "You'd best keep that."

"And just what am I to do with it?"

"I have absolutely no idea, but Bruadair seems to think you should have it. You two can come to some sort of agreement later."

"I shudder to think what that might entail," he said faintly, "but I'm learning not to argue with your country." He looked at her hand in his for several minutes in silence, then at her. "So, whilst I was being tormented in the lists, what did you do? A nap was involved, I hope."

She shook her head. "I was given the tour by Freasdail. I was very briefly introduced to people I don't remember, saw chambers that I don't remember the use for, and was offered food I couldn't bring myself to eat." She winced. "I think Freasdail took pity on me and stopped when perhaps I looked as if I might soon weep. Or, rather, Ceana found me and ordered him to let me breathe."

"I knew there was something odd about that woman," Rùnach said with a snort. "Too canny by half."

"She is," Aisling agreed. She paused and considered her next words for quite some time before she felt equal to releasing them out into the hall. "I was curious about how she'd come so quickly," she said carefully. "I was assuming, perhaps badly, that she hadn't known what was to happen here until fairly recently. So I asked her how she got here."

"And?"

"She said she had a map." She paused. "They all have maps."

"Maps," he repeated slowly.

"Maps that wouldn't mean anything to anyone else," she said, wishing with a fair bit of enthusiasm that she'd never had the conversation to start with. "I probably should have stopped there, but I had to know more."

"Curiosity is a dangerous thing."

"Spoken like one who's had his fingers burned more than once," she said grimly.

He smiled very briefly. "I wish I could deny it, but I can't. Very well, so they—and I'm assuming that would be all these spinners we seem to be surrounded by—and who are they, do you think? Ceana, we know already. I recognized my grandmother Brèagha's Mistress of the Cloth and waved across the room to the wizened granny who spins for Eulasaid, but didn't recognize any of the others."

"I think they're just as you say, those in charge of spinning for various important households," she said. "I haven't had the chance to meet them all, but they seem to have some interest in the fate of the world beyond the norm."

"Interesting," he said, sounding far too interested for his own good. "We'll have to investigate that later. But I interrupted you. All these important spinners have maps, but . . . ?"

She pushed herself to her feet. "I have to walk."

The path sprang to life as if it had been poked with a sword. Rùnach laughed a little and heaved himself up. He left his crown behind, propped his sword up against his shoulder with one hand and took her hand with his other.

"Go on," he encouraged. "Maps?"

She took a deep breath. "They're maps that don't display the locations that maps normally indicate. Maps with odd markings on them, or so I understand."

He looked rather ill all of the sudden. "Is that so?"

"It is," she said. She paused. "She said she would show me hers, did I care to see it."

"Did she?"

"You're doing it again," she said miserably. "That thing where you answer questions with other questions."

"I think I'm about to vomit on your lovely floor," Rùnach said thickly. "I'm trying to comfort myself with my most annoying habit."

She pulled her hand away, then threw her arms around his neck. She closed her eyes and held on to him as his arms came around her. Breathing was important, she decided, but perhaps less important than remaining upright. She held on to him until a cramp in her back left her with the choice of either continuing to cling to him and shake, or pulling away and walking upright to luncheon. She chose the former, then looked at him.

"I think we might have to find a side door to this place sooner rather than later."

"Are you thinking what I'm thinking?"

"Why don't you tell me what you're thinking?" she countered.

He took a deep breath. "I'm thinking it's very coincidental that there are maps in the world that aren't maps that a normal lad or lass would recognize."

"I agree."

"And it's further quite coincidental that I have a book of scratches in my pack, a book created by Acair of Ceangail, who it would seem has an interest in Bruadair's magic."

"Oh, Rùnach," she said, pulling away from him but taking his hand. She laced her fingers with his and was grateful that his hand was no steadier than hers. "You don't think Acair's scratches might be a map. Not in truth."

He dragged his sleeve across his forehead, then looked at her. "The witchwoman of Fàs seemed to think so, didn't she?"

"Perhaps that was indigestion from tea," she said, wondering how many more excuses she could invent before she ran out of them. "Or she was having us on."

"I chopped wood for her," he said wearily. "She doesn't take that lightly."

"And you would know," she said.

"I would," he agreed, "having had many answers from her over the years in return for adding to her wood pile. Besides, she liked you rather a lot, I'd say. She wouldn't have lied to you." He looked at her helplessly. "She's a very committed diarist."

"And collector of hair ornaments," Aisling added. "How can you doubt a woman with those sorts of hobbies?"

"I wish we could," he said with feeling, then he sighed. "I would like a peek at Mistress Ceana's map, but perhaps later. I suggest we now go puke our guts out, have some supper, then walk along the shore. What do you think?"

"I think you're daft."

"And I think we may have stumbled upon something that merits further investigation. Tomorrow. After you've recovered from today and I've recovered from the thrashing your great-grandmother just gave me in the lists."

Aisling smiled. "She didn't."

"I'll tell you about it once I've recovered from the embarrassment of being knocked fully upon my arse by a woman half my size."

Aisling laughed. "I wish I'd seen it."

"I'm sure she would repeat the exercise for your pleasure, if you asked her," Rùnach said dryly. He looked over his shoulder, then back at her. "Your steward is awaiting your pleasure. Perhaps we can filch something portable to eat and see if the ocean truly does lie beyond that rise out there."

An hour later, Aisling found herself standing on the edge of the ocean, breathing deeply of air that filled her lungs and soothed her soul. The words a ship's captain had once said to her came back to her suddenly, that she was one for whom seeing the sea spelled doom. She sighed a little at the thought. It was a fate she could readily accept, especially if it included the man standing next to her.

Rùnach was looking up the coast, thoughtfully, as if he considered things he hadn't before. He looked at her, then blinked when he apparently realized she was watching him. He smiled.

"Aye?"

"Nothing," she said easily. "Just happy to have my two favorite things here together."

He smiled and turned to pull her into his arms. "I would like to show an appropriate amount of gratitude for those sweet words but, again, we have an audience. Very fierce, those lads of yours."

"I haven't met them yet."

"I think they're trying to be discreet."

"Not discreet enough if you keep seeing them," she pointed out.

"Well, I have a terrible habit of always looking in the shadows," he admitted, "so perhaps I'm not the best one to offer an opinion. They do seem to be armed with not only steel but spells, so I'm not about to discourage them. But I will look for a decent place to thank you at some point today. Perhaps they won't swoon if I hold your hand for a bit."

She nodded and walked with him along the shore until the sun had dipped well below the mountains to the west. She turned and walked back the other way with him, watching not the sea but the bluff to her left. She finally stopped because she realized why it looked so familiar.

"Rùnach?"

"Aye, love."

"I think your grandmother was here, in this very spot."

"I think so too."

She looked at the spot in front of her and realized what had struck her as unusual. There wasn't a great amount of color, but there was more than she'd seen in the usual spots in Bruadair.

"We should go back."

Aisling looked at Rùnach in surprise. "Why do you say that?"

"I'm uncomfortable." He smiled briefly. "Besides, it's getting dark."

She supposed that was as good a reason as any. She nodded and walked quickly with Rùnach back up the hill and through the forest. Somehow, the shadows didn't seem nearly as benign as they had earlier in the afternoon.

"Do you think a battle was fought here?" she asked when the hall was again in sight.

"It makes you wonder, doesn't it? I suppose we could ask Muinear when we have a chance."

"I wonder why your grandparents were here."

"That," he said with a smile, "is a question I think she would definitely answer without much prodding. Apparently she tried to school my grandfather in a little magicmaking and he wasn't a very good student."

She smiled in spite of herself. "I don't doubt that. Well, at least it gave your grandmother time to walk on the shore and see the view."

"Our view, I think," he said slowly. He looked at her. "That bluff would be a lovely place to build a house, don't you think?"

She leaned up and kissed him. "Aye," she said simply.

He put his arm around her shoulders. "Let me escort you inside and in front of a fire. I have a little errand to run."

"To the kitchens?"

"To the lists," he said seriously. "It won't take long, I don't imagine."

Aisling nodded and continued on with him. It made her wonder, however, just what had drawn the king and queen of Tòrr Dòrainn into a land not their own and left at least Sìle attempting to use his own magic.

It was very odd.

Perhaps there were more maps out in the world than she feared.

Sixteen

Rùnach decided that there was a fair bit of irony that he'd had a horrible night's sleep in the very place where sleep should have come easily.

Then again, it was entirely possible he simply thought too much.

It was thoughts that had kept him tossing and turning until he'd finally given up any hope of slumber before dawn and taken to pacing along passageways until he'd reached the great hall. Fires had been burning merrily in hearths made of crystal and stone, servants had been industriously sweeping the polished floor, and not a single soul had asked him to leave. He'd been welcomed with smiles and pleasant greetings, queried about his need for sustenance or music, and left to himself when he'd declined both.

He'd paced until he thought he could give an accurate measure of the length and breadth of the great hall, then left it and took to finding other things to count. He wasn't a counter as a rule, but he had to do something to keep his thoughts from straying in directions he didn't care for.

What if the innards of his book *were* a map?

What if they were a map not of places, but of spots in the fabric of the world where there might be . . . he hardly knew what to call them. Flaws? Missing threads?

Portals?

What if Acair's plans included not only stripping Bruadair of its magic, but stripping every country in the world of whatever magic it had? What if he intended to do that through the portals that the dreamspinners and their allies spread throughout the world used to travel from Bruadair and back home again as easily as stepping from one room to another?

The thought left him feeling profoundly chilled.

He realized he had almost plowed over Aisling and Muinear only because he lost his balance. He steadied himself with his hand on a wall and attempted a smile.

"Sorry," he said. "I was thinking."

"Take his arm, Aisling," Muinear said, taking his other arm. "We'll take him to the library and tuck him safely in a corner. I think they'll allow breakfast to be brought there if we ask nicely."

Rùnach didn't protest. A chair was sounding particularly appealing. If he found himself snoozing over a book on unremarkable Bruadairian sheep, so much the better. And Muinear owed him a perch in a comfortable chair after what she'd put him through the night before. Necessary, but intensely unpleasant.

He was quite happy to be escorted to where he might have a chance to distract himself with something to read, though the journey to that chamber didn't take as long as he'd hoped it might. They paused in front of a set of doors, then the doors swung open as if commanded to.

He stepped inside, then froze. He gaped at the library's contents, then looked at Aisling. She was yawning.

"Interesting," she offered, shutting her mouth abruptly. "Fascinating."

Rùnach laughed. He walked into a library that for all intents and purposes was a copy of Bristeadh's, down to the carpet on the floor. There were wheels and echoes of wheels and things that looked like wheels but were obviously just curved bits of a deep, dark wood that left him reminding himself that grown men did not skip across floors of libraries to touch and pat and pull books from shelves. In a palace that was full of endless amounts of light, this was the perfect place to spend an afternoon with a good book or sit at a long table and commence a serious study, all accompanied by warm tones, comfortable chairs, and just the right amount of muted light.

And then he realized something else.

Some of the books seemed to be less than corporeal, if such a term could be used for them.

He looked at Muinear in surprise. "What's this?"

"Copies of every book in existence in every library, great and small, in the world."

He retrieved his jaw that had fallen down for the same reason he'd refrained from skipping, because he thought it might behoove him to look like an adult. "How does it work?" he asked, wondering if a swoon would be looked at askance. "Though I have to admit that I'm not precisely certain why I'm daring to ask."

"Afraid?"

He couldn't help a smile. "My lady Muinear, I'm not sure you're the one to be asking that after what you inflicted on me yesterday. I'm certain I'm not the one to be answering that."

"Call this penance, then," she said with a smile. "Aisling, darling, let's go spin and leave your lad to his gaping, shall we? Rùnach, you'll be fine on your own?"

"Um," he said, searching for the right thing to say.

They laughed, then left him without a backward glance.

He wasn't sure how much time had passed by the time he realized time had passed. Hours had gone by, no doubt. He had roamed happily through stacks, warming himself thoroughly by the thought of Soilléir learning where he'd been and suffering a fair bit of envy over it. Then again, knowing Soilléir, he had likely contributed heavily to the tomes that found themselves actually being housed on those endless shelves.

Of course, that warmth of smugness had only lasted until he'd come face-to-face with the thought he'd been trying to avoid all morning, namely that there was a book in his pack that he knew he needed to open sooner rather than later and contemplate in a new way what lay inside. He wasn't sure the palace would permit such a thing without screeching, but he knew he needed to try.

He rose, thanked the librarians profusely for their aid, then left and went to retrieve his book from his backpack. He tucked it under his arm, then went in search of somewhere that wouldn't kill him for cracking the damned thing open.

He wandered through the hallways unmolested until he found himself suddenly standing in front of a doorway. There were things placed on the doorframe, runes of might and power from a source he didn't recognize. It wasn't evil, that much he thought he could say with certainty, but it was certainly dark.

The door opened and a man stood there. Rùnach studied him

for a moment or two. He had runes on his hands and face, runes of power and magic and darkness.

"Who are you?" he asked.

"Uabhann," he said mildly. "I am Dread."

"Ah," Rùnach managed. "An interesting thing to be."

"I have sent you dreams before."

"That," Rùnach said with feeling, "I do not doubt in the slightest."

"Come in," Uabhann said, beckoning for him to enter. "I don't get very many visitors."

Rùnach imagined he didn't. He walked into the man's chambers and blinked in surprise. He could have been standing in the midst of any suite of rooms favored by a cultured gentleman. In fact, he wasn't entirely sure he hadn't seen that same style of sofa in the headmaster of Buidseachd's private solar. He thought he might like to know how that could possibly be, but perhaps later, when he was certain he would toddle back out that doorway alive.

He accepted a seat in front of a roaring fire, then didn't protest the further offering of what looked to be a glass of port.

"Not poisoned," Uabhann assured him. "In case you were wondering."

"The thought crossed my mind."

"That thought crosses everyone's mind."

Rùnach almost laughed, but he thought that might be inappropriate. He sipped instead, thanked his host for the excellence of his libations, then set his glass down on the table at his elbow. He looked at the man sitting across from him, wearing runes that were only barely visible, and surrounded by a darkness that wasn't necessarily evil.

"How long have you been at this?" he asked politely.

"At what?"

"The business of nightmares."

Uabhann smiled. "Long enough."

"Don't suppose you gave my father any, did you?"

"I imagine I did, Prince Rùnach."

Rùnach acknowledged the recognition with a nod. "I should thank you, then, for he had terrible ones."

"Most were of his own making," Uabhann said. "Guilty conscience, you know, troubling his sleep. I just added a few threads here and there when necessary."

Rùnach didn't doubt it. He considered, then decided there was no sense in not asking for what he needed.

"I have a book I need to look at."

"Something nasty?"

"Fairly. And I'm afraid that if I open it in the great hall, I'll bring the whole place down around my ears."

Uabhann rubbed his hands together. "Sounds delightful. Let's have a look here, then, shall we? Sìorraidh and I have an understanding, as you might imagine."

Rùnach didn't dare speculate, but he imagined they did indeed. He nodded, then took the book in both hands. He had to admit that he was nervous about opening it anywhere. He had very vivid memories of his grandfather's glamour protesting the action. Loudly.

"I'm not evil, you know."

Rùnach looked at him. "I never said you were."

"I make people uneasy."

Rùnach imagined he did. Uabhann wasn't handsome, which Rùnach supposed was his saving grace. In his experience, evil had a very attractive face, which was what gained it entrance where it might not have found an open door otherwise. He shrugged.

"You don't bother me."

"Not as ugly as your sire, eh?"

"Actually," Rùnach said, "you're quite a bit uglier than my sire, if you don't mind my saying so."

That was an understatement, he had to admit. He was hardly any judge of male beauty, he supposed, but he had two good eyes and he could tell the difference between a troll and a faery. His father had been terribly handsome and all the more dangerous because of it.

Uabhann only smiled. "I'll accept the compliment. Thank you."

"But still I don't think you're evil," Rùnach added.

"Perhaps your sight is clearer than most."

"And perhaps you force people to see things they wouldn't like to."

Uabhann lifted his eyebrows briefly. "Perhaps." He sat back and looked at Rùnach. "I do like the light," he admitted, "but I do my best work in the shadows."

"That seems reasonable," Rùnach said. "No darkness, no appreciation for light."

"What do you prefer, Prince Rùnach?"

"Rain."

Uabhann looked at him, then smiled. "I see I'll need to plan a bit more to entrap you, won't I?"

"Is that your goal?"

"We've been without a First for almost three decades now," Uabhann said with a shrug. "Aisling comes from a long line of powerful, canny women. Don't want her being bamboozled by a pretty face."

"I thought the hall doors would kill me if Bruadair didn't like me," Rùnach said.

"Her," Uabhann said distinctly. "They would have killed her. You, Your Highness, have a far different test to pass."

"Any hints?"

"Do you need hints?"

"They might be useful."

And then he felt something tugging at his soul, though perhaps that was a poor way to put it. There was something calling to him, singing with a song that was almost too tempting to resist.

Calling to his pride.

His ego.

His mighty magic.

It was tempting to trot out a few spells for Uabhann and show him just what he was capable of—

He looked at Uabhann and let out his breath slowly. "I see."

"Oh, laddie, I don't think you've but begun to see, but there you have it." He shrugged. "I make people uneasy."

"I can see why."

Uabhann looked at him. Well, through him, actually. Rùnach decided that perhaps he would do well to tread carefully around that one who was obviously not precisely what he seemed to be.

"Your half brother has dark dreams."

Rùnach wondered if he should not bother looking any further at his book when apparently a veritable font of tidings was sitting right there in front of him. "Are you encouraging that?"

Uabhann smiled. "The idea has occurred to me."

Rùnach suspected it had done more than just occur to the man in front of him. "How did you come to be here?"

"My father was a dreamspinner," Uabhann said, "and his father before him. Where our line began, I hesitate to say for the source is not pleasant." He paused and looked at Rùnach. "My grandfather's grandfather was reared . . ." He paused again. "The locale is not pleasant either. Let us simply say that it gave him a unique perspective on evil and all its incarnations."

"I won't speculate."

"You likely shouldn't." Uabhann gestured toward Rùnach's book. "Let's discuss that instead. What is it besides something nasty?"

"A book I created of spells to counter my father's spells," Rùnach said slowly, "a book I didn't realize had been lost. When I found the book where I hadn't left it, I quickly realized the innards were missing and had been replaced with what the covers currently hold."

"Who lost the book?"

Rùnach considered. "*Lost* was perhaps a poor choice of words. I left it in the care of the witchwoman of Fàs, but she didn't guard it very well." *Or at all* was what he didn't add and likely didn't need to add.

"I've wandered in that woman's dreams. They're as tangled as her hair, if you're curious."

"I was and I'm utterly unsurprised. The twistings and turnings of just her conversation are alarming."

"I believe you. So, what's inside your little book now?"

"Scratches."

Uabhann rose. "Bring it over to the table by the window, if you like." He shot Rùnach a look. "It keeps the sunlight lovers happy."

Rùnach imagined it would. He took his book over, set it down on the table, then looked at Uabhann briefly. Bruadair's spinner of nightmares only watched him without expression. Rùnach cast caution—and his hope of continuing to breathe, it had to be said— to the wind, then opened his book.

The chamber didn't shriek, but he felt something shift. Uabhann peered at the contents, then whistled softly.

"Isn't that interesting."

"Is it?"

He looked at Rùnach from the same ageless eyes Aisling had. "You don't have a clue what's there, do you?"

Rùnach leaned on his hands. "I'm guessing it might be a map of portals."

Uabhann laughed a little. "Portals. Haven't heard them called that in years. Sounds like something Muinear would call them."

"What would you call them?"

"Doorways," Uabhann said with a shrug, "but I haven't much of an imagination. I like my nightmares to be fairly straightforward without undue fuss accompanying them."

Rùnach would have laughed, but he suspected Uabhann was utterly serious. Suddenly, Uabhann turned and made a bit of a bow. Rùnach looked over his shoulder to find Aisling standing there just inside the doorway.

He was tempted to make a bit of a bow himself.

He wondered if she would bloody his nose if he did so, but decided that he would chance it. He made her a low, courtly bow, then hoped he wouldn't straighten to find her fist in his face. Instead, she was looking at him with less irritation than an expression that seemed . . . unsettled. He frowned immediately.

"What is it?"

"I felt something . . . shift."

"What does Bruadair have to say about it?" he asked, then he shook his head. He could hardly believe he was talking about a country as if it were an entity. At least in Tòrr Dòrainn, the flora and fauna were all that made their opinions known. He was beginning to think that Aisling's entire country had a mind of its own.

Aisling smiled at Uabhann, then looked at Rùnach. "It's silent on the matter," she said, but she looked almost haunted by the fact. She looked at Uabhann. "I hesitate to speak."

"In front of me?" Uabhann asked in surprise. "I've heard things that would turn this wee elven princeling's hair white, if that eases you any. You may say whatever you like. I guarantee you I won't be shocked."

"I don't want to erode any confidence in, ah, or rather about, ah . . ." She stopped. "I don't want to speak amiss."

Uabhann gestured to the book on his table. "You're not going to do anything worse than the author of that has already done."

"I don't *want* to do anything worse than what he's done."

Uabhann smiled. "And that, my lady, is one of the many reasons why you're the First."

Rùnach leaned against the table and looked at Aisling. "I think you may speak freely here."

She took a deep breath. "I think Bruadair is growing weaker."

He blinked. "What?"

She shrugged helplessly. "Here the magic is very strong, stronger than anywhere I've felt it." She looked at him. "Can you believe I just said that?"

"I can," he said with a smile. "You, a simple weaver with no magic."

"Is that what she believed?" Uabhann interrupted incredulously.

"I'll hire a king's bard to do justice to the tale," Rùnach said seriously, "for it will take a very skilled one to tell it properly." He looked at Aisling. "So what do you think?"

She wrapped her arms around herself. "I'm not even sure how to describe it." She gestured at the table. "When you opened that book, because I'm assuming you just did, the magic shuddered. As if it prepared for an attack."

Rùnach felt the book behind him shudder a bit at her words, a sensation that he had to admit was one of the most unwholesome things he'd ever had the misfortune of experiencing in a lifetime of numerous unwholesome things. He looked at the book behind him, then at Uabhann.

"Interesting."

"Very." Uabhann made Aisling another bow. "If you'll permit me an opinion, I think the others should come and see what's here. I'll go fetch them, if you like."

"Thank you," Aisling said. "Do you mind if we stay here?"

"Of course not," he said. "The First and a prince of Tòrr Dòrainn in my humble chambers? I must be dreaming. Good ones, for a change," he threw over his shoulder as he walked across his chamber and out the door.

Rùnach looked at Aisling. "Interesting friends you have here."

"They say he's the most intimidating of them all," she said very quietly. "No one likes him very much."

"Ah, courtly intrigues," Rùnach said with a smile. "Lovely. What do you think of him?"

She looked at him steadily. "I'm not afraid of the dark."

He smiled and reached out to pull her into his arms. "I know you're not. I think Master Uabhann would be very pleased to hear that."

"Will he mind if I ask for extra werelight when he's around, do you think?"

He laughed. "I daresay he'll find a way to tolerate it." He pulled back and looked at her. "Your eyes are the same color, you know."

"As Uabhann's?" she asked in surprise. "Are they?"

"It seems to be a characteristic of several of the spinners I've met so far," he said, "which admittedly isn't all that many."

"Inbreeding back in the mists of time?"

"An ability to see more clearly than others?"

"Are you always going to answer questions with questions?"

"Should I, do you think?"

She leaned up, kissed him quickly, then smiled at him. "It's reassuring."

"Thankfully," he said. He leaned back against the table, then drew her over to lean with him so he could watch the door. It occurred to him that he was doing it, but he supposed Aisling wouldn't notice.

Only she did.

"I think we're safe here," she ventured.

"Bad habits developed over a lifetime of looking over my shoulder."

"I understand."

"I imagine you do," he said quietly. He put his arm around her shoulders. "We'll try to see to things so we don't have to do that anymore, Aisling."

"Do you think we'll manage that?" she asked, looking at him with those pale, fathomless eyes of hers. "To rescue the magic of an entire country . . ."

"Or tinker with the dreams of an entire world," he said with a smile. "Which do you think is more difficult?"

"Do I have to answer that?"

"Shouldn't you?"

"You're doing it again."

He smiled. "I'm trying to distract you. I'd rather use other methods but your steward is standing at the doorway and I think his brow is beginning to pucker. Best for me not to irritate the man with the keys to your schedule right off, wouldn't you agree?"

"My schedule," she said with a faint laugh. "What a thought."

It was something to think about, though, and he supposed it wouldn't do for the others to see him sitting so casually with the leader of their exclusive group, so he dropped his arm from around her shoulders and put his hand over his book. Aisling shot him a warning look, which he responded to with a quick smile. He supposed she might have had something to say to him, but the entire council of dreamspinners was suddenly standing there in a little semicircle in front of her. Freasdail slid in from one side and made Aisling a very low bow.

"My lady," he said, "I have come to see if you need refreshment. Wine? Biscuits? Little cakes soaked in lemon juice and sprinkled with delicate sugars?"

"Sounds lovely," said a voice. "Freasdail, set a course for the kitchens and leave the girl room to breathe."

Rùnach watched Bristeadh come to stand at the side of the group and shoo Freasdail off. Surprising, but what did he know about the political machinations of dreamspinners and their servants? Bristeadh looked at his daughter and smiled.

"Your companions are here, daughter. What do you need from them?"

Aisling nodded. "The prince of Tòrr Dòrainn was looking for an opinion on something."

Rùnach faced the gaggle of dreamspinners gathered there. He'd already encountered them as a group before, but at a distance and through the haze of terrible spells. They were a much friendlier-looking group at the moment. He cleared his throat.

"I have a book—"

Well, apparently that was enough of an announcement for them. They crowded around him to see just what sort of book he had. He unveiled it to reactions ranging from gasps of horror to murmurs of appreciation. The last was from, of course, Uabhann. And then the suggestions came at him from all directions.

"Pull it apart."

"Someone fetch a book knife!"

"Take it out of the cover first, naturally."

Rùnach couldn't bring himself to argue when Aisling's compatriots began to assault Acair's writings, if that's what they could be called. There was a bit of jostling, much discussion and rearranging of sheaves of paper, some low arguing, but all of it left Rùnach standing to the side, watching in horror as something emerged there on the table.

A map of the world, the current Nine Kingdoms being given especial attention.

"Oh, my," someone said faintly. "Whose book is this again?"

"Acair of Ceangail," Uabhann said, stroking his chin thoughtfully. "Bloody brilliant, isn't he?"

"If you like that sort of thing," said a woman who looked as if she'd first touched a spinning wheel several centuries earlier. "Gauche, if you ask me."

"But effective," Bristeadh said quietly. "Rùnach, what do you think?"

Rùnach found several pairs of eyes on him. He didn't bother to count them, though he supposed he might be able to do so later from memory. He took a deep breath.

"I think my half brother is trying to take over the world."

Seventeen

※

Aisling wandered aimlessly through passageways, wishing she could have found someplace to sit. Actually it wasn't so much the sitting that she wished for as the surcease from thinking.

Rùnach's bastard brother had made a map of the world.

That wouldn't have troubled her before, most likely because she never would have been the wiser as she'd sat in the Guild and woven her endless lengths of cloth. If she'd seen his map, she likely would have silently criticized his cartographer skills and gone about her business. But now she knew what the map actually was, that Acair had made particular marks on the map that corresponded to particular kingdoms where there were portals known only to dreamspinners and those select spinners apportioned to royal houses.

Or at least they had only been known to them before.

She didn't want to think about how Acair had found out where those portals were or what else he knew.

She jumped a little as she realized Muinear was walking down the passageway toward her. She smiled and went into her great-grandmother's embrace.

"Thank you," she said, though thanks seemed particularly inadequate.

"Ah, my love," Muinear said, pulling back and kissing her on both cheeks, "I'm so happy you're finally here."

"And I'm so happy you're alive," Aisling said frankly.

Muinear laughed a little. "Iochdmhor is powerful, true, but she has so little imagination that it was an easy thing to leave her thinking she had the victory."

"I would like never to see her again," Aisling said, "no matter how easily fooled she might be."

"Oh, not easily," Muinear said, her smile fading, "but done readily enough, I suppose. In the end, darling, she is just a little witch who will fade into obscurity. There have been and will no doubt be in the future those with much more power than she." She took Aisling's arm. "I thought you might like to see your chamber at sunrise. Sunset is better, perhaps, when the light is full west and you have twilight to look forward to, but sunrise is lovely as well."

"My chamber?"

Muinear smiled. "Yours, my love. I didn't have a chance to show it to you yesterday and Freasdail had left the honor of it to me." She started to walk, then apparently realized she was pressing on alone. She paused. "What is it?" she asked.

Aisling hardly knew how to voice her thoughts. "I'm not sure where to begin." She looked at her great-grandmother. "Were you in truth the First?"

"For centuries, until your grandmother took my place." She

nodded toward to her right. "Let's walk, Aisling, and I'll tell you of it, what there is to tell."

"Are you afraid I'll bolt?"

Muinear smiled. "Nay, my girl, not that. Though I hope it was clear enough yesterday that you *can* walk away from your birthright. There are other paths you could choose."

"And who would take my place?" Aisling asked reluctantly.

"For the moment? No one." She paused. "We would begin a search for someone with the right temperament and the requisite magic, but whether or not we would find him or her—well, we would continue on as we have been until that person was found. And our line would end." She smiled. "Sometimes that happens, in spite of our actions or lack of action."

"Who was the first dreamspinner?"

"My grandfather's grandmother," Muinear said. "Your lad could likely find you all the details you want in his wonderland of a library, or if we manage to do what we must, we'll spend long evenings during the fall in front of my fire, talking of those who have come before. I will tell you this, Aisling: every last one of the men and women who came before you and put their hands to that wheel felt as if the task was too great at first."

"I'm not sure I'm equal to even thinking about the task," Aisling said faintly, "much less how to accomplish it."

"Come look at your chamber, then, love, and see what you think."

Aisling nodded and continued on with her. She wasn't blind to the deference everyone she passed showed her great-grandmother, nor could she deny that she was shown the same deference.

Well, perhaps a bit more.

"I keep thinking I should look for Rùnach behind me," she said.

"Oh, I imagine he receives his share of courtesies. Lovely man,

that one. I imagine he accepts them politely but doesn't need them
for the sake of his ego."

"Nay, he knows who he is."

"Do you, my girl?"

Aisling took a deep breath. "There are times I'm not sure."

"What was the first spell you used, Aisling?" Muinear asked.

"Do you not know?"

"I think you know the answer to that already."

"What I think is that there must be a very select dinner group
comprised of you, Soilléir of Cothromaiche, Uachdaran of Léige, and
perhaps even Sìle of Tòrr Dòrainn, who meet regularly and discuss
how best to torment those with much less knowledge than you have."

Muinear laughed. "You might be surprised to learn how close
that is to the truth. And you forgot Queen Brèagha and Eulasaid
of Camanaë."

Aisling started to ask her just how many people she knew, but
she shut her mouth around the question. She wasn't entirely sure
she hadn't heard Rùnach ask that same thing of various souls over
the course of their journey. He had never been particularly happy
with the answer, so perhaps it was best she remain ignorant. She
looked at Muinear.

"If you'll have the tale from me," she said, "I'll tell you. Rùnach
and I had just escaped Gair's hiding hole in the mountains using a
rune of opening Còir of Tòrr Dòrainn had gifted Rùnach. We
dropped into a river that carried us away—in truth, I was sure it
would drown us. There were things in that river—" She shivered.
"Unpleasant things. So I said the last thing that came to mind
before I thought I would simply consign myself to a watery grave."

"What was that?"

"I wanted light." Aisling shook her head at the memory. "And
the magic gave me light."

"Of course it did, love," Muinear said gently. "I'm sure it was happy to be of use to you."

"I believe it was."

Muinear stopped in front of a simple door made of a pale, blond wood. "Light, Aisling, is what allows us to see, gives us hope. I think you'll find the same thing here."

Aisling took a deep steadying breath, then nodded. She waited until Muinear had opened the door, then stepped inside.

And she caught her breath.

She walked into the chamber and stopped in the middle of it, in front of a wheel that looked so much like the one she'd made from Soilléir's spell of essence changing that she had to look at it twice to make certain it wasn't. She put her hand on it, felt Bruadair sigh a little at the touch, then looked around her. She turned around, looking at walls she had first thought were covered with tapestries . . . only those tapestries weren't cloth. They were made of events.

She turned around and around until a shaft of sunlight came through a ceiling partly made of glass and lit up her wheel. It shone through one of the scenes as well, turning it into something less than reality but slightly more than a dream.

Unbidden, the memory of the first time she'd touched a spinning wheel came to her. She had been standing in the very humble home of a widow, looking at her worn, wooden wheel, and knowing that if she touched it, she would die. But she'd reached out to it just the same, sending it spinning without touching it at all.

A vision had come to her of standing on the edge of a cliff she now realized was the bluff outside the palace. The sky had been full of colors, colors she had never before seen and suspected she never would again if she didn't do something to save Bruadair, and scenes of battle, scenes of sorrow and delight—

Much like what she was looking at presently.

She looked for Muinear. "What—"

"The world," Muinear said with a smile. "As it passes by."

"And what is my task?"

Muinear sat in a comfortable chair Aisling hadn't noticed until that point. "Tasks," she corrected gently. "Your most important task, of course, is to oversee the other dreamspinners, adding your own touches to what they send out. It is their task to provide the weavers with something to weave for more substantial intrusions into the events of the world."

"Weavers?" Aisling echoed. "There are weavers?"

"*You* have weavers, Aisling, who weave what you and the Council will spin. You will learn to pull threads from what passes before you here in this chamber, as you've learned to find bits and pieces of things along your way here."

Aisling put her hand to the little purse she'd been given in Cothromaiche only to realize she'd left it in her chamber. She looked at Muinear in alarm, but her great-grandmother shook her head.

"Not to worry. No one will disturb your things." She considered the moving scenes for a moment or two, then looked at Aisling. "We take our turns here in the world, Aisling, for whatever length of time we're allotted. Part of the task of each soul who takes breath is to contribute something to the body of creative work, if I can call it such a pedestrian thing. All the tales written, the songs composed, the mighty deeds done, the magic wrought, all those things make up the fabric of our world, becoming a grand tapestry of the Nine Kingdoms. Part of your task is to decide how that tapestry is best woven. Though, I hasten to add, you need not do the weaving yourself."

"Thankfully."

Muinear smiled. "I understand. I far prefer to spin as well. You can, of course, weave your own tapestry—and you will—but that will come later, when you have the leisure to see how you might draw on what you see that moves you."

"Single words and simple thoughts?"

"You've been talking to Soilléir, I see." She smiled. "He is a master at letting the world go on its way without interference, though in this instance, he has been almost as involved as the rest of us. There are times when the fate of the world hangs in the balance that you must perhaps do things you might not otherwise." She sat back and smiled. "So, what do you think of your chamber?"

Aisling sank down on a stool in front of her wheel. "I'm not sure what to think. I don't even know where to begin."

Muinear cocked an ear, then looked at the doorway. "Your answer might be arriving, I daresay. I'll go—"

"Nay," Aisling said, holding out her hand to stop the woman from rising. "I'll answer it."

It was Rùnach. She held open the door and motioned for him to come inside. He did, then stopped so suddenly, he almost lost his balance. He looked around with wide eyes.

"Well," he said finally.

"I couldn't agree more."

"May I?"

Aisling looked at Muinear, but her great-grandmother only waved her on.

"The chamber is yours, my love. Make use of it how you will."

Rùnach reached for her hand briefly. "This is . . . unbelievable."

She couldn't answer. All she could do was watch him as he walked around the chamber, pausing to look at the scenes being played out there in front of him. He lingered an especially long time in the spot where the sun shone. She realized with a start that he was looking at her.

"Your eyes are the color of the sea."

She looked at him in surprise. "What?"

"The sea in the south," he clarified. "That sort of bluish green that has color but doesn't." He smiled. "I've been trying to decide for some time now, actually, just what color they were."

"Well, that's settled."

He smiled, then his smile faded. "I'm sorry to interrupt, but I'm wondering if you would be willing to come look at something and give me your opinion."

"You look so serious," she murmured.

He hesitated, then shook his head. "Just come and see what you think."

She took his hand and walked with him to the door. He paused in front of Muinear's chair.

"Would you care to come, my lady?"

She popped up out of her chair with the energy of a woman a fraction of her age. "Of course, Rùnach. Where are we congregating?"

"Uabhann's chambers, if you don't mind."

Aisling watched her great-grandmother take Rùnach's arm. "I never mind. He is one of my favorite people. So many interesting things rattling around in his head."

Aisling didn't dare ask what those things might be, but she was happy to exchange a look with Rùnach before he nodded and walked with them down the passageway that led toward a chamber she wasn't entirely comfortable with. Then again, Muinear had a point. Lord Dread was full of all sorts of observations that he seemed to take genuine delight in.

She expected to find the entire collection of dreamspinners in Uabhann's chambers, but it was just him standing next to his table, leaning on his hands as he looked at the map that he and his cohorts had put together the night before. He looked over his shoulder when he heard them come inside his chamber, then immediately turned and made her a bow.

"Oh," she said uncomfortably, "you don't need to do that."

"Yes, my lady Aisling, I do," he said seriously. "If you'll permit me the privilege."

Well, if there was anyone she didn't suppose she would be arguing with, it was Uabhann. She nodded, smiled as best she could, then looked at Rùnach and waited. He took a deep breath.

"I've discovered something."

"On the map?"

He nodded. "Unfortunately. Or perhaps not, if we look at it the right way. Let's just say I think we've solved the mystery of where the magic is being drained from. Where's it's going *to* is another story, but perhaps for now that is less important than this."

"Stanch the wound first?" she said quietly.

"Exactly. Let me show you what I've seen."

She stood with Rùnach at the table and looked at the map. It didn't look any different—or any less unsettling—than it had the night before. She glanced at Rùnach.

"How do you think Acair discovered all this?"

"I would like to say he eavesdropped on someone far more intelligent than he, but I'm afraid he's canny enough to have mapped this out all on his own, damn him for it just the same." He sighed and gestured to the map. "What do you see?"

She looked but saw nothing different from what she'd seen the night before. The world was there, outlined faintly as if borders didn't matter as much as the portals to be found within those borders. There was nothing that stood out, nothing that seemed any less unsettling than what she'd already dealt with the night before. She looked at Rùnach and shrugged helplessly.

"It looks the same to me."

"So I thought this morning. And then I realized there was something tucked into the pocket I'd made on the inside of the back leather binding."

"Clever you."

"Aren't I?" he said wryly. "It was covered with a spell, but apparently Acair is equally clever because he unraveled it. Or his mother did it for him. The material point being, there was something tucked inside that pocket." He took a folded sheaf, unfolded it, then smoothed it out. "Does this look at all familiar?"

She took the page but saw nothing but more scratches. The sheaf was thinner somehow, though, as if it had either been made poorly or had been meant to go over something else. She studied it, then looked at the map laid out on the table. "If I could hold the entire thing up to the window—"

The table began to glow, which made her jump.

She looked at Uabhann in surprise. "Did you do that?"

He inclined his head. "Night light. Very useful for keeping nightmares at bay."

And he would certainly know. She looked at the table, looked at the sheaf in her hand, then held it over the map to see if it might match anything there.

She was somehow unsurprised to find it did.

She was, however, very surprised to see how when she laid it down, there was a particular spot in Bruadair that was emphasized. She pulled her hand back because she feared its trembling might disturb the entire puzzle. She took an unsteady breath, then looked at Rùnach.

"The Guild?"

He nodded. "I think so."

She looked at Muinear. "Did you know?"

Muinear looked, for the first time Aisling could remember,

actually troubled. "I didn't. Rùnach, are you certain that is where the siphoning is occurring?"

"I'm more sure than I think I would like to be," he said slowly. "But there is only one way to find out for certain."

"Agreed," Muinear said.

"I'll leave Aisling here—"

"Of course you won't," Aisling said, before she thought better of it. And after she'd thought better of it, she looked at him with an expression she hoped said all she couldn't say. "You won't."

"It won't be safe," Rùnach said seriously. "Acair will likely be there. Sglaimir, assuredly."

"But I know the Guild," Aisling said.

"You'll spend the rest of today telling me what you know, then. I'll leave tonight and see to it."

"But—"

"I've already been there once, Aisling. And it's not as if I'm planning to go knock on the front door and alert the Guildmistress to my intentions. I'll slip over the walls—"

Muinear shook her head. "In this, my boy, I have to be the bearer of very evil tidings. There is absolutely no possible way to enter the Guild without Iochdmhor knowing you have. The spell is impenetrable."

Aisling watched Rùnach frown and wished she had the wherewithal to join him. All she could do was stand there and feel the cold hand of doom come to rest on her shoulder.

"Not even with a change of essence?" Rùnach asked carefully.

"Impenetrable," Muinear repeated. "We've tested it a thousand ways with every spell possible." She looked at him seriously. "Even with a spell or two of your father's, if you're curious. And don't tell Uachdaran or Sìle that their collection is a little less secure than they might want to believe."

Aisling would have smiled but she was too busy trying to simply breathe. There was no worse hell than the Guild . . .

"I can't let Aisling go back inside," Rùnach said quietly. "Lady Muinear, there are simply things you cannot expect me to do."

"I'm not sure, Rùnach my lad, that you have any choice."

He looked ashen. Aisling wasn't entirely sure she didn't look the same way. She took a deep breath and pushed aside thoughts she didn't want to entertain.

"Let's say we could find a way inside the Guild," she said, "what then? If we stop the leak, we stop any more magic from leaving, but that doesn't solve getting back what's already gone."

Rùnach turned to sit on the edge of the table. "True enough. For all I know, there's no way to get it back."

"But it has weakened Bruadair," she said quietly. "I can feel that."

"But if we stop the flow—"

She shook her head. "It will take centuries to rebuild what has been lost, if it could even be rebuilt." She took a deep breath. "We'll have to call it back."

He grasped the edge of the table and looked at her. He looked paler than he had, if such a thing were possible.

"I don't think I have a spell for that," he admitted slowly. "Well, save my father's spell of Diminishing."

"And what does that do?"

"It's what he used to drain mages of their power," he said grimly. "It was what Acair tried to use on me in front of my father's bolt-hole."

"It wasn't very well done," she said.

"One could hope Acair hasn't refined it since then," Rùnach said seriously, "though I wouldn't be surprised to learn he had." He considered, then shook his head. "I don't know, Aisling. I think I could perhaps draw all the rivers of magic back into Bruadair, but what do I do with them then? I know my father's spell, but I can't guarantee what it will do here and I'm honestly not sure I dare use it."

"I wouldn't suggest it," Uabhann said. "Very nasty things come with that spell, if you don't mind my saying so." He shook his head. "The dreams your father has." He shivered. "Unpleasant."

Aisling was tempted to smile. "And do you help them along?"

"Well," he said modestly, "that *is* what I do. But in Gair's case, unless I'm feeling particularly cheeky, I just leave him to his own devices. He frightens *me*."

Rùnach patted the table next to him. Aisling was happy to lean for a bit, even happier to have his arm around her.

"I have been thinking about the magic that's already gone," he offered. "What's been unraveled, if we can call it that."

"Unraveled," she echoed. "What a thought."

"It is," he agreed. He paused, then looked at her. "It occurred to me that perhaps there is a way to call it home."

She knew what he was getting at before he even said the words. "You think I can spin it back here."

"It seems logical," he said, "though I can't believe I'm saying as much. The thought is not so much ridiculous as it is terrifying."

"It might be difficult to contain something that's been loosed," she said, finding it hard to speak for the sudden dryness in her mouth.

He shot her a wry look. "Well, we could make a journey to Shettlestoune, I suppose, and ask my father how that goes, but I think I might have enough experience with it to agree with you." He looked off into the distance for several minutes in silence, then looked at her. "It would be interesting, though, wouldn't it, if you could draw it all back here to Bruadair."

"That would be a fairly large bobbin, I imagine."

·

"I daresay." He continued to look at her. "It might be good to have help."

"Can you spin?"

He smiled, pained. "You know I can't. But I imagine you could think of a few spinners, couldn't you?"

She wrapped her arms around herself. "This is becoming a very uncomfortable conversation."

"Your brother's lady wife, Princess Sarah," Muinear put in carefully. "She's a spinner, isn't she?"

Aisling watched Rùnach look at Muinear for a moment or two in silence, then let out his breath slowly.

"She is."

"Are you thinking to have her come here?" Aisling asked in surprise.

Rùnach shook his head. "Sarah spun my father's power when it was hanging in the air between him and someone else, which is what I think your great-grandmother is getting at. But that was just a single person's power and all she had was a spindle." He paused. "I don't think she has the power to create a wheel of sunlight, which you do. That might be enough to do what's needful."

"Soilléir will frown at me if I do that again."

"But Bruadair won't," Rùnach said.

"There is something else you might want to consider," Muinear said, "not to throw a pole between the spokes of your tidy wheel or anything."

Rùnach smiled faintly. "My lady?"

"If you discovered this, Rùnach my dear, don't you think it's possible others might have discovered the same thing? Or have known about it long before now?"

Rùnach dragged his hand through his hair. "The thought has occurred to me."

"What about the thought that there might be those looking for you to attempt to slip over the Guild's walls?"

He sighed. "What else am I to do?"

"We," Aisling said, though it was the last thing she wanted to say. "What else are *we* to do."

Muinear looked for the first time slightly weary. "I think, children," she said with a sigh, "that you'll need to go to Beul, but I'm not sure you can go as you are."

"More patina?" Rùnach asked grimly.

Muinear smiled briefly. "I noticed that Soilléir had applied a bit, which didn't surprise me. But nay. You'll need to do something a bit more drastic, I think."

"More drastic than a change of essence?" Rùnach asked in surprise. "Is there such a thing?"

"Well," Muinear said slowly, "if you were the Guildmistress and you were expecting someone, let's leave aside who for the moment, to attempt to come into your domain, what's the last thing you would expect?"

Aisling felt Rùnach go very still.

"I would never expect someone to simply walk in," he said. His expression was very grim. "Shall I give myself up to the Guildmistress and allow her to chain me to a loom?"

"Nay," Muinear said softly. "I think that perhaps Aisling should."

Aisling had no idea if the conversation continued past that point, because she did the most reasonable and useful thing she'd done in at least a score and seven years.

She fainted.

Eighteen

❧

It could be said that there were occasions when reminding oneself of all the miserable places one had been and terrible situations one had survived was quite useful. It gave a certain perspective to the dire straits currently being contemplated. Unfortunately, there were just some situations that couldn't be made any less horrifying, no matter what one tried.

Rùnach looked at the Guild in front of him and wondered if he were equal to thinking of anything miserable and terrible enough to possibly mitigate the horrors he fully expected his current locale to offer.

And not to him.

"I don't like this," he murmured, not for the first time.

"I don't see any other possibility," Bristeadh said very quietly, perhaps for the fourth or fifth time.

Rùnach had lost count.

"Let's raze the damned place and see what's in the cellar," Rùnach suggested.

"I won't dignify that with a response."

Rùnach would have looked at his love's father, but he'd been having the same conversation with the man for hours. He'd seen the absolutely haunted look in Bristeadh's eye. He didn't suppose seeing it once again would solve anything. He also imagined that allowing the man to see the same look in his own eye wasn't going to do anything useful.

He looked at Aisling who was standing a pace or two away, as still as if she'd been a statue. He couldn't begin to imagine what was going through her head. She'd fainted at the thought of going back into the Guild, though she'd claimed that had been because she'd been overwhelmed by lack of food and too much excitement over spinning and, well, other things she hadn't been able to articulate with any success.

Rùnach suspected she'd been lying through her teeth.

He shook his head, something he'd been doing for hours. He looked at Bristeadh and shook his head again.

"I can't do this," he said. "I can't let her go back inside there. Not like this."

Bristeadh looked at him for several minutes in silence, then sighed. "All I can say, son, is that I understand exactly what you're feeling."

Rùnach closed his eyes briefly. "My sympathy for you is complete. I'm not sure how you managed this."

"There was no other alternative, Rùnach," Bristeadh said, then he cleared his throat as quietly as possible. "Better the Guild's horrors where she would be anonymous than out in the world where I had no means of protecting her. We didn't dare even leave her in Ciaradh given what had happened to my mother-in-law. At least Iochdmhor had no idea who she was at the time, so she was relatively safe. Miserable, but safe."

"And now?"

"I don't know what Iochdmhor knows. She was obviously at my house recently, but whether or not she connects that place to me, I can't say." He lifted one shoulder in the slightest of shrugs. "I don't think any of us are safe, but I imagine we never expected we would be."

"And if she connects you with Aisling?"

"Then she'll slay me on the spot," Bristeadh said, "though I don't think she will. Far better to make me pay dearly for not returning with her prize as quickly as I should have."

Rùnach suppressed the urge to shake his head again. Their plan was to have Bristeadh drag Aisling into the Guild and present her as a trophy, Rùnach hard on his heels with a sorry tale about wanting to collect the bounty on her head given that her parents had refused to pay him what they owed him. There were more variables with the plan than he cared for, mostly concerning Aisling's foster parents. There was no way of knowing whether or not they'd talked to the Guildmistress after he and Aisling had visited.

He didn't like uncertainty. He and Keir had gone over every possible scenario before going to Ruamharaiche's well, endlessly and behind their mother's back. She had done the same thing with Keir, but Rùnach had never been included in the conversations. His brother was older than he was by several years, so he'd known that Sarait was trying to spare him any distress. Of course Keir had divulged everything she'd said just the same and they'd factored it into their plans and into the plans they had made with their mother. Every damned possibility had been accounted for.

Well, save the one that Gair would slay his three middle sons whilst taking their power with a single word.

Rùnach had no desire to make that same mistake again, but there were simply too many variables to account for them all. The

Guildmistress, Sglaimir, Acair, and the magic sink itself: all things he couldn't predict and couldn't control. And he with magic that wasn't what he wanted it to be, Aisling with her essence as hidden as she and Muinear could hide it, and Bristeadh without any magic at all.

What he wouldn't have given for a contingent of powerful relatives, though he supposed if his grandfather arrived on wing he would simply attempt to order things about to his satisfaction and make an unholy mess of it all.

He looked at Bristeadh. "I don't like this."

"What other choice do we have?"

"None," Rùnach said, resigned. "But I don't like it."

Bristeadh put his hand on Rùnach's shoulder briefly. "There is no one else to do this, Rùnach."

"What of the other dreamspinners?" Rùnach asked wearily. "What of her bloody steward? Has he no magic?"

"Don't you think that if there were any other way, I would take it?"

"You, without magic?" Rùnach said, perhaps a bit more sharply than he'd intended.

"I would be fighting to the death to keep her from that accursed place if it took all my strength to my last breath," Bristeadh said evenly. "As I believe you would do. Unfortunately, Aisling is the only one who can do this. She is the First."

"Then sell me instead," Rùnach said. The words came out of his mouth and he realized they were completely daft, but once they were hanging in the air in front of him, they made perfect sense. "We'll use a spell of essence changing and you can return me in her place and I'll see to things." He looked around himself. "Where is that damned Soilléir when you need him?"

A throat cleared itself from behind him. "Here."

Rùnach wasn't at all certain that was a welcome voice. He looked over his shoulder to find standing behind him none other than Soil-léir of Cothromaiche himself, dressed as a fop. He frowned.

"How did you get here?"

"The usual way."

Rùnach supposed it might be useful to ask a few pointed questions about Bruadair and its environs, but he suspected he would have the same answers he'd had at Inntrig, which were none. He looked over Soilléir's shoulder to find Ochadius of Riamh standing there, dressed like a palace guard.

"What are you doing?" Rùnach demanded. "Escorting us inside?"

"I have other things to see to," Ochadius said hoarsely, "though if you find Acair, tie him up and leave him for me. I have a few things to repay him for, should I have the good fortune to find his throat within reach of my grasping hands."

Rùnach winced. "I appreciate the time you bought us at Taigh Hall."

"Happy to have been of service. Now, if you all will excuse me, I'll be off to make my own pieces of mischief."

And with that, he walked away and disappeared into the darkness.

Rùnach turned to Soilléir. "Make me look like Aisling. I'll do what needs to be done, slay them all, then she can walk in and see to whatever's left."

Soilléir looked at him for far longer in silence than Rùnach was comfortable with. He started to speak, but stopped when Aisling put her hand on his arm. Rùnach realized only then that she had come to stand next to him.

"I must go."

Rùnach closed his eyes briefly, then looked at her. She looked so calm, he flinched. He reached for her hand and pulled her into his arms, holding her close. She wasn't shaking; he was. He looked over her head at Soilléir.

"Very well," he said quietly. "We'll go as planned."

Soilléir's expression was very serious. "I've done what I can."

"I know."

"I can do no more."

"I know that too. Stay out of sight."

"Are you protecting me now?" Soilléir asked with a faint smile.

"Yes," Rùnach said simply.

Soilléir looked a little winded, which Rùnach supposed was nothing more than he deserved. If they survived the day, he supposed he might look back on that moment and enjoy his erstwhile host and mentor's inability to catch his breath.

He looked at Bristeadh. "Ready?"

Aisling's father nodded. Rùnach realized that Aisling was watching him, which made him wish he dared hold her one more time. Not one last time, but just once more before they walked into darkness he didn't want to try to imagine. But he knew the time for that had passed and there was nothing to be done but walk forward. He couldn't even bring himself to call the start of the battle, he simply waited for Bristeadh to take the lead and march them straight into hell.

It was almost as terrible as he'd imagined it would be. Bristeadh walked out of the shadows, dragging Aisling by the arm, and marched across the road right up to the Guild's front gates. Rùnach followed hard on his heels. The Guild guards were an unfortunately alert lot, surprisingly alert, actually, given that it was only a couple of hours before dawn.

That made him extremely nervous.

They were allowed in, however, without any fuss. He trotted out his best imitation of his grandfather, but even that didn't do anything to mitigate his unease. He stood in the Guild's vestibule, affecting a look of boredom laced with disdain coupled with a bit of outrage, and wondered how that might go over with anyone who was watching.

Time passed with excruciating slowness, though he supposed he expected nothing else. He waited with a fair bit of manufactured impatience until the Guildmistress herself sauntered into view. It was an effort not to flinch. If nothing else could be said about the woman, it had to be said that Iochdmhor of wherever she'd come from was terrifying. For a moment, he had the most overwhelming urge to fling himself forward and confess all his crimes.

Then again, his father had inspired that sort of thing now and again, but Rùnach was fairly sure Gair had used a spell. He didn't sense any magic coming from the woman who'd stopped in front of them and was looking at Aisling as if she'd been something recently scraped off the bottom of her shoe.

"I heard, but didn't believe," she drawled. "I see I was mistaken." She looked at Bristeadh. "You were successful."

"It took longer than I anticipated, madame."

Rùnach found himself under her scrutiny next.

"And what are *you* doing back here, merchant?"

"Her parents were unwilling to reimburse me for my goods and my time," he said with a careless shrug. "Since I provided an escort for these two over the past several hours, I thought you might want to perhaps reward me for my trouble."

"I daresay I might," she said, looking at him as if she didn't quite see him. "I think I might want to repay you handsomely for your efforts." She looked at the guard to her right. "Take George to the dungeon."

Rùnach realized that's what Bristeadh was being called only after realizing that the Guild had a dungeon and that Aisling's father was going to be put in it. He forced himself not to react as Bristeadh was led off. A rescue would be accomplished soon enough if he could simply keep Aisling—

"And you," the Guildmistress said, stepping close to Aisling and looking at her with an unwholesome light in her eye, "you, little runaway. Know that if it were my decision, I would have you flayed to within an inch of your life." She stepped back. "Unfortunately, that decision is not mine. Guards, take her to the sinner's dorm."

Rùnach hardly dared attempt to identify the look in the woman's eye, but there was definitely madness lurking there. It took all his willpower to keep from pulling Aisling behind him, but he forced himself to remain still as she was taken roughly by the arms as if she were somehow thought capable of overcoming everyone in the Guild and needed to be restrained.

Which, he supposed, might well be the case in the end.

"We'll go with her," the Guildmistress said easily, "then I'll show you a guest chamber where you can rest from your journey. We'll discuss payment in the morning."

Rùnach inclined his head because it was expected. He followed along after the guards and had to suppress the urge to knock one of them across the room after the man shoved Aisling so hard inside a chamber that she went sprawling. The door was slammed and locked without delay.

"And now you, good sir," the Guildmistress said. "Follow me, if you will."

Rùnach ignored the hair standing up on the back of his neck and followed her without balking. That she didn't look back at him even once made him wonder, but what was he to do? He had to be inside and this was the price he had to pay.

He was shown into a surprisingly luxurious chamber, though he realized he shouldn't have expected anything else. Appearances needed to be kept up, no doubt.

The Guildmistress stood back and smiled. "Only the finest," she said smoothly.

Rùnach hesitated, but hopefully so slightly that she hadn't noticed. He crossed the threshold and walked into the middle of the chamber.

The door slammed shut behind him and a key turned in the lock.

He stood where he was for a moment or two, wondering why he was in the slightest bit surprised, then walked back over to the door and made a great production of rattling the knob.

"Let me out!" he shouted.

"It's for your own safety, of course. I'll keep a guard here for the remainder of the night, again for your protection."

"Well," he said loudly, "unorthodox, but I suppose there is merit to it."

She made no comment, but he hadn't expected anything else. He made himself at home on a chair and wondered how long he dared wait before he picked the lock, disabled the guard standing outside, and went about his business.

He didn't dare wait long.

Two hours later, he deposited his very pedestrian lock-picking tools in his pocket, thanking his late brother Gille for having decided it would be a brilliant skill for them all to have, and very quietly opened the door.

The guard there whirled around. Rùnach would have apologized for shoving the heel of his hand into the guard's nose, then following that up with the hilt of his sword against the man's head, but he supposed there was no point. He dragged the man inside and deposited him on the bed. It would probably be the best night's sleep the poor fool had had in years.

He substituted the man's cloak for his own and hoped that would be enough to at least keep other guards at bay long enough for him to get close enough to render them likewise useless. He left the chamber, locking the door behind him, then walked down the passageway in the direction he'd come earlier.

Guards only nodded to him, which he supposed was nothing short of a miracle. He nodded back, complaining occasionally about the earliness of the hour and the quality of the buttery offerings. No one questioned him as to why he was roaming the passageways, so he continued on until he had no choice but to make a decision between Aisling and her father.

There was no choice.

He found the dormitories through sheer dumb luck and perhaps only because he continued to wander until he found the shabbiest part of the Guild. He knew he shouldn't have suspected anything else. He wasn't even surprised to find there was no guard at the door, though he wouldn't have been surprised to find the chamber itself full of men armed to the teeth, waiting for him.

Instead, it turned out to be a rather small chamber full of only a handful of beds stacked three high. He closed the door softly behind him and wasn't sure where to begin looking—

Someone took him by the arm.

He almost jumped out of his skin. He was vastly relieved to see it was just Aisling. He was less relieved to see that she hardly seemed to be breathing. He took her hand quickly, but her fingers were like ice. He understood completely. He had a case of nerves he hadn't had since the last time he'd gone inside his father's private solar to nose about in his books whilst his father had been napping in his chair. He was too old to have to remind himself to breathe, but there it was.

He opened the door silently, looked out into the passageway, but saw nothing out of the ordinary. He drew Aisling out of the chamber behind him, then flattened himself against the wall.

"My father," she whispered. "We must find him."

He looked at her. "I don't think we dare—"

"I can't leave him there."

"We won't," he said quietly, "but if we go now, we'll likely wake the whole damned place."

She looked at the ceiling for a moment or two, then at him. "If we don't survive, he likely won't either."

"I didn't want to say it, but aye."

"Then let's see that we survive."

"Any ideas where to start?"

"I would say her private chambers, but I'm not sure I can stomach that to start with," she said grimly. She paused, then looked at him, dismayed. "I thought that perhaps once we reached the source of the—what would you call it?"

"Sink?"

"Aye, that. I thought perhaps the closer we came, the easier it would be to sense it, but I don't feel anything. Beul is almost empty of any magic I might be able to call on."

"That might be to our advantage," he offered. "Perhaps our adversaries will find themselves in the same situation."

"One could hope," she agreed. "But that doesn't aid us now. I suppose all we can do is roam the halls and see what we find."

"I take it you never did this before?"

She closed her eyes briefly. "Nay."

He didn't dare ask for the particulars. "Let's just walk," he suggested, "and see if we run into anything interesting."

An hour later he regretted heartily having suggested that. If picking the lock on his luxurious accommodations had been easy, and slipping down the passageway slightly less easy, then trying to find from where Bruadair's magic was being drained was almost impossible. They had hidden in various corners, overhangs, and empty chambers until Rùnach had wished they'd had a better idea coming inside where to look.

He finally leaned back against a doorway with Aisling and looked at her. "Any ideas?"

"I—"

The doorway opened suddenly behind him and he went sprawling across the threshold. Aisling fell alongside him with a squeak. She scrambled to her feet, then hauled him up to his. He smiled apologetically, then plunged the hapless, no doubt quite innocent, Guild guard who stepped into his line of sight into insensibility. He flexed his fingers a bit, wishing he'd been more accustomed to that sort of thing, then realized Aisling wasn't moving. He looked at her quickly, but she was simply standing there, gaping at something in the distance. He frowned, then turned to look at what she was seeing. He caught the door before it closed loudly, then let it slip shut with a soft click.

"I didn't know this was here," she whispered.

He imagined she couldn't help but wish she didn't still.

It was a garden, or, rather, it had been a garden. He suspected that in times past it had been an absolutely spectacular place. The only light there was from a dawn that had apparently bloomed whilst they'd been roaming the halls, but even that light revealed a glorious setting. He could see skeletons of trees and shrubs, long stretches of earth where flowers had no doubt been planted in pleasing patterns, numerous places to sit and enjoy the beauty there.

Now, it looked as the rest of Bruadair did, as if death had breathed on everything in sight and killed it without mercy.

In the middle of the garden lay—or, rather, had lain—a fountain. The only reason he knew that was that although the top two tiers were obviously missing, the bottom basin was still intact. It was enormous, actually. He supposed he could have stretched himself from one side to the other and scarce been able to keep himself out of the water. He realized with a start that the bottom basin was definitely not empty, and it wasn't water that filled it.

Aisling started forward, but he stopped her with a hand on her arm. She looked up at him.

"That's it," she murmured. "You know what I'm talking about."

He did. It was where Bruadair's magic was being syphoned off to go heaven only knew where and through who knew which countries. He took her hand.

"I don't want you falling in."

She shivered. "I suppose that's a possibility."

"Not one I'll let happen," he said. "Let me go first."

She nodded, but didn't release his hand and didn't walk anywhere but beside him. He supposed there was no convincing her to do anything other than that.

He approached the fountain. It took no especial powers of observation to see that magic was indeed being drained into the lowest bowl there. Or, rather, that magic had once been drained there. Echoes of it lingered against stone that had turned black. Rùnach knew the stone had been a beautiful slate blue before because there were patches of that color still visible amid the ruin.

"What to do now?" Aisling asked quietly.

"Well," a voice said from behind them, "why don't you let me suggest a few activities?"

Rùnach whirled around almost knocking Aisling over. He caught her by the arm and wasn't sure what to do with himself. If he put himself in front of her, he might accidentally push her into the vortex behind him. If he left her beside him, she would be out in the open and more unprotected than he might like. Because he wasn't facing the Guildmistress, he was facing Acair of Ceangail.

Acair seemed to be considering something, though Rùnach didn't dare speculate what. He wasn't reaching for a spell, which perhaps was the best they could hope for at the moment.

"How did you get inside Bruadair?" Rùnach asked.

"Bribed a border guard. You?"

"The same."

"Bloody ugly country," Acair said with a shudder. "At least

what I've seen of it which, fortunately, hasn't been all that much."
He looked at Aisling, dismissed her, then looked back at Rùnach.
"Let's cut out the chitchat, shall we? Give me what I want and I'll
let you and your little wench there live."

"What do you want?" Rùnach asked. "Or should I bother to ask?"

"I want what we all wanted, even you, little brother," Acair
said. "Father's spell of Diminishing."

Rùnach supposed there was no point in denying what Acair
was saying, though the only reason he had wanted his father's
spell had been so he could counter it. The only reason. He might
not be able to say anything else in his own defense, but in that, he
could defend his motives without hesitation. He shrugged.

"You should have just taken it from my book—oh, wait." Rùnach smiled, pained. "You couldn't get past the spell locking those
damned pages together, could you?"

Acair threw a rather pointed spell of death at him, but Aisling
caught it and spun it around what was left of a small, rickety
wooden table. The table made a horrendous squeak as it collapsed
in on itself. Rùnach looked at Acair. He was gaping at Aisling.

"What . . ."

"Too complicated for you to understand," Rùnach said regretfully.
"But what you might be able to understand is that you won't have
anything from me if I'm dead."

Acair shook his head. "I'm continually baffled as to why I didn't
kill you when you were a lad—nay, I know. Because then I couldn't
have what I want. Yes, I understand, Rùnach. But I'll have it now, I
believe."

Rùnach scratched his head. "You, against us? How quaint."

"Oh, it's not just me," Acair said softly.

And apparently it wasn't.

Nineteen

❧

Aisling could hardly believe what she was seeing, but there was no denying it. Rùnach's bastard brother, Acair, stood there, flanked by none other than the Guildmistress and, of all people, Sglaimir the usurping king. Acair nodded crisply to Sglaimir.

"See to them. Or have that horrible woman there do the deed. You said she has magic, though I've seen no indication of it."

"Neither have I," Aisling said before she thought better of it. "I don't think she has any skill but cruelty."

Acair looked at her briefly, then nodded reluctantly. "There is that, and it makes me a little queasy to agree with you on anything, but given that I intend to kill your lover there, perhaps that camaraderie won't last."

"Bloody hell," Sglaimir complained, "do you *ever* shut up? I'm surprised your father didn't slay *you* simply to spare himself having to listen to you blather on and on."

Acair looked at him coldly. "You forget yourself, my lad. *I* am the reason you find yourself on your comfortable perch."

"Lad," Sglaimir echoed in disbelief. "I'm a century older than you are, you idiot!"

"And I was working great magic when you were still trying to set your ugly sister's skirts on fire!"

Sglaimir's mouth fell open. "*You* wouldn't recognize great magic if it came up to you and bit you on the arse!"

The conversation, if that's what it could be called, deteriorated from there. Spells began to fly again amongst the trio in front of her. Or, rather, between Acair and Sglaimir. The Guildmistress seemed to have very little magic of her own, or perhaps she didn't know how to use what she had. Aisling honestly didn't care which it was as long as the woman refrained from any demonstration of what she could or couldn't do.

She found herself catching more than one stray spell on the dagger Soilléir had gifted her, as it seemed to function quite well as a spindle. Rùnach absently reached up and batted away everything else that came their way. Obviously his time in the lists with Muinear hadn't been wasted.

Acair's spells were nasty, true, but they were unwieldy and didn't seem to work as he intended them to. Aisling was surprised, but then again, it was Bruadair after all. The only thing she didn't find reassuring was how weak her country's magic was in the garden. She wasn't sure she could count on any of it to aid her.

She leaned closer to Rùnach. "What do you think?"

"If the fate of the world weren't at stake, I might be looking for a chair to use whilst watching the spectacle."

She smiled. "What do you think of their spells?"

Rùnach seemed to stop just short of stroking his chin. "Standard fare for your country, wouldn't you say? They definitely seem to be expecting different results from what they're getting. You would think by this time they would have realized what they can and cannot do."

"Maybe they've spent too much time talking," she said, "and too little time doing."

He shot her a brief smile. "I think you might be right. I wonder how much longer they're going to go on and what we can do until they stop?"

"I'd sit on the edge of the fountain, but I don't think we dare," she said.

"I don't think so either." He cleared his throat loudly. "Just so I'm clear on it, what is it you're doing here?"

The Guildmistress pointed at Aisling. "We want her."

"Why?" Rùnach asked. "What could she possibly have that you want?"

"*I* don't want her," Sglaimir said bluntly. "I want a throne. Actually, I'll have the one I'm sitting on, the one *you* promised me, Acair you treacherous bastard, if I would help you get in and out of the borders."

"You could have done that with just gold," Rùnach put in.

"Shut up," Sglaimir snarled at him before he turned back to Acair. "I have spent *years* aiding you in this stupid plan to strip Bruadair of its magic, which has done nothing but leave me in an ugly city with no proper subjects to rule over. And all the while I've been waiting for you to find that spell of your father's which I don't believe exists—"

"Oh, it exists," Rùnach said.

Aisling elbowed him, then ducked with him as Sglaimir tossed a rather wobbly spell of something their way. Aisling watched it drift past them, then looked at Rùnach.

"What was that?"

"I have no idea," he said with a shrug. He looked over his shoulder as the spell fell into the vortex behind them. "I just don't want to follow it to where it's gone. Let's move away from this thing, shall we?"

She was happy to do so, especially given that the two mages standing thirty paces away from them didn't seem to be paying them any heed. She supposed she and Rùnach might have even managed to escape the garden if that had been their desire while Acair and Sglaimir continued to argue. Or perhaps not. The Guildmistress sent her a look that had her freezing in her tracks in spite of herself.

The Guildmistress clapped her hands together sharply. "Stop it, you fools," she said. "Have you forgotten what it is we're doing here?"

Aisling watched the two men in front of them snarl out a few more curses before they put up their spells, as it were. Sglaimir was obviously furious at what he no doubt considered being double-crossed. Acair, apparently the perpetrator of that injustice, was looking at the would-be king of Bruadair as if he simply couldn't believe what he was forced to endure. The Guildmistress was one Aisling couldn't quite bring herself to look at too closely. She hoped she wouldn't pay a price for that as time went on.

"My father's spell is more powerful than anything you've ever used," Acair said stiffly.

"It's apparently more powerful than anything *you've* ever used," Sglaimir shot back, "given that I've waited almost twenty years for you to find someone besides your sire to share it with you!"

"I've been waiting as well," the Guildmistress said, turning to face Acair as she stood alongside Sglaimir. "And perhaps you've forgotten this, but you promised *me* the throne."

"What?" Sglaimir exclaimed. He turned and glared at the Guildmistress. "You want my throne?"

"Well, why do you think I was allowing you to use my bloody

garden?" the Guildmistress demanded. "Out of the goodness of my heart?"

Aisling wondered if it would take all day for the three in front of her to wear each other out so she and Rùnach could go have a rest. That the battle seemed to be limited to arguing, though, made her a little nervous.

Aisling leaned closer to Rùnach. "Does this seem too easy to you?"

"I hate to say it, but it does," he murmured. "Sglaimir's a fool and Acair hot-tempered." He shook his head. "The Guildmistress is the one I don't understand. It doesn't seem as if she has any spells, yet here she is in the company of these two."

Aisling started to agree, then realized that the Guildmistress was watching them as if she had heard everything they'd said. She felt suddenly quite cold, but that could have been from simply being where she was.

Rùnach cleared his throat. "And what do you want, Guildmistress," he asked politely. "We know what the lads want and you seem to want the throne as well, but surely that isn't all."

The Guildmistress's smile didn't reach her eyes. "I want power," she said. "As do all good mages."

"A mage," Rùnach said with an indulgent smile. "Is that what you call yourself?"

Well, whatever she called herself, she apparently wasn't without spells. Aisling was surprised enough to watch her spew one out to be caught unawares. She almost didn't stop it from wrapping itself around not Rùnach, but she herself. She took the first cut of thread, turned it back toward the Guildmistress, and let the spell itself do the work. She was a little surprised to find that Bruadair was only standing by, watching, if she could put a name to what her country was doing. Fortunately, the Guildmistress was also soon standing there, merely watching. Aisling supposed that as long as the woman wasn't moving or speaking, she could be safely ignored for a moment or two.

Aisling looked at the other two in time to watch Sglaimir suddenly strike Acair full in the mouth, sending him sprawling backward. Acair's head made a terrible noise as it struck against a rock. He groaned, then was silent. Sglaimir then turned to Rùnach, his chest heaving.

"Shall I do the same to your little wench there," he panted, "or should she just sit to the side and let us be about our business?"

"And what business it that?" Rùnach asked politely.

"Why, the business of your father's most famous spell," Sglaimir said. "What else?"

Rùnach rolled his eyes. "I wish the damned thing had never been created."

"Well, it was and I intend to have it," Sglaimir said angrily, "so you can either hand it over easily or less easily. Your choice."

Aisling felt herself be suddenly robbed of air and only Rùnach's quick hands caught her from toppling back into the bottom of a fountain that she realized with alarm had no bottom. Rùnach jerked the spell off her—she didn't bother to identify what it was—and pulled her behind him.

"Go, when his attention is on me."

"I—"

"Just out of his sights."

She supposed that since her alternative was to stand behind Rùnach and perhaps find herself knocked into that magic sink, shifting off to the side wasn't unthinkable. Besides, if she was out of the way, she might be able to aid in ways she couldn't otherwise.

But it made her uncomfortable to slither off the field, as it were. She stopped next to a pillar, out of the midst of the battle, but didn't care for standing along the sidelines and watching. She wasn't sure how she could possibly help Rùnach short of simply standing behind him and adding power to his as Uachdaran had done for her when they had dropped Rùnach's magic back into him.

Rùnach caught a spell before it struck her, then flung it back at Sglaimir who stumbled backward into the Guildmistress. That seemed to be enough to break her free of what had been binding her. She angrily shoved him away from her.

"Not her," she snarled. "Just kill him."

Sglaimir stopped in mid-spell and looked at the Guildmistress. "What is it with *that* one? She makes me nervous, but what's the point of her?"

"She ran away from me," the Guildmistress said flatly, "and no one runs away from me."

Aisling supposed that might be enough to send the woman into a frenzy, but she didn't dare hope that was the extent of her interest.

"That's all?" Sglaimir asked incredulously. "That's the only reason you wanted her?"

"I was told to watch her," the Guildmistress conceded. "That she was important, though I wasn't given the reason why."

"What idiot told you that?" he demanded.

"I did," Acair said, cursing as he sat up. He clutched his head and looked blearily at Sglaimir. "Can you possibly be any more stupid? She's important because people want her! Why do you think we marched out into the wilds of this ridiculous country to look for her? Didn't you see the spell that guarded her house? She must have something someone wants and if people want her, I want to get to her first."

Aisling exchanged a look with Rùnach. He sighed lightly, then shook his head. She couldn't believe that such a trio had managed to strip Bruadair of its magic, but perhaps they'd been aided by dumb luck.

Sglaimir blinked. "Which people?"

Acair hauled himself to his feet, then leaned heavily against a pillar. "I do business with many, too many to remember ridiculous details such as this. All I know is someone at some point told me to look for a weaver in your guild with odd eyes. She's the only one who fits that description."

"So you're telling me that I've turned my country into this ugly wreck because you thought you found someone important," Sglaimir said slowly.

"Nay, I had you turn this country which was never yours into an ugly wreck because I wanted its magic," Acair said briskly. "That silly wench there is another matter entirely, but since we have her here, I think we should discover who she is."

Aisling found three pairs of eyes fixed on her. She had the first moment of regret she'd ever experienced over not having learned to use her magic in any meaningful fashion. She was tempted to run, but a voice stopped her.

"I know who she is."

She looked past Sglaimir and watched a tall, grey-haired man step out of the shadows. She wondered how long he'd been standing there.

Sglaimir whirled around, then stumbled backward in surprise. "You—"

Aisling almost said the same thing because she recognized the man as well. He was the border guard she and Rùnach had given money to on their way into Bruadair. He was also the border guard she had given money to on her way out of Bruadair however many fortnights ago it had been.

The man waved his hand and Sglaimir crumpled to the ground. Aisling didn't bother to look to see if he breathed still. There was something about the older man standing there that made her extremely uneasy.

He looked at the Guildmistress and smiled. "She's the First Dreamspinner, Iochdmhor, and you're a fool."

"The what?" the Guildmistress echoed, looking down her nose at him. "And who are you to insult me that way?"

"I know who he is," Rùnach said. "He's Carach of Mùig. Unless I'm mistaken."

"Never said you weren't clever, lad," the man said. "But powerful? You are nothing compared to your father."

"I take that as a compliment."

"You shouldn't."

"Who are you," the Guildmistress demanded, "and why have you come to disturb our parley?"

"Oh, I suppose you might call it that," Carach said with a smile, "but I wouldn't bother. To introduce myself, I'll just say that I'm young Sglaimir's grandfather."

"Oh," the Guildmistress said. "I didn't know."

"Of course you didn't know," Carach said, looking at her as if she possessed no wits whatsoever. "Why would I want you to know?"

"Familial affection?" Acair offered.

Acair went flying, landing on his back in an undignified sprawl. Aisling felt very cold all of the sudden. She supposed that was terror. It wasn't just an angry bastard of Gair's they were dealing with. She could look at Carach and see the layers of his life built up over centuries, only the layers weren't haphazard or unkempt. They were the layers of a man who had methodically and deliberately chosen evil every single time when a choice was offered him. She wasn't even sure what to call the magic she could see running through his veins, but whatever it was, it was very dark.

"I didn't ask for you to come here," the Guildmistress said stiffly, "so if you'll be off—"

"Oh, I don't think 'tis me who'll *be off*, my dear," Carach said. "I have come for that girl there because she will spin the world's power out of the very earth on which we stand, then hand it over to me because I tell her to. You were instructed to keep her safely captive in your guild, which you have done fairly well until recently. But now that I have her and unlimited power at my fingertips, I have no more need of you."

Aisling realized her mouth had fallen open only because she heard some sort of noise come from within herself. She thought it might have been a scream, but she wasn't sure she was equal to identifying it. All she could do was watch the Guildmistress go rushing across the garden, absolutely not under her own power, and fling herself into the fountain.

She disappeared with a long wail.

Sglaimir heaved himself to his feet and started to run, but he met the same fate. Aisling would have run as well but before she could force herself to move, she found herself in Carach's sights—

Until Rùnach stepped in front of her.

"Why don't you dispatch me first," Rùnach said quietly. "If you have the courage to."

Aisling was still looking for the courage to do something, *anything*, when she found her hand taken. She didn't have the time to even protest that before she was stumbling along the portico and being pulled down behind what looked remarkably like a crypt. She realized her rescuer was none other than Acair of Ceangail.

"You," she managed.

"I know," he said, looking thoroughly unsettled. "It must be something I ate for breakfast, which I actually didn't have because you and Rùnach—damn you both to hell—were at this business too early for my stomach."

Aisling felt a shudder run through her and she wasn't sure if it was for herself or Rùnach. She eased up to peek over the edge of the stone but Acair jerked her back down.

"Are you mad?" he whispered. "Don't let him see us. He'll suck us dry and leave us as husks if he can."

"Can he?" she managed. "Take our magic, I mean. Does he have that spell?"

"Diminishing? No idea, though I imagine he has something very much like it."

"Why does everyone want that horrible spell?"

"Power," Acair said distinctly.

"Is there never enough for you black mages?"

"Never," he said grimly, "which is why we'll let Rùnach distract him long enough for me to clunk him over the head and render him senseless. Then I'll take *his* power. Yours, too, if I can manage it. I imagine by that time, Rùnach will be so exhausted, he'll hand his over freely."

She very much doubted that, but supposed there was no reason to say as much. She looked at Acair skeptically. "I thought you didn't have that spell."

"Oh, I do." He paused, then shifted. "Mostly."

"I don't think it works with just *mostly*. Why don't you go help instead? I think you can do that with only part of a heart and a full tally of rudeness."

"You have a point there," he conceded. "My mother has no manners and my father was—is, rather—an arrogant whoreson. I'm operating under reduced circumstances, if you will."

She frowned at him because in spite of everything, she had the feeling he wasn't completely without the odd redeeming quality. "I don't trust you."

"Very wise."

"Don't make any sudden moves," she whispered sharply. "You won't like what happens to you otherwise."

He blew out his breath. "Trust me, I've seen your handiwork on my older brother. I'll just sit here like a powerless lad and let your lover there die for us. And as to the old bastard who'll be killing him, if you weren't paying attention, that's Carach of Mùig. A very nasty sort, old as death. I'm not entirely sure my father didn't steal a few of his spells." He nodded. "There's a bit of revenge here, I daresay."

"Then go help!"

Acair looked torn. "I might sally forth and step on what's left of the victor's neck. We'll see."

He stopped speaking, at least to her, which she supposed was a good thing. Then again, perhaps that was because Carach of Mùig had tossed a spell of death their way and Acair apparently had a keen sense of self-preservation. He drew a spell of protection over them, which Bruadair protested with a screech. He glared at her.

"You do it."

She drew a net of loveliness over them that Carach's spell didn't care for in the least.

To her dismay, neither did Rùnach's.

She realized that he was using magic that wasn't at all pleasant and spells that he couldn't possibly have learned anywhere but from his father's book. She watched in horror for far too long before she couldn't let him continue. She stood up to stop him, but Acair pulled her back down in spite of her protests.

"He's Gair's son," Acair said coolly. "What did you expect?"

"For him not to destroy himself with your father's spells," she said, shaking off his hand. "I'm not sure he sees—"

"Aye," Acair said quietly, "he does. Look."

She watched Rùnach stop, then take a deep breath. Acair cursed him, but Aisling felt a sigh come from deep inside her. Rùnach continued to counter Carach's spells, but he was no longer using things that were causing Bruadair to shrink from him. Unfortunately, even with her country's attempts at shoring up his strength, Aisling could see that he was weakening.

And Carach's spells were unyielding, as if they had come from the deepest mines of the dwarf king's palace.

"That's a nice blade."

She blinked and looked at Rùnach's half brother. "What are you talking about?"

"I'm looking for spoils," he said philosophically. "Rùnach's sword. Where'd he get that?"

Sword. Aisling leaped to her feet. "Rùnach, your sword!"

He looked at her blankly, as if he'd heard her words but simply couldn't understand their meaning. Aisling shook off Acair's hand and rushed out from behind the crypt. If she could just get to his sword, or convince him to draw it, or perhaps even use the knife stuck down the side of his boot—

Without warning, Carach of Mùig backhanded Rùnach, sending him stumbling to one side. Before Aisling could rush forward or Rùnach regain his balance, Carach had pulled the knife from Rùnach's boot and turned.

Aisling watched that spell-laced blade coming toward her, accompanied as it was by Carach's spells she could scarce bear to look at, and knew she was going to die.

And still the blade came.

Twenty

Rùnach spun around to the sound of a slap. He realized only then that it hadn't been Carach of Mùig's fist across his face to make that noise, it had been his knife going into Aisling's chest—

Nay, not Aisling's.

Acair's.

He could hardly believe his bastard brother had taken a blade meant for Aisling, but there was no other conclusion to come to. He realized at that instant that he had less than a heartbeat to decide what to do and do it before Carach made his next move.

He didn't even attempt a breath. He simply took the first thing that came to hand, a spell of elven glamour as it happened, and wove it over his foe. He slammed the edges of it into the ground, anchoring it without apology to the faintest hint of Bruadarian magic, then covered it with a spell of containment.

Carach whirled around and looked at the spell in surprise. Then he shot Rùnach a look of disbelief before he laughed.

"You have no idea who I am, do you, boy?"

"You might be surprised," Rùnach said.

Carach ripped aside the spells as if they'd been threadbare cloth. Rùnach refused to be baited. Mockery had been one of his father's favorite weapons against him and his brothers. It was difficult to ignore, but not impossible. He steeled himself for the next wave of terrible things and wasn't at all disappointed.

The only thing that aided him, he decided after an eternity had passed, was that he had spent an afternoon with Uachdaran of Léige having Carach's own spells thrown at him. At least he wasn't surprised by anything he saw presently.

He was surprised, however, by the things that he found himself reaching for. Again. He had already used half a dozen things of his father's, terrible spells that should have had the mage facing him backing up a pace, at least.

Bruadair was silent, as if it understood what he had to do.

He wished he'd had another choice. He didn't want to think about what the cost to his soul would be if he didn't do something besides use vile magic to fight vile magic.

And then something happened that he hadn't expected at all. He realized abruptly that Carach had lost his hold on his own magic, as if it had been a dream he'd been able to cling to for only a few minutes after he'd woken.

The look on Carach's face once he realized he was reaching for dreams was almost worth the time he himself had spent in Uachdaran of Léige's lists.

Aisling was spinning his power out of him. Rùnach might have considered pointing out to her that even Diminishing couldn't compare to what she was doing, but he thought it was best that he just keep his damned mouth shut. Besides, it wasn't only Aisling manning the tiller, as it were. He could see Bruadair's magic swirling around her just as it had when she'd first encountered it in an underground river where they had been on the verge of drowning. Now, Bruadair seemed to aiding her, however faintly, in rescuing itself.

Carach was not pleased.

"Stop it, you . . . you . . ."

"Dreamspinner," Aisling said crisply. "The First Dreamspinner, if you want to be exact. You are trying to rob my country of its birthright and I will not allow it."

Rùnach thought he might want to find somewhere to sit very soon. If he managed to see his grandmother Brèagha again, he would ask her to paint that woman there just as she was at present: a slender, pale, impossibly beautiful barrier between a black mage and the destruction of an entire country.

She was breathtaking.

Carach took a step back, then whirled to look at Rùnach. "I will not submit."

"Then draw your sword," Rùnach said with a shrug, "and let's see if that's just for show or not."

Perhaps it wasn't a fair fight. Rùnach's last encounter on any serious level had been with Scrymgeour Weger, after all, and that after several days of a brutal training regimen. It took him less time than perhaps it should have to disarm Carach and leave him standing there, swearing furiously.

"Rùnach, move!"

He looked at Aisling in surprise, then spun around to see what she was pointing at. He leapt out of the way of tendrils of magic that were slithering out from the fountain. The stench that accompanied that magic reminded him so sharply of what his father had loosed, he almost lost his gorge. Aisling pulled him out of the way and held his arm tightly as the magic felt for Carach. It surrounded him in an embrace he obviously wasn't going to escape, then drew him inexorably to itself.

He went over the edge of the fountain and into its depths with a shriek.

Rùnach pulled Aisling into his arms. He wasn't surprised to find he was the one shaking, not she. He stood there with her until he thought he could speak without weeping.

"Thank you," he managed.

She tightened her arms around him so quickly, he lost his breath, then she pulled back and looked at him. "You're welcome. But I had help."

"I think you were the one offering help," he said. "You were magnificent, by the way."

She lifted her chin. "I decided I wasn't going to look at the ground anymore."

"Weger would be impressed."

"I'll tell him."

"I think he'll notice before you can." He nodded toward the fountain basin. "We should close that."

"Wait," she said, taking his arm before he could walk away. "We can't yet."

"Why—oh."

She nodded. "Oh."

He resheathed his sword. "What can I do?"

"I'm not sure yet," she said slowly. "Let me see if I can spin the magic back here, then we'll decide what to do with it."

He nodded, then watched her consider. He supposed it wouldn't be a terrible thing to sit for a moment or two, so he found a handy stone bench and availed himself of it. He looked down to find his bastard brother lying at his feet, gasping as if each breath were his last.

He reached over and yanked the knife from Acair's body, then healed him with the first thing that came to mind. Acair put his hand over his chest, sat up, and glared at him.

"Fadaire?" he accused.

"It was all I could think of in a tight spot," Rùnach said with a yawn. "Shut up and let Aisling work, would you?"

Acair patted his chest suspiciously. "You put something inside there."

"I wouldn't have bothered. It's probably leavings from the blade. Soilléir gave it to Aisling so I can't guarantee what was on it."

"I feel an undue warmth in the vicinity of my heart."

"Heartburn from all your vile deeds," Rùnach said. "And still shut up."

Acair fell silent, thankfully. Rùnach watched Aisling continue to spin. He realized Acair was watching as well because his half brother was making the sort of noises a body makes when it's on the verge of a faint.

Aisling had created a flywheel and bobbin out of air and sunlight and was spinning magic back from the fountain. She looked over her shoulder.

"Help."

He pushed himself to his feet and strode over to her. "How?"

"Things are coming with it that I don't like. What can you do?"

"Pick them out as I see them?"

"Perfect."

And so he did. He realized that Aisling had done the same thing as she'd been spinning his magic out of him, which led him to believe that whatever darkness had been left inside him was of his own making. Muinear would have something philosophical to say about it, he was sure of that.

Time passed in a way he couldn't measure. He worked with what Aisling was spinning until he was almost blind from a weariness he suspected was exacerbated by the spells he'd used against Carach of Mùig. At the very moment when he thought he might have to unman himself by begging Aisling for a rest, the last of Bruadair's magic was drawn from the fountain. Aisling sighed deeply, then fashioned a loom of sunlight. He would have told her that he was beginning to suspect she'd found her favorite medium with which to create otherworldly things, but he was too damned tired to.

"A rest?" he asked hopefully.

She shook her head. "I'm fine. I'll sleep later." She paused. "What of you?"

"If you can continue, so can I," he said, hoping that would be the case.

She leaned over, kissed him, then smiled. "I love you."

"I think you've inspired me to bear up for at least another quarter hour."

She laughed a little, then began to weave what she'd spun until it was an enormous piece of fabric that sparkled with endless facets of light and shadow. She looked at him and sighed.

"What now, do you suppose? A dwarvish spell?"

"That seems a little indelicate," he said slowly, "don't you think?"

"What would you suggest?"

"Mist?"

"Can you do mist?" she asked.

"Today, Aisling, I think I can do anything."

She smiled and stepped back. "Then the task is yours, my love."

He considered, then decided he couldn't make a bigger fool of himself than he had by using his father's damned spells earlier. He posed a silent, casual question to Bruadair's magic that was spread out on that loom in front of him and was almost surprised to find the decision of what to do was left up to him.

If he managed to survive the rest of the day without weeping, he would be very surprised.

He gathered the cloth of magic, infused it with the spell for creating a healing mist his grandfather had learned from his own land, then flung the magic up into the sky. He watched, open-mouthed, as it spread almost instantly farther than he could see. And then, to his utter surprise, magic fell like rain.

Or, rather, mist.

Aisling laughed, then put her arms around him and held him tightly. "Beautiful."

He held her close, closed his eyes, and wished for nothing more than any place to lie his sorry self down and sleep for a fortnight. He sighed and looked at the fountain.

"We need to close that portal still."

"Will you?"

"Will Bruadair mind a Cothromaichian spell—or perhaps not." He had known Bruadair had a mind of its own when it came to things inside the border, but now that magic was drenching everything the country's opinions were undeniably clear. He took the spell he was given, wove it over the portal, and felt to his bones how the entire doorway calcified, then sealed itself closed with a faint click.

He thought he might have to sleep not for a fortnight, but a solid month. He yawned, covered his mouth as an afterthought, then put his arm around Aisling's shoulders.

"Let's find somewhere to sit."

"Let's find somewhere to nap."

He smiled and kissed her hair. "That too." He yawned again, then walked with her to where Acair stood, still looking terribly unsettled. Rùnach wasn't at all prepared to forgive him—he was a complete bastard, after all, in every sense of the word—but perhaps leaving him alive wasn't beyond the realm of possibility. He considered, then looked at Aisling.

"What shall we do with him?" he asked.

"Do?" Acair echoed. "What do you mean, *do*? As if either of you had the power to *do* anything with me!"

Rùnach looked at Aisling. "You could give him nightmares. Well, not you, exactly, but you have people who do that sort of thing."

"I'm not afraid of nightmares," Acair said haughtily.

"Nay, not nightmares," Aisling said slowly. "Something less dark."

"Unicorns and dancing elven maidens?" Acair asked sourly.

Aisling looked at Rùnach. "Unicorns?"

"I believe those definitely *are* creatures from myth," he said with a smile.

"I don't know," she said slowly. "I think perhaps there are things in this world we haven't investigated yet—"

"Spare the world any more of your quests," Acair interrupted.

Rùnach looked at him coolly. "You know, you're not helping your case any. You did, after all, try to steal all the world's power."

"I'm my father's son," Acair said with a shrug. "And my mother's. It's in the blood."

"Why did I avoid it?"

"Too much of your mother in you," Acair said. "I can't help that."

Rùnach looked at the half brother who had made his life so miserable as a youth and supposed that perhaps even Acair couldn't help some of his predilections. After all, both his parents had been less than stellar souls. But that didn't mean he couldn't do a little penance and then retire quietly to a little spot in some obscure country where he could at least refrain from attempting to undo the world.

"We could have him go round and apologize to those he tried to use for his own nefarious purposes," Aisling suggested.

"And why," Acair said in disbelief, "would I do that?"

"Because," Rùnach said, "I know all Soilléir's spells of essence changing and if you don't, I'll turn you into a gargoyle for your mother's front porch. Or, better still, a servant to the faeries of Siabhreach."

"Oh, please nay," Acair gasped. "Those mindless flutterers? Rather take that blade and put it back in my chest where you found it." He looked at Aisling narrowly. "You, woman, forget I pulled you behind that bit of stone and saved your sorry life. What was I thinking? And now look who's arrived to complete the misery of the morning!"

Rùnach looked to his right to find Soilléir standing a few feet away, looking as if he'd done nothing more taxing with his morning than linger over a cup of tea. Which, knowing Soilléir, he likely had. Rùnach smiled.

"What do you think?"

"I'm not surprised," Soilléir said pleasantly. "But I knew what you two could accomplish together." He moved to stand next to Aisling, then looked at Acair. "Prince Acair."

Acair snarled a curse at him.

Aisling looked at Soilléir. "We're thinking of sending him off to repair the damage he's done. What do you think?"

"I think what I always do," Soilléir said with a smile. "If there were no evil in the world, what would there be for good men to do?"

"Ah, kill me now," Acair moaned. "I want to find a dull blade and fall upon it when you start with that rot."

"And what would you know of it?" Aisling asked.

"My mother has an entire book of his sayings," Acair said with a shudder. "An extremely thin volume, but there you have it. She has no taste. And look, you have yet more witnesses over there. Perhaps that might cause you to hesitate before doing me any injuries."

Rùnach looked to his right and realized Acair spoke the truth. There was Bristeadh, looking very much worse for the wear, Muinear, and even Uabhann. The latter was sending meaningful glances Acair's way.

Acair shifted closer to Aisling. "Who is that lad?"

"He's the dreamspinner in charge of nightmares."

"Thought I recognized him."

She looked at Acair seriously. "Go do good."

"I'd rather perish."

"Your choice, of course."

He considered, then nodded shortly to her. "If I see someone on the verge of death, I'll give him a good kick to help him along. It's the best I can do." He looked at Rùnach. "My thanks for my life, damn you to hell for it."

Rùnach smiled. "I have a lifetime of torment to repay you for."

Acair scowled at him, then walked away. He gave Muinear a wide berth, shot Uabhann a look of faint alarm, then left the garden.

Rùnach watched the door close behind him, then sighed as Aisling went to embrace her great-grandmother. He looked at Soilléir.

"Well?"

"I wasn't worried."

"You don't lie well."

Soilléir smiled. "Very well, I was worried. But I'm not surprised you were successful. Very resourceful, the two of you."

Rùnach studied him for several minutes in silence. "Have you ever used a spell of essence changing in a fight?"

Soilléir shifted. "Why would you ask?"

"I'm curious."

"Shouldn't you be careful what your curiosity leads you to ask?"

Rùnach smiled. "I know what you're doing."

"It's my favorite technique."

"Unfortunately, it's one you taught me quite well, which renders it perhaps less effective than you might hope."

Soilléir sighed. "Perhaps. And perhaps I'll tell you one day, when we've absolutely nothing else to discuss."

"You inspire me to entertain you regularly at my table."

Soilléir smiled and clapped a hand on his shoulder. "I would hope you would." He stepped away. "I think you should rescue your lady before Uabhann monopolizes her. I think he's looking for new ideas to use in his craft."

Rùnach shuddered to think of what sorts of things Uabhann might find interesting, no matter what Muinear had said about him. He looked around the garden once more, breathed in deeply of the wholesome, rich air, and was grateful for the gifts he'd been given. Light, darkness, the ability to govern both of them within himself.

And the chance to spend the rest of his days with a woman who loved him in spite of both.

Twenty-one

✲

Aisling walked along the same street she had traversed so often during her time at the Guild, only now she wasn't sure she had ever seen anything more beautiful. Beul was drenched in magic that still hung over the city like a mist. She had the feeling that mist was healing the country—nay, she knew it was. The entire land of her birth was sighing in relief, as if it had been perishing of thirst for years and had finally been offered sweet water. It was without a doubt one of the happiest days of her life, made all the more lovely because she was walking next to the man who had made it all possible.

"I didn't."

She looked up at Rùnach and smiled. "Of course you did," she said, "and how did you know what I was thinking?"

He smiled wryly. "You've told me so half a dozen times in the past hour. I've disagreed at least that many."

"You closed the portal."

"You quite handily took Carach's magic away from him before he killed me."

She smiled. "Then perhaps we can consider it a joint accomplishment."

He nodded and fell silent, but she had the feeling it was a silence inspired by more than weariness. She continued on with him for a bit longer before she looked at him.

"You're thinking."

He smiled briefly. "Barely." He hesitated, then shook his head. "I'm not thinking anything very useful."

"I'm coherent enough to listen," she said. "Barely."

He breathed out a huff of a laugh. "I understand, which is why I'm not sure I want to clutter up the day with my thoughts, but I will if you can bear it." He considered, then shook his head again. "I suppose 'tis simply my past intruding on the pleasure of the present, but I didn't like what was coming out of that fountain." He looked at her then. "Too much like what my father loosed, truth be told."

"But it's sealed shut now," she said slowly. "Don't you think?"

"I'm sure of it," he said, sounding very sure indeed.

"That magic took what I'd spun out of Carach and pulled it into the fountain with him, if that worries you," she said.

He closed his eyes briefly. "It did, actually." He stopped, turned her to him and put his arms around her. "It concerned me greatly."

She understood. The evil Gair had loosed had trickled through the Nine Kingdoms for years before Rùnach's siblings had managed to shut the well Gair had opened. Rùnach had every reason to be unsettled to think another source of it had sprung up. She held him tightly for several minutes, ignoring the people that walked around them as they stood in the middle of the thoroughfare, ignoring how all she wanted to do was find a flat place to lie down on and sleep for a fortnight.

"Wed me?"

She laughed a little. "Aye."

"I just wanted to make sure."

She pulled away and looked at him. "Was there any doubt?"

"You still have that enspelled handkerchief my cousin gave you. I feared you might feel the need to scratch a wobbly *rescue me from Rùnach* on it before I managed to get you to an altar and there he would come to save the day."

"He didn't save my country."

"He didn't save my sorry arse this morning, either," Rùnach said with a weary smile, "so I suppose neither of us needs him. But perhaps what we do need is a cup of ale and a scrap of floor. And look you, there is a likely lad to ferry us to such a place if we're fortunate."

Aisling looked over her shoulder to find that a carriage had suddenly stopped in the street behind them. She supposed it was indicative of the morning she'd had that her first instinct was to fling a spell of containment at the driver. She realized that perhaps Rùnach was feeling something along those lines because he had pulled her behind him and had his hand on his sword.

"Perhaps a ride to a fine inn?" a familiar voice suggested. "It'll cost you a gold coin, though, if you want to be anonymous."

Aisling smiled at Ochadius's son as he tipped his hat up so she could see his face. "That seems like a bargain."

"If you only knew," Peter said. He inclined his head. "Lady Aisling. Prince Rùnach. Perhaps a ride free of charge considering what you've done this morning."

Rùnach looked up at him. "Do you know?"

"Your Highness, I think everyone knows," Peter said, smiling. "I won't say my father went so far as to make a general announcement, but he has noised the tidings about. He has also taken the finest rooms in the finest inn in Beul for your pleasure." He hesitated, then looked at Aisling. "My lady Aisling, he has been much more discreet about your presence here, which he suspected you might prefer. You being who you are, of course."

Aisling put her hand on Rùnach's arm before he could speak. "I think that would be best."

Rùnach handed her up into the carriage, then climbed in and sat next to her. "Aisling—"

"Rùnach, I don't want anyone to know."

He studied her for several minutes in silence. "I'm not the one who stripped the whoreson of his power."

"Which I did with Bruadair's help only after you had weakened him to the point where I could without his noticing until it was too late for him to do anything about it."

"I don't want the credit," he insisted.

"And I couldn't take it even if I wanted it, which I don't." She took his hand in both hers. "Rùnach, you and Ochadius can step out in front of the crowd and tell them that you saved their country for them because you loved it and the souls who were born to it. And that will be the absolute truth. Ochadius has done things that have held the country together until today when you stopped what was taking Bruadair's magic, fought its bitterest enemy, and sealed shut a fountain that was obviously more than just a portal."

"Aisling," he said with a sigh, "you know it isn't as simple as that."

"What I know, my love, is that you were born to put on court clothes and dazzle people who will thereafter fall over themselves to please you. I was born to stand off-stage and watch."

"And manage the dreams of the world."

"Well, I suppose that, too," she agreed.

He leaned over and kissed her, then looked into her eyes. "Single words and simple thoughts?"

"Where have I heard that before?"

He smiled and sat back. "You and Soilléir are more alike than you realize, I'm afraid." He sighed deeply. "Very well, I can see the sense in it. I'm not sure most Bruadarians even believe there are dreamweavers, much less dreamspinners. Anonymity may be vital to your calling, but I want you to know that I don't like the idea of taking credit for any of this."

"I know," she said simply. "Which makes all the difference." She leaned her head on his shoulder. "A carriage ride without worrying about the destination or who is following us," she said wearily. "Astonishing."

"It is," he agreed.

"I'm not sure I can stay awake any longer."

"Then close your eyes, love. I'll keep you safe."

"You have so far," she murmured, then found that she was simply too exhausted to say anything else.

She wasn't entirely sure that she didn't sleep, because it seemed like just a moment or two later that the carriage had come to a stop and she was crawling unsteadily back out of it. She looked blankly at the inn in front of them for a moment or two before she realized where she'd seen it before. It was the one where Rùnach had rented a chamber days earlier. For all she knew, he might find some of his missing gear still there. The things he'd bribed the madam of ill repute with, she supposed he would never have back.

They thanked Peter for the ride, then walked inside where they were shown to a large gathering chamber. Aisling was faintly surprised to find it was full of people waiting for them. She was even more surprised to realize who was there.

"Half an hour," Rùnach murmured, "but no more."

"Truly?"

He smiled and squeezed her hand. "They'll understand."

"We could invite them north for supper in a day or two," she said. "Don't you think?"

"Let's make it in a fortnight or two and we might be awake enough to make coherent conversation," he said wryly. "Here, lean on me and we'll prop each other up until we can make our escape."

Aisling would have been happy to do so, but she and Rùnach were immediately led to a bench that was perhaps the most comfortable thing she'd ever sat on. She accepted a very decent mug of ale which she hoped would keep her awake long enough for her to greet their guests.

Ochadius was there, looking very much worse for wear but holding the hand of a woman Aisling could only assume was Alexandra, the crown princess of Bruadair. King Frèam and Queen Leaghra were in the company as well, but she wouldn't have recognized them as what they were if she hadn't met them before. They were dressed in homespun and seemingly quite happy to pass themselves off as simple country folk.

The rest of the chamber's occupants were far from that, though. Rùnach's grandparents, Sìle and Brèagha, were there, along with Miach of Neroche and Rùnach's sister, Mhorghain. Aisling was happy to see them both and grateful they seemed perfectly willing to ignore her yawns. She was introduced to Frèam and Leaghra's niece, Sarah, and her husband, Ruith, whom she knew from having met him at Seanagarra.

It occurred to her at one point that she had family there herself. Muinear was sitting on a chair near the fire, watching her with a smile, while her father, cleaned up from his early-morning adventures, stood behind his wife's grandmother with his hand on her chair. Uabhann was sitting in a corner, as usual, blending in with the shadows. Aisling didn't want to try to imagine what he was turning over in his head at the moment. Hopefully she wouldn't find the events of the morning making an appearance in her nightmares.

She was fairly sure that at some point food was brought and extra chairs provided. She was far less sure that she hadn't closed her eyes once too often while her head was resting against Rùnach's shoulder and slept. If she woke, she couldn't tell. It all felt like a dream.

All she knew was that at one point Rùnach patted her awake and no one seemed to find that unusual. She and Rùnach made their excuses to various royal personages, extended an invitation to come to dinner in a few days, and promised visits during high summer when the king and queen of Bruadair intended to commemorate their return to the throne.

"Let's go now whilst another round of ale is being served," Rùnach said under his breath. "Hurry."

She hurried only to realize that their escape might not be made so easily. She only knew that because they had run bodily into Sìle of Tòrr Dòrainn who was waiting by the latch.

"I see you're off."

"Grandfather, Aisling needs to sleep and if I don't find some-where to sit where I needn't speak for at least a fortnight, I will break down and weep."

"And how will you travel back to Aisling's keep?"

"We'll shapechange."

Sìle frowned. "Far be it from me to tell you what to do—and if you snort at me over that, Rùnach, I will insist on satisfaction—but I would caution you against it. I must admit—very reluctantly—that shapechanging did not go very well for me the last time I tried it within these borders."

"You, Grandfather?" Rùnach said in mock surprise. "Shapechange? I thought you said elves don't ever shapechange."

"Especially not in Bruadair," Sìle said promptly, "which was where I decided that very thing several centuries ago." He looked at them from under bushy white eyebrows. "I don't suppose I need to tell you how to get along in your own country, especially not after this morning, but for myself, I will take my lovely bride and walk."

"Want company, Grandfather?" Mhorghain called from across the chamber.

"Yours, aye. Those rambunctious lads, perhaps not, but that leaves me without our lovely Sarah to escort if I ban Ruithneadh." He shrugged. "I'll take Miach and Ruith if I must."

"Thank you, Grandfather," Ruith called dryly from across the chamber.

"I helped you dig your garden, whelp."

"You helped *Sarah* dig our garden and the plants that are there are for use in dyeing her wool. How do I benefit?"

Rùnach took Aisling's hand and pulled her out the door. "I can't bear another moment of listening to anyone say anything. Well, you, of course. But anyone else? Nay, please no."

She smiled and ran with him down the stairs and out into the street. She pulled up short at what was waiting at the curb.

Iteach and Orail stood there with wings on their feet, harnessed to a sleigh that had wings on the runners. It was even more magnificent than the one Sìle had created for her in Seangarra when he'd determined she was too tired to walk anywhere. She looked at Rùnach in surprise, but he only shook his head with a rueful sigh.

"Elves might not shapechange, but elven grandfathers have absolutely no problem apparently negotiating with your magic to provide comfortable transportation for a sleepy dreamspinner and the man who loves her."

She turned and put her arms around him, then smiled up at

him. "Let's go home," she said. "Courtesy of your grandfather and our shapechanging horses."

"We lead a charmed life."

"I believe, Your Highness, that we do."

She soon found herself sitting in a luxurious conveyance she never would have dared dream about earlier in the year, holding the hand of an elven prince she would have been convinced during the same time belonged safely tucked in a book on fables and myths. She closed her eyes as Iteach and Orail pulled them gently up into a mist that seemed to fall everywhere but on them and tried to stay awake so she didn't miss anything, but the pull of dreaming was too strong.

She closed her eyes and surrendered to it.

Twenty-two

❧

Rùnach walked along the same shore his grandmother had painted all those centuries ago and marveled at the course his life had taken. He couldn't quite believe a year had passed since he had stood on the shores of Lake Cladach and resigned himself to an ordinary, magicless life in the garrison of an unimportant lord.

He looked up at the house he had built Aisling on the bluff where he'd envisioned it the first time he'd looked at his grandmother's painting of the same scene. Very few doors, endless amounts of light, baskets of wool and silk and whatever other sort of fiber he could find for Aisling that he thought she might enjoy. Gardeners had been imported and saplings planted. And if his grandmothers had arrived at various times and spent copious amounts of time digging in the dirt with both him and his lady wife, who was he to have argued? He had been a score of years without family about him. The privilege of enjoying their company was an unexpected joy.

He realized with a start that his favorite family member was walking down the path from the house toward him. He went to wait for her at the bottom of the path instead of climbing to meet her only because he knew she savored her moments on the shore where she could put away the fabric of the world and simply breathe.

She walked into his arms and sighed. "I thought you might be here."

"Waiting for you," he said gathering her close. "How are you?"

"Happy," she said, sounding very much that. "A little tired, but I think a walk along the ocean's edge will cure that."

He nodded, then took her hand and walked toward the water. She didn't seem inclined to speak, but he expected nothing less. Selecting threads to make up the tapestry of the world was quite often a difficult business, which he knew she had expected. He was happy to walk with her when she needed it and offer the exceptionally rare single word and simple thought when she requested it. Soilléir came to supper regularly. Rùnach supposed all those years at the man's elbow had done more to prepare him for his current life than he ever would have imagined they would.

He breathed deeply of the lovely sea air and thought back over the last year of that life. It was difficult to believe so much time had passed.

He had been a little surprised initially that Aisling hadn't taken longer to recover from her work of spinning all Bruadair's magic back into itself, though perhaps she'd had help from sources that valued her light magical touch. He'd slept for close to a se'nnight, then stumbled through the subsequent fortnight feeling as if he'd been trapped in a dream. It had occurred to him at one

point that perhaps that was simply his reality tapping him firmly
on the head and telling him to wake up. Accustoming himself to
living in a dreamspinner's palace had been an adventure, to be
sure. If he hadn't grown to manhood in a land full of mythical elvish happenings, he might not have survived it.

As time had passed, he supposed he'd done his bit, removing
spells that blocked the magic here and there and lending a hand
where needful. He had definitely made his share of visits to various
and sundry rulers of affected countries—accompanied, to his surprise, most often by his grandfather Sìle—to smooth over where necessary and chastise where appropriate. Acair had come to a handful
of those meetings, looking utterly unsettled and periodically rubbing
his chest as if something inside it vexed him. Heartburn, Rùnach had
supposed, from not only memories of his foulness but perhaps tummy
upset from being subjected to stern moral lectures from the king of
Tòrr Dòrainn. Rùnach had enjoyed both thoroughly.

Bruadair had seen its share of happy events as well. Frèam
and Leaghra had been restored to their throne, Alexandra and
Ochadius had been married in a glorious ceremony, and Beul had
become less a hellhole and more what it had been in the past, a
bustling city with a grand tradition of very fine, exclusive cloth
sought by the finest courtiers in the Nine Kingdoms.

His own wedding had been much quieter, attended by those he
and Aisling loved, and celebrated in a great hall where it was difficult to make out the ceiling for the dreams hovering there.

He smiled at the memory, then realized that there was something
in the air that sounded a great deal like a melody he recognized from
somewhere. He listened for a bit longer, then pulled up short.

"Rùnach?"

He considered, then looked at his wife. "Do you hear that?"

"The song?"

He blinked in surprise. "Is it a song?"

"Of course," she said with a smile. "The palace sings it occasionally. I think it might be a thread running through the tapestry as well, but I haven't had time to investigate. You're welcome to, if you like. Why do you ask?"

He laughed a little because he couldn't help it. "Sgath was humming that tune the evening I left for Gobhann all those many months ago. I've heard it, or thought I heard it, here, but I couldn't place it."

"I wonder where he heard it?" she mused.

"I wonder," Rùnach said with a snort. Obviously he was going to have to make a visit with Aisling at some point and ask his grandfather how he'd known, but he had the feeling Sgath would only smile and talk about fishing.

He, however, would think of wheels that went around and around, drawing visions and lives into their centers, blending lives and hopes into the endless tapestry of dreams his wife spun.

"Rùnach?"

He smiled, kissed her softly, then nodded down to the edge of the sea. "Nothing. Just thinking pleasant thoughts. Shall we walk more?"

"A bit more," she said, "then I want to show you something." She smiled, but her eyes were full of tears. "I found my mother's thread in the tapestry."

He looked at her in surprise. "Did you? I didn't think she had spun."

"She didn't spin anything." She smiled, her eyes bright with tears. "It was a dream."

He rubbed his free hand over his face, then pulled her into his arms so she wouldn't see him weep. How he, son of a black mage, had come to stand in a place of wonder and hold the woman he was wed to in his arms . . . well, he hadn't done anything to merit it and wasn't sure how he would ever repay anyone with a hand in it.

Dreamer's daughter that she was.

He would ask her what that dream had been later, when he thought he could speak successfully. For the moment, he simply held her until the sun set and the sea breezes seemed to suggest a return to a warm fire and a glass of something equally warm.

"Home?" she murmured.

He nodded, took her hand, then walked with her back up the shore.